ALSO BY IRIS JOHANSEN

LIVE TO SEE TOMORROW

LIVE TO SEE TOMORROW

IRIS JOHANSEN

ST. MARTIN'S PRESS ⚓ NEW YORK

LIVE TO SEE TOMORROW. Copyright © 2014 by Johansen Publishing LLLP. All rights reserved. Printed in the United States of America. For information, address St. Martin's Press, 175 Fifth Avenue, New York, N.Y. 10010.

www.stmartins.com

Design by Omar Chapa

Library of Congress Cataloging-in-Publication Data

Johansen, Iris.
    Live to see tomorrow / Iris Johansen.—First Edition.
        pages cm
    ISBN 978-1-250-02004-8 (hardcover)
    ISBN 978-1-250-02003-1 (e-book)
    1. United States. Central Intelligence Agency—Officials and employees—Fiction.   2. Women intelligence officers—Fiction.   3. Kidnapping—Tibet—Fiction.   4. Women journalists—Fiction.   I. Title.
    PS3560.O275L58 2014
    813'.54—dc23

                                                                    2013047079

St. Martin's Press books may be purchased for educational, business, or promotional use. For information on bulk purchases, please contact Macmillan Corporate and Premium Sales Department at 1-800-221-7945, extension 5442, or write specialmarkets@macmillan.com.

First Edition: April 2014

10 9 8 7 6 5 4 3 2 1

*Who can say for sure that one will
live to see tomorrow?*

—TIBETAN PROVERB

LIVE TO SEE TOMORROW

CHAPTER
1

HONG KONG

Why didn't she think of this city as home? Catherine Ling wondered as she looked down through the clouds from the window of the jet approaching Hong Kong. Other people would have found it strange that she had never regarded this exotic, wonderful, terrible city as her home place. She had spent her childhood here on the streets struggling, sometimes starving, always having to use her mind and wits just to stay alive. It was only when she was fourteen and had been chosen by Venable to go to work for the CIA that she had left the city. Perhaps it was because she had never been at ease enough to think of it as a haven. Wasn't a home supposed to offer safe haven?

Her cell phone was vibrating, and she frowned as she looked down at it.

Venable.

Should she ignore it? She had no desire to argue with him right now. Venable hadn't wanted her to go to Hong Kong to be with her son. He'd had that job for her to do in Guatemala City, and he could be as stubborn as he was devious. But if she didn't get the argument settled now, she'd have to face it when she was with Luke and Hu Chang after the plane landed. Venable would keep trying until he reached her. He never gave up.

"What is it, Venable?" she asked curtly as she accessed the call. "I can't talk very long. I should be landing within the next fifteen or twenty minutes."

"I know. I timed the call that way. It had to not be enough time for you to smolder and build up resistance and just enough time to spark that mind of yours into gear."

"I'm not going to Guatemala City. Forget it."

"I've already forgotten it. I've sent Tolliver. I really didn't want to send you there anyway. You were much more suited for this other job I've had in mind for you for the last week. It just had a few awkward ramifications I didn't want to deal with."

"And where was this job?"

"Tibet. I decided that since you were so determined to go to Hong Kong, I'd give you work closer to there."

"Bullshit. It may be close in distance, but it's a world away in every other aspect."

"Unfortunately, that's true. And this one isn't going to be easy. If I didn't need you, I'd give it to the local guy and let you take your vacation."

Her voice was soft. "Let?"

He chuckled. "Wrong word. I'll rephrase it. I wouldn't try to persuade you to postpone your time with your son. There were a few headaches connected to bringing you into it. I actually was looking for another agent even though you're as close to perfect as I could get."

"No," Catherine said with precision. "Not Guatemala. Not Tibet."

He continued as if he hadn't heard her. "But I decided to leave it up to fate. If you'd agreed to Guatemala, I'd accept it. If not, you were mine."

"You're not listening to me."

"I'm listening to every word. Believe me, if you weren't so good, I'd let you out of this one. As I said, bringing you in may be a major headache."

"Good. Then you won't feel too disappointed if I refuse the assignment. Venable, for God's sake, what can I say to convince you that I'm going to spend these next few weeks with my son and my friend, Hu Chang. Then I'm going to take Luke back to Louisville to start the school year. Period. End of discussion."

"Not quite. You've not allowed me to offer my side of the discussion. Have you ever heard of Erin Sullivan?"

"No. Yes." Memory was stirring as she made the connection. "She's a journalist. There was some kind of big fuss about her a few years ago. I didn't pay much attention to it. You were keeping me busy down in Venezuela at the time."

"Not exactly a fuss. She won a Pulitzer for her stories about the earthquake at Qinghai Province in Tibet a few years ago." He paused. "She also worked side by side with the monks and the Chinese soldiers rescuing the victims of the quake. By the time the Chinese government decided that Erin Sullivan was gaining too much star power and influence among the Tibetan people, it was too late. The villagers throughout the mountains were regarding her as their angel of mercy.

"Very admirable. And dangerous. China doesn't appreciate interference in their policies in Tibet. But she's an American, and that gave her an umbrella of safety. She had no desire to be an activist. She didn't consider it her place. She just helped where she could."

"So why are we talking about Erin Sullivan?"

"Unfortunately, she's become a problem for us."

"How? You said that she's not trying to stir up trouble."

"Sometimes people cause turmoil just by being what they are." He added dryly, "If an angel of mercy becomes a victim, then that means a martyr. Martyrs can ignite wars."

She stiffened. "And has Erin Sullivan become a martyr?"

"I don't know. I don't believe it's gone that far yet. What we do know is that she disappeared on her way to write a story about an orphanage in the mountains two months ago. She hasn't been seen since."

"Why hasn't her newspaper raised hell?"

"She's freelance."

"She just dropped off the face of the Earth?"

"I didn't say that. There have been rumors."

"Rumors from what source?"

"The same source that sent me a tip that the unrest and revolt building among the Tibetans because of Sullivan's disappearance might cause an upset with big brother China if it wasn't addressed. It wouldn't take much to do that. China has always been more ready to attack than negotiate."

"And China was responsible for Sullivan's disappearance?"

"Not that we can confirm."

"Stop pussyfooting around. If she's been missing two months, you must have an idea where she is. You wouldn't want to send me in blind if you didn't. She's an American citizen."

"And Tibet is still a wild and desolate land where anyone could be lost for decades and never found. We've been making inquiries and tapping our sources."

"Sources, again. What sources, Venable?"

"Have I piqued your curiosity, Catherine?"

"No, I've been trained to question and probe. You had a hand in that training." But she had been caught and held by the story of Erin Sullivan. It made her angry. She hated the idea of good people being thrown to the wolves as the journalist probably had been. She supposed she should be accustomed to the lack of fairness in the world by now, but she never got used to it. "And I won't let you lure me into searching for her out of sheer curiosity. I left my son for over three weeks while I pulled your hot potatoes out of the fire in Colombia. I want Luke to remember that he has a mother who cares about him. I'm sure whoever you send after Erin Sullivan will be competent."

"You've told me yourself that you have to walk carefully around your son to make sure that you don't overwhelm him. He got along without you for nine years just fine while you were searching for him."

"You know he didn't get along fine. Rakovac tried to destroy him and almost succeeded." She felt a ripple of pain as she remembered the torment of those years after Rakovac, a Russian criminal, had tried to punish Catherine by kidnapping her two-year-old son. He had kept him for nine long years and tried to turn him into everything that Catherine would hate. She had only recently managed to free Luke, and they were still tentative with each other. "He survived, but I probably won't know how damaged he is for years. Yes, he's had to be independent all his life just to avoid Rakovac's abuse, but now he has to know I'm there for him."

"He has his tutor, Sam O'Neill, and Hu Chang."

"I'm his mother, dammit."

"A mother who Luke isn't sure he knows what to do with," Venable said bluntly. "He knows about surviving neglect and torture. He knows about a man who put a gun in his hand when he was a small child and took him on guerrilla raids. He doesn't know about normal relations."

"He's learning," she said fiercely. "Every time we're together we get a little closer. Yes, I have to be careful not to let him know how much I—" She stopped. She wouldn't reveal to Venable the aching frustration of having to restrain the deep, boundless love she felt for Luke. She wanted to reach out, touch him, smother him with the affection that had been stolen from both of them. She couldn't do it. Luke was older than his age in many ways, but his lack of experience in ordinary emotions had stunted him, and he was only now beginning to open to her. She had to hold back, respect that reticence. But God it was hard.

"Do you think I don't know why you've been letting me send you on assignments during these last six months?" Venable asked softly. "I believe Luke may be as torn and confused as you are about how to make the adjustment. You both have to occasionally step back and take a deep breath before you take another step forward."

"Very perceptive," Catherine said dryly. She wasn't surprised that Venable had studied her situation and come so close to the exact truth. No one ever underestimated Venable's cleverness. "And a convenient explanation for you in this case. Abandon my Luke and go off on CIA business because it's good for us as well as the country. No deal, Venable."

"Think about it. Look Erin Sullivan up on the Internet. Get to know her."

"The hell I will."

Venable chuckled. "I think you will. I'll get off the line now so you can check her out before your plane begins its descent."

"Wait." She had just thought of something else. "You said bringing me into the mission would cause you big problems. Why?"

"I was wondering when you'd ask that question. It all has to do with my source. He doesn't want you involved."

"Why not?"

"You'll have to ask him."

"And how am I supposed to do that when you won't tell me who he is? I take it you've changed your mind." She stiffened as she began to have an outrageous suspicion. "Just who is your source?"

"Someone you know very well," he said quietly. "Hu Chang."

"What the hell? What's Hu—"

But Venable had already hung up.

What did Hu Chang have to do with Erin Sullivan? He might slide in and out of political situations like a Las Vegas magician if he chose, but he seldom chose. At least, she didn't think he often dabbled in the fates of nations any longer. What did she know? After all these years, he was still an enigma to her. She had met him when she was only fourteen and had been on the streets selling information to the highest bidder. He had been a practitioner of Chinese medicine, and they had bonded and become friends. She had not learned until later that Hu Chang was also the foremost creator of poisons in the world and sold them to the highest bidder. By that time, it had not mattered to her. He was her friend. He had saved her life, and she had saved his. Two solitary people who had found one person they could trust to make the loneliness go away.

He doesn't want you involved.

Well, dammit, she didn't want to be involved.

But why did Hu Chang want to close her out?

She pulled out her computer and flipped it open.

The next moment, she had drawn up the story of the Qinghai earthquake. The second story she accessed she saw the photo of Erin Sullivan. She was standing beside a monk and a Chinese soldier, and she was frowning as she stared down at the wreckage below her.

Catherine had thought she'd be older, but the woman looked to be close to her own age. She wasn't over thirty, perhaps a little younger. She was tall, slim even in the bulky, cold-weather garments she was wearing. She had on a black, hooded jacket and matching pants and brown, fur-lined boots. A strand of copper red hair had escaped her hood and lay on her forehead above eyes that were large and a gray-green hazel. Not a beautiful woman, but she had an interesting bone structure and a full, wonderful mouth. Her expression was mature and intelligent and troubled as she looked down at the devastation in the valley below.

Who wouldn't have been troubled? Catherine thought. Several thousand people had been killed in that quake. She quickly scanned the info about Erin Sullivan. She had been an Army brat who had traveled all over Europe and the Middle East with her parents. She had earned a scholarship to Stanford University, majored in languages and journalism, held several minor jobs in cities around Europe, and

found a niche in a small television station in Calcutta, India. She
had worked three years traveling for the station in Pakistan and
Tibet, then had quit and become a freelance journalist. According
to the story, she had traveled to the quake site on her own to write
the story. Then she had stayed to help with the rescue that was being
conducted by the monks of the area and the Chinese soldiers who
had been sent from Beijing to help. They had needed all the help
they could get because the soldiers had become disoriented and
physically ill because of the altitude. Erin had worked in these mountains, and the altitude was no problem for her. Both the Tibetan
monks and the Chinese soldiers had nothing but praise for her.

Clearly a remarkable woman. Why would someone want to
target her?

"We are going to land." The smiling, Asian flight attendant
was standing beside her seat. "Please put away all electronic de-
vices."

"Sorry." Catherine nodded, shut off her computer, and slipped
it in her bag. She glanced out the window. They should be on the
ground within a few minutes. She hoped Hu Chang would be
there to meet her. She would see him walking toward her with a
faint, mocking smile on that face that was totally ageless. She had
questions to ask him that he might not answer. She could never tell
if he would dance around or give her the simple truth. As if any truth
was simple with a man so complicated.

"Just what the hell are you up to, Hu Chang?" she murmured.

DAKSHA PALACE
TIBET

"Get *out* of here, Jafar." Erin Sullivan's voice was shaking as
she gazed at the young boy in desperation and fear. She had been
stunned when she had seen the boy slip over the windowsill into

her bedroom only moments before. Stunned and sick with panic. "You should never have come. I'll get out on my own."

"I should have come. I was sent." Jafar's huge brown eyes were glowing in his small face. "I heard the calling, and I went to my father. He told me to follow the spirits. You can't get across the mountains on your own. I will lead you from this dark place."

His father had told him to come to this hellhole? Jafar couldn't be over eleven or twelve years old, Erin thought, agonized. She had grown to know Jafar and his family during the weeks she had spent in his village, but she had not dreamed they'd sacrifice their son like this. Perhaps she should have realized it could happen. Like the rest of the people in his village, Jafar was full of dreams and the belief that good would always triumph in the end. Erin knew better. Not here, not anywhere where Paul Kadmus could reach out to crush and mangle. But she wouldn't be able to persuade the child to leave her by using fear. The dreams were too strong, the belief too ingrained. She thought quickly, searching for a way that he would understand.

"Your father should not have sent you to me. I must fight this battle alone. My special spirit told me that's the only way to gain a higher plane of enlightenment."

He frowned. "But this is a dark place. We've heard stories that they hurt you here. *He* hurts you." He looked at her face. "You have bruises."

She couldn't deny it. The ugly stories must have been driven from the palace like ice pellets in the wind. Find an excuse. "Suffering sometimes cleanses the soul."

He was gazing at her doubtfully.

She changed the subject. "Jafar, how did you get past those soldiers and into the palace? Could you get out the same way?"

He nodded. "I crawled down a drainage pipe underneath the palace that goes from the compound wall to the courtyard. It leads toward the road that goes down the mountain. My father said the monks who settled in our village after Kadmus drove them out of this palace told him about it." He smiled proudly. "I was like a shadow. No one saw me."

She hoped to God no one had seen him. "You're very clever, Jafar. I'm sure that you were just as invisible as you claim."

"As invisible as Shambhala." He nodded solemnly. "I can take you out of here the same way. Once we reach that far mountain, no one will find us."

And the minute anyone discovered Erin was gone, Kadmus's mercenaries would be after her, and the boy would be considered collateral damage. She had experienced just how brutal Kadmus could be. She couldn't risk it. "No, I can't go with you." Her hands closed on his thin shoulders, and she looked him in the eye. "I thank you with my whole heart. You have been very brave, and you must tell your father that no one else from the village should come here. I will leave this place on my own." She gave him a quick, hard hug. "You have to go now. Good-bye, Jafar, safe journey."

He didn't move. "But the spirits want you free. My father said that was true. He said you had helped our people to live, and now we must help you."

"You have helped me. When I'm ready to go, you've told me how to leave this place." She was searching frantically for a way to make him go. She didn't know how much time she had before Kadmus would show up. She was allowed the freedom of the ancient palace on this barren mountaintop because he considered it a safe prison, but he never left her alone for long. "Go now, please, Jafar."

He nodded slowly. "But I will return if you don't come to us soon. I told you, the spirits sent me to lead you from this place. And I don't think the spirits want you to be hurt. That's the work of the demon who took you." He turned and slipped out the window.

Erin crossed to the window, but he'd already disappeared.

Madness. Bravery. Sacrifice.

The cold was biting, and the distant mountain was shrouded in icy mist.

Let the boy reach the mountain. Let him get back to his village.

Oh, let him *live*.

Then she heard the shot.

Her body jerked as if the bullet had struck her.

No. No. No.

"What did you expect, Erin?" Paul Kadmus was strolling out of the mist toward her from across the courtyard. He was carrying Jafar's limp body. "If you wanted someone to save you, then you should have chosen someone besides this crazy kid." He threw the boy's body on the ground in front of her window. "But he's probably the only male specimen in the mountains who would be willing to go up against me."

There was a bullet hole in the center of Jafar's head, and Erin couldn't take her eyes from it. A few minutes ago, he had been vibrantly alive and now this . . .

"He wasn't crazy," she said dully. "He believed he was doing what was right. He had a calling. His people don't consider age a factor in moving toward true enlightenment. I wasn't going with him. I was afraid that you or your men would do this. You didn't have to kill him, Kadmus."

"No, it was a pleasure." His face revealed the same fierce enjoyment as he looked up at her. Those craggy, high cheekbones and deep-set blue eyes were riveting, but even before she had realized what lay behind that face, she had never thought him handsome. She had always sensed the evil.

"You're becoming used to the usual forms of torment, Erin," he said mockingly. "I wanted to see your face when I gave you a new and different wound. Aren't you tired of fighting me? This boy would never have had reason to die if you'd given me what I wanted." His gaze went to the gold necklace around her neck. He said softly, "Tell me, Erin."

"There's nothing to tell you." Her shaking hand instinctively went up to cradle the carved, eight-sided lotus that hung from the chain. "If you want this thing, take it. I don't want it. I've told you before, you can pick one up like it at any market in Tibet."

"Not like that one." Kadmus smiled. "And I don't want your pretty necklace. I want to know who gave it to you. I want you to take me to meet him." His boot nudged the body of the boy at his feet. "And then we won't have to kill any more of these simpletons who think you're some kind of Mother Teresa. Wouldn't that please you, Erin?"

"You'd still kill anyone who got in your way."

"True. But they wouldn't get in my way if they didn't put themselves between you and me." His gaze met her own over the boy's body. "Where did you get that necklace, Erin?"

"I told you, I bought it at a market in Qinghai Province."

He sighed. "I was hoping that the boy might be a breakthrough." He turned on his heel. "But I'll just have to think of something else that will bring about the same result." He looked over his shoulder, and added quietly, "You do know it will be very bad for you tonight, Erin? I'm very angry that you're being so stubborn."

She tried not to show the tension his words brought. He always used the anticipation of pain to make the torture even more devastating. It was a small victory to not let him see that psychological whip had an effect on her. "I know," she said steadily. "It won't make any difference. The answer will be the same."

She saw a flicker of anger cross his face. He muttered a curse, then strode across the courtyard. A moment later, he was lost behind the veil of icy precipitation.

Were they going to leave the boy lying there in the courtyard? Probably. Kadmus would like the idea of her seeing Jafar's body every time she looked out the window. Because each time she saw that poor boy's body, it would hurt her.

It *did* hurt her. But what did her pain matter, she thought impatiently. A child had died. A life had been taken. A soul had taken the next step.

Smother the pain.

Say good-bye.

Say a prayer for that brave boy who had died to try to free her.

The faith of his village was Buddhist, and she didn't know any Buddhist rituals. But prayer was prayer.

"Please, God, take him," she whispered. "Care for him. He was so good here with us for the little time we had him. You're lucky to have him back. He gave his life to save mine. How often do you get someone who would do that? He deserves anything you can do for him." The tears were stinging her eyes. "Good-bye, Jafar. You have a great spirit. Your parents would be proud of you. You'll be with me always . . ."

She was wiping her wet cheeks with the backs of her hands as she turned away from the window. Kadmus would be coming soon, and he mustn't see that she'd been weeping. It would be a triumph, and she wouldn't allow the atrocity he'd committed tonight to give him that victory.

Start the mantra.

No triumphs tonight.

Close your eyes.

Go away from this place.

Suspend all hatred. It would get in the way.

Withdraw into yourself.

Nothing can really touch you.

She sat down in the chair facing the door and began to prepare herself for what was to come.

CHAPTER
2

HONG KONG

Hu Chang hadn't come to meet her.

Catherine smothered disappointment when she saw Sam O'Neill, Luke's tutor, as she got through customs. "Hi, Catherine." He took her carry-on case and duffel bag. "Good to see you. I hear you've had a rough week or so."

"It wasn't wonderful," she said dryly. "None of them are. You know that, Sam." Sam was a retired CIA agent and a fine teacher. He had been Catherine's first choice as both a tutor and bodyguard for her son. "I got through it."

"You always do." He smiled as he led her toward the parking lot. "And very well, I'm sure. Venable knows how lucky he is to have you."

"I'm a valuable commodity to him, but I'm not the only agent who can give him what he wants."

"That sounded defensive."

"Did it? How has Luke been doing?"

"Intellectually, superb. He's learning in leaps and bounds. Of course, Hu Chang has a lot to do with that. He not only sparks and challenges, but he thinks outside the box and makes Luke come with him." He grimaced. "I haven't had much time for ordinary studies. Hu Chang has him in his lab most of the time. Luke's be-coming a chemical whiz."

"Intellectually, superb," she repeated. "What's that supposed to mean? What are you leaving out?"

"Nothing. I'm Luke's teacher, I'm used to judging his mental capability. I haven't had the opportunity to monitor his psycho-logical condition. You'd have to ask Hu Chang about that." He saw her expression, and said gently, "I'm not dodging the question. From what I've seen of Luke, he's seemed enthusiastic, happy, and full of life. Just what you'd want him to be." He paused. "He asks about you. Not often. It just comes out of the blue sometimes. He asks if I'm sure you're safe. And I've heard Hu Chang and Luke talk about you."

"Are you trying to comfort me, Sam? I don't expect Luke to worry and wonder about me. I wouldn't want him to do that." But she was grateful that Sam had confided those little signs that Luke had not forgotten her. "And Hu Chang cares about Luke or he wouldn't bother teaching him. I should be grateful he's dominating Luke's every thought." She heard the way that sounded, and said, "I *am* grateful."

Sam raised his brows.

"Okay, I'm protesting too much."

"Yes, you are. I believe you're feeling a little like a fifth wheel."

"Maybe. Luke's life goes on, and I always seem to have to catch up. Look, I'm grateful that you came to pick me up, Sam, but I'd—"

"You're wondering why Hu Chang didn't come instead."

"No, Hu Chang always does what he wishes." But she would have liked him to have wished to see her as much as she wanted to see him. It seemed like a long time since she had been with Hu Chang. "I never expect anything of him."

"Very wise. How well you understand me, Catherine."

She stopped, her gaze flying to the man walking across the park-ing lot toward her. "Hu Chang." She felt a surge of joy and took an involuntary step toward him. Then she halted and said offhand-edly, "Not really, you can still surprise me." She watched him come toward her, every step lithe and graceful. He was wearing black as usual, black trousers, black tunic that somehow was faultlessly elegant. His shoulder-length dark hair shone in the lights of the parking lot. He was only a few inches above middle height but appeared taller. When she was fourteen, she had thought he was an old man, but that was because his night-dark eyes seemed to hold all the secrets of the world. She didn't know how old he was; his high-cheekboned face seemed totally ageless. He had told her once he was part Russian, part Mongolian, and he looked neither except for those black eyes. All she knew was that she had seen him do amazing physical acts, and his endurance was incredible. She knew he had lived long enough to travel the world and learn a great deal. She knew he had delved into dozens of philosophies and accepted bits and pieces of them. She knew that he let her into his life more than he did any other human being.

Yet she did not ever know what he would do next.

"Why did you even bother to come? I didn't need anyone to pick me up. And who's taking care of Luke if both of you are hov-ering over me?"

"Your son can take better care of himself than many men three times his age," Hu Chang said. "And you're being rude to Sam, who is just obeying my orders."

"I'm not being rude to Sam. He has his orders. He wouldn't have left Luke by himself if he'd known that he'd not be with you. I'm being rude to you."

"I'm glad you made that clear," he murmured. "But let's permit Sam to leave you now that I'm here. He doesn't have to listen to you abusing me. I'm sure it embarrasses him."

"Actually, it's entertaining," Sam said with a grin. "And en-lightening. But I take it you want me to go watch over Luke while she does it?"

"That would be less humiliating for me." He inclined his head. "If you would be so kind."

"No problem." He turned to Catherine and handed her the handle of her roller bag. "I'll see you later."

Catherine watched him stroll away from them across the parking lot. "Why did you send him to pick me up?"

"My car is over there. The gray Mercedes. I would carry your bags, but you're obviously feeling fiercely independent and a little resentful. You may carry them yourself."

"Thank you," she said as she fell into step with him. "Why did you send Sam?"

"Because you've had a bad time for the last few weeks, and I wanted you to see a friendly face when you got off the plane."

"So you took Sam away from guarding my son and sent him to furnish the friendly face? Why would you do that?"

"Because I was busy and couldn't do it myself. Of course, my expression is seldom described as friendly, but you wouldn't care about that." He opened the passenger door of the Mercedes for her. "You're much too discriminating."

"No, I wouldn't have cared. But you seldom feel it necessary to pick me up. Why this time?"

He smiled, his gaze meeting her own. "Perhaps because I wanted to see you. Is that too difficult to believe?"

She felt a melting deep inside her as she looked at him. She had wanted to see him, too. All the years of friendship, all the bonds that nothing could break. This city was not home, but being with Hu Chang came close. "No, I believe that's true. But perhaps it's not the entire truth. Did you send Sam because he was ex-CIA, and you thought I needed protection? Or did you have a problem with Luke that you wanted to solve before I saw him?" She got into the passenger seat. "Get in the car and tell me the rest of it."

He smiled with genuine amusement. "I have missed you, Catherine." He came around the car and got into the driver's seat. "You're

an unending delight." He started the car. "But you shouldn't demand that Sam watch over Luke night and day. It's not healthy for
Luke."

"Too bad. It's healthy for me not to have to worry about him. I
lost him once when a scumball targeted him instead of me. It's not
going to happen again."

"You'd worry anyway," he said quietly. "You're afraid he'll
walk away and never come back. You're wrong, Catherine, he's not
going to leave you. Only a fool would abandon a jewel like you.
Luke is not a fool."

"Bullshit. He doesn't have to be a fool. He's a boy who was told
all of his childhood by that bastard Rakovac that all the pain and
misery he was going through was because of me." She looked at
him. "Are you trying to change the subject? You didn't answer my
question."

"I'll answer it now. Yes. And yes."

She stiffened. "What's happening, Hu Chang?"

"That's another question." He took out his phone and started to
dial. "Forgive me, I have to call Sam before he gets too far."

"Why? What's he—"

"Sam, don't go to my shop in the city." Hu Chang spoke into
the phone. "Luke is at the Golden Palace. I had your bags transferred there after you left to go to the airport. Yes, everything is all
right. We'll join you shortly." He hung up and started to back out
of the parking space. "You may explode now, Catherine."

"I'm not going to explode," she said through her teeth. "Why
did you move Luke to Chen Lu's palace? Wasn't it safe for him in
the city?"

"Probably, but Chen Lu has a security force that's top-notch,
and she's been missing Luke since we left the island. I thought it
wouldn't hurt to have him visit her. Unless you object?"

"You tell me, should I object?" Not about the visit itself. Catherine knew that Chen Lu had a genuine affection for Luke after his

stay with her sometime ago. She had been born in Dublin, Ireland, and she and her husband had acquired vast wealth and fallen in love with Hong Kong many years ago. She had taken the name Chen Lu and bought the wonderful Golden Palace on an island outside Hong Kong, where she'd lived since her husband's death. Catherine liked her as much as Luke did, but the woman was totally devoted to Hu Chang and would do anything he asked. "The first thing you mentioned was the security on the island. What are you up to?"

"Safeguarding your son. Safeguarding my friend, Catherine." He sighed. "Though I fear you will refuse to be safeguarded. You are most stubborn."

"Why should you have to safeguard either one of us?" She was silent, thinking, putting together the puzzle. "And what the hell do you have to do with Erin Sullivan?"

"Ah, you've made the connection. I knew you would." His lips tightened. "Just as I knew Venable would not keep you out of it if it suited him. I will have to think of a fitting way to punish him."

"You obviously told Venable not to tell anyone you were his source. Why?"

"You were the only one I was concerned about. There was a possibility that he wouldn't tell you unless he wanted to use you. Evidently, he wishes to use you."

"I wasn't interested. I told him to go to hell."

"Excellent. Then I don't have to discuss it with you. Should I make reservations for you and Luke on the next plane for the U.S.?"

"And will you stay here with Chen Lu?"

"For a little while perhaps."

She was silent. "What did you tell Venable? Why did you contact him?"

"I knew he must have contacts in Tibet. I wanted information."

"Did he give it to you?"

"With a little prodding."

"What else?"

"I wanted him to send a CIA agent into the mountains of Tibet who had a modicum of sense and would obey orders." He smiled. "Someone who clearly wasn't you, Catherine."

"And do what?"

"Just be available in case a backup was needed."

"Your backup?"

"Have I ever required assistance?"

"Yes," she said bluntly. "I remember one time Venable had to bring in an F-18 to stage a distraction."

"But that was by my intention."

She ignored that remark. "Are you going after Erin Sullivan?"

"But you're not interested."

"Tell me."

"Yes."

"Why? Do you know her?"

"I've never had the pleasure of meeting her."

"Is it because she's some kind of glorified activist or something?"

"When have I ever involved myself with activists? They usually end up dead. That definitely puts a pall on a relationship."

"Why?" she repeated.

He shrugged. "I was asked to intercede in her situation by a man I respect."

"Who?"

"A friend of long standing."

Blank wall. "Then why doesn't he go after her?"

"There are problems for him."

"Because he'd rather you risk your life? What kind of a wimp is he?"

"Wimp?" Hu Chang tilted his head. "That is amusing. He's probably the most dangerous man either one of us will ever meet."

"All the more reason why he—" She met Hu Chang's gaze.

This was going to go nowhere. Change direction. "What is Sullivan's situation? Venable didn't seem to know. Do you?"

"I have an idea where she is. So does Venable."

And he wasn't about to tell her. "Listen to me. I won't ask you any more questions about Erin Sullivan. But if you think that something about her 'situation' is going to pose a danger to me or Luke, then I should know about it. Why did you move him to Chen Lu's island?"

He was silent. "Merely as a precaution. There's no danger to either of you as yet. That doesn't mean there might not be in the future. There may be certain tentacles that reach out and try to grab. You'll be safer on the island than any other place if you choose not to get on that plane to the U.S. Probably safer than there, too. I've never found the U.S. any too secure. Too many laws and ways to get around them. Lawless countries have a basic frontier mind that—"

"Tentacles?"

"Very sharp, very deadly tentacles," he said softly. "That's why I told Venable I didn't want you involved. Tentacles can do terrible damage to a woman as wonderfully beautiful as you. I could not bear the thought of it. I'm glad you're not going to let Venable draw you into this. It's more comfortable than having to be the one to do it." He was parking the Mercedes at the pier. "I've arranged to rent a speedboat to take us to the island. You'll be with Luke in a little over thirty minutes."

"Good." She moistened her lips. "Don't do this, Hu Chang. Let Venable handle it."

"But I will do it so much better." He smiled as he got out of the car. "And it requires a certain delicacy that only I can offer." He opened her car door. "You know that no one has a more exquisitely subtle touch than I do."

"Your 'subtle' touch would have a hell of a time fighting against those damn tentacles."

"No, it wouldn't. Any one of my poisons could make any battle exceptionally short-term."

"If you had the time and proximity to administer it." She paused. "At least, tell me that you're not having to fight Beijing."

"Not directly."

"Hu Chang."

"Perhaps not at all." He helped her into the speedboat. "One can never tell." He added gently but firmly, "But whatever the confrontation, you will not be present. Do you understand?"

"Perfectly," she said curtly. "I have no intention of letting either you or Venable rope me into this. If you're going to be fool enough to risk your neck, why should I care?"

"Because that is the nature of our relationship. Now hush and relax, and I will tell you what a splendid few weeks Luke has had under my magnificent guidance . . ."

•   •   •

Catherine could see Luke waiting on the pier as the speedboat approached the island. He was dressed in black trousers and a loose white shirt, and his dark hair was lifting in the strong breeze. He smiled and waved. She had seen him only a few weeks ago, but he looked taller, older than his eleven years. She felt a pang at the thought that she had missed those weeks.

God, he was beautiful.

God, she loved him.

She lifted her hand and returned his wave. "Did you tell him to come and meet me?" she asked Hu Chang.

"No, stop thinking that Luke has to be prodded to come to you," Hu Chang said. "If he is here, it is because he was eager to see you. I never interfere with his free will."

"If Chen Lu didn't suggest it."

He sighed and shook his head. "You're impossible." He drew next to the dock, and one of Chen Lu's servants jumped forward to secure the boat. "Think what you like. You will anyway." They both watched Luke run down the dock toward them. "But for someone who has to be forced to come and greet you, he appears to be in a great hurry to get over here."

"Catherine?" Luke was standing before the boat, his eyes sparkling, his cheeks flushed with color. He had never called her Mother since she had rescued him from Rakovac, and that was okay with her. She would be friend or mother or anything else he wanted her to be as long as he let her stay in his life. "I've been waiting for you." He reached down and took her hand and pulled her from the boat to the dock. "Hu Chang says that you might be tired and that maybe we should stay here at the Golden Palace for a little while."

"I'm not tired." She stood staring hungrily at him. Don't be too obvious. Don't make him feel uncomfortable. "But we can stay for a week or so if you like. You always liked it here."

He grinned. "After the fire here, I got to replant a lot of Chen Lu's garden. I kind of feel as if it's mine. I like being at Hu Chang's shop and lab, too. But it's different."

"Every place is different." She wanted to reach out and hug him, hold him. "We just have to enjoy what we can wherever we are at any given time."

His smile faded. "Hu Chang said that you would have come sooner but that your friend, Eve Duncan, was in trouble, and you had to help her. Is she okay now?"

She nodded. "She's home and safe. But I had to stay and find her." She moistened her lips. "I wanted to come right here to you, but she helped me when I needed to find you, Luke. I couldn't let her down."

"I know that. I like Eve." He was silent. "If you'd told me, I would have come to search for her, too."

"That was my job." She smiled. "You're just a kid, Luke. Wait a few years."

"I don't feel like a kid." He frowned. "I guess I don't know what that would be like."

"I know you don't." That had probably been the wrong thing to say. The rough life he had lived had burned the childhood out of him. Occasionally, she saw flashes of it that she celebrated, but they were rare. "And I hate it that I can't give that back to you."

"Why? You can't miss what you've never had. Hu Chang says that you grew up on the streets, and that doesn't sound much better."

"I was free, you were a prisoner."

"There is no use arguing with her, Luke." Hu Chang was getting out of the boat and strolling toward them. "She grew so accustomed to feeling guilty that she couldn't save you that she's not reasonable on the subject."

"I'm completely reasonable." Luke and Hu Chang were exchanging glances, and Luke was smiling, she realized with a pang. There was a closeness, an intimacy between them that was shutting her out. "And you both realize there are differences in—"

"Catherine." Luke chuckled as he took a step forward and took her hand. "I can't realize the difference. It's hard for me to imagine your running around Hong Kong, hunting for food, and just trying to stay alive. I can only think of you strong and beautiful, the way you are now."

"I have no trouble imagining your life when you were with Rakovac." Her hand closed tightly, lovingly, on Luke's. He had made the first physical move, so she felt safe about responding. He wouldn't think that she was demanding more than he wanted to give. "But I don't like to remember it."

"I don't mind remembering Rakovac," Luke said. "I never let him win after I got old enough to fight him." He added fiercely, "And I like to think about your killing him. I wish I could have seen it."

"Luke, that's not the thing to say to make Catherine feel better about the normalcy she evidently wants for you." Hu Chang was ushering them toward the ornate golden gates that led to the front door. "Though I agree in your case she gave you a gift beyond price."

He nodded at the servant who swung open the gates. "Come along. Is Chen Lu waiting in the garden, Luke?"

Luke nodded. "She wanted to show Catherine how much all the plants have grown since she was here."

"I thought as much. You take her along to Chen Lu." He fell back and took out his phone. "I'll join you later. I have a few arrangements to make."

Catherine stiffened, her gaze flying to his face. She knew what that meant. He was getting ready to move. She had hoped to have more time to persuade him. How much time did she still have? "You'll join us for dinner?"

He smiled. "Of course."

There was no "of course" about it, she thought grimly. But he wouldn't lie to her. "We'll see you then." She let Luke lead her toward the magnificent palace gardens. "Are the plantings as wonderful as Chen Lu thinks, Luke? There hasn't been that much time for growth. Those acres of wonderful trees and plants were a blackened ruin only months ago."

"They're much better now." His tone was distracted. "Hu Chang and I have been working in his lab on a special fertilizer. It's pretty good."

"You didn't tell me."

"It was going to be a surprise." He looked over his shoulder at Hu Chang. "You're worried about him. What's happening?"

"I'm not really worried as much as—" She met his gaze. Her first instinct was to protect him, but that instinct was wrong. Not by lying to him. From the moment she'd gotten him back, she'd promised she'd always be honest with him. It was the only way their relationship had a chance of surviving. "Hu Chang has a friend who is in danger, and he's thinking about going to help her."

"Are you going with him?"

"No," she said quickly. "I wouldn't do that."

"Why not? You told me once that being CIA is something like being a soldier. Isn't it your job?"

"No, it's not. And Hu Chang doesn't want me to go."

He thought for a moment. "Then I think I'll go with him."

"No!"

"Why not? Hu Chang's not like you. He wouldn't be afraid of anything's happening to me. He knows that I can take care of myself."

And Catherine knew that, too. He'd been forced to learn how to survive in the guerrilla warfare into which Rakovac had deliberately thrust him. It just hurt her to even think of subjecting him to anything resembling that again. "Luke, Hu Chang wants to do this alone. And I don't want him to go at all. I'll try to talk him out of it."

"Can you do it?" He slowly shook his head. "I don't think so."

She didn't think so either, and she was starting to feel the beginning of panic. She felt backed into a corner. She was frightened to death that Hu Chang would disappear into those damn mountains. Now, she was afraid that Luke would find a way to try to go after him. She had seen the strong bond that had formed between them.

Hu Chang's not like you.

No, he wasn't. He didn't agonize, he accepted. And she knew the fascination Hu Chang could weave when he chose. He would not take Luke with him, but that didn't mean Luke wouldn't follow.

"I'll work it out." She had no choice. Like it or not, she had been tossed in the middle of this brouhaha. "Trust me, Luke."

"I will," Luke said gravely. "And will you trust me, Catherine?"

She looked at him in surprise. There was something beyond the obvious in that question. What exactly did he mean?

"There's Chen Lu." Luke had looked away from her as they went around the corner.

Chen Lu was sitting on a bench in the garden. Pure white hair framed a face that was youthful, vivacious, and full of vitality and didn't look a day over forty. She was dressed as usual in a magnificent silk caftan, and she jumped to her feet with a broad smile.

"Catherine. Welcome. At last an audience that can appreciate my garden." She still had a strong Irish accent in spite of her years in Hong Kong, and her eyes were sparkling with humor. "Hu Chang and Luke just dumped their noxious brew into the ground and took off back to the city to their lab." She threw out her arm. "You remember how blackened and burnt-out it was. All my beautiful roses and tropical plants . . . I thought it would take years." She shook her head. "New life. Resurrection."

"Yes, it's beautiful." Catherine was stunned as she looked around the huge acreage. She had been here when the replanting had taken place. In spite of all the money Chen Lu had put into the rebirth of her precious garden, Catherine, too, had thought it would take years. But the plants appeared to be surprisingly mature, and the blooms were vivid and splendidly healthy. "Wonderful." She turned to Luke. "Noxious brew? Oh, that special fertilizer?"

"Hu Chang had an idea for a better fertilizer than Chen Lu's gardeners had put down." Luke smiled proudly. "He let me help create it. He said I did well."

"Yes, you did." Chen Lu chuckled. "My gardeners were stunned when they saw what my roses were doing a week later." She pulled Catherine to the bench. "Sit down and enjoy the scents. You look as if you need to just relax for a while." She turned to Luke. "Would you run and tell the cook we'll be ready to eat in an hour and a half?"

He nodded and took off down the path toward the palace.

Chen Lu watched him affectionately. "What a sweet lad. It's good to have him back. I've missed him."

"So have I." Catherine smiled. "And you can't have him back for more than a week or so, Chen Lu."

"We'll see. Something's brewing, or Hu Chang wouldn't have brought him to me." She tilted her head. "I don't suppose you'd like to tell me what it is?"

"I'm not sure."

"And you're not talking. That's fine. I'll find out eventually."

She was silent. "I remember that a man visited you when you were last here. John Gallo. He didn't come with you?"

"There was no reason for Gallo to come. He has his life, I have mine."

"Ah, and he was becoming too possessive?"

"It hadn't gotten that far. I have enough problems without dealing with a relationship."

"That might interfere with your independence." Chen Lu laughed. "Well, there's no threat here. You can relax. You need to just sit here and let all the tension kind of . . . unkink. You have thirty minutes before you have to go to your room and dress for dinner." Her lips curved in a mischievous smile. "I'll even be quiet, and you know what a chore that is for me."

"A terrible burden," Catherine agreed. "But I can go to my room now, Chen Lu. The same one?"

"Yes, but in thirty minutes." She closed her eyes. "Now, hush, and breathe deep. Let all these glorious scents soothe you. Are they not wonderful?"

"Magic." A thousand aromas, all potent and delicious and intoxicating. She made her mind go blank. Thirty minutes. Then she'd start to think about Luke and Hu Chang.

And Erin Sullivan . . .

DAKSHA PALACE
TIBET

Pain.

"Where is he, Erin?" Kadmus whispered. "All the agony will stop if you just tell me."

"Go to hell."

"Now is that a fitting way for you to speak to me? All those peasants who think you're such a boon to humanity would be so disappointed in you. You're supposed to be everything angelic and serene."

"Take these handcuffs off me, and I'll show you serene."

"I'm tempted, but you made me quite angry before I decided they were necessary. I don't want to kill you before I get the information I need." He frowned. "You should have broken long before this. I'm getting very impatient, Erin."

"I can't tell you what I don't know. I told you where I got the damn necklace."

"But it wasn't the answer I wanted. I thought you'd be more cooperative after I shot that stupid kid. Oh, well, I'll get there." He looked objectively at her naked body. "The right breast this time, I think . . ."

She tensed as she saw the flame come closer. She could bear this. At least he wasn't using the ropes.

Relax.

Close out the pain.

Go to the place where there is no pain.

She could feel the heat of the flame as it came slowly nearer to her nipple.

Close it out.

Help me, Cameron.

The flame touched her.

Searing pain.

Cameron!

CHAPTER
3

Catherine slammed the door of the elegant suite Chen Lu had assigned her. The young servant girl jumped to her feet and smiled at her. "I'm Susan Mei. How may I—"

"I don't need help." She had forgotten that Chen Lu always supplied her guests with servants. She had to get rid of her quickly. She only had forty-five minutes before dinner. "Thank you. You may go. I'll tell Chen Lu that you did everything splendidly."

The girl's smile faded. "Perhaps I could run your bath? I've already laid out your caftan. I thought that ivory with the gold would be—"

"That will be fine." Chen Lu always supplied her guests with what she deemed suitable evening clothes. "No, nothing more." She smiled. "Perhaps another time." She opened the door. "I'll ask for you if I need you."

The girl reluctantly left the room, and Catherine closed the door.

The next moment, she had pulled out her phone and was dialing.

"How is Chen Lu?" Venable asked when he answered. "A delightful woman. I always wondered if she and Hu Chang were—"

"How do you know I'm at the Golden Palace? Did you have me followed?"

"No, I had Hu Chang followed. You're bound to be with him, and that's where he took the boy today." He paused. "Why are you calling? Let me guess. You've found that Hu Chang is going after Erin Sullivan. Tell me, did you persuade him to let you go with him?"

"No," she said curtly. "You know better than that. Hu Chang doesn't change his mind."

"That's right, and you have no intention of going on this mission anyway, do you? You made that clear."

"Stop being smug. I'm mad as hell. You're using Hu Chang and Luke to back me in a corner."

"No, I have nothing to do with that happening. Those chess pieces were all on the board before Erin Sullivan was taken. I just recognized an opportunity. I needed you, and you were vulnerable."

And she couldn't deny that was true no matter how frustrating it was to her. "This isn't what I wanted. I may still refuse the damn mission." She paused. "But I need to know details, so that I can judge my chances of coming out of it alive and the amount of time I'd have to be away from Luke."

He was silent. "Details are sketchy."

"Which means I could end up dead."

"I have faith in you."

"Bullshit. Give me what you have. Who took Erin Sullivan?"

"We believe she's being held by a mercenary by the name of Paul Kadmus. He has over fifty men under his command and runs roughshod in the villages in the interior. Actually, he calls himself General Paul Kadmus. If he could get away with the title of emperor, he would. He has a gargantuan ego and a king complex. He's been operating in the mountains of Tibet since Vietnam and thinks he owns them."

"Vietnam?" She stared at him in shock. "That's been over for something like forty years."

"It takes a long time to establish a dynasty for the emperor," Venable said sarcastically. "Kadmus was only a kid when he was captured by the North Vietnamese. He was in prison for over two years and became very bitter against the U.S. When he finally got out, he went to Tibet and set himself up to run his own show. Theft, murder, torture. Governments came, governments went, but as long as they paid him, he got the job done."

"And no one sent soldiers into the mountains to capture him?"

"They found it economically and militarily disastrous. No one knows those mountains like Kadmus. They decided to pay tribute instead. He has fingers in several pies around the country, both criminal and legitimate. He's become one rich bastard."

"You could have sent a hit man in to get him."

"Yes."

"But he made you an offer you couldn't refuse."

"Several offers. Tibet is a difficult country, and Kadmus was useful on occasion."

"Until he snatched Erin Sullivan. The publicity probably made him too hot for you to handle."

"It wasn't the publicity. She's an American citizen. No one can be allowed to victimize an American citizen."

And he believed every word he was saying, she realized. He was both cynical and a master manipulator, but he had a code, and he stuck by it. It was the only reason she had been able to work with him all these years. "And is he victimizing her? Why did he kidnap her?"

"We don't know." He paused. "We believe she has something he wants. Is he victimizing her? Yes, there have been reports of torture."

She went still. "You didn't tell me that."

"You weren't ready. You'd have accused me of playing on your sympathy to keep you from being with your son." He added grimly, "But we've got to get her out of Tibet pretty damn quick, or it won't be in one piece."

"Unless she gives him what he wants."

"I don't believe that's an option. She's held out this long."

She changed the subject. "Where is he keeping her?"

"Utset Province. Daksha Mountain, an ancient palace deep in the mountains. It was taken over by the monks when the local royal family was killed off by a warring neighbor. Kadmus moved in and kicked out the monks a couple years ago. It's practically inaccessible from the outside."

"Then how would you get me in?"

"A helicopter that will let you out on the left slope of the mountain. You'd have to climb up to the plateau from there and find your own way into the palace. I can give you a map of the location of Kadmus's troops within the gates and the outside sentries. There's a drainage pipe that we thought would be a possible way in, but we've crossed that out now."

"Why?"

Venable didn't speak for a moment. "A young village boy used it to try to get in to rescue her. He was killed, and the pipe may have been discovered as an entry source."

She felt sick. "A young boy . . ."

"So you'll probably have to climb the compound wall and come in through the roof of the palace."

"And how am I supposed to get her out?"

"That's up to you."

"Thank you." But she'd probably prefer it that way. Planned exits had a habit of going to hell when you were on the spot. "The helicopter?"

"The pilot can stay in the area if you don't alert Kadmus's men. If you do, he has orders to leave. Kadmus has missile launchers."

"My alternative?"

"There's a village on the mountain, but it's controlled by Kadmus. You'll have to leave the area and head for one of the other mountains. The closest one is Milchang Mountain. Sullivan might know a village that will shelter and hide you until you can get out of the country. Otherwise, you trek across the mountains until you get to a place where we can set down a helicopter."

"Time?"

"Best-case scenario, you're in and out in three hours with Sullivan in tow. Worst-case scenario, you're hiding in the mountains for four to six weeks until we can get to you."

"It had better be a best-case scenario." She paused. "How soon can you get me there?"

"You're going to go?"

"I didn't say that. How soon?"

"I could have a man pick you up on the dock in three hours. I have a helicopter ready, packed with all the emergency equipment you'll need at a heliport in town. You'll be in Utset Province in four hours if the weather holds."

"Is there a chance it won't?"

"There's always that chance. High altitude, misty snow when it's not a blizzard, freezing temperatures. Kadmus had a reason for establishing his headquarters there." He added quietly, "And a reason why Erin Sullivan's chances are going down the tube with every passing day. Are you going to help improve those chances? She deserves it, Catherine."

"We all deserve it." But some deserved the chance to survive a little more than others. Erin Sullivan had earned that preference when she had saved all those victims in the earthquake. There was such a thing as payback. "It had better be that best-case scenario, Venable."

"Yes."

"And you get me out of here without Hu Chang knowing that I've gone, or it's no deal."

"No problem."

"Liar. I can see big problems from start to finish. I'll be on the dock in three hours." She hung up.

She was an idiot. She should not be worrying about anything or anyone but her relationship with Luke.

You told me once that being CIA is something like being a soldier. Isn't it your job?

Yes, it was. She had made the decision which way she wanted her life to go a long time ago. For a person of her background in Hong Kong, there had been only two paths, and she had turned her back on the corruption that would have been the easy choice.

And besides Erin Sullivan, there was Hu Chang, who would be going after her if Catherine did not. She would not be able to stay on the sidelines and worry about his running up against a bastard like Paul Kadmus.

All right, decision made.

She got to her feet and headed for the shower. She had this evening with Luke, and she would forget everything else and live for the moment. It was how she had always tried to deal with every adversity, and this one might be shaping up to be one nightmare of an adversity.

Just live for the moment and hope for that best-case scenario.

•   •   •

"Catherine is lighting up my garden tonight," Chen Lu said to Hu Chang. Her bemused gaze was fixed on Catherine and Luke, who were going down the steps of the terrace to the garden after dinner. "She was tired when she arrived, but she seems to have made a rapid recovery."

"Perhaps too rapid." Hu Chang lifted his wine to his lips. "We'll have to see."

"You'll have to see," Chen Lu said. "I have nothing to do with the complicated relationship you have with Catherine. It sometimes bewilders me, so I prefer to not think about it. You're the one who analyzes and studies. I just enjoy."

"I know." Hu Chang smiled faintly. "That's a great and wonderful gift. And may you continue to enjoy it for the foreseeable future."

"I intend to do that." She laughed as she reached over and

touched his hand with affection. "With the help of my friend." Her gaze returned to Catherine. "That ivory brocade is magnificent on her. I thought I preferred her in color, but that caftan makes her dark hair and gold-olive skin seem to burn in contrast. She's truly beautiful, isn't she?"

"Yes." He nodded. "And you're right, she seems extremely high-voltage tonight." He paused. "I'm going away tomorrow morning. Before dinner, I talked to Garret Flannan, your head of security. I told him to put on extra personnel and assign special security to Catherine and Luke while they're here. They don't go anywhere alone." He met Chen Lu's gaze. "See to it."

Her smile faded. "Trouble? I suspected as much." She grimaced. "Tell me I'm not going to have to plant another new garden. I was most upset when you let it be destroyed by that terrible man who came after you, Hu Chang."

"Just a precaution." He smiled. "And there will always be terrible, troublesome men who come after me. If you want to avoid the problems I bring to your doorstep, you could always throw me into the streets."

"Not likely," Chen Lu said. "I'm not that kind of fool. What's a paltry garden or two compared to the gift you bring me?"

"You still have no regrets?"

"Not yet." She was silent a moment. "When I do, I'll come to you and beg one of those poisons that you sell for so much money." She lifted her chin and smiled. "Or perhaps for old times' sake, you'll give it to me for nothing."

"Perhaps I will. If I'm still around."

Her smile faded. "I don't like the sound of that."

"Life moves quickly and changes every minute. One can never be sure." He rose to his feet. "I have a few preparations to make for my trip. I believe I'll go and say good night to Catherine and Luke." He crossed the terrace and started down the steps. "You'll remember to make sure Flannan does as I told him?"

"Don't be ridiculous; of course I will." Her Irish accent deepened with emotion as she added, "And I'm not going to like it one bit if you're stupid enough to get yourself killed. What would I do without you? I like the idea of a choice."

"I'll remember that," Hu Chang said. "And I'll do my utmost to oblige."

•   •   •

"Hu Chang is coming." Luke was looking over his shoulder. "I thought I heard his footstep."

"Heard?" Catherine looked down at him. "He's yards away, and how would you know it is him?"

"He taught me," Luke said. "It was fun, like a game. We worked all day in the lab, but after dinner, we would sit outside the shop. He would point to someone in the crowds in front of the other shops or the market and tell me to concentrate, listen to the sound of that person's footstep so I'd recognize it if I closed my eyes."

"Why?"

"He said it might be useful." He shrugged. "Besides, it was fun. It was a puzzle. It took a long time, but I got pretty good at it."

"And what else did Hu Chang teach you?"

"All kinds of things," Luke said vaguely. "He knows a lot of stuff. But you know that, don't you?"

"Yes, I do. But he never taught me anything like that." She turned as Hu Chang caught up with them. "What have you been teaching my son?" She made a face. "Besides creating miracle fertilizers and heaven knows what other concoctions?"

"To concentrate and use his six senses." He nodded at Luke. "Or any others that he might discover. I detest wasting a skill. He's exceptionally good at focusing."

"I was telling him that you never taught me anything like that."

"You were my friend, not my apprentice. One must let a friend decide for themselves." He said to Luke, "Though sometimes an apprentice can become a friend as long as the respect remains. We will consider that possibility when I return."

Catherine stiffened. "You're leaving?"

"Not until morning. I only came to say good night."

She tried to hide her relief. "But I'll see you in the morning?"

He nodded. "It will be early. About four, I think."

"But I'll be able to talk to you."

He smiled faintly. "Talk. Not persuade." He glanced back at Luke. "You will guard her?"

Luke frowned. "If you think I should."

"Always," Hu Chang said. "It is your duty and your privilege." He turned away. "Sleep well." The next moment, he was walking away from them.

She wanted to go after him. She felt sad . . . and wrong. She had never lied to him even by omission.

Luke was watching him, too. "You said he wouldn't go."

She nodded. "And I meant it. He won't be leaving you, Luke."

"But he just said that—"

"It will be all right." She started back toward the palace. "I told you, I'll take care of it."

•　　•　　•

Two hours later, spray mist was striking Catherine's cheeks as Agent Les Caudell guided the speedboat through the harbor. He was a small, fiftyish man with gray-streaked hair and compact, muscular body who hadn't smiled once since he'd picked her up fifteen minutes ago.

"Is everything ready? When I called Venable back, he said that you'd also be flying the helicopter." Catherine's gaze was fixed on the lights of the city in the distance. "I want to be out of Hong Kong within the hour."

"You're in a hurry. You won't be so eager once we cross into Tibet," Caudell said dryly. "That area where I'm going to drop you is hell on Earth. Just substitute ice for flames."

"You're familiar with it? Good."

"As familiar as I can be. I've been assigned to Kadmus for six years."

"What do you know about him?"

"Not much. He likes it that way. He makes sure that the villagers don't talk to outsiders."

"How?"

"They disappear, and when they're found, they lack body parts."

"That would be effective. Who's Kadmus's chief enforcer?"

"They come and go. Kadmus has a nasty temper. At the moment it's Peter Brasden, a South African mercenary. I asked Venable to e-mail you photos of both Kadmus and Brasden. Brasden walks very carefully around Kadmus, but he likes power, too, and might be lured to sell him out."

"I don't intend to be around long enough to lure him to do anything. Venable said that my best bet would be to get into the palace through the roof. Is the roof guarded?"

"No, but you'll have a hell of a time getting through the guards in the courtyard. Brasden keeps them in tip-top shape, and he doesn't tolerate carelessness. He knows it could be his neck if he did."

"Where does Kadmus keep Erin Sullivan?"

"She's allowed the run of the place, but he's given her quarters in the south wing."

"Run of the place? Are we sure that she's a prisoner?"

"We're sure," he said grimly. "I think he likes the idea of making her feel that no matter what she does, she's totally in his power. She tried to escape twice and paid a high price."

"How do you know?" She gazed at him shrewdly, then guessed. "You bribe someone in the palace. Can he help me?"

"No, I wouldn't ask him. I've worked too hard to establish a connection." He added, "But I can give you a map of the palace and the times the guard changes."

"Don't be too generous," she said sarcastically. "How much will a map of the palace help me?"

"Very little. It's kind of a small palace. Only nine or ten rooms and scantily furnished. Kadmus would probably be more comfortable evicting the monks from the bigger monastery on Milchang, the next mountain over, but he likes the idea of living in that moth-eaten grandeur." He gave her a cool glance. "And I'm giving you what I can afford to give. I'm not sacrificing one contact and certainly not my life to make it easy for you. Venable thinks you're some super-duper agent who can whisk down and pull Sullivan out of that hellhole. You're a legend here in Hong Kong, but legends die just like anyone else."

She stared at him in surprise. "You're angry. Why?"

He was silent, then finally said, "It's stupid sending you in alone. A Special Forces team might have a chance. You're going to get her killed."

"No, Venable is right. I might get myself killed, but I represent less threat to Kadmus than an attack force. Venable would get another chance if I screw up." She smiled crookedly. "Maybe he'll send you in, Caudell."

He didn't answer.

Then she understood. "Why, you wanted to be the one who went after her," she said softly. "Did you offer?"

"Yes," he said curtly. "Venable turned me down."

"Why? You have the connections, you know the country. You've got to be good if Venable assigned you to Kadmus."

"But I'm not a legend." He paused. "And he thinks I'm too emotionally involved to function efficiently."

"Really? Because you hate Kadmus? Or that you're overly sympathetic toward Erin Sullivan?"

"Both."

She looked at him thoughtfully. "But you never wanted to go and fight that scumbag on his own turf until Sullivan came on the scene."

"Dammit." His voice was suddenly harsh. "I *like* her. Okay? I've been in Tibet for six years, and I'd heard about her, watched her, as she traveled to the villages and monasteries on stories."

"Did you ever meet her?"

"No, that wouldn't have been according to recommended procedure. You know we don't hobnob with the media unless we need to use them." He paused. "But I watched her at the earthquake zone. She was . . . something else."

"So I've been told."

"And did they also tell you what that son of a bitch has been doing to her?"

"Only that it's bad, and we have to get her out right away." She stared him in the eye. "And I will find a way to get her out, Caudell. That stuff about my being some kind of legend is pure bullshit. I'm just a damn good agent, and I'm probably the most stubborn woman you've ever met. That works pretty well sometimes. I'm not going to ask you to give up your contact. We've got to give Sullivan an escape hatch if it doesn't work well this time. But I've got to know if your resentment is going to interfere. I can't afford to let that happen."

He was silent. "You get her out of that place, and I'll stay on that ledge until they bring out the big guns." He grimaced. "No, maybe even a little longer."

"No, this isn't going to be a suicide mission. I'll need you later. You leave us on our own and get out of there if you have to do it. What kind of equipment do you have for me aboard the copter?"

"Cold-weather protective gear for both you and Sullivan, Emergency equipment, first-aid pack, radio, usual weaponry. Have you ever been on your own in conditions like that?"

"Not in those mountains. I've been working in South America lately. Four years ago, I was on a mission in Mongolia. I nearly froze to death before I got to the rendezvous. Not pleasant."

"You'll find it less pleasant to be stranded in Kadmus's little kingdom." He docked the speedboat at the heliport. "You'd better hope you get out of there in time for a pickup."

"I haven't been hoping anything else since I told Venable I was on board." She jumped out of the boat and followed him to the cream-and-tan helicopter. "What info does Kadmus want from her? You must know something."

"He wants to find a man. He thinks she knows where he is."

"Find whom?"

"How the hell do I know?" he asked harshly. "I told you, she won't tell Kadmus. But he won't give up."

"No names?"

"No names." He opened the door of the helicopter. "If you get her out, you can ask her yourself."

"I will." She got into the helicopter. "Because, unless I kill him, Kadmus is just going to go after her again if he still thinks he can get what he wants."

Who the hell was the man Kadmus wanted to find?

And what was his value to the son of a bitch?

A friend asked me to bring her out, Hu Chang had said.

Why? Because he was the same man for whom Kadmus was searching? Was he was afraid Erin Sullivan would break and reveal his location?

Or maybe Hu Chang's friend was just some charitable philanthropist who had been touched by Sullivan's plight.

He's probably the most dangerous man either of us will ever meet. That didn't sound like anyone who might be driven by humanitarian aims.

Guesses. With Hu Chang, one never knew.

"Let's get moving." What she did know was that Hu Chang was not going to be pleased when Chen Lu handed him her note in the morning. By that time she had to be deep in Tibet.

•   •   •

GOLDEN PALACE

Hu Chang recognized Catherine's handwriting at the first glance. Forceful, scrawling, every stroke finished but impatient and brimming with vitality.

"Catherine gave the note to her maid last night and told her to give it to me at breakfast," Chen Lu said. "And you're not to scold the poor lass. She just obeyed orders."

"I would never be so rude. Obedience is a fine quality." He tore open the envelope. "One that Catherine has never developed."

"And you would be disappointed if she did." Chen Lu poured tea into a cup. "You like her just the way she is."

"Not entirely." He quickly scanned the note. "She still has much to learn if this is any sign." He kept his face totally expressionless as he tossed the note on the table. "Where is Luke?"

"In the garden. I thought there might be a disturbance, so I sent him on an errand with the head gardener." She met his gaze. "Is there a disturbance, Hu Chang?"

"Oh, yes. On the scale of an earthquake." He rose to his feet. "I think that I will go and make adjustments to accommodate it. Tell Luke I will talk to him soon."

He moved quickly down the hall toward the library. Keep control. Don't let emotion interfere with intellect. Do not think of Catherine at Daksha Palace.

Not possible. He could do that with anyone else but not with Catherine. She was too much a part of him to block her out.

He sat down in the executive chair at the desk and reached for his phone. He quickly dialed Venable. "Where is she now?" he asked bluntly. "Has Catherine contacted you since she left here?"

"You sound a bit upset," Venable said. "My, my, and you're usually so serene."

"I told you that she was not to be involved in this. Have you heard from her?"

"They should be arriving at Daksha Mountain at any moment. My pilot will contact me when she starts for the palace." He paused. "And I will not cancel the mission, Hu Chang."

"As you wish, but all actions have consequences."

"Threats?"

"Statement."

"I take it that you just found out about it. A note?"

"A very brief and concise note." He quoted, " 'I'm on my way to get Sullivan out. It shouldn't take long. Take good care of Luke, or I'll never forgive you.' "

"Not exactly touching or sentimental. Typical Catherine. She stated her purpose, then tried to tie your hands and protect Luke at the same time. Did she do it?"

He didn't answer. "Does she have a chance?"

"Catherine always has a chance. It's at least fifty-fifty. I'd give her better odds if she wasn't on her own once she reaches the palace. If she gets back to the helicopter in one piece, she'll be home free."

"You will call me the minute she takes off from the mountain." He paused. "You threw too many ifs into that answer. I do not like ifs, Venable. I will not tolerate the idea that poor planning or rashness would cause me to lose her. You would not like my response to that possibility."

"Threats, again? This is Company business. We'll do what we have to do."

"And so will I." Hu Chang hung up and leaned back in his chair. Stifle the anger unless it was needed. Difficult. Very difficult. Anger was burning inside him, and he wanted to embrace it. Anger against Venable, against Kadmus, against a world that had created a special creature like Catherine, then tossed her into an existence where she could be destroyed at any moment.

Accept.

Release.

Consider consequences and look beyond the present to how to save the situation if it became necessary.

Catherine should have landed by now and be on her way to the palace.

The chances are fifty-fifty.

The muscles of his stomach clenched.

Banish fear. Look beyond.

And summon help.

His lips twisted as he looked down at his phone.

Modern technology at its best.

And not worth anything to him at the moment.

He closed his eyes.

Concentrate.

Look beyond.

One minute.

Two minutes.

Beyond . . .

He was *there*.

Cameron!

CHAPTER
4

She couldn't *breathe*.

This damn altitude.

Catherine took several deep breaths to fill her lungs as she moved up the slope toward the palace. It was still dark and snowing. Both good things to hide her from the sight of the guards. She'd slipped the white protective parka and suit on in the helicopter, and she hoped she blended into the landscape. She'd also memorized the guard stations as well as the layout of the palace. There should be a sentry a hundred yards around the next bend . . .

Go around him or kill him?

It would be easier to avoid, but she might have to face him on the return trip to the helicopter with Erin Sullivan.

Get rid of him now.

No gun. Silence. Knife or injection.

He'd be dressed in the same layered garb she was, and injection would be too chancy. She took out her knife and glided toward the bend.

There he was, holding an AK-47 and facing the road leading down the mountain. Tense, huddled with cold, standing near the rocky path to the palace. He was probably wishing he was the hell out of this weather and back at his quarters.

Move silently. Unless his instincts were superb, he shouldn't know she was behind him.

His instincts sucked.

Three minutes later, she lowered the guard to the ground and wiped her knife on the snow before she returned it to her holster. The guard wasn't supposed to be relieved for another forty-five minutes. It should give her enough time.

Maybe. No place to hide the body anyway. Just his absence from his post would set off an alarm.

She set off up the path. The wall to the north was the least guarded according to Caudell. Climb it. That would put her into the courtyard. Get rid of the guard at the steps leading to the roof. There was another staircase across the roof that led down and emptied into a hall approximately ten feet from Erin Sullivan's quarters.

And that might be the most dangerous part of the mission. Catherine could count only on herself. Erin Sullivan was a wild card. She might panic and cause them both to go down.

Stop worrying. She had freed hostages before and not lost them.

Focus on getting to that roof.

Then she'd concentrate on Erin Sullivan.

She checked her watch. The guard in the courtyard was due to be changed in thirty minutes.

She had to take down the guard and get Erin Sullivan out of the compound by that time.

Her pace increased to a trot as she headed for the north wall.

Thirty minutes.

It was going to be damn close.

•   •   •

SEVENTEEN MINUTES

Catherine pressed back against the wall of the stairwell as she slowly opened the carved-wood door that led to the hall of the palace.

The scent of mildew, spice, and the candles in sconces on the walls assaulted her.

No one in the hall. Caudell had said Sullivan had the run of the place, but she hadn't been sure that could be correct. She hoped that he was right. It would help if she didn't have to spend time picking that lock. It could mean the difference between success or failure, and that meant life or death.

No time to waste. Find out. She'd still have time to get out of here if rescue wasn't possible. She moved out of the stairwell to the door.

The door swung open.

Darkness.

"Again, Kadmus?" The woman's voice was weary. "Come ahead, it won't do you any good."

"Erin Sullivan?" Catherine asked softly as she moved into the room toward the bed and shut the door. "Catherine Ling. I've come to get you out of here. I'm going to turn on my flashlight. Please don't ask questions. I don't have time to answer them." She turned the flashlight on the dimmest setting. "I have to make sure you're Sullivan and able to travel."

She could see the woman tense, heard the sharp inhale of her breath. "I'm Erin Sullivan."

Catherine focused the light on her face. "Yes, you are. Bad bruises. Anything worse?"

"Burns. Pulled muscles. No broken bones." She swung her legs to the floor. "This isn't one of Kadmus's tricks? Who sent you? Cameron?"

"Cameron? I don't know any Cameron. I'm CIA." She opened

her backpack, pulled out a pair of boots, and tossed them to her. "Put these on. We don't have time for you to put on anything else but a parka. Where's Kadmus? You thought I was him when I opened the door."

"His bedroom is in the other wing." She smiled bitterly. "But he likes to surprise me. He thinks it weakens me psychologically." She already had the boots on. "Where's the parka?"

Catherine tossed it to her. "We'd better hope that this isn't one of the nights he chooses to do that." She checked her watch. "Come on. I've got ten minutes to get you over the wall and down the mountain to the helicopter."

Erin was on her feet and awkwardly shrugging into the parka jacket. "Who else is here?"

"No one." She headed for the door. "Hurry."

"You're crazy," Erin said. "Kadmus has more than fifty soldiers at this compound. We'll never make it."

"We'll make it." She turned, and said fiercely, "I have a son, and I intend to go home to him. And I can't leave you because I'll just have to come back for you. So get your ass in gear and help me."

Erin gazed at her for an instant. Then she was moving after her. "Which way?"

"The roof."

"One of Kadmus's men guards the staircase down to the court-yard."

"Not any longer."

"What about the wall?"

"I have a fireman's ladder that's attached to the top." Catherine was in the stairwell and running up the curving stone steps. "Listen, I know what I'm doing. No matter what happens, I need you to do what I tell you. Will you do that?"

Erin nodded. "Yes."

"Then don't talk until we get out of the compound. No noise. Just follow me."

"Right. I'll do—" When Catherine gave her a glance, she shrugged. "Sorry."

Erin Sullivan had nothing to be sorry about, Catherine thought. Considering her condition and the hell she had gone through, she was behaving with extraordinary guts and intelligence. She just hoped Erin didn't make a careless mistake that would blow it for both of them.

She was on the roof and running toward the exterior staircase. Still no one in the courtyard, and she had stashed the guard's body beneath the staircase.

Erin Sullivan was her shadow as Catherine flew down the stairs, then dashed toward the north wall.

Seven minutes.

They reached the wall, and Catherine pushed Erin toward the fireman's ladder she'd fastened to the top.

"Up and over," she whispered. "And then straight down the slope toward the—"

"And what do we have here?"

Catherine froze as she turned to face a tall, blond man in a navy parka. The accent had been South African, and he had to be Brasden. He was smiling and pointing an automatic weapon at them as he strolled forward. "Going for a stroll, Erin? And who is your friend?"

Two more steps, and he'd be within range. Catherine had to get him to take those steps. "Climb the ladder, Erin. Get over the wall and take off. He won't shoot you. Kadmus wants you alive."

Erin didn't move.

"You promised me that you'd do what I told you. Do it."

Erin started to quickly climb the ladder.

"Stop, you bitch," Brasden said harshly. He took three steps toward the ladder. "I won't kill you, but I'll put a bullet in your—"

Close enough.

Catherine did a karate kick that struck him in the throat, then leaped forward, and her hand came down on the side of his neck.

He fell to the ground.

Catherine grabbed his automatic rifle and hit him in the head with it. The next instant she was on the ladder, pushing Erin ahead of her. "Move!"

Erin didn't speak. She was climbing quickly and reached the top of the ladder.

Catherine was right behind her and reversed the ladder. "Three minutes," she whispered, and she pushed Erin toward it. "Head for the helicopter. Don't wait for me. I'll be right behind you, but I may have to stop to clear the way."

Erin nodded and started down the ladder.

Catherine glanced back at Brasden. Was he stirring? She'd hit him hard, but he'd been wearing that damn parka. It had probably cushioned the blow.

No time to worry now.

She followed Erin down the ladder and jumped the last three rungs. Erin was streaking over the hard-packed snow ahead of her in the direction of the north ledge.

Good. No hesitation. They just might get out of this alive.

Catherine tore after her, past the body of sentry she'd had to kill on her approach to the palace, down the rocky path to—

A bullet whistled past her. Then more gunfire, shouts as the gates of the compound were thrown open.

Shit.

It didn't matter whether Brasden had recovered from the blow she'd dealt him or that the other guard she'd taken down had been found. They were blown.

She cast a glance over her shoulder.

The moonlight was glinting on the two missile launchers that were being carried out of the compound.

No way she could take them down.

And they could blow the helicopter out of the air.

She put on speed and caught up with Erin.

"We're not going to make it," she said. "I have to tell the heli-copter to take off without us. Once we get off the plateau and can't be seen, head for the road that leads down the mountain."

Erin didn't argue. "I know that road. There are a few places we could hide if we get past the village. But it's the—" She broke off as another spatter of bullets rained around them. "There are at least two guards who patrol that road."

"Not right now. They'll all be headed here." She pulled out her phone. "Caudell, take off. There's no way we'll be able to make it before they blow you out of the sky."

"I can wait a little—"

"Take off. *Now.* But if you can put on a show after you get a safe distance away we could use the distraction."

"You've got her?"

"I've got her." She added grimly, "And I'm going to keep her. I'll be in touch." She hung up. They had reached the edge of the plateau, and Erin was half running, half sliding down the slope. Catherine followed her.

Dammit, Caudell hadn't taken off. The idiot was trying to give them a chance to fool Kadmus that they were on board the copter. The soldiers from the compound would be here in just a few min-utes, but they were out of sight now that they'd left the plateau.

If they could get down the rocky path toward those few stunted trees in time, it might work.

Erin was already flying toward those scrubby trees.

And Catherine had asked her if she could function, she thought ruefully.

Erin slipped on the ice, tumbled, fell to her knees, and hit the ground!

For an instant, she didn't move but then she was on her feet again and running.

They reached the trees just as the helicopter lifted off the ledge.

Shouts!

Shots!

Soldiers appeared at the edge of the plateau and began to run down the slope toward the ledge.

"Come on, we can't stay here," Catherine muttered. "We have to get down this road before they stop thinking we might have made it to that helicopter."

They *ran*.

The helicopter roared over the heads of Kadmus's men, then turned and headed toward the side of the mountain.

More shouting.

Catherine glanced over her shoulder.

Oh, God, they were loading the missile launcher.

Caudell showed himself for the briefest moment, then flew again behind the outcropping of the mountain.

A moment later, a missile blew that stony outcropping to bits.

"Enough, Caudell," Catherine murmured. If he played hide-and-seek any longer, his chances of making it away from the mountain intact were nil.

Erin was looking back, too. "What is he doing?"

"Giving us time. Where's this village?"

"Straight ahead. But we can't go through it, or they'll send word to Kadmus. He has everyone on this mountain terrified." She nodded at a side path. "That will take us around the village. There's a cave near there that was used by the monks for prayer vigils over a hundred years ago. Everyone has forgotten about it by now. We should be safe there for a little while."

"If everyone's forgotten it, how do you know about it?"

"I was told." Erin looked at her. "By someone I trust. The cave is there, Catherine."

Another missile explosion.

Dear God, Catherine hoped desperately that was the mountain being shattered again and not the helicopter. She turned and started down the path that went around the village. "Then let's go find it."

· · ·

"You're not going to like this," Venable said when Hu Chang picked up the phone. "So I'm going to say it fast, then let you explode or offer a suggestion."

"I will not explode," Hu Chang said. "You've lost Catherine. Does Kadmus have her?"

"I don't know. She got Erin Sullivan out of the palace, but they weren't able to make it to the helicopter before all hell broke loose. She told Caudell to get out, and she'd contact him later."

"But you don't know if Kadmus captured them or if she's still trying to get away from him. That is inexcusable."

"It's only been an hour. Even if she's free, if she's anywhere near Kadmus, she won't use phone or radio since he could pick up the signal. I'm exploring the situation."

"Not good enough."

"You have contacts. Perhaps you can have them put their ear to the ground and get answers."

"I don't want answers. I want Catherine back in one piece. I want Erin Sullivan to survive. I want Kadmus dead. Is that understood?"

"Do you think I don't want that, too? First, we've got to find them."

"You should never have lost them." Hu Chang was silent, trying to control himself. "You should never have lost Catherine. Now, you will do everything you can to locate her and let me know every step of the way."

"And what will you do?"

"I will find her."

"And you'll return the favor and inform me of any progress you make?"

"Perhaps. If I have use for you. Otherwise, stay out of my way."

"Dammit, I told you that we're on the job searching for her."

"I have little faith in you."

Venable drew a deep breath. "Look, you'll need me. Kadmus has a small army. If necessary, I can send a support force into the area."

"I'll have my own support force."

Venable muttered a curse. "Shit. No direct confrontation. You're not to cause an incident with Beijing."

"Do you believe China owns Kadmus? I think not. But it would not matter to me. I find it interesting that it matters to you. And that's why I have little faith in you." He hung up.

He sat there for a moment, calming the anger and fear. For many years, he had worked on obtaining complete control of mind and body, and he'd had considerable success.

But not where Catherine was concerned. She was the exception to every rule.

Gradually, serenity returned, and he could ponder the options.

Contact Cameron now or wait?

Wait. He'd already told him of the possible problem. He'd get into position for action before he involved him directly. And perhaps Cameron already knew. Hu Chang was never sure about him at any given time. Cameron probably preferred it that way.

But there was one thing he had to do immediately.

He got to his feet and strode out of the study in search of Luke.

DAKSHA, TIBET

The cave was almost inaccessible. It was hidden behind a screen of trees, and once they reached it, they found the opening behind it covered by boulders and smaller rocks. It took Catherine and Erin almost thirty minutes to clear the opening enough to crawl inside the cave.

It smelled of wood rotting in a pile of against the far wall. Other than that, Catherine smelled nothing but the dirt on the floor and the moss on the stones beside the opening. She lit her flashlight and let the beam play around the space. "It's not as small as I thought from the outside, but those monks wouldn't have been able to do much more than pray and sleep." The area was barely eight by twelve, and the roof of the cave was about ten feet high. "Definitely, no group prayers."

"No," Erin said. "But it's safe, isn't it? No . . . predators?"

"No, all the predators seem to be on the outside," Catherine said. "Maybe a few jumping spiders. They're the only ones that live this high up."

"Safe . . ." Erin's voice was a weak breath of sound. The next instant, she was sliding down the stony wall of the cave and closing her eyes. "I think I'll let you take care of the spiders. I'm very . . . tired."

"Erin?" It occurred to her that Erin had been very slow helping to clear the cave entrance. Catherine dropped to her knees beside her. "You had a fall back there. Were you shot? Hurt?"

"No, I'm just tired." Erin opened her eyes. "I'll be fine in a little while." She tried to smile. "I'm sorry. I'm not as strong as I was before Kadmus started to work on me. It doesn't take much to exhaust me. I'm glad I was able to keep up."

"You more than kept up. You were ahead most of the time. You have nothing to be sorry about," Catherine said. "You told me at the palace that there was nothing seriously wrong with you. Was that a lie?"

"No." She paused. "I do have a dislocation in my shoulder that's extremely painful. It slipped out of the socket again when I fell. And the index finger on my right hand is broken. The rest is manageable."

Catherine felt a surge of anger. Just the matter-of-fact way Erin had mentioned those injuries made the thought of their being inflicted the more terrible. "That son of a bitch. Why didn't you tell me?"

"We were in a hurry. You wanted to know what condition would keep me from being able to help free myself." She looked her in the eye. "Nothing would have kept me from doing that. If

I'd had a broken leg, I would still have made it here. I didn't have the slightest doubt that I'd hold out until we were safe."

Catherine grimaced. "I would have had a small doubt or two if I were you. Why were you so certain?"

Erin shrugged. "I don't know. I just knew I'd do it."

"Adrenaline?"

"Maybe something like that." She added quietly, "And, besides, I wouldn't want to let you down. You seemed very passionate about getting home to your son. I'm sorry that everything went wrong."

"So am I. But we'll work through it." She got to her feet. She shrugged off her backpack and dropped it to the ground. "But right now I'd better go back and erase any sign of our footprints. When Kadmus figures out that we definitely weren't on that helicopter, he's going to go on the hunt. He may have started already." She started toward the cave opening. "I should be back in thirty minutes or so, and I'll see what I can do about that shoulder and finger."

"Be careful."

"Always." She smiled grimly back at her. "There's no way I'd let Kadmus catch us now. You're out of that hellhole, and you're not going back."

"No, I won't let myself be taken. Not again." She closed her eyes. "Don't hurry. I'll just sit here and rest until you come back."

The finality of Erin's words sounded ominous. She had no doubt undergone mental as well as physical torture and would take any other path rather than go back to it. Who could blame her? Catherine would feel the same. She just hoped that Erin meant that she would not give up her life but would be determined to take Kadmus's.

"I won't be long." Catherine strode out of the cave and picked up a branch from beneath one of the sparse trees in the grove. She pulled out her knife and cut it down to a manageable size for her purpose. She moved swiftly back up the path.

Keep busy. Work fast. Do the job at hand. Don't think of that bastard or what he had done to Erin Sullivan. Venable had told her that there was torture involved, but it was always different when you actually met the victim. It was doubly upsetting when the victim was Erin Sullivan, and the courage shone beacon-bright through that hideous darkness surrounding her.

"I was right to come, Luke," she whispered as she started carefully brushing the traces of their footsteps from the stony path. "I didn't want to leave you. I thought I'd be back almost before you missed me. But it was right that I got her out."

But Erin Sullivan wasn't out yet. Now they had a long, difficult way to go before they escaped. She mustn't think of Luke or Hu Chang or anyone else right now. She had to concentrate on a plan to get them through the mountains to a point where Caudell could pick them up.

If the helicopter hadn't been blown to kingdom come.

She didn't think that last shot had gotten Caudell, and she hadn't heard any more explosions as they had hurried down the path toward the village.

So assume that Caudell was alive and had told Venable that Erin was alive and free and running for her life. Catherine could not use any electronic device to request pickup unless she knew that Caudell was in the immediate area. Surely, they would stay close in case she was able to communicate.

She couldn't assume anything except that while she remained on this mountain, Kadmus would be able to zero in on her if she tried to reach anyone. She'd have to get off this mountain, and even then, it wouldn't be certain.

Think about it. Work it out. She was competent, and Erin Sullivan was not going to be a handicap. They'd get away from this mountain that Kadmus thought he ruled.

She just hoped she got the chance to kill the bastard before they did it.

CHAPTER
5

DAKSHA PALACE

They weren't on the helicopter," Brasden said as he strode into Kadmus's library. "I've interviewed several of our men who had different vantage points, and none of them saw anyone but the pilot on board. That means they're still on the mountain."

"I told you that was what happened," Kadmus said impatiently. "That pilot was behaving like an asshole. He was trying to divert our attention." He gazed coldly at Brasden. "And he was successful. You were a fool."

"The helicopter was the biggest threat. I had to focus attention first on—" He stopped as he saw Kadmus's expression. "I sent men to search every cranny of the mountain as soon as I suspected that they were—"

"And you haven't found them."

"Not yet." He moistened his lips. "But we've started to question the villagers. So far we haven't had any luck, but—"

"Luck?" Kadmus repeated harshly. "I don't pay you to rely on luck. I want answers. Naturally, you wouldn't get answers from those villagers. I've taken care over the years to make sure that they wouldn't do anything that would be against my interests. They'd turn Erin Sullivan over in a heartbeat if she'd gone there."

"I thought that boy you killed was—"

"He wasn't from my village. I own this mountain."

Kadmus believed he owned the whole damn world, Brasden thought sourly. And, if he had his way, given time, he'd do it. That was okay. Brasden would ride on his coattails and eventually find a way to steal it away from him. Right now, he'd have to play meek and subservient. He'd screwed up royally by letting Sullivan be taken away. "I thought as much, but I thought it would do no harm to interrogate a few villagers. There are a few monks and the old lama who are still there." He paused. "I told you that it was a woman who got Sullivan out. The bitch was very, very tough. Do you have any idea who sent her?"

"I have an idea or two. Yes, she was tough. She made you look like a weakling."

Brasden choked back his anger. "I know you've been questioning Sullivan about the man who gave her that necklace. Do you suppose he sent the woman and the helicopter?"

"It's possible. Not likely. He would probably let Sullivan die before he risked himself. It's rare that he makes any contact at all. Sullivan was the exception. If he'd sent two more people to free her, that would be two more people I could possibly break. He wouldn't permit himself to be that vulnerable." His hand knotted into a fist. "But I could have made Sullivan talk. I just needed a little more time."

"I'll get her back."

"Yes, you will," he said with soft menace. "Or I'll toss you off this mountain." He frowned. "It could be CIA who sent her. We've been hearing that they've been investigating her disappearance."

"It was dangerous to take an American citizen. Naturally, it would cause an uproar."

"It was safe enough for me. No one has been able to touch me in all these decades. I *had* to have her."

"Why?" He paused, then said persuasively, "Perhaps it would

help if I knew what value she has for you. Who are you trying to locate?"

"The only person that knowledge might help is you, Brasden. And I'm not sharing this with you." Kadmus gave him a cold glance. "I've told you that my dealings with Sullivan are personal and private. Don't ask me again."

Brasden backed off. "Just trying to be helpful."

"Then find her and the woman who took her. I want constant electronic surveys of the entire area. Send out patrols to monitor any possible transmissions." He added through his teeth, "Bring her back to me. Now get out of here and find them."

·   ·   ·

"That's done," Catherine said as she came back into the cave. She carefully rolled the boulders back in front of the opening. "It wasn't that difficult. The path was almost pure stone and—" She stopped. "Were you sleeping? Is the cold getting to you?"

"No." Erin struggled to a sitting position. "But I was dozing. I haven't been sleeping lately."

"I can see why, with Kadmus paying you midnight visits." She walked over and knelt beside her. She lit her LED torch, and the cave was suddenly flooded with light. "But I'm surprised you were able to doze now. I couldn't, not until I unwind. The situation isn't exactly restful."

"You told me to trust you." Erin smiled faintly. "I do trust you, Catherine. I feel safe with you."

She wrinkled her nose. "Now that's a responsibility."

"Your fault. You got me out of that hellhole, and now you're stuck with me." Her smile faded. "It's going to be hard to get out of here, isn't it? How hard?"

"On a scale of one to ten, eight," Catherine said. "But at least it's not ten. But don't ask me how we're going to do it. We'll worry about that when Kadmus's first feverish search activity passes us by. Providing it does pass us by." She took out her gun and her knife and laid them on the ground beside her. "And if it doesn't, then we'll worry about it." She dug into her backpack and brought out the first-aid kit. "But let's get your wounds fixed up so that you'll be in better shape to face them. Shed that parka, and I'll take a look at your shoulder."

"Could you help me with it?" She unzipped the parka. "It's still dislocated, and there's a good deal of pain. Not as bad as the first time Kadmus did it."

"Kadmus didn't pop it back into the joint for you?"

"No, I did it myself the first time, but he dislocated it again. He liked the idea of constant reminder."

"How did the dislocation happen in the first place?"

"He was using the ropes on me."

Catherine's gaze flew to her face. "Ropes?"

"He said it's a torture he learned from the North Vietnamese. The arms are tied up and back until the elbows are forced together. It cut off circulation. The pain is excruciating, then he would rotate my arms until they dislocated."

Catherine glanced away from her, trying to control her rage. She carefully pulled the parka off her. "Son of a bitch."

"Oh, yes." She unbuttoned her shirt. "Without question."

"How did you manage to pop it back in by yourself? You have first-aid experience?"

"No, I've always thought I should go take a course. But then I kept putting it off."

"Then how did you know?"

"Someone . . ." She grimaced with pain. "Told me . . . what to do."

"Who?" Catherine was trying to keep her talking as she neared the final motion that would send it back into the socket. She could see the agony twisting Erin's face. "Someone at the palace?"

"No." She drew a deep breath. "Just *do* it."

Catherine sent the bone back into the socket. Erin jerked, and cried out, "Cameron!"

"Are you okay?" Catherine asked. "I think it's back in place."

Erin nodded. "It will be fine. Thank you."

"You're welcome," Catherine said. "Now give me your hand." Catherine quickly unbound the crude wrapping around the index finger. "Not a compound fracture. That's good." She quickly splinted it, then rebandaged. "But it's a bad break."

"Kadmus bent it backwards until it broke."

"You'll have to have it rebroken and set when we get you to a hospital." She sat back on her heels. "Anything else? You mentioned burns?"

"Five. Breasts and thighs. I can do that myself. Do you have salve?"

Catherine handed her antiseptic salve. "If you can handle it, I'd just as soon you do. I'm getting angry. I want to go back to the palace and see how much Kadmus can take before he—" She stopped and fought for control. "But that would be stupid, and we're not going to give him any chance of getting his hands on you again." She dug into the backpack again. "There are always nutrition bars in these backpacks. I think we need them."

"Perhaps we should save them in case—"

"Now. You've gone through hell, and you need to stoke up." Catherine found a bar and handed it to Erin. "There are several." She made a face. "Evidently, my pilot, Caudell, wasn't at all sure of the best-case scenario for which I was hoping. Finished with the salve?"

"Yes." She handed the tube back to Catherine. "It feels very cooling."

"Only the best for the Company. Of course, only the CIA would put you into a position where you might need meds." Catherine had been trying to avoid looking at the vicious burns Erin was treating. It made her too furious. "Before you eat that bar, bundle up in that cold-weather gear I gave you. You need to layer quickly."

Erin picked up one of the garments. "They appear so thin . . ."

"Space-age and high-tech and wonderfully efficient. The sleeping bags fold down to the size of a woman's small purse."

"Kind of James Bond stuff?"

"If James Bond ever got himself into a situation like this. He was always too slick. But I have to be able to move without freezing my ass off, and Venable always has a way to make sure I move. You should be careful to keep that shoulder as warm as possible. Dislocations are particularly susceptible to frostbite." She laid out the two sleeping bags. "We should sleep as much as possible during the day while the temperature is higher. Even with high-tech gear, it will be hard to fight off the cold enough to sleep once the temp plummets."

"When do you think we'll be able to try to get off the mountain?"

"Maybe a day or two. I'll go out tonight and scout out what's happening in Kadmus's kingdom. But we'll play it by ear." She looked at her. "But you're the one who knew about the village and this cave. You may be able to tell me more than this map they gave me."

"I knew about the village because I heard Kadmus talking about it."

"And this cave?"

"Someone told me about it."

Catherine's brows rose. "When it's been lost for decades? Were you familiar with this mountain before Kadmus brought you here?"

"No. The closest I've ever come is the village on Milchang, the next mountain. I did a story on their herd of goats—"

"Then how did you know about this cave? Who told you?"

"Does it make any difference? I knew, and we're here. Isn't that enough?"

Catherine looked at her with frustration. It was clear Erin didn't want to reveal her source. "It would be enough if I could be sure that what you said was true about this place being forgotten for all that time. It wasn't forgotten by the person who told you about it. I don't want Kadmus to be able to tap into the same source."

She shook her head. "He won't be able to do that."

"I hope not." Catherine sat down and leaned back against the stone wall. She was suddenly bone tired. She had been going on sheer adrenaline for too long, and now that there was a break in the action, strength was beginning to ebb away from her. "To help you, I have to know everything, Erin. It's dangerous to keep me in the dark."

"I know it's not fair," Erin said quietly. "I'm sorry, Catherine. There are things I can't talk about."

"I'm sorry, too." She paused. "Who is Cameron?"

Erin stiffened. "Cameron?"

"You asked me if it was Cameron who sent me when I showed up at your room at the palace. And that was the name you screamed just now when you were in pain."

"Did I?" She shook her head. "I didn't even realize it. I must trust you very much to have done that. I suppose it was an automatic—"

"I accept that. But I know you remember asking me if Cameron sent me to get you away from Kadmus."

"Yes, I remember doing that."

"So who is Cameron?"

She didn't answer.

"Another blank wall?" Catherine asked wearily. "Okay, but you're making things more difficult than they have to be."

"You're wrong. Difficult or not, my refusal to tell you about Cameron is exactly what it has to be. It can't be any other way."

"Then I'll have to work around it." She bit into her nutrition bar. "But if I find that your silence is putting me at a disadvantage, I'm not going to be pleased." She changed the subject. "You've spent years here in Tibet. Can you think of anyone here who might be willing to help us?"

"No one I'd permit to do it. A day before you came, a boy from a village on the next mountain came to try to rescue me. I'd helped some of his distant family members at the earthquake site. So brave . . . so young." She tried to steady her voice. "Kadmus shot him. His body is still in the courtyard below my window. I won't let that happen again. I'm on my own." She suddenly smiled. "No, I'm not on my own. I have you, Catherine."

"Yes, you have me. But under the circumstances, it might be better if you have a few more people in your corner."

"Better for you, too," Erin said, troubled. "You wanted so much to get home to your son."

"I'll still get home to him. It will just be a little later." She finished her bar. "And it's not as if he's not being well taken care of. I have a friend, Hu Chang, who is extraordinary, and Luke adores him. My son probably isn't even missing me."

"A son always misses his mother."

Catherine shrugged. "We have a rather guarded relationship. We were separated for nine years. There are a lot of bridges to mend."

"But not guarded on your part." Erin was studying her face. "You love him very much."

"To the last beat of my heart." She tilted her head. "What about you? I scanned your dossier but I saw no mention of immediate family. No children?"

She shook her head. "My parents are dead. I was married when I was in college. It was all sex and rock concerts and pot. But when we came down off the high, we found out that we wanted different things."

Catherine suddenly chuckled. "It sounds weird to hear you talk about pot and sex. I was led to believe that you were some kind of Mother Teresa icon."

"Not willingly." She grimaced. "Look, all I did was what anyone else would do when faced with a catastrophe like Qinghai."

"But not everyone did do what you did," Catherine said. "You went beyond any reasonable limits."

"I was there," she said simply. "It had to be done. I knew some of the people in those villages. You would have done the same."

"Perhaps. What happened after pot, sex, and rock and roll?"

"Charlie wanted to be a stockbroker, and I wanted to become a journalist and wander the world. We parted ways, and after a few years, I ended up in Tibet." She smiled. "Sometimes I wish there had been a child, but I wasn't prepared to be a parent anyway. It took me a long while to learn responsibility. How about you?"

"I wanted a child. I'd been alone all my life, and I wanted desperately to have someone of my own. Then when Luke was born, I knew that it wasn't about what I wanted. It was what was best for him."

"Your husband?"

"He was CIA, much older than me, a real good guy. He was shot by the same criminal who kidnapped my son."

"And kept him for nine years?" Erin asked softly. "And you never stopped looking for him?"

"Not for a minute, not for a second." Catherine took out her phone and pulled up the map of the mountain she'd already stored. "There doesn't seem to be more than one very perilous road down this mountain, which links it to the next mountain in the range. Do you know of any other road? Do you remember Kadmus mentioning one?"

Erin shook her head.

"Then we need your mysterious source who told you about this cave to step up to the plate."

"Sorry," Erin said gravely. "I can't promise that either."

"I know you can't. We're hardly accessible for advice or anything else." She knelt and wriggled into her sleeping bag. "Don't worry, I'll think of something."

"We could always parachute off the mountain. You seem to have everything else in that backpack."

"Actually, that's not too out of the question." Catherine thought about it. "The Internet can give you directions to do anything. I'd have to see about the process you have to use to make—"

"I was joking."

"I know, but some of the best ideas come out of the blue." She smiled. "Would you jump off this mountain if I asked you, Erin?"

"Yes, why not? I promised you I'd do anything you told me to do."

She meant it. Catherine was amazed and touched. "That was in a situation of immediate peril and emergency. I'm not perfect. I'll do my best, but I believe you should draw the line somewhere."

Erin shook her head. "You deserve to have my trust. You risked your life to come get me out of that hellhole. I might question. I might suggest. But in the end, I'll do what you want me to do." She sighed. "Though parachuting off the mountain may be a stretch."

"I'll see what I can do about avoiding it. With that shoulder, it could prove extremely painful." She pulled the zipper of her sleeping bag up to her throat. "Crawl into your sleeping bag and try to nap. Don't worry, I'll hear anyone if they come down the path toward the cave."

"CIA training?"

"Partly. Partly pure instinct. I've had to sleep with one eye open since I left the cradle."

"Have you?" Erin was pulling up the zipper and settling as comfortably as she could. She closed her eyes. "Sad . . ."

"Life."

"Not all life is sad."

"Not if we try to help each other make it better." Catherine waited a moment, then asked softly, "Who is Cameron?"

Even half-asleep, the question caused Erin to tense. "Not fair, Catherine."

"I told you that I wasn't perfect. Who is Cameron?"

"I'm going to sleep now."

And Catherine would not try to keep her awake. Erin had suffered too long, and the escape had put her on the edge of exhaustion. Catherine had felt obligated to try to break through the silence that might be dangerous for both of them, but she would not pursue it. She had done what a good CIA agent would do. Now she would do what a decent human being would do.

"Sleep well, Erin."

·   ·   ·

"Where the hell are you, Hu Chang?" Venable asked testily when Hu Chang answered the phone.

"Do you not know? You've been having me followed for some days."

"Of course, I have," he said bluntly. "You've always been the key to controlling Catherine. I couldn't just let you wander around."

"I'm disappointed." He glanced at Tashdon, the pilot in the cockpit seat next to him, but the man was tactfully ignoring his conversation. "I thought I might have some small importance of my own. Since my self-love is seriously damaged, I believe I'm going to hang up."

"Where are you? Dammit, I haven't been able to trace you since you left the Golden Palace."

"Because I didn't wish your man to tail me. The situation has become very delicate, and I won't have you sticking your far-from-subtle fingers in the mix. I only answered your call to make sure you knew that I will make myself available if you have any information I can use. Do you?"

"Not at the moment."

"Good-bye."

"Wait. Where are you?"

"At the moment, I'm in a helicopter flying over Kham Province in Tibet. That would make me approximately halfway to my destination."

"Daksha."

"Perhaps. I repeat, good-bye, Venable." He hung up, and his gaze shifted out the cockpit window at the blinding brilliance of the snow-covered mountains.

"Hu Chang?"

He didn't look behind him. "I thought you would be too curious not to eavesdrop. However, you should have exercised restraint considering the risk to life and limb I've taken in inviting you to be my guest."

"I *was* curious, Hu Chang."

He got to his feet. "Then I suppose I might as well come back there and decide if I'll answer your questions, Luke."

• • •

Cameron.

Darkness.

Cameron.

Swirling intensity.

Cameron!

"Good God, you're a determined woman." A man's deep voice, half-impatient, half-amused. *"I really didn't want to do this, but it seems I have no choice."*

Cameron.

"I heard you. Now open your eyes and say hello properly."

Catherine slowly opened her eyes.

No cave. No sleeping bag.

No cold.

A room furnished with rich Persian rugs, leather chairs, books . . .

A fire burning in a huge fireplace.

And a man in jeans and close-fitting black shirt standing before that fireplace, his body outlined by the flames. She couldn't make out his features but they were framed by close-cut dark hair, and she got an impression of symmetry.

Beautiful, she thought drowsily.

Power.

Electricity.

Grace.

Energy.

All beautiful . . .

"Thank you." He stepped forward, and she could see his face. "I think you're beautiful, too, Catherine." His brilliant blue eyes were glittering with humor, his lips curved in a smile, and his entire expression was alive with exuberant vitality. "But I don't think either one of us prefers to rely on that particular asset." He sat down in the leather armchair and stretched his legs out before him. "However, I admit I've been enjoying watching you since you entered into my life. You're like a wonderful symphony with exquisite passages of pure serenity, then magnificent crashing drama." He made a face. "Unfortunately, I seem to have become fascinated by you."

Crazy, she thought hazily. All this was crazy.

"Not crazy," he said. "Like almost everything else, it has a perfectly sane basis if you accept certain parameters."

She closed her eyes. "I'm dreaming. I'm in the cave and sleeping. I will now wake up." She opened her eyes.

No cave.

Fire, warmth, beauty. And that man was still here.

He shook his head. "I set the rules, Catherine. You called me, and I came. But you have to play my game. I didn't really want to contact you. I thought it would be much better to work through Erin." He chuckled. "But you wouldn't stop, and I couldn't resist you."

"I called you?"

He nodded. "Richard Cameron, at your service. You were curious, and you thought that I was someone you should know about. So you kept turning it over and over in your mind, and you wouldn't let me go."

"Bullshit."

"No, true." He added softly, *"Actually, I could have resisted you, but I didn't want to. I thought it might be worth it to me to get to know you. You evidently thought the same, though not for the same reason. I'm delighted to meet you, Catherine Ling."*

"Cameron." She tried to think, tried to reason. *"A hallucination brought on by stress and my desire to—"*

"Wrong. Take a step outside the box, Catherine. You've done it before."

She was silent. Something was strange here that had nothing to do with dreams, and stress had never made her lose her mental balance. What else could it be? She went over the possibilities and came up with an answer. *"Mental telepathy. We've been experimenting with it, and so have the Russians, Chinese, and half a dozen other countries. But if it's mental telepathy, then you've brought it to a highly sophisticated level."*

"You have no idea. Very good, Catherine."

"Two years ago, I was present at the testing of a young Italian girl who was the pride of the CIA think tank. They brought twenty-two agents to Rome to test her and teach us how to handle a possible mental infiltration. It turned out that she could read the minds of several of the agents, but I wasn't one of them. And she couldn't read those other agents from a distance of more than a football field. I take it that you're not that close?"

"Correct."

"And there have to be elements of hypnotic suggestion for you to have set up a scenario like this."

"I wanted you to feel welcome. You're accepting this better than I hoped."

"I'm not accepting fact, only possibility. I know that mental telepathy has been tested and exists. It's rare, but I've seen the experiments. But I also grew up on the streets of Hong Kong, where a belief in angels and devils is a way of life. "

"And which do you think I am?"

"You tell me." She thought about it. *"I think Erin believes you mean*

her well. She thought you might rescue her." She was sifting through every-
thing, trying to put the entire picture together. "Are you the 'friend' who
asked Hu Chang to go after Erin?"

"I told him that it would please me. I left the decision to him."

"Why didn't you go after her yourself?"

"I couldn't allow myself to do it." He shrugged. "There are certain rules
I have to go by."

"Hu Chang said that you were the most dangerous man either one of us
would ever meet. Why the hell couldn't you go after Erin?"

"Rules."

"But your rules didn't keep you from sending Hu Chang out to do the
dirty work."

"No." His lips twisted. "Unfortunately, that option is allowed and
even encouraged. I just have to choose wisely and decide if it's worth a pos-
sible death to accomplish the goal."

"You decide? Yet you just said your hands were tied. Not consistent,
Cameron. What government do you work for? What agency are you with?
China? Russia? Great Britain? You sound American, but that doesn't mean
much. Kadmus was born American, and he works for everyone who has the
cash to pay him. I don't think Venable knows about you, or he would have
told me. He doesn't let me go in blind."

"That's good," he said. "And Venable doesn't know I exist. Though I
think Caudell may have suspected at times. He knows there's someone who
was occasionally there before him."

"Who do you work for?" she repeated.

"It's an international organization with worldwide membership." He
smiled. "I assure you that you've never heard of it. I'm not going to interfere
with anything the CIA is doing unless they interfere with me."

"What do you do for them?"

"Too much and too little."

"That's no answer."

"No, it isn't. It's a skill at which I've become an expert." He was silent

a moment, then added wearily, "Okay, I act as a sort of Guardian, trouble-shooter, and executioner. In a way, our duties are similar in scope. I'm not going to go into details with you."

"Is it some kind of commercial organization?"

"In many ways." He held up his hand. "No more, Catherine."

"Yes, there's going to be more," she said fiercely. "I'll stop asking about your damn organization, but I have to know about Erin. She was being tortured because she wouldn't tell Kadmus what he wanted to know about a man he was searching for." She stared him in the eye. "Was that man you, Cameron?"

"I think you know it was."

"Why does he want to find you?"

"Because I am who I am. Kadmus has been searching for me for a long time."

"That's vague as hell. And why did Erin feel she had to keep him from finding you?"

"Because she made a mistake, and she wouldn't let us suffer for it."

Catherine could feel her frustration rising by the minute. He was answering her, but the answers were totally unrevealing, and she knew if she delved any deeper, he would close up. "And yet you couldn't go after her and get her away from that bastard?"

"I did what I could."

"The hell you did."

"It was a risk I wasn't allowed to take," he said quietly.

"You son of a bitch; I saw what he did to her."

"And so did I. I was with her every time he touched her," he said. "I taught her how to block out the pain. It was all I could do for her until I found the right person to go after her."

"Hu Chang."

"Yes." He paused. "It was going to be Hu Chang. Until I found out about you. You were always there in Hu Chang's mind. I became very familiar with you. And, to my regret, I knew it had to be you who went to get Erin."

She stared at him in shock. "You're telling me that you were pulling the strings? No way."

"I'm very good at it. I could have lied to you about that. I know the idea of manipulation would be salt on a wound. But I'm trying to be as honest as I can be." He leaned his head back on the leather armchair. There was a lazy, sensual, catlike grace in the movement. "You'll probably never trust me, but you have to be able to work with me. As I said, I was going to deal through Erin, but you wanted to be in control." The thread of steel in his voice suddenly belied his indolent position. "That's not going to happen. I'll always be in control. It's what I do. It's what I am."

"Not when you hide away and just play around with these mental hi-jinks. When you come out in the daylight and do something with your own hands, then you can show me why you deserve to be in control."

"Catherine." For an instant there was a flash of anger in those glittering light eyes. Then he relaxed and smiled. "Hold your tongue. It's sharp as that knife you carry in that sheath on your calf. For a moment, I actually felt pain. It's been a long time since I permitted myself to get that annoyed. You're arousing all kinds of emotions." He held her gaze. "I'm tempted to arouse a few interesting emotions in you. That would be very . . . satisfying."

A wave of heat.

Breathlessness.

A swelling and tingling in her nipples.

"And that's only physical," he said softly. "That's satisfying, too, but emotional response can tear you apart."

She drew a deep breath. She had been caught off guard, and she was still shaken. "You're not in control. Not of me, not of Erin. As for that childish little display, next time I'll be prepared, and it won't happen."

He was silent. Then he chuckled. "It was hardly childish. But I'll try to keep it from happening again." He paused. "Unless I decide to heed your suggestion and show up in person."

"Show up for sex but not to save Erin from being tortured?"

His lips tightened. "You're doing it again. I'm not going to make excuses. I had only two options with Erin. I've told you the one I chose."

"What was the other option?"

"To kill her," he said simply.

"My God."

"You asked." He sat up straight in the chair. "And now we have to deal with what's important. I want Erin off this mountain."

"So do I."

"And I will help you in any way I can to get her away from Kadmus's men and out of Tibet. But that's not going to be good enough. Take her back to the U.S. and hide her until I send someone to kill Kadmus. She won't be safe while he's still alive." He paused. "I admit I had hoped that you might take care of that when you went after Erin."

"It was Erin who was important. I didn't give a damn about Kadmus at the time."

"I thought as much, but there was a chance."

"In that charming little scenario that you said you contrived? Too bad. I did what I could."

"And you did it brilliantly."

"Then do some more contriving and come up with a way that we can skirt Kadmus's men and find our way to a place where I can safely contact Caudell. It was you who told Erin about this cave, wasn't it? Can't you come up with something else useful?"

"I'm trying. It takes research . . . and consultation. But I'll manage to do it given a little more time."

"We don't have time. Kadmus is on the hunt. Who's to say he won't find this cave and catch us off guard."

"I won't allow that. I'll know long before he gets to you and warn you."

"How?"

He shook his head. "I'll warn you," he repeated. "Relax. Try to sleep." He smiled faintly. "And don't try to pull me back here. I have Hu Chang to deal with, and I need to concentrate on keeping him from storming the mountain to get to you."

"Hu Chang?" She stiffened. "He's in Hong Kong. I told him to stay there and take care of Luke."

"And I'm sure he will do it but in his own way. You might have had a chance of keeping him at bay if you'd been able to make that helicopter." He got to his feet and moved toward the fire. *"And we both have a good deal of trouble persuading Hu Chang to do anything he doesn't want to do."*

"He mustn't come here."

"Back to square one. Then we must get you off this mountain." He was only a dark silhouette against the leaping flames again. But now she knew him, the power, the charisma, the hard edge behind that velvet, sensual surface.

And the danger of which Hu Chang had spoken.

"I hope not to you, Catherine," he said gently. *"I'm trying not to hurt you."*

Dammit, she had forgotten he could read her mind during the conversation that had transpired. *"I wouldn't let you hurt me."*

"It's time for me to leave and let you come to terms with all that I've bombarded you. You've taken it extraordinarily well, but then I knew you would." He chuckled. *"I'm looking forward to our next meeting."*

"And I'm looking forward to you making it up to Erin for covering your ass and not going in and getting her away from Kadmus. I can't see why—"

Cold.

No fire.

No cozy, book-lined room.

No Cameron.

She knew when she opened her eyes it would be to see Erin in her sleeping bag a few yards away and the stark dimness of the cave.

She wouldn't open her eyes and face that reality yet. It would come as too much of a shock, and she had to assimilate all that Cameron had said and revealed. It was all weird and difficult and frustrating . . . and frightening. No, not frightening. She wouldn't accept fear. It was just that she'd felt momentarily helpless when she'd realized that her thoughts were transparent, and he could create a scene for her that didn't exist down to the last detail.

It shouldn't have that effect on her. Mental telepathy was just a gift that had to be dealt with like any other weapon. She was sure Cameron was unusually adept, but she'd find a way to understand and learn to cope. It was only those damn marvelous good looks and powerful personality that kept getting in the way. He was undoubtedly the handsomest, most intensely sexual man she had ever met, and as a woman, she instinctively responded to it. She would have to ignore that—

She had a sudden thought that brought a smile to her lips. What if Cameron wasn't what she had seen? What if he'd created his appearance as he had the rest of that inviting scenario? Hell, maybe he was really as ugly as Mr. Hyde or the Hunchback of Notre Dame.

She definitely liked that idea.

"Nasty, very nasty, Catherine."

She felt a ripple of shock. "Go away. Now. I won't have this."

Laughter. "I'm going. I was just staying to make sure you were all right . . ."

Was he gone, she wondered crossly a few moments later. How could she tell? One thing was certain—she could not count on keeping anything secret from the bastard.

Well, she would just have to learn to adjust until she found a way to close him out. Since he supposedly was on Erin's side, anything he learned from Catherine should not be damaging to her.

Maybe. If he was telling the truth, if he was not twisting perceptions.

If she kept questioning, she would get nowhere. She would put suspicions aside and be wary but cooperative. She would work for a solution of her own to the dilemma but take help when given.

Decision made.

She turned over in her sleeping bag and settled down to nap. She wanted to wake Erin and ask her a hundred or so questions, which she probably wouldn't answer. Not now. Let the woman sleep a little before she had to face the barrage.

Catherine doubted if she would sleep again, but she would try.

She had to have all her strength and mental acuity for the next few days.

Hu Chang.

Don't think of him now. She had enough to worry about without borrowing trouble. If she managed to get off the mountain, Hu Chang would have no reason to try to come and save her.

Stay away, Hu Chang.

CHAPTER
6

MILCHANG MOUNTAIN

Catherine was everything he had thought she would be, Cameron thought.

He smiled with amusement as he stood up from the boulder where he'd sat down to mentally build their rendezvous. He started up the icy path toward the plateau where Hu Chang's helicopter would land.

No, she was more, he amended. Brimming with fire and intelligence and emotion and completely her own person. It had been a stinging, lively, and tumultuous encounter, and he had enjoyed every minute of it.

When he hadn't wanted to kill her.

Or take her down and have sex with her until they were both out of their minds.

He was readying at the thought.

Control.

Not easy. From the moment he had caught glimpses of Catherine in Hu Chang's mind, he had been aroused and stimulated beyond belief.

How long had it been since he had wanted a woman this much?

He couldn't remember. Maybe never.

Not only desire but intrigue and excitement . . .

Control.

Concentrate on Erin Sullivan. She had to be protected. He probably should not have even sent Catherine to rescue her. He had known at the time that he was having a physical and emotional response to her.

But, dammit, Catherine Ling was the one who should have gone. All his experience had pointed to her as having the best chance. She had the instincts of a prime warrior. It was not because of that sexual response.

But now she was here, and they were going to have to interact.

Interact in what way?

He was tired, too much had been demanded of him during the last year. Didn't he deserve a reward?

Discipline. He only deserved what he could take and what he allowed himself.

He must not allow himself to take Catherine Ling.

•   •   •

"So why did you feel it necessary to eavesdrop on my call with Venable, Luke?" Hu Chang asked as he came back and sat down beside Luke in the rear of the helicopter. "Why did you not come to me and ask what you wanted to know?"

Luke was silent, then said slowly, "You didn't want to talk to me about Catherine. I have to know if she's safe, Hu Chang."

"She's not safe. I told you that when I gave you the choice whether to come with me." He smiled faintly. "And you said that you would have gone after her by yourself. The answer pleased me." He added ruefully, "But your mother would not have been pleased either by the question or the answer. And she will be in a rage that I brought you with me. She told me to take care of her son. Yet how can I take care of her son unless he is under my eyes? Since I had to journey to help her it was a paradox."

"That you solved." Luke suddenly grinned. "You could have left me with Chen Lu. You wanted me with you."

"You are usually good company. However, you will have to prove yourself to me. You are not a child. You've lived a hard life, but I will take no excuses for disobedience when it could hurt our Catherine."

Luke's grin vanished. "When I'm in the lab, don't I do what you tell me? Do you think I'd do less for Catherine?"

"No, but a warning does no harm. You might become overenthusiastic. It happens in the young."

"Rakovac put a gun in my hand when I wasn't even big enough to hold it. He wanted to teach me to kill so that he could hurt my mother. When he first took me on guerrilla raids in Russia, I was afraid. After a while, I was excited and began to think of it as a game," he said. "Then later, I saw the deaths all around me, and it was no longer a game." He looked Hu Chang in the eye. "I will not be overenthusiastic. I will only do what I have to do to save Catherine."

"Tell me why."

He frowned. "Because she could die if I don't. That's a strange question, Hu Chang."

"Not so strange. Then you're not looking for a grand adventure?"

He shook his head. "I told you, Catherine could die."

"And is she worth saving, Luke?"

"Of course she is. She's a fine agent, a good soldier, and I owe her for saving me from Rakovac."

"Very cool and logical. Do you know why I think she's worth saving? Because it would be a barren world if I didn't see her smile at me. She came to me, and I suddenly discovered how lonely I had been. She fills so many places in my mind and heart that I can't conceive of life without her." He lifted his shoulder in a half shrug. "Yes, we owe each other many debts, but that's only surface. She is worth saving because she hears my soul speak, and I hear hers." He added softly, "Do you hear her soul speak, Luke?"

"I . . . don't know what you mean."

"I think you do hear, and that's why you wanted to come to find her." He smiled. "And I brought you with me because it's time you admitted to yourself that you hear her. There's nothing like enduring hardship and danger to clarify emotions. Perhaps before this is over, you will tell her that you hear her."

He moistened his lips. "I don't know what you want from me." He made a face. "And you're talking weird. Catherine would laugh at me if I started talking about hearing souls."

Hu Chang nodded. "That is true. You don't have my eloquence and gift of words. Pity. But you might be able to make her understand in your own crude way."

Luke shifted his gaze to the snow-covered mountains outside the window. "Are we almost there, Hu Chang?"

"That's a disgustingly trite and overused phrase," Hu Chang said. "But I'll answer you anyway since you're scrambling frantically to fend off my own questions you find awkward. Yes, we'll be landing soon."

"Where?"

"On a plateau near the top of one of those mountains at which you've been looking so admiringly."

"How close will we be to Catherine?"

"Not close enough. But we'll be met by a man who will be able to help us to locate her. He's the man who sent this fine helicopter and pilot to bring us here. His name is Cameron, and you must be polite to him though he may confuse you."

"Confuse me?"

"Yes, I know youths of your age are so blasé and wise that they find it difficult to believe that anything can bewilder them, but you may be surprised. Just flow with the tide."

"You're talking weird again."

"Then you must forgive me. My heart is heavy, and it is difficult being both wise and witty." He leaned back against the paneled wall of the cabin. "I will rest and be myself by the time we arrive at our destination."

Luke was silent. "I didn't mean that you were really weird." He added awkwardly, "And you're always wise. You're the smartest man I've ever met."

Hu Chang didn't open his eyes. "But you've had a limited acquaintance. Still, you've been lucky enough to have many hours in my exceptional company. That makes up for many lapses. I take it this is your gauche way of apologizing?"

Another silence. "Yes."

"I will consider accepting it. No, because of the circumstances, I will generously forgive you."

Silence.

Hu Chang sighed. "I can sense you fretting. What is it, Luke?"

"'Gauche.' I don't know that word. What does it mean?"

Hu Chang was aware after the last nine years spent in Russia there were many English words that Luke didn't know, but the boy was voraciously curious about them. "Inept. Which is something you must never be again while we are on this journey. There must be respect and competence. And if you give it to me, there will be trumpets and fireworks and many wonderful things." He opened his eyes and smiled. "And the most wonderful thing of all will be that we have our Catherine back."

DAKSHA PALACE

"I *have* it." Brasden strode into Kadmus's library and threw down a photo on the desk. "I had Mark Nagle, the man who handles your West Coast operations, call his contact at Langley. There was a top secret operation going on in this area. Catherine Ling was to be in the center of it."

"Catherine Ling . . ." Kadmus gazed down at the woman staring back at him from the photo. "Beautiful. Fierce." He read the brief dossier. "And exceptional. You're sure that she's the agent who took Sullivan?"

"She arrived in Hong Kong yesterday."

"Coincidence?"

"I only saw her for a moment in the darkness, but I'd swear it was the same woman in the photo."

Kadmus couldn't take his gaze from the photo. He could feel the rage searing through him. Catherine Ling was not smiling, but he could feel the mockery behind that intense expression.

Mocking him? Mocking the fact that he'd not been able to stop her from taking Sullivan. It was irrational, but the thought would not leave him. He had been beaten by a woman and he could—

"Kadmus?"

"Get out of here, Brasden," he said through his teeth. "Find her. Find them both and bring them back to me."

"I know you want Sullivan alive. What about Catherine Ling?"

"I want her alive, too."

Torturing Erin Sullivan had been a necessity, but it had given him a certain pleasure. It would be a pure, intense pleasure teaching Catherine Ling she could not make a fool of him. "I want to spend a long, long time with the bitch before I cut her throat. Maybe watching her suffer will make Sullivan more cooperative."

"I'll be delighted to assist," Brasden said grimly. "I know you don't want excuses about me being taken off guard by her, but it's true. Ling won't ever be able to take me down again."

"We'll talk about participation later. First, you have to find them. I want a lead within the next four hours." He didn't look up from the photo as the door slammed behind Brasden.

Catherine Ling.

She was as alluring as one of the high-priced whores he paid at

that house in Beijing, but he had no desire for her. Her skin was
glowing, golden satin, and her lips were full and beautifully shaped
and she was all fire . . . and mockery.

Mockery.

The rage was pouring through him. She had taken away Sullivan and was standing in the way of his reaching the lotus gate. He
ruled these mountains, he could take or crush or kill at will, but it
was not enough. He wanted more, and he would get it.

The ultimate power.

He reached into the top drawer of the desk and took out the
black velvet jewelry box. His fingers caressed the softness of the
velvet. He always liked to anticipate before he opened the box.

How many times had Erin offered to give him her necklace?
She had never understood why he didn't want it.

I don't need it. I have my own lotus necklace, Erin.

He opened the box and gazed down at the eight-sided lotus
pendant on the gold chain. There were still faint traces of blood on
that chain. He had decided not to clean it after he'd yanked it off
the neck of the priest from whom he had taken the necklace. He
had found out many things from that fool of a priest but not enough.
But this necklace gave him a sense of his own power and a vision of
what was to be.

Shambhala.

Just thinking about it brought the heady joy that it had the first
time he had found out that it could be within his reach.

And he could still have it.

Erin Sullivan would have given in eventually if he'd been able
to work on her a little longer. Then he would have found the
Guardian, and he would have been on his way.

And it had all stopped because this bitch had stepped in and
snatched Sullivan. It was intolerable. The rage was rising and crest-
ing and rising again as he thought of the things he wanted to do to
Catherine Ling.

tion, but then we talked, and I realized that he was a man capable of mental telepathy and God knows what else. He's some kind of troubleshooter for an organization that could be corrupt or just the usual bureaucratic conglomerate." She stared Erin in the eye. "And you're involved with them in some way. Innocently, I hope. Because Cameron impresses me as one dangerous customer and more ruthless than you could imagine."

Erin shook her head. "And Cameron impresses me as being far more wonderful than you could ever imagine."

"Wonderful? Oh, for God's sake, Erin. Are you infatuated with him? I can see that anyone would be a little dazzled by those good looks, but this is a man who let you be tortured for weeks and didn't raise a hand to help you."

"He helped me. You don't know what you're talking about."

"No, I don't. I don't know anything about a person who could have a gift that strong and complex. I don't know why Kadmus wants him bad enough to do what he did to you. So why don't you tell me?"

"Because I promised Cameron I wouldn't do it," she said simply. "And I won't, Catherine."

Catherine drew a deep breath. "Cameron's already told me bits and pieces. It seems that he's going to deign to communicate with me until we get you away from Tibet."

"I told you that he helped me." Erin smiled. "And now he's going to do it again. As I said, he's wonderful." She saw Catherine's expression and shook her head. "And I'm not infatuated with Cameron. I admire him more than I can say, and I hope someday we can be friends. Right now, I'm sure he can only look on me as someone who's brought him big-time trouble."

"I'd say that the opposite is true," Catherine said dryly. "And I'm not sure that you've not been influenced by a little mental manipulation. Can you deny that's possible?"

"No, but I trust him. He wouldn't do that to me without reason."

"You're sure about that?"

"Yes," she said with certainty. "As for that mental manipulation, I blessed it every moment I was with Kadmus." She gazed at Catherine's skeptical expression. "Listen, to me. After Kadmus kidnapped me and brought me to Daksha, I knew it was going to be terrible. I've never been more frightened. But that first night, Cameron came. I'd known he was capable of mental telepathy from our other encounter, but I hadn't thought it was possible for him to be able to do it from great distances. Suddenly, I wasn't alone any longer. Do you know what that meant to me? He told me he couldn't come for me, but he would help me through it until he could get me away from Kadmus. By the time he left, the panic was gone."

"He said he taught you to block the pain."

"Yes, and when I couldn't do it, he was there to do it for me. He stopped all pain and wrapped me in a kind of joyous peace." She paused. "He was with me during the most terrible moments of my life. I couldn't be any closer to anyone than I am to him. So don't tell me that he shouldn't have done a little mental hocus-pocus to help me to survive."

"No, I won't tell you that." Her lips thinned. "But I will tell you that he should have tried to get you out himself."

"He wasn't permitted. I understood."

"Well, I don't."

"It wasn't his fault. I made a mistake. He could have just let me suffer for it. He didn't do it. He came to help me. And, in the end, he sent you, Catherine."

"He did *not* send me. I took the mission of my own volition."

Erin smiled and nodded.

"It's true." And she wouldn't be able to convince Erin that Cameron hadn't influenced that decision. She might not be infatuated with him, but she obviously had a king-size case of hero worship. Was that how Cameron had planned it? She was fanatically grateful, and nothing could bind her closer to Cameron and his interests. Catherine might never know. The intimacy between them bred by those months of torture and captivity was probably unexplainable to anyone else.

"Worry about Kadmus," Erin said gently. "Don't worry about Cameron. He'll help us, Catherine."

"I have to worry about him. He's a wild card." She made a face. "That's an understatement. But I'll try to accept him the way you see him." She thought about it. "No, that's not going to work. I'll just play it by ear."

"You do that." Erin settled back down in the sleeping bag. "It will be all right."

"I don't suppose you'll tell me about that first encounter you had with Cameron?"

"No, that would be breaking my word. Any information has to come from him."

"I suspected that was going to be the way of it. And I'm not too sure that he can help as much as you seem to think. Since he managed to supply us with this home away from home, I asked him if he could find a way to get us off this mountain. He said that he'd have to consult someone or other. That didn't give me a high degree of confidence."

"He'll do it." She yawned. "I'm going back to sleep. I feel much better now that I know I don't have to keep clamming up when you're questioning me about Cameron. I hated closing you out."

"But you did it. You're still doing it."

"Because I promised him," she said drowsily. "But he took care of that, and now the two of you can work everything out . . ."

The next moment, Erin was back asleep.

She was glad Erin was so confident, Catherine thought ruefully. She wasn't at all sure that she could work with that arrogant son of a bitch.

Too much power.

Too much charisma.

And far too much sexuality.

Erin may not have been influenced by that potent combination, but Catherine had been. He had been everything gentle with Erin, but she could not see him being that way with her.

Of course, she would work with him. She could overcome personal barriers. She just had to understand more about her antagonist. The only information she had received from her conversation with Erin was just a confirmation of what Cameron had told her. She needed answers to other questions.

The details of the encounter between Erin and Cameron would tell her a hell of a lot. Everything seemed to have stemmed from that meeting. Where had it taken place? Probably somewhere in these mountains since Erin seemed to work almost exclusively in the provinces of Tibet.

And what had happened then that caused Kadmus to have zeroed in on Erin?

Okay, concentrate on those two questions and forget everything else.

Except Richard Cameron. If she couldn't solve his connection with Erin, she could search for answers about him. Should she call Langley and tell them to dig as soon as this present emergency was over?

No, Erin would regard that as a betrayal when she had suffered tremendously to keep his identity secret.

Catherine could just drop the subject of Cameron once she had Erin safe.

That wasn't an option either. Kadmus wasn't going to stop until he found Cameron, and he'd continue to search for Erin to use as the key. So that meant she'd have to deal with Cameron until Kadmus was dead.

Langley was out, but there was another possibility.

Hu Chang.

He considered Cameron a friend, and Hu Chang did not accept

friends lightly. He would know everything, or as close as an outsider could come to everything, about who and what Cameron really was.

Hu Chang. She had been trying to keep herself so occupied that she wouldn't think about him. As Cameron had said, if she had been able to extract Erin immediately, then there would have been no problem. But there was no way that Hu Chang would not come after her if she wasn't able to get out of here within a short time.

Stay away, Hu Chang. I'm working on it. Just take care of Luke and give me a little more time.

· · ·

"We are landing, sir." The helicopter pilot, Tashdon, called back to Hu Chang. "We should be down in just a few minutes. And I can see Cameron coming across the plateau."

"Indeed?" Hu Chang rose and came forward to the cockpit. "Where?" Then he saw Cameron striding toward the place where the helicopter would set down. The snow was swirling around his black-garbed body, but he moved through it with swift, athletic grace. There was a boundless energy, a burning vitality, to every step. He was everything Hu Chang remembered. It was good to know. He would need Cameron to be exceptional to get Catherine out of this quandary. "Our friend, Cameron, appears to be in good form, Tashdon."

Tashdon gazed at him in surprise. "But he's always that way. Cameron never changes."

"How long have you worked with him?"

"Five years."

"And you've enjoyed it?" he asked curiously.

"Not always. But it's been my privilege." He added, "You'd better sit down, sir."

Hu Chang sat down and buckled the seat belt. Tashdon's reply had been in the same tenor as Hu Chang had run across in other members in Cameron's circle. Devotion. Respect. Fear? Yes, he was sure that there were elements of fear. And that respect was almost fanatical.

He observed that truth again a few minutes later after he had left the helicopter and was walking toward Cameron across the hard-packed snow. Tashdon had scurried ahead and was hovering in front of Cameron protectively. "I've delivered them as ordered," Tashdon said. "Is there anything else, Cameron?"

"No, you've done very well. I don't need you any longer."

Tashdon smiled with relief. "I'm glad you're pleased."

Hu Chang said, "Go back to the helicopter and bring the boy to meet Cameron."

Tashdon looked at Cameron.

"Go ahead," Cameron smiled. "I'm not going to make you take him back to Hong Kong, Tashdon." He turned to Hu Chang. "Did you think I would?"

"No, I wouldn't permit it. But I thought two friends should have the opportunity to meet alone before there were intrusions. You knew about Luke?"

"Yes, though not from you warning me."

"I thought there was a good chance you might break your word to me and take a peek. It seems I was correct."

"I told you I would honor your privacy whenever possible. It was not possible. I had to make sure that you weren't going to be doing anything that would interfere with my getting Erin out of here."

"That is why I am on this deplorably uncomfortable mountain."

"No, your objective has changed. You're only thinking about Catherine Ling."

Hu Chang nodded slowly. "You have a right to be concerned. My prime objective is not yours. But if I do not have to sacrifice Erin Sullivan for Catherine, then I will be happy to expand my goal."

Cameron's gaze shifted back to the helicopter. "I believe we'll be able to do that. In fact, I don't think that Catherine will let anyone take Erin from beneath her protective wing until she's safe."

Hu Chang said quietly, "You could take her away from Catherine."

"I'm not sure that I could."

"Really?" Hu Chang's eyes narrowed. Cameron was not inclined to underestimate himself, and they were both aware of his capabilities. "It's true that she's extraordinary, but I wasn't aware that you'd discovered that."

Cameron glanced back at him. "But I find I don't want to be forced to take Erin away from her. I might have to kill her, and that would upset my friend, Hu Chang."

"Yes, I would be so upset that I would seek and find a way to kill my friend, Cameron."

Cameron chuckled. "I do like you, Hu Chang. No one intimidates you, thank God."

"And you're bored to extinction with people who allow you to intimidate them."

He grimaced. "Not extinction. That's one of the prime things that I'm not permitted."

"But bored nevertheless." He watched as Tashdon opened the helicopter door and gestured for Luke to jump out. "Your fine, competent pilot is an excellent example. He seemed quite normal until he got near you. He was almost subservient, eagerly subservient, but subservient nonetheless. Have you been indulging in a little brainwashing?"

"God, no," Cameron said violently.

"Then I have to admire your ability to handle him. He'd obviously do anything for you. When he was hovering so protectively over you just now, was he asking if I was a possible threat?"

"You caught that? Tashdon always regards it as his duty to make sure that he doesn't deliver anyone who might be dangerous to me." He shook his head. "Even though I ordered him to bring you." His lips twisted bitterly. "Haven't you heard? Nothing must happen to me."

"Yes, I've heard," Hu Chang said. "And I tend to agree. Of course, with the exception that will exist if I decide that you're interfering with my retrieving Catherine."

Cameron laughed and slapped him on the back. "Exception noted. Now tell me why you brought the boy."

"He belongs to Catherine and, though extraordinary, he needs schooling in many areas. I thought this would be an excellent training ground." He paused. "And why did you not try to stop me?"

"I was curious. I wanted to see her son." His smile widened. "And I wanted to see her tear into you when she discovered you brought him. It will be interesting to see how you handle it."

"Indeed it will," he murmured. He gestured to Luke, who was now only a few yards away. "Luke, I would like to present my friend, Richard Cameron. He has just told me how amused he is going to be to see your mother's reaction to my bringing you along."

"That's not kind," Luke said. "I think everyone knows she's going to be very angry." He took the last few steps to stand before Cameron. "Hu Chang says that I should be polite to you. I can't do that if you're going to wish bad things to happen to him."

"I was joking." Cameron's gaze was raking Luke's face, his expression intent. "Though it will be something to see."

Luke was silent. "I have trouble with jokes. Sometimes I can't tell . . ." He looked at Hu Chang. "Hu Chang will tell you."

"I don't believe I'll have to tell Cameron," Hu Chang said. "I think he's already understanding more about you than I want him to know. Back off, Cameron."

"I'm out," Cameron said. "It was the quickest way. Though it appears you're the one who has done a little manipulating. You must think a good deal of him." He smiled at Luke. "Politeness isn't necessary between us. I have great respect and admiration for Hu Chang, and I'm looking forward to getting to know you. I think you're going to be a great help."

Luke looked at him for a long minute. "You're not lying to me?"

Cameron shook his head. "Though you'll never be certain until I prove myself to you, so I won't try to persuade you." He turned to Tashdon. "Get going. No electronic communication until you're completely out of the area. Go back to Hong Kong and refuel and stand by for further orders."

"Yes, Cameron. I'll be ready." Tashdon turned and strode swiftly back toward the helicopter.

"He acts as if you're his boss," Luke said as he gazed after the pilot. "Are you?"

"Not exactly. He works for hire, but he wants to please me. I can count on him to obey orders." He met Luke's eyes. "Can I count on you?"

Luke was silent. "Yes, if you don't do anything that Hu Chang doesn't like."

"That's not good enough." He looked at Hu Chang. "We've already discussed possible differences of opinion and agreed there's no problem. But I can't take you with me unless you agree to belong to me even if it's only for a short time. Will you do that?"

"Belong to you?" Luke frowned. "I don't like the—"

"Agree, Luke," Hu Chang said. "We need him, and it's only until we get Catherine back." He gazed at Cameron. "If it makes you feel better, Cameron told me the same thing several years ago, and I conceded my independence until I had what I wanted. It was not a totally unpleasant experience."

"Not for me either," Cameron said. "Luke?"

Luke slowly nodded. "Okay."

"Good." He turned away. "Now grab your gear and come along. We have a long hike up the mountain."

"And where are we going?" Hu Chang asked.

"I have quarters I use occasionally on this side of the mountain where we can be comfortable until we're ready to move. But we can't do that yet. I have some research to do." He smiled over his shoulder. "Catherine told me that I should find her a way to get off Daksha Mountain, and I have to obey."

Hu Chang stiffened. "You've been in touch with her? I thought you were dealing through Erin Sullivan?"

"How could I resist? Catherine is a warrior. I feel a kinship for her. Erin is strong, but she endures and hesitates to attack. It's her basic character, and I've had to make allowances all through these months." He paused. "But now I have Catherine. Her basic instinct is to make a judgment, then attack. It will be much easier."

"You have Catherine?" Luke repeated, puzzled. "Does that mean she said she'd belong to you, like you asked me to do?"

"No, not yet." Cameron laughed. "I have that pleasure to look forward to."

"I would not count on it," Hu Chang said dryly.

"But I do count on it. I would not have thought you would agree, my friend. But in the past, you found I could supply you with something you wanted, and you chose to run the risk." He started up the trail. "I just have to find the correct bargaining chip . . ."

It was two hours later that Hu Chang caught up with Cameron on the curve of the mountain trail. "How much longer?" he asked. "The boy is struggling."

"I know," Cameron said. "He's very strong. But the altitude is a killer if you're not accustomed to it."

"And you haven't stopped to let him rest."

"Has he complained?"

"No."

"Good. I didn't think he would."

"You could help him," Hu Chang said. "You could ease it."

"But I won't." Cameron turned and strode forward around the curve.

It was nearly an hour later that he stopped in front of a sod hut balanced on the edge of a cliff overlooking the valley. He stood waiting, watching as Hu Chang came up the trail. "The boy?"

"Five minutes behind me."

"But you didn't wait for him."

"No, I knew what you were doing. It was a test, and I wouldn't cheat Luke of his victory."

"A test you would not have given him?"

"Perhaps, perhaps not. But Luke agreed, and I knew you were no easy taskmaster."

"Any resentment?"

"No. Curiosity. Why did you wish to test him?"

"You brought him on a man's job. I wanted to see if he could do it."

"That's not all."

He was silent, watching as Luke came around the curve, staggering, catching himself, then trudging on. "No, I wanted to see if he was truly her son in spirit as well as body. When I saw that you had trusted him enough to have given him that magnificent gift, I thought he might be."

"But you had to see for yourself."

"You might have been blinded by your affection for his mother."

"And why was it so important to you?"

"I have no idea." He smiled brilliantly. "But it appears that it is." He strode toward Luke, and called, "You did very well. I've known men who have grown up in these mountains who have had trouble on this trail."

Luke stopped, weaving on his feet. His face was flushed, and his breathing was labored. "It . . . hurts. It was a . . . long way. I kept throwing up, and it hurt to breathe. At first, I thought I hated you."

"But you changed your mind."

"You were making it, Hu Chang was making it. Why should I hate you because I couldn't?" He glared up at him. "So I forgot about hating you and just did it."

"Very sensible of you." Cameron's voice was uncharacteristically gentle. "May I say that you have my admiration." He held out his hand. "And I'd like to shake your hand. Would that be all right with you?"

Luke hesitated, then slowly took Cameron's hand. "You're not making fun of me?"

"Why should I do that?" He looked directly into Luke's eyes. "You belong to me. Your pain is my pain. Your victory is my victory." He shook his hand, then released it and put his arm around Luke's shoulders and led him toward the sod hut. "I have great pride in you. Can't you feel it?"

Luke nodded. "Yes, I think so. I feel . . . warm."

Cameron's eyes were twinkling. "And that's a good thing in this frigid air. Soon you'll be inside, and you'll feel even warmer. You'll notice that the altitude sickness is gone now."

"Yes, why?"

"It happens that way sometimes. You'll be a little tired, but that exhaustion will slip away like a thief in the night." He opened the door of the hut. "And now you and Hu Chang can heat us something to eat while I stay out here and concentrate on finding a way for us to get to Catherine. Or better still, for Catherine to get to us." He glanced at Hu Chang. "I was able to make considerable headway on the hike up here."

"A contact?" Hu Chang asked.

"Yes, I had to sift through half a dozen false leads, but I came up with Sadiki, an Egyptian monk who visited this area thirty years ago. I believe he knows enough to help us." He smiled again at Luke. "I think Sadiki is the one. Give me a little time, and I'll be able to give Catherine a way out."

"I don't know what you're talking about," Luke said. He added thoughtfully, "But I think you do know what you're doing. It's like Hu Chang in the lab. I have no idea how he knows what to put into his potions, but I know they will do what he says they'll do."

Cameron's lips twitched as he inclined his head. "I appreciate being compared to Hu Chang, but I'm no brilliant chemist. I'm only a poor soldier trying to do his job."

"Come along, Luke." Hu Chang drew Luke into the hut. "I fear my friend Cameron is choosing to be deceptively humble. I don't want you exposed to such deceit."

Cameron's smile faded. "No deceit. Simplification, perhaps." He turned and strode several yards away and sat down and leaned against a scraggly pine tree. "Take the boy inside. This shouldn't take me more than forty or fifty minutes."

But Luke was hanging back, staring at Cameron. "Why is he staying out in the cold? He's just sitting there. He should come in where it's warmer."

"Don't worry. He doesn't feel the cold," Hu Chang said. "He trained himself a long time ago not to let heat or cold bother him. I believe he has to remind himself that he can't stay out in either too long."

"Peculiar . . ."

"That he is, Luke." His gaze narrowed on the boy's face. "But you like him, don't you? It's impossible not to like Cameron when he exerts himself. In spite of how tough you had it today, he did make an effort with you."

"Yes, I guess I do. I . . . liked it when he said he had pride in me. That made me feel . . . I liked it."

Hu Chang had to pull the boy aside to close the door. He was still gazing at Cameron with that puzzled, bewildered, fascinated expression Hu Chang had seen on other people's faces when confronted by Cameron. Hu Chang didn't know how much of that fascination was engendered by Cameron's charismatic personality or what seeds he had insinuated into the boy's mind during that time when he had been face-to-face, talking to him. Something had definitely been going on in that moment.

"It's all right to like Cameron, Luke. But one must always keep a sense of one's own well-being when around him. Don't try to please him too much." His lips twisted. "Or you'll end up like that pilot, Tashdon. Now, let's find what rations are available and have them ready for Cameron when he comes back in." He started toward the camp stove across the room. "And hope that he finds out something valuable from that monk, Sadiki . . ."

CHAPTER 7

"Catherine."

She tensed.

"You're not answering. I know you're not asleep. Turnabout is fair play," Cameron said. "I answered when you called me. Now I'm calling you."

He was suddenly there before her. The same cozy room, the fireplace and deep leather chairs. He was standing in front of the fireplace, and he was just as riveting as she remembered.

"I thought you'd forgotten about us," she said dryly. "It's been hours since you did your precision hit, then took off."

"You knew I didn't forget," he said softly. "That can't happen any longer. Though I can see that you've been fighting accepting our very uneasy alliance."

"I don't like anything about it, but I particularly don't like that you can 'see' anything in my mind. It's an intrusion I won't permit."

"I can understand. We may come to an agreement later. But at the moment, I have to be close to you, know everything you're seeing and feeling."

"Not fair."

"But efficient and necessary. You want off Kadmus's mountain, and there's no easy way. I have to make sure that I don't have to step in too soon."

"Too soon? Oh, yes, that's right. Your job description doesn't permit you risking your neck."

"That's right." He grimaced. "And that's been thrown at me a thousand times. Why does it bother me when you do it?"

"I have no idea."

"Neither do I, but it makes me uneasy." He added, "But we'll drop it for the moment. It's always a challenge talking to you, but I have to get on with extricating you from that cave. How strong is Erin?"

"I'd think you'd know. You've been such buddies."

"I'm not leaving you to go to her and probe. It would be inefficient. Assess her for me."

"I bound her dislocated shoulder and splinted her broken finger. She has other wounds that will give her pain but not impede her from normal activity."

"What about abnormal activity?"

She tensed. "Is that the way it's going to be?"

He nodded. "It will be a rough path out. Can she make it?"

She thought about it. "She can do it. Strength doesn't always depend on the physical. She shouldn't have been able to keep up with me when we were escaping the palace, but she did. I'll help her, and she'll do it. Tell me what we're up against."

"I've contacted Sadiki, an Egyptian monk who visited Tibet about thirty years ago. The palace was being used as a monastery at that time and he stayed with the monks for a year. He traveled the entire mountain when he was there, and in the end, he knew more about the mountain than the monks who lived here. The road that leads off the mountain runs along the edge where most of the habitats and village exist. There are three roads that branch off from the one you took, but they'll be watched by Kadmus's men."

"You're not being encouraging. What's the alternative?"

"Go inland. From where you are, you can climb up to the top of the mountain. Kadmus wouldn't expect you to take that route. Once you get to the top, you'll find it strewn with huge boulders and crevices. Make your way north through them and in about a mile, you'll see a path that winds around and down. It's rough and narrow and slippery, and there are gaping crevasses that can send you hundreds of feet down."

"Wonderful. And how far do we have to go?"

"All the way to the bottom, where it exits at a hot spring."

"It goes clear to the bottom of the mountain? That far? But does it dead-end there at the spring? Or will it lead to a path that will connect to a road that will bypass any of Kadmus's roadblocks?"

"It doesn't exactly dead-end, but there isn't any path to take you away from the hot springs."

"That sounds like a dead end to me."

"The hot springs are the way out. The primary pool flows down through several passages and eventually joins with another small hot spring in a valley in Milchang, the next mountain over. You could be picked up there and taken up to the hut."

"What hut?"

"Just a place near where I can arrange to have a helicopter pick you up and flown out." He smiled. "It's icy cold up there and snows almost all the time, but you might welcome a little cold after the hot springs."

"How hot are those springs?"

"They vary from being very hot to lukewarm. There's an underground river that runs alongside the spring and occasionally feeds it. The river would be icy cold and would cool the springs at those points. But it could be scalding hot four feet away from where the river flows into the spring. You'll have to stay close to the river side."

"And hope that the river still feeds it the same way it did thirty years ago."

"There is that. I did a geographic check, and the possibility is good that the conditions are the same."

"That's comforting. How deep is it?"

"Deep enough to swim in some areas. Wading depth in others."

"It sounds like hell for Erin and bad for me. There's no other way?"

"It's the safest. Otherwise, you'll run into Kadmus's men."

"And I won't be stumbling over them around those springs? How do I know that Kadmus doesn't use those springs for his private spa?"

"You wouldn't stumble. And, according to reports, neither Kadmus nor any of the villagers ever go to the springs. I doubt if he even knows they exist. He just took over the mountain a couple years ago, and the villagers wouldn't *tell him about them. No one but the monks knew anything about the springs, and they were thrown out of their monastery by Kadmus."*

"It might be possible." She thought about it. It was an unusual and probably dangerous solution to the dilemma. But possibly less than the one presented by hiding here or trying the mountain road. "Okay, it's a go. We'll be on our way as soon as it gets dark. Erin has had a sound sleep and she should be as good as she'll ever be."

"And what about you?"

"I slept a little. It's all I'll need. The adrenaline will carry me." She paused. "Until I get to you on that other mountain. You may be able to judge how long it will take us, but I don't have any idea. But when we make it, you'd better be there when we end this marathon swim."

"Don't worry, I'll see that you're met."

"No, I want you there. You take the risk for once. After what Erin's going to go through, she deserves to have a reward at the end. Though God knows I can't see that you're any prize."

"But then you haven't explored my many talents."

"I've been exposed to one of them, and I can't say that I appreciate it. Will you be there?"

"I'll think about it. You'll be met." He added, "At any rate, I'll be with you all the way. Sadiki has an excellent memory of that journey and was able to transfer that memory to me. I'll try to guide you and save you a few falls."

"You're going to whisper in my ear?"

"That would be delightful, but I'll stick to the present communication. Just don't ignore me, Catherine. I'll have the overview, and I'll be right."

She was silent. "I won't ignore you."

"What a concession."

"It is a concession. I don't like the idea of not having full control." She gazed challengingly at him. "Like you, Cameron." She waved her hand dismissingly. "So gather up your cozy fire and other paraphernalia and all that soothing mind crap and hit the road. I need to wake up Erin, check her over, and get her prepped for the trip."

He chuckled. "I hear and obey. Anything else?"

"Yes, be there when we fight our way through this."

"Possibly . . ."

The fire flared, then was gone.

The next moment, so was Cameron.

"Very theatrical," she said sarcastically. "You can do better than that."

"Definitely. I just didn't want to dazzle you."

"Out. I'll accept your bullshit only when I'm on the road and at risk."

"You would never have known I was still here if you hadn't decided to insult me. Later . . ."

Was he gone?

She couldn't worry about it. She had things to do. She sat up and wriggled out of the sleeping bag. The next moment, she was kneeling beside Erin. She shook her gently, "Hey, rise and shine." She wrinkled her nose. "Though the shine part will be pretty difficult considering what I'm going to throw at you. But we'll have to take what we get."

Erin sat up and yawned. "What are you talking about, Catherine?" Her eyes suddenly widened with alarm. "Trouble?"

"Yes, though I guess it depends on what you call trouble. Your hero, Cameron, came calling. And I'd say he's big-time trouble . . ."

·   ·   ·

"There's moonlight," Erin said quietly as she helped Catherine roll the huge boulder back to hide the opening of the cave. "Is that going to be bad or good for us?"

"It could work either way." She smiled at Erin. "I'm going to consider it lucky. It will help us to find our way to that crevasse at the break in the boulders on the mountaintop. After that, it won't matter. There won't be moonlight once we start down into that darkness. Too bad. We need to see where we're going. Cameron said that the winding path down to the hot springs is killer."

"You brought your flashlight." Erin frowned. "But not much else. You left the sleeping bags and everything that—"

"We can't afford the extra weight. And it won't do us any good once we reach the springs. We'd have to leave them there anyway." Catherine carefully brushed their footprints away from the cave opening until they reached the stone path. "If everything goes wrong, we can try to make our way back to the cave."

"You took your gun."

"That's not something I consider expendable. Besides, we have to take the road to make it to the crest of the mountain. I might have to use it if the road is patrolled." She threw the branch away. "Though if given a preference, I'd prefer knife or hands. A gunshot would be heard all over this mountain and the next in this clear air." She moved ahead of Erin on the trail. "I'm hoping they'd expect us to be going down, not up the mountain. I'll keep the pace slow and steady on the trail, so that you can conserve your strength. After we reach the top, I can't promise anything. No conversation until we reach the top."

"Okay." She was silent a moment. "But you don't have to be so careful of me. I won't hold you back."

"I know you won't." She smiled faintly. "But I prefer you don't kill yourself to keep from doing it. Now, hush."

Silence.

The cold wind striking their faces.

The bright moonlight as icy as the snow on the ground.

Isolation.

Ten minutes.

Fifteen minutes.

Twenty minutes.

The wind was sharper, more merciless the higher they climbed.

Catherine could hear the sound of Erin's breathing behind her.

Her own breathing was probably heavier and more labored, she thought. Erin was more accustomed to the altitude than she. But at least she wasn't sick and dizzy as she had been the last time she'd been

this high in the mountains. It would have been difficult to function. She would have done what was necessary, but it would have—

Laughter.

She stopped short, her gaze flying to the curve of the trail up
ahead.

Conversation. Chinese. Vulgar. Obscene. Boasting.

It was either two of Kadmus's soldiers or a phone conversation.
She listened. Only one voice.

A phone conversation. She hadn't thought that Kadmus would
allot more than one sentry for this stretch of road.

But the road was so narrow, they couldn't go around him without being seen.

Erin had nudged closer to her.

Catherine shook her head and held up her hand to indicate she
was to stay. Then she moved cautiously forward.

The conversation was continuing, and so was the laughter.

Keep on talking. What else is there to do on this barren mountainside to amuse yourself? Keep on talking . . .

She had reached the curve of the road and stopped, pressing
back against the stone.

Don't be facing this way.

Please, I need a break . . .

And she got it!

He was leaning back against the stone face of the mountain and
facing the valley. Not as good as if he had his back to her, but she
could work with it.

She took off her gloves and stuffed them in her pocket.

Hit him low, bring him down, use her hands on the carotid
artery.

He laughed again.

Wait until he hung up. She didn't want to alert whoever he was
talking to in the compound.

He talked a few more minutes.

He hung up.

She moved!

He didn't see her until she was almost on him. He grunted as he dropped the phone and tried to turn toward her and raise his AK-47. But she had already tackled him, and he was falling. She was astride him as he hit the ground.

Her hands tore open his coat and fastened on his throat.

His eyes were glaring up at her as his fist struck her cheek. "Zai—"

The curse was cut off. She had reached the carotid.

Five seconds later, he was dead.

She took a deep breath and sat back on her heels. Death was never easy, and she never got used to it. It didn't matter if it was kill or be killed. It still sucked.

She got to her feet and ran back to Erin. "Come on, I need your help."

"What happened? I didn't hear—" Erin stopped as she saw the soldier huddled on the ground. "Dead?"

"Very."

"Then I don't see why you need me."

"I want you to help me roll him off the mountain."

"What?"

"I can't leave him here, there's no place to hide him. If someone checks up on him, then it will lead them to this post. If he's just not here, then they'll have to look for him. That will take time. We need time." She was already struggling, tugging him toward the edge of the cliff. "Don't help me with this. I don't want your shoulder to go out again. When I get him in position, just help me roll him off the cliff . . ."

"What if someone sees him fall or maybe—"

"Don't second-guess." She tried to catch her breath. "I think that he should fall fairly straight down, there's no slope or—Help me. Take his shoulders. I'll do his lower body."

"Right." Erin was there pushing. A moment later the body slid silently over the side of the cliff.

She straightened. "What next?"

"We erase signs of struggle and his header over the cliff. Then we erase our own footprints. That's all we can do without using up time we can't afford. Come on, get busy."

Five minutes later, they were moving up the trail again.

Erin shivered. "I'm still seeing that soldier tumble off the mountain. I was hoping that we wouldn't be forced to do anything that violent."

"And I was almost sure we'd be faced with something like it," Catherine said. "We've been pretty lucky since we got away from Kadmus."

"Yes." She didn't speak for a minute. "Do you think we'll run into any other sentries on this road?"

"I doubt it. But I have to be prepared." She said gently, "You're doing great, Erin. I couldn't have done without you back there."

"Yes, you could." She made a face. "It just would have taken you longer." She looked up the road. "How far to the top?"

"I'd say another ten minutes. Any problem?"

"No." She quickened her pace. "I'm fine. Let's get up there. It's always easier going downhill."

. . .

The top of the mountain looked like a moon landscape. It was flat, not jagged, and the surface was covered with huge boulders, craters, and rocks.

"It seems our monk, Sadiki's, memory didn't fail him," Catherine murmured. "But the way down might not be as easy as you hoped, Erin. It looks pretty rough to me." She started over the rock-strewn surface. "Those big boulders, there should be twisting passages between them going down . . ."

"According to Sadiki."

"And according to your friend, Cameron. Let's see if he's right."

"*Of course I'm right, Catherine.*"

"You're back. There's no *of course* about it. It's all hearsay."

"*But expertly-well-researched hearsay. And I'm not 'back.' I've been with you all along. It just wasn't wise to interfere in the arena you obviously own. Besides, you resent my intrusion.*"

She kept moving quickly toward the boulders. "Yes, I do. I don't really know either your intentions or your parameters of power. You could be some nut one of those think tanks tossed out who decided to throw in with a group equally crazy."

"*That's true. Move faster, Catherine. I'm figuring that you have perhaps forty minutes to get down to the hot springs before Kadmus's soldiers start pouring up here.*"

"I am moving fast." *But her pace instinctively became even faster.* "And I was allowing thirty minutes."

"*But you did such a fine job of disposing of that sentry. It should allow you a little more time. You did everything right. I'm lost in admiration.*" *He paused.* "*The path should be right ahead, between those two boulders. I won't communicate again other than to give you directions or information. You're going to need to concentrate.*"

"Good."

She was entering the narrow darkness between the boulders. She could see nothing. But the twisting path was sloping downward she realized with relief.

"Catherine?" Erin was behind her, moving cautiously.

"I'm going to turn on my flashlight as soon as I'm sure that we're below the surface and there aren't any cracks between these boulders for light to escape. I hope you're not claustrophobic. There's barely room to move in this passageway."

"No, but it's hard to breathe, isn't it?" She paused. "But Cameron was right, wasn't he?"

"Yes, but we won't know how right until we get down to those hot springs. As soon as we're able to see better, we've got to put on more speed."

Silence. "Is that what Cameron told you just now?"

She stiffened. "Erin?"

"He was with you, wasn't he? You were so quiet, and I realized that Cameron was there."

"Oh, no, not you, too. I'm having enough trouble dealing with Cameron and his so-called talents."

"I don't have any talents. But I've been so close to Cameron that it would be strange if I didn't sense him near me. Only now he's not as close since he's with you."

"And do you resent that?"

"No, why should I? Cameron always makes the right decisions."

"I believe I'm beginning to feel ill."

"May I help?" Erin asked, concerned.

"No, that was sarcasm." Catherine turned on her flashlight. It did little good. Because of the twisting downhill narrowness she still couldn't see more than a few feet ahead before the next turn. But at least, they weren't in complete darkness. She would have to be cautious that there wasn't a falloff beyond one of those turns.

"No time. Go for it. I'll help you."

Was that Cameron's sense of urgency or her own?

Both.

But it was her instincts on which she had to rely. She was still far from the springs that could be their salvation. And who knew what hazards might stall their progress when they reached them?

And Kadmus could be hot on their trail.

Throw caution to the winds. Rely on luck, Sadiki, and yes, even Cameron.

"Stay close," she tossed to Erin over her shoulder as she began to move at a half run through the passage. "We're on our way."

●　　●　　●

"They're on the move," Brasden's eyes were bright with excitement. "We have a sentry reported missing north of the village."

"Missing?" Kadmus said. "What the hell do you mean missing?"

Brasden shrugged. "What I said. Li Kim was on guard on the upper road, and we weren't able to reach him by phone. I sent two men up to his post and he wasn't there. No signs of struggle. He was just . . . missing. We're searching for him now. And for Ling and Erin Sullivan. There has to be a connection. They were probably hiding up there near the top and decided it was time to make a break for it."

"And where are you searching now?"

"Down the road leading past the village to the bottom of the mountain."

"Down?" Kadmus gazed thoughtfully up at the top of the mountain. "Why would Ling have taken Erin Sullivan up there anyway? Because it would have been the most unlikely place for them to hide?"

"It makes sense."

"No, it doesn't. It's a dead end, and Catherine Ling is no fool. Was the top of the mountain searched?"

Brasden frowned. "Yes, I wouldn't forget that."

"But you wouldn't have done it with the same care as more reasonable escape avenues."

"Perhaps not," he said reluctantly. "But it doesn't matter. They're on their way down. They disposed of the sentry, but we have a heavy force all the way to the main road. We'll get them."

"What if you don't?" Kadmus asked harshly. "And what if they were going up, not down?"

"Why would they do that? As you said, dead end."

"How do I know? Maybe they arranged to have a helicopter pickup there."

"We detected no electronic transmissions."

"Don't argue with me. There are always ways to get around problems. Ling was on that road for a reason. She got rid of the sentry for a reason."

"You're telling me to abandon the village and road leading down—"

"Don't be an idiot. I'm just telling you that road could be taken in either direction." He was still gazing at the mists shrouding the top of the mountain. *Are you up there, Catherine Ling?* It would be unexpected. A red herring? Or something more dangerous? He didn't know enough about the mountaintop to be certain. He'd only gone up there once after he'd taken over the palace and property. He'd been unimpressed. "You keep your search going as you've begun. I'll take a few men and climb to the top and look around." He turned and started to cross the courtyard. Then he stopped and glanced back. "And rout out one of those monks who are still living in the village and send him after me. Maybe that old lama who refused to leave his precious mountain. He might be able to tell me more about that area."

"It's only a bunch of boulders and rocks."

"Send him," Kadmus said. "Right away. Bring him to the sentry post." He strode over to the jeep parked near the compound gate. He would only be able to take the vehicle a short distance before the road narrowed as it neared the top. That didn't matter. Speed was important now.

I thought there was only one way out. Did you find another one, bitch?

It won't do you any good. You can't get Erin away from me. It was meant to be. I was meant to have it all.

Shambhala.

·   ·   ·

"How are you doing, Erin?" Catherine's words were coming in gasps. Her own lungs were tight, her breath almost nonexistent.

It seemed as if they had been running down this twisted, spiraling path, for hours. If she had felt like this, what must Erin be feeling? "It can't be much farther."

"Promises. Promises," Erin said breathlessly. "I'm okay. Except that my legs feel like spaghetti." She drew a deep, shaky breath. "And I didn't expect all these weird echoes down here. I guess I should have, it's sort of a cave, after all. But it's like being in a giant fun house."

"Without the fun." The echoes had also startled Catherine when she had first noticed them. "Anything else?"

"I'm dizzy from all these twists and turns. But then I bet you are, too."

"Yes. But it would be worse if the incline were straight—" She stopped. "Do you smell something?"

Erin sniffed, then stiffened. "Something's dead."

"No, though I can see how you might think that. It smells like rotten eggs." She sniffed again, then said eagerly, "Sulfur smells like rotten eggs. And hot springs are full of sulfur. We have to be close. Hurry."

"What else have I been doing?" Erin asked ruefully. "But you may be right. I'm feeling warmer."

Dressed as they were in this cold-weather gear, they were going to feel a good deal warmer as they got closer to the springs, Catherine thought. Even in extreme, frigid temperatures, the area surrounding a hot springs could be seventy degrees or much higher. "You've lived and worked in Tibet for a number of years. You probably know more about these hot springs than I do. I've only taken a bath in one of the springs up north, and then I was in and out. Cameron said they could be scalding. Have you ever run across that?"

"Once. But only in spots, and you can move away from the area, and you're comfortable again."

"But you weren't deep inside a mountain. Conditions could be different."

"I don't know about that. But the hot springs here in Tibet could be less hot because they weren't created by volcanoes. The Himalayas were formed by two tectonic plates shifting and coming together millions of years ago. One of the side effects was the forming of a network of hot springs throughout the mountain range."

Catherine found herself smiling. "I only wanted to know if we could get scalded. I forgot you were a journalist until you started spouting volcanoes and tectonic plates."

"I was interested," Erin said. "But what you mustn't ever do is submerge your head under the waters. There's an amoeba that exists under those conditions that can enter your sinus passages and cause a deadly brain disease that could kill you."

"Thanks for telling me," Catherine said dryly. "Cameron failed to mention that little threat. A warning would have been nice."

"Why make you worry? I wouldn't have let it happen to either of you."

That jarring intrusion again. She would never become accustomed to it.

She ignored him. "Anything else I should know, Erin?"

She shivered. "Snakes. I've heard there's a species of snake that can live in the hot water."

Steam was beginning to pour through the passage and perspiration was beading Catherine's face. "Poisonous?"

"I don't think so."

"It would be nice to know."

"It's not relevant. They're rarely found outside Qinghai Province."

"I think it's safe, Erin," Catherine said. "Snakes may be the last thing we should worry about at the moment. God, that sulfur stinks. We must be right on top of—" She broke off as she rounded the corner.

Billows of steam drifting upward from a large dark pool.

Heat.

Sounds of running water.

The foul, ever-present stench of rotten eggs.

"This sure isn't like the last hot springs where I bathed," Erin said. "The sun was shining, the sky was blue, and the mountains were magnificent. This looks . . . menacing."

"It's the darkness. The unknown can be frightening." And those billows of steam coming from that darkness seemed something from a sci-fi movie. She bounced the beam from her flashlight around the stone bank of the spring, then to the water itself. "Listen. That rushing sound. Can you tell where it's coming from?"

Erin listened. "To the right. But it's very faint."

Catherine lifted the flashlight and aimed it to the right.

A break in the solid wall of the mountain.

Yes!

The waters of the spring appeared to be trickling through the break and down . . .

"Come on. That could be our way out."

"Or not," Erin said.

"Well, I don't see anything else. Hurry." She was shedding her parka and shirt. "Get rid of all your outer clothes. They'll weigh you down when you're in the water. You can keep on your underwear." She was down to her thermal undershirt and tights. She tucked her gun and knife in her boots, loosened the shoestrings and tied them around her neck. "Leave your clothes here, but you'll need your boots. They're hard to replace and we can't afford to have our feet cut to ribbons once we're outside. Slip anything you want to keep into the boots."

Erin followed Catherine's example and tied the boots around her neck. "I'm ready."

"What about that gold necklace you're wearing? Don't you want to take it off and put it in your boot?"

"No, I won't lose it." She touched the necklace. "It's very strong."

"Whatever. Stay here. I need to test the waters." Catherine put her bare foot in the spring and slipped from the stony bank. "Warm.

Not hot. But it may change the farther we go. My feet are touching the bottom, and so far, the waters are only up to my chest."

"I'm coming in."

"No, let me go a little farther. There's no way that it's not going to hurt those wounds but I want to make sure there's no additional acidic—"

"No, you don't have time to baby me." Erin slipped into the water and inhaled sharply. "You're right, it does smart a bit. It's nothing I can't deal with." She waded toward Catherine. "Let's go."

There would obviously be no arguing with her. "We'll try to stay side by side as much as possible. If it narrows down, you go ahead. I need to keep an eye on you."

"That's going to be hard. I can barely see you through this steam."

"It should get less if that passage leads closer to the outside." She was almost to the break in the wall, and the beam of her flashlight was playing deep into the dark cavity. "Except for the water, it looks almost like that twisting path we took to get down here."

"Then we shouldn't have a problem."

"I appreciate your optimism. I hope you're right." Her heart was beating hard as she plunged down into the water within the passage. It was difficult to be optimistic at the moment. They had moved very quickly since they had left the mountaintop, but it might not have been quick enough. They had to try to make up more time in this steaming cauldron. She could only hope that Kadmus had not moved at top speed when they found the sentry or that his chosen direction was not toward the mountaintop.

·   ·   ·

The lama Padma Nagtal's face was now as red from the blood streaming down his cheeks as the color of his crimson robe.

"I do not know any more," he said hoarsely as he tried to struggle from his knees to his feet and regain dignity. "I have told you all."

"And did you tell the Americans about that passage, too?" Kadmus punched him in the stomach and knocked him back to the ground. "Did they come to you in the village and beg for a route to freedom?"

"I did not see them. I would not have risked the lives of my people in the village to save foreigners."

"But you didn't tell me about that passage down the mountain when I sent you and the rest of your stinking brothers away from my palace."

"You did not ask."

He kicked him in the face. "And there is no way that they can get away once they reach that hot spring? You say there is no opening to the outside."

"There were only a few, almost forgotten, texts concerning the hot spring in our library." He paused. "The library that you burned. None of the texts mentioned any way to leave that spring once reached. Since neither I nor my brothers considered it our duty to explore that place of cold and fire, I must assume that the texts were correct."

"Assume? I don't assume anything." He bent down. "And I'd burn your library again, old man. All those books meant nothing."

"Except when you needed them." He met Kadmus's eyes. "And someday men like you will find you have nothing and will search for our holy books to find your way."

"Fool. I will own the world. I'll not need you or—"

"We've found the sentry." Brasden hung up his phone as he approached. "Dead. He was found in the brush about five hundred feet down the mountain. What do we do now?"

"What I planned before. Search all the possible roads down the mountain. But I'm taking eight men with me to the top. I think our lama's help warrants that increased force, don't you?"

"It's still only a rocky hole in the mountain."

"Then we'll chase them down to the bottom of that rocky hole.

We'll go so fast and hard that there's no way they'll escape." He took out his gun. "But first I have something else to do." He pressed the barrel to the lama's temple. "Good-bye, holy man. We'll see who reaches his special paradise first."

He pulled the trigger.

CHAPTER
8

I t's getting colder." Erin was panting with effort as she forced herself through the water. "We must be away from the mountain. Could we slow down?"

"No." It hurt her to say the words when she knew what Erin must be going through. "Not until we reach the hot springs at the other mountain. Even then it will be dangerous."

And when would that be, she wondered. It seemed as if they had been wading, half swimming and crawling forever down this rocky water passage. It had just narrowed again, and Erin was ahead of her crawling through shallow water on hands and knees over the rocky ground. Catherine's own hands and legs were scratched and cut from the sharp rocks.

"Cameron, you'd better have been right about this damn spring."

"I'm right." Soothing gentleness, removal of all pain. *"You're not too far. Keep her going."*

"I don't hurt anymore. Is that one of your tricks?"

"One of the better ones."

"Well, don't waste it on me. Take care of Erin."

"I've already done it. I had to attend to her first. She's my responsibility."

"No, she's my responsibility." She added wearily, "But I'll let you share. I'm too tired to argue."

"You've had a rough—" He stopped, then said sharply, "Tell Erin to stop. The floor of the cave falls off just ahead. She won't be able to see—"

"Catherine!" Erin suddenly plunged forward, hitting her shoulder on the stone bank as she fell.

Water.

Water up to Erin's shoulders.

No, up to her neck!

Panic jolted through Catherine as Erin's words came back to her. Never let your head go under the water. Brain disease and death.

"Erin, hold on to the bank." She was crawling frantically forward. "Tread water. I'll be there in a second."

"Having trouble," Erin gasped. "It's deep here. And I can't hold on to those stones. I think my shoulder popped out again when I hit it against the bank when I fell."

Dammit!

Catherine threw her flashlight into her boot and dove after her in the water.

Hot. The water was hot.

"And it will get hotter. Get her to the left side of the passage. There's cold water flowing in there."

Catherine grabbed Erin and pulled her toward the left. The water didn't cool until she was almost to the edge of the water. "Why didn't you tell me you were boiling like a lobster?" she asked as she held Erin above water.

"There seemed to be enough problems to tell you about," Erin said. "And I wasn't scalding."

"Yes, there is that." She took her flashlight from her boot. "Let's see how far this stretch of water goes . . ." The water was wider, deeper, and the sound of rushing water was clearer.

"Cameron?"

No answer.

"We're on our own? Fine. I didn't need you anyway."

She grabbed Erin under the chin, carefully keeping her head above water, and started to propel them both through the water. "Look, try to kick, but let me do the rest."

"I don't have any choice." Erin began to kick rhythmically. "I'm sorry, Catherine."

"For what? It's not as if you could keep that shoulder from going out again. If we're going to blame someone, let's blame Kadmus."

Erin chuckled. "I'll second that motion. I'll just add it to my list and—" She stiffened. "My God, did you hear that?"

"Yes," Catherine's pulse had jumped, then began to pound hard. Shit.

Voices. Men's voices. Shouts. Curses.

Coming from behind them.

"Kadmus," Erin whispered. "I was hoping—"

"Me, too." Catherine began to swim harder, stronger. "But we didn't luck out. We have to get out of here."

"By all means, but it may not be as bad as you think. These passages act as one huge echo chamber. They could still be on their way down."

She had just remembered that echo syndrome herself, and relief was pouring through her.

"It's bad enough, Cameron."

She said out loud to Erin, "Echoes. We'll make it."

"That's right, why didn't I think of that?" She added, "I think the water is getting cooler again."

"Not too bad."

But it was cooler. What was happening? All they needed was to be dumped in an ice pool instead of hot springs.

No, the water was getting warmer again and rough, very rough. She had to struggle to keep Erin's head above water.

"Move left. There are rocks ahead. Grab hold of them and pull Erin up with you."

"I don't see—"

"Do it!"

She moved left. A moment later, she saw the group of four or five rocks ahead. The water was pouring, gushing around them.

"Grab them."

She grabbed desperately for the rocks with her free hand. She curled her arm around the smallest and scooted up the flat face of the rock, pulling Erin with her.

A blast of cold air cut her like a knife.

Outside. They were outside.

"Keep crawling. Go down the rocks on the other side. You'll be able to manage the flow there. If you'd stayed on that course, you'd have gone down that small waterfall and there would have been no way to keep from dunking both of you underwater."

Bright moonlight. She could see the waterfall pouring down into a wide pool. It was small as Cameron had said but the force could have been deadly.

She crawled over the rocks and then down the other side.

Cold. So cold.

Then she was immersed in water again. Warm water.

She sighed with relief as she pulled Erin down into the water.

"Does this mean what I think it does, Cameron? Are we away from Kadmus's mountain? Have we reached Milchang and the other hot spring?"

"Of course, I told you that you'd make it. Keep swimming. Hurry. There's a bank about thirty yards away. You have to get out of this area right away. Kadmus will have found your clothes back on the bank and will start trying to put everything together."

"I am hurrying." She was so tired she was numb, but she had to ignore it. Keep moving. Keep swimming. Keep Erin well and afloat. "She'll need help. You'd better have someone there to—"

"Hush. Stop worrying. Just get her to the bank."

"Catherine?" Erin's voice was weak. "Is it going to be—"

"It will be fine. We're almost there. You've been great. Just hold on a little longer."

"You're the one who's been holding on."

"Hey, I couldn't let that Pulitzer Prize brain be taken down by some crummy amoeba." Keep going. Shouldn't she be seeing that bank by now? Mountains. Moonlight. Water.

There it was!

And on the bank dressed in black parka and gear was Richard Cameron. All power and grace framed against those harsh mountains. Light, glittering eyes, that face that had held her fascinated during their strange mental encounter. He was the same, yet not the same. But definitely more than she had envisioned.

"You said you'd send someone else."

"You were insistent. What could I do?"

"I was right. Erin needs you."

"So I'm here." She was close enough to see his smile. *"Now come the last few yards and let me take care of both of you."*

"Just Erin. And, now that we're away from that damn mountain, you get out of my head."

"As you wish. But it was much simpler . . ."

"Cameron?" Erin had caught sight of him on the bank. Her face lit with a radiant smile. "God, I'm glad to see you. Now I know everything will be all right."

He ruefully shook his head. "Erin, after all you've been through? I'm flattered but a little bewildered. The sight of me should make you anything but optimistic."

"My fault. All my fault."

"Shh." He grabbed a dark covering of some sort from the ground. "Now get out of there and let me wrap you up. The minute you're out of that spring, you're going to be subject to freezing temperatures."

"I'll help." Catherine swam closer to the bank and steadied Erin. "Watch her shoulder."

"I'll do that. I really don't need your instructions, Catherine." He reached down and lifted Erin out of the water, enveloping her in the cover with the same motion. He wrapped her carefully, even covering her damp hair. Every movement was done with the most exquisite gentleness Catherine had ever witnessed. Was this a glimpse of Cameron's treatment of Erin during those days of horror? For the first time, she was beginning to understand the woman's blind devotion to him.

Cameron glanced at Catherine. "Satisfied?" He shook his head resignedly as he saw that Catherine had levied herself onto the bank. "I brought a cover for you, too." He gestured to the dark cloth on the ground. "If you'd been more patient, I would have given you—"

She was already wrapping herself in the blanket. "Warm. Very warm." Her hands were running over the material. Not plastic. Not ·cloth. Somewhere in between. But it was blocking both sharp wind and frigid cold and seemed to be completely retaining her body heat. "It's working better than the space-age tech stuff they issued to get me through the mountains. I've never seen anything like it."

"There is nothing like it. A friend invented it."

"What is it?"

He ignored the question. "Cover your head. Don't bother putting on your boots. They aren't going to do you any good until they dry out. Just run for the jeep and tuck yourself in with the blanket." He picked up Erin and carried her toward a jeep parked a distance away.

Catherine jumped to her feet and was right behind him. "Put her in the backseat and let her stretch out. I'll cover her and make sure she's—" She stopped. Cameron was already carefully settling Erin in the backseat.

He gently stroked Erin's cheek. "I'd reset your shoulder, but we don't have time. The road is rough, but I'll make sure you don't feel the pain."

"I know you will," she said quietly. She glanced at Catherine. "Get in the car, Catherine. You heard him, we don't have much time."

"I believe we established that fact a long time ago," she said dryly. "We didn't need him to repeat it." She got in the passenger seat. "Let's go, Cameron."

"Cover up," he said briefly as he slipped into the driver's seat and started the jeep. "I'll put on the heater, but it's not going to do much good for a while."

She tucked her feet beneath the blanket and drew it tighter around her. The action brought immediate warmth. "Why didn't you bring one of these covers for yourself?"

"I'm used to the weather. I spend a good deal of my time in Tibet."

"Why?"

He smiled. "I find it fertile ground."

"Really?" She gazed out at the barren landscape. "Then you must be as innovative as Hu Chang about promoting growth. I can't see how anything could grow here." Her gaze narrowed on his face. "But that isn't what you mean, is it?"

"I admire Hu Chang. I understand his latest experiments have been very successful. Mine aren't nearly as promising. I guess it depends on what you're trying to grow."

She was too tired to decipher oblique meanings. "We heard Kadmus back there, and you said he wasn't as close as we thought. How near is he?"

"I'd judge from the sound of the cadence of those echoes that he's just reached the hot spring in the mountain. We have a sizable head start."

"Judge? How the hell can you even guess?" She shook her head. "No, don't try to explain. I'll just accept it for right now. I'll explore it later."

"I'm sure you will," he murmured.

"Does that head start guarantee that Kadmus isn't going to catch up with us?"

"No guarantees. It depends on how much information he was able to gather about the hot springs or if he's searching blind. But it does give us an excellent chance of avoiding him until I can get you a flight out."

"Why?"

"I know this mountain very well. I've used it for exits before. Kadmus will be running around frantically trying to gather information from the villagers and sending his men all over the mountain."

"Villagers?" Erin repeated from the backseat. Her voice was tense. "You know what that means, Cameron."

"I've told the monks from the monastery to lead them inland. They'll do what I say," Cameron said gently. "Kadmus won't find anything but empty villages. They won't be hurt, Erin."

"Good." She relaxed. "I couldn't stand—"

"I know," Cameron said. "He won't find anyone to question until after I get you away. Which would make it nonproductive for him to use force on anyone."

"Except you," Catherine said. "You're talking about getting us out. What about you?"

He shrugged. "Perhaps I'll go with you. Probably not. I'll make a decision later."

"And we're supposed to leave you on this mountain surrounded by Kadmus's men?"

He smiled. "Would you stay and do battle by my side, Catherine?"

"Don't be stupid," she said curtly. "If you decide to do something that crazy, why would I try to stop you? I've got a life to live and a son to raise."

"That's true. But you have warrior instincts that cause you to do unreasonable things on occasion. You'd be foolish to risk either. Just as it was foolish for you to come to rescue Erin."

"But you said I had nothing to do with that decision, remember? Pure manipulation." She grimaced. "Not that I believe you."

"Oh, I think you might believe it." He paused. "But I would never do anything to convince you to come and do battle by my side. That would have to come from you." He met her eyes. "But, oh, what a battle that would be, Catherine."

Power.

Excitement.

Magnetism.

Heat.

She had to force her gaze away from him. "The only battle I intend to fight is to get Erin to a safe place." She glanced at Erin in the backseat. Her eyes were closed, and she was breathing deeply, steadily. "I think she's asleep. Your work?"

"No, but it makes it easier for me to shelter her from the pain. This road is going to get bumpier."

It was already rough. The jeep was bucking like a bronco, but Cameron seemed to have perfect control. "How long will it take us to get to this hut?"

"Another fifteen minutes. From this side of the mountain, the road winds in and out like a snake and crosses through a dozen passes. That's good because it will be almost impossible for Kadmus to track us if he starts at that hot spring. Though the road is clearly accessible by vehicle. That's what I planned on him doing. But, if by some bad luck, he starts at the road on the other side of the mountain, we might have a harder way to go."

"Why?"

"The trail goes straight up the mountain and leads directly to the hut. They could take the vehicles as far as the plateau, but then they'd have to go on foot the rest of the way. It would take hours, but they'd be able to locate us fairly simply."

"It's an Achilles' heel," Catherine said. "But if he's coming through the hot springs, there's no reason for him to go clear on the other side of the mountain."

"So one would suppose. And I left clear tracks on the first few miles of road. We'll have to see. And the trek up the mountain on foot would certainly discourage them. It's even rougher than this road. Hu Chang wasn't pleased that I chose that path."

"What?" She stared at him, stunned. "Hu Chang?"

"Yes, we had a disagreement about certain difficulties regarding the—"

"When?"

"This afternoon."

She drew a deep breath. "Let me get this very clear. Hu Chang is here, on this mountain?"

"Yes, he's at the hut waiting for you. Well, not exactly waiting. I didn't tell him I was going to go and fetch you. But when I left, he probably deduced that it was something to do with you and Erin. Hu Chang is a brilliant man, and he would be able to put two and two together."

"May I ask why you didn't tell me?"

"You were worried about his coming after you. It was better for your concentration that you didn't know that he was already on the scene."

"Did you help him get here?"

"Yes, but don't underestimate Hu Chang, he would have been able to get to you without me. I just furnished the means."

"But he wouldn't have been able to get here as quickly."

"I don't know about that. He's an amazing man."

"I wanted that amazing man to stay safely in Hong Kong," she said sharply. "That's why I came after Erin, dammit."

"He was certainly one of the prime reasons why you did it. But there were several others."

She could feel the anger begin to mount. "Look, you had me to get Erin off Kadmus's mountain. You didn't need Hu Chang. Why couldn't you have left him out of it?"

"Because he's my friend, and he deserved his chance to save you," he said simply. "I first brought him into this because I thought he was the best possibility to free Erin. I was wrong. It was you. But because I was wrong, I couldn't close him out once the decision to use you was made."

She stared at him in frustration. "You're impossible. And probably nuts. You have no right to make decisions and try to shape the whole world to suit yourself."

"Not the whole world." He smiled faintly. "Just my part of it."

"I'm not part of your world, and neither is Hu Chang. So you can just stay away from us."

He shook his head. "Hu Chang became part of my world years ago, and he understands there's no going back. And you came into my life as a sort of gift from Hu Chang."

"The hell I did."

"Why else are you here?"

"Because of Erin and that bastard, Kadmus."

"I rest my case."

He meant that everything that had happened to Erin and Kadmus had been done because of the entire ugly scenario that had revolved around him.

And he was right. She didn't know how or why it was true, but Cameron was the center. "I won't have it, Cameron," she said unevenly. "I have to tolerate your help to get Erin out of here and make sure that Hu Chang is safe, but after that, I want you out of my life. I haven't known where I was with you since the moment you appeared. You and Hu Chang probably share some strange bond, but I want no part of it."

"I hope I can keep you free of it," he said soberly. "And you're much safer not knowing more than a few shallow things about me. But I don't believe you'll allow that to keep on. You're curious, and you think you can't be in control unless you have the entire picture." He added, "Sometimes, the entire picture isn't pretty."

"I can do without the entire picture. You'd probably turn out to be like that portrait of Dorian Gray who turned into a monster."

He suddenly chuckled. "Let's see, you've compared me to Jekyll's Hyde, the Hunchback of Notre Dame, and now I'm Dorian Gray? You're full of literary insults. At least you haven't gotten obscene."

"That could come." She was trying to regain her composure. "You had no right to bring Hu Chang here."

"I only allowed him to come." He glanced thoughtfully at her expression. "You care as much about him as he does for you. I thought you might. I knew it would be dangerous to try to step between you."

"You didn't step between us. And you'd better not have put Hu Chang in any danger by—"

"Shh, you're getting too upset. You've gone through hell tonight, and you don't need to—"

"I'll get upset if I choose. You're not in control of that either."

"You're right. Feel free to sit there and fume. We should be at the hut within a few minutes, and the two of you will be able to discuss how unfair and overbearing I am." He added, "But while you're doing it, you might remember that Erin is free, and you and Hu Chang have a way out because of who I am and what I can do, overbearing or not."

There was no anger in his tone, only weariness. She could feel her own anger ebbing and tried to hold on to it. He might have helped getting them away from the mountain, but she resented that she'd had to rely on him. She'd had to struggle to remain independent. And bringing Hu Chang here was completely out of the bounds of—

"It's how I run my life," he said quietly. "For every act I take, I have to strike a balance. So many balances you can't imagine."

"Then tell me."

He shook his head. "Hu Chang knows some of it. He can probably be persuaded to share it with you. Though it would be safer for you if he didn't."

"I wouldn't try to persuade him. He'd laugh at me. I would reason with him." She had a sudden thought. "Why would it be safer? You said once that you'd had two choices after Erin was captured, and she was becoming a danger to you. One was the one you chose, the other was to kill her." She paused. "You're saying that you would do the same to me if I learned too much about you?"

"God, I hope not, Catherine." His voice, his face, suddenly held the same glowing, tenderness she had noticed earlier when he was caring for Erin. "It's the last thing I want. I'll do everything I can to avoid it. I'd take the most extraordinary steps possible to prevent that from happening."

"As you did with Erin?"

"No, you'd be much more difficult. I'd have to stretch . . ."

"To keep from killing me."

"It won't happen."

"You're damned right it won't."

He chuckled. "Then we're agreed. Now all I have to do is convince you to see things my way."

"Bullshit. Stay out of my mind." She tore her eyes away. "How soon can we get off this mountain?"

"Possibly tomorrow. Kadmus's men will be streaming across the road from Daksha to this mountain as soon as he's convinced we made it over here. They'll be setting up and beginning the search. I'll send one of the villagers down to keep an eye on them and report back to me. Unless there's an emergency situation, I'll have a helicopter here by tomorrow."

"He'll detect any electronic signals."

"No, he won't."

She touched the blanket covering her. "Another whiz-bang invention? You can block the signal?"

"No, I won't handle it like that. It would raise questions that would send ripples and I avoid ripples. Too much could go wrong."

The answer led to a flood of wild and improbable possibilities. "Then I'm not going to ask you how you're going to do it."

He nodded. "That would be best."

"Though I might ask Hu Chang."

"Not best, but totally characteristic. You'll do what you have to do." He paused. "Just as Hu Chang did what he had to do. You might remember that when you find yourself in a fury with him."

"I'm not angry with him. I'm angry with you."

"But that may change. I'd be glad to share that fury with Hu Chang, but it would hurt you more than it would either one of us."

"What are you talking about?" Her gaze was narrowed on his face. "I don't understand a lot of what you say, and that annoys the hell out of me. But that sounded remarkably like a warning."

"Not a warning." He was slowing the jeep and pulled it over to the side of the road. "Just sincere advice from someone who cares." He gestured to the hut across the road. "There you are. I'll leave the headlights on so that you can see Hu Chang, and he can see you." He got out of the car. "He must have heard us coming. I'm sure he'll be out here any minute."

"Cameron . . ." Erin dazedly lifted her head. "I must have fallen asleep."

"Yes, you did." He opened the rear door. "And just as well. It saved you from hearing Catherine scold me." He picked her up and started for the hut. "It was most disturbing."

Erin chuckled. "I can see that it bothered you."

"Catherine never scolds." Hu Chang stood in the doorway, the light from the fire within the hut outlining his body. "But she's been known to tear strips from those who displease her." His gaze was searching the darkness beyond the brilliant headlights. "Catherine?"

Warmth.

Memories.

Love.

And after all the worry, and frustration and anger he was here in front of her, unhurt, a few yards away.

"You shouldn't have come," she said unevenly as she struggled to get out of the car. "You deserve to have a strip torn off you. You should have waited in Hong Kong."

"I'm not good at waiting." She could hear the humor in his voice. "In that, I'm like you, Catherine. What is that ugly garment that you have about you?"

"Something that your friend, Cameron, gave me. It's very warm, but I think that I'll come into that hut and get my feet warm."

"Good idea." Cameron said as he passed Hu Chang with Erin. "Hu Chang, I think I'm going to have to tap your medical skills. Erin is going to need some attention."

"I'll be in soon," Hu Chang said. "I believe there's something that I have to discuss with Catherine. I'm guessing that you didn't do it on the way here."

"And interfere with your business? I wouldn't do that." His smile had an element of mocking mischief. "But get it over quickly. She's been through a lot tonight."

"I should have been with her. I was not pleased when you left here without saying a word."

"If I'd needed you, I would have used you." He entered the hut. "Turn off the headlights when you come in. I only left them on so that Catherine could—Ah, that's what I was expecting."

Luke had pushed past him and stood in the doorway. "Catherine?"

"Oh, my God."

She stared at him, stunned. She felt dizzy, drunk . . . and terrified. She couldn't breathe. "Luke. What are—"

"I can't see you. The light's in my eyes. Are you okay?" He was coming toward her. His hair was mussed, and his expression was strained. "Hu Chang said that we'd get you out safe but then Cameron left and I didn't—"

"I'm fine." She ran toward him. "You shouldn't be here. You have no business—" She touched his hair. It was soft, warm from the fire. "It's all wrong. You shouldn't have let him bring you, Luke." She looked over her shoulder at Hu Chang, and said fiercely, "Dammit, you knew better that to risk him. What insanity led you to do this?"

"He wanted to come," he said simply. "Sometimes it's best to follow desire instead of reason."

"And sometimes it's better to be responsible and do what's right. I'm not going to forgive you for this, Hu Chang."

"Then I must bear the pain."

"No!" Luke said. "Stop it, Catherine." His dark eyes were glittering in his taut face. "Don't you blame Hu Chang. I'm the one who decided I was going to come. I would have come after you whether he'd brought me or not. You were in trouble, and you were alone. I needed to be with you."

"Tell her why, Luke," Hu Chang said.

"I can't tell her what I don't know. Hu Chang talked a lot of weird stuff about souls speaking and how I had to learn . . ." He frowned. "Well, I haven't learned what he wanted me to learn. All I know is that I'm here where I should be, and I'm going to stay with you until it's over." He stared her in the eye. "You're not going to send me away, Catherine."

"Luke, this is crazy. You're scaring me to death." She stared at him helplessly. "You're my son, you're only a boy. I can't stand by and let you—"

"I've tried to listen to you, Catherine. But you don't know me." He swallowed. "I know who you want me to be. I'll never be able to be him. I can't be anyone but me, what I am," he said unsteadily. "Maybe you could get to like me that way, too. But you can't do it unless you see me for who I am."

She gazed at him, stricken. "Luke, I love you. I think you're wonderful. I'd never want you to be anything you didn't want to be."

He repeated, "You don't *know* me. If you let me stay, maybe you will. I promise I won't hide anything from you."

Oh, God, she had the feeling she was on the edge of a precipice. It could be a disaster, or it could be the beginning of something . . .

She didn't know. She could only follow Luke's lead. She was afraid to do anything else. "Look, I have to find a way to keep you safe. But I promise I won't hide anything from you either."

He smiled. "You don't have anything to hide. I knew that from the minute you came to get me from Rakovac. It was all there out front." He took a step closer and gave her an awkward hug. "I'm glad you're safe, Catherine. Next time, I'll be there to watch out for you." He turned and started to trot back into the hut. He stopped and turned to Hu Chang. "You see that she gets out of the cold. Can't you see she's barefoot?"

"It's been called to my attention."

She watched as Luke disappeared into the hut. What had happened just now? She was bewildered and frightened, and yet, there was the tiniest seed of hope.

"I only wanted to do what was best for him. I wanted him to have a normal life after what he'd gone through," she whispered. "But was I doing it for him or for myself? Have I been such a coward that I came close to losing him, Hu Chang?"

"You will have to answer that for yourself," he said quietly. "I can only say what I've told you before. He was born of a remarkable mother, and his hard life honed and sharpened him until he, too, is remarkable. You have to accept that remarkable people have to be allowed their space."

"And all the rules and guidelines are thrown out the window? I tried so hard to let him know I didn't want to smother him."

"He knows that. He's worked it all out for himself. He's even put you both in a position where you'll have to work the rest out together." He smiled faintly. "You should be proud of him."

"Proud? I'm terrified."

"And proud."

"Yes, I think so." She was remembering Luke's expression, his intensity, the sincerity. It had shocked her, but there had also been another sheer primitive emotion that could have been deep maternal pride. "I don't know. The last thing I needed was to have to start reworking a relationship under these circumstances." She whirled on him. "And you could have helped. You could have tried to persuade him to stay in Hong Kong."

"I could have," he acceded. "But he is your son. Would you have listened and obeyed?"

No, and neither would the boy she had faced tonight.

Hu Chang said softly, "He has been thinking, and waiting, and this was his time."

"What about Cameron? He got you up here, didn't he? Why did he permit it?"

"You will have to ask him."

"But he did know you were bringing Luke?"

"I'm sure you've found that it's difficult to keep anything from Cameron."

"Why would he—"

"You're having trouble blaming me, so now you attack Cameron?"

"Why not? He has broad shoulders. I'm sure he can take it."

"Hu Chang!" It was Luke calling from the doorway.

"Ah, yes, the boy is still concerned about your bare feet." He waved. "We're coming. Catherine decided it wasn't worth her time to chastise me. We'll be right in." He reached into the jeep and turned off the headlights. Darkness except for moonlight and the faintest light streaming from the tiny window of the hut. "You'd best hurry. Luke will be upset with me if you've developed frostbite. He had a lesson from Cameron earlier on resistance to the elements, but I don't believe he relates it to you."

"Cameron, again." She moved quickly toward the hut. Her feet felt ice-cold now that she had become aware of them. "I don't want Luke's learning anything from Cameron."

"You'll have a hard time keeping Luke away from him. The fascination has started to take hold." He shook his head ruefully. "Once that happens, it's all over."

"You're speaking from experience?"

"Yes."

"It would take a lot to fascinate you." She stopped at the door. "I have to know about Cameron, Hu Chang."

"You know more about him than a good many do right now."

"Bullshit. Not enough. He can do anything with Erin, and he

might be as dangerous as Kadmus to her for all I know. I have to
know everything if I'm going to protect her."

He stared at her thoughtfully. "Are you sure that's all?"

"What do you mean?"

He tilted his head. "It's no more than I expected. He's curious
about you. He'd naturally make an effort to draw you closer. Fascination . . ."

She stiffened. "No way. I just have to know. Will you tell me?"

"I'll consider it. Although there could be some element of threat
connected to it."

"You mean that old chestnut about 'if I told you, I'd have to kill
you'? Cameron's already used that on me."

"Really? He threatened you?"

"No, he said he'd try very hard not to kill me." She smiled recklessly. "So you see, you have nothing to worry about."

"I'm beginning to see many things." He opened the door for
her. "And one of the things is that you may need more knowledge
than I thought necessary to get you through the next weeks."

"Then talk to me, tell me about Cameron."

"I'll consider it," he repeated. "Now go over to the stove and
warm yourself while I go talk to Luke. He was rude to me just now,
and that's not to be tolerated. I must make it clear to him that emotions must be controlled."

Catherine watched him move across the room to where Luke
sat by himself on a pallet before she turned to the corner where
Erin was settled. She, too, was lying on a pallet and still covered by
the black blanket. But her underclothing had been stripped off and
lay in a neat pile beside her.

Cameron was gently drying her hair and looked up at Catherine. "You took long enough. How are your toes? It doesn't take
long to get frostbite up here."

"Cold. A little numb. But I'm beginning to feel them again."
She made a face. "Everyone seems to be worried about my feet,

even my son." She came closer and looked down at Erin. Her eyes were closed, but they opened, and she smiled.

"Hi, how are you doing, Catherine?"

She smiled back at her. "Better than a couple hours ago."

"Me, too."

"Hu Chang will be over here to take a look at you in just a minute. He's a wonderful physician, and he'll fix you up. He had to go over there and give a stern reprimand to my son for not being respectful to him." She chuckled. "With all hell going on around us and Kadmus licking at our heels, he still felt bound to teach Luke."

"He's right," Cameron said. "Discipline is important. You can't let it lapse just because the battle hasn't started."

"That's your son?" Erin was looking across the room at Luke. "He's beautiful, Catherine."

"Yes, he is."

Erin's face was troubled. "But he shouldn't be here. I told you what happened to Jafar."

"And it scared me to death." She looked at Cameron. "But the death of children doesn't seem to bother Hu Chang or Cameron. They're the ones who decided that he should be here."

"Cameron?" Erin was looking at him. "Is this the way it has to be?"

"The boy will be safe, Erin," he said quietly. "I promise you."

She gazed at him a moment, still frowning. Then she nodded. "Then I know it will be okay. But it still worries me."

Cameron gazed quizzically at Catherine. "And you?"

Did he expect her to give him the same trusting reply just because he'd made a promise? Yet, for some strange reason, that promise had given Catherine a sense of security and relief that had no basis on reality. "I don't know it will be okay. But Luke and I will get through it together." She fell to her knees and took Erin's hand. "And we'll take you with us, Erin."

Cameron chuckled. "You notice she's leaving me and Hu Chang

behind in the dust. She's not any more pleased with us than you are."
He looked beyond Catherine's shoulder. "It seems that Hu Chang is
finished with your son and is coming to tend Erin. She won't need
you. Why don't you get out of those clothes and warm up?"

She didn't move. "When will you have word about Kadmus?"

"Soon. I'll let you know."

"We should take turns standing guard."

"We'll discuss it later," he said firmly. "I had the pilot who flew Hu
Chang in bring you and Erin clothing. It's on the chest over there. You
can't fight for Luke or Erin or anyone else bundled up in that blanket."

She hesitated and got to her feet. "You're right." She turned
toward the chest. "But it's a very good blanket, Cameron. Fantastic.
I'm still curious about your friend who gave it to you."

"Among a thousand other questions," Hu Chang said as he
stopped next to her. He gazed down at Erin. "So you're the woman
who has been causing so much trouble. Now it seems I have to put
you back together."

She smiled. "If you think it's worthwhile."

"You are worthwhile. I made that decision before I even started
on this endeavor." He knelt beside her. "And since Catherine has
seen fit to champion your cause, I have no choice."

"You make your own choices." Catherine looked over her shoulder. "But Erin and I will be glad to have you along."

Cameron gave a mock shudder. "I appear to be in isolation."

She didn't answer as she moved toward the chest. She was still
angry with both of them, but Hu Chang belonged to her. She had to
forgive and work with him. Cameron was an entirely different matter.

Different. Oh, yes, he was definitely different.

However, the gleaming white cold-weather gear that he had
ordered for her was the best quality and worthy of the slopes of St.
Moritz. Glamorous as was the outerwear, the undergarments were the
same practical issue that Venable had ordered and that she was now
wearing.

The first priority was to get out of the wet clothes she was wearing
and into the clean dry garb. Privacy was not an issue. There was none
in this tiny hut. Forget about it. The only person she might be concerned about was Luke, and he was turned on his side and clearly dozing. She dropped the blanket and stripped off the wet clothes in two
minutes. It took her less than that to replace the bra, T, and tights. She
towel-dried her hair, then rubbed her feet vigorously until it revved
up the circulation. She put on the rest of the clothes except her boots.

Done.

She sat down before the stove and tried to finger comb her hair
but it was too stiff from the chemicals of the hot springs to behave.
She looked like a wildwoman and stank like rotten eggs, but this
was the best she could do.

"And a very good best it is."

Her gaze flew to the other side of the room. Cameron was leaning against the wall, sitting slightly apart from where Hu Chang
was attending Erin.

"Peeping Tom, again? This time in more ways than one, Cameron."

"It interested me that you had no false sense of modesty." His smile was
*purely sensual. "And so I decided to benefit from it. Rotten eggs or not, you're
fantastic, Catherine."*

*Heat. Her breasts swelling, tightening. A tingling in her palms and be-
tween her thighs.*

"Not me," he answered the question she hadn't asked. *"You're a very
responsive woman. I was lucky enough to strike the right note."*

*He was probably telling the truth. She couldn't deny that he'd had a
strong sexual effect on her from the beginning. How could she when the bastard
could read her mind? "I'll get over it. That note will get very sour the longer you mess with my head."*

*"I've been thinking about that. I find I'm reluctant to have you get over it.
Suppose I guarantee that I won't 'mess' with you unless I find it necessary to save
you or Erin? It worked pretty well traveling through the hot springs, didn't it?"*

"No, I always knew you were there."

"Only because that's what I wanted. I thought it might give you a feeling of safety. I didn't want you to feel alone."

"Look, I don't need you to make me feel safe. In the end, it always has to come from me." She added, "And it's totally ridiculous for you to try to seduce me when we're struggling just to get Erin out of here."

"It's not actually seduction. I'm just paving the way."

"Then, stop. Go find out what's happening with Kadmus."

"In a few minutes. I have one of the villagers on the way up to the hut now."

"How did—Never mind." She paused. "Then let's concentrate on Kadmus and forget about your libido."

He chuckled. "Don't worry, I'll do my job. I was even considering devoting myself entirely to boring duty and discipline. But that was before I spent so much time with you. I've been entirely too good for too long. I've decided I need a reward."

"And I'm the prize? Screw you, Cameron."

"Oh, I do hope so." His smile lit his face with mischief and humor. "And now I'll bow out and leave your mind alone." He got to his feet. "But you may find that you miss that kind of contact. It's much more efficient."

"Not a chance."

He shrugged as he slipped on his parka. "Hu Chang did miss the contact after our time together several years ago. But he's more cerebral and less emotional." He headed for the door. "We'll have to see."

Catherine watched the door close behind him and felt an odd sense of loss. More mental hijinks? Or was that a natural aftereffect of dealing with a man who bewildered and challenged her more than anyone she had every encountered?

Hu Chang did miss the contact after our time together several years ago, Cameron had said.

Which meant that Hu Chang had become closer to Cameron than she had imagined.

And that Hu Chang was the one who could probably answer most of her questions.

And she wanted those answers now.

She got to her feet and crossed to where Hu Chang was still kneeling by Erin.

"How is she?" she whispered as she looked down at Erin. There was a faint flush on her cheeks, and she appeared asleep. "She looks better."

"Of course, she's better." He closed his leather medicine duffel. "I've healed everything physical I can heal. She will need rest and perhaps a little additional surgery. He was very cruel to her. Her mind will take longer, but she's very strong." He drew the cover higher about her throat. "And Cameron will help her. Just being with him is a healing factor for her."

"I noticed."

Hu Chang tilted his head, his gaze on her face. "And you do not like it."

"No more than I like his influence on Luke." She met his gaze. "Or you."

"Why?"

"It frightens me. Luke is a child, and there's reason for him to fall under Cameron's influence. But not you, Hu Chang."

"You have nothing to fear. Cameron and I have an understanding. He won't break his word unless I do something that threatens his objectives."

"What word? What objectives? I need to know more, Hu Chang. Don't push me away. Tell me."

He stared at her for a moment. "You are very weary. You need to rest."

"I'm tired and pissed off, and I'm worried. I won't be able to rest until I get rid of two of the three."

His gaze shifted to the door. "Where did Cameron go?"

Her gaze narrowed on his face. "Why do you think I should know?"

"He was joined with you while I was working on Erin." He

smiled faintly. "I'm familiar with Cameron when he's in the joined state. I was with him for a number of months and allowed to get to know him fairly well. He was not joined with me or Erin. Therefore, it must have been you."

"It was," she said curtly. "He went to meet with the villager he'd set to watch Kadmus and his men."

"And managed to irritate you exceedingly before he left."

"He does that very well. I think he enjoys it."

"He enjoys *you,*" Hu Chang said softly. "Beware." He rose gracefully to his feet. "But since he will be gone for a while, we will have time to talk." He moved to the stove and sank to the floor in front of it, his legs crossed tailor fashion. "Come. Sit with me."

She sat down beside him. "Not too close. I still stink from the hot springs."

"Yes, you do. Ask me if I care."

"No." The warmth of the fire. The closeness that always bound them together. She felt herself begin to relax. "But it scares me to risk offending you. You might throw it in my face someday."

"That is true. But it is a poor weapon and not likely to be of value." He looked away from her and into the leaping flames in the stove. "Ask your questions, Catherine. I will answer what I know and what I consider safe for you."

"Let's begin with how you came to know Cameron. You never mentioned him to me." She added ruefully, "Not that you're ever very communicative. When did you meet him?"

"Several years ago at a monastery in Amdo Province. And I did not mention him because silence was part of the agreement I made with him. It was one of the more important demands he made. I was not to mention him or anything that I saw or experienced at the monastery."

"Yet you're willing to talk to me now."

"Cameron has interfered with your life. He almost took your life. You have a right to know why."

"What did you have to do with that monastery?"

"I had heard stories that the monks of this particular monastery had been formulating rare herbal mixtures for close to nine hundred years. I wanted to learn what they were and if I could use them in my own potions."

"I should have known." She shook her head. "Well, was it worth your while? Did you find a brand-new poison?"

"That was not what I was seeking."

She stiffened. "Hu Chang . . ."

He nodded. "Life not death. At that time, I had not yet found the final ingredients for the potion I gave to Chen Lu to extend and reverse her cell regeneration. It was frustrating me. I thought that the monastery might be the answer." His lips twisted. "But I couldn't get permission to study with the monks. The monastery was completely isolated, and the lama would permit no one, not even other monks from the area, to visit it. I had to find some way to go around the lama. I was getting quite desperate."

"I've never seen you desperate."

"But it was to be such a magnificent potion. An elixir that would extend life fifty to a hundred years? It was exciting even to me. I had to get in to see if those monks had some ingredient I didn't. I stayed there in the province and began to research a way to do it."

"Richard Cameron?"

"Yes, I watched, I listened, and I found Cameron." He smiled reminiscently. "Though one who was not as dedicated as I would not have been so fortunate. I just heard a word here and there about the Westerner who moved around the mountains and villages. Strange words . . . about a Guardian, a protector, a warrior . . . But those words held boundless respect and an element of fear. Then I saw him at the monastery with the lama. I saw the same respect from the lama and no fear. Most unusual from a religious figure that prestigious. Over the next weeks, I found that Cameron held a special place in the affections of the lama and those monks."

"And you decided to use him."

"That was not possible. I had already taken Cameron's measure and knew that he was an extraordinary man. I knew I would have to negotiate." He grimaced. "If I was to avoid having to plead. So I went to him as he was leaving the monastery. He was as tough and sharp as I thought he would be. It took me three days to persuade him to even consider interceding for me. On the fourth day, he started asking me questions about myself. I had no idea about his gift at that time. If I'd lied, I would not have stood a chance. I did not lie. On the fifth day, he said that he would persuade the lama to let me have access to records and the herbs the monks used . . . on condition." He smiled. "And so it started."

"What conditions?"

"You do not need to know. I will not break that promise."

"It's not important. Okay, let's go on. I want to know about Richard Cameron. I was thinking about going to Langley and getting a complete dossier, but I didn't want to upset Erin."

"It would have been useless. There are no records on Cameron."

"There are always records. You just have to know where to look and tap all the organizations."

"No records. No DNA info. No fingerprints. No retina scan. Nothing. When the committee chose Cameron as Guardian, they spent a good deal of time and millions of dollars erasing his former existence. If, by any chance, he does leave anything traceable, a cleanup crew goes in immediately and takes care of it."

"What?" Her eyes widened. "No records? That doesn't happen."

"Test it. When you get back to civilization, discreetly check it."

"I will." She latched on to the one word that might be the key. "Committee. What committee?" She thought about what Cameron had earlier told her. "When I was questioning him about what country he was working for, he said something vague about an organization. An organization would have committees."

"Yes, it would. Only in this case one committee."

"Then what organization? What's its purpose? What's its name?"

"He never mentioned a name to me."

"But did you guess?"

Silence. "I guessed. But I never confronted him with it. It was one of the conditions of my stay with Cameron that I would not question anything that I wasn't told."

"I know you. That's not a condition you would ever accept."

"Then you don't know me as well as you thought. I came to Cameron because he had a treasure beyond imagination, and I needed what he could give me." He added, "I studied with him and the monks for five months. I received what I came for, and I did not quibble about his rules. It was worth it to me."

"And do you regret it now?"

"No, not for a minute."

It was clear he wasn't going to talk about this committee. Back to Cameron. "Why did they concentrate such an effort on erasing Cameron's background?"

"They wanted him to remain completely untouchable. It had taken them a long, long time to find someone of his caliber and character, and they were determined to protect him at all costs. The only way they could assure that was to remove him from the grid. He has false documents for every country on Earth, which are exchanged frequently."

"It sounds very efficient . . . and lonely."

"I'm sure that the committee provided therapy for any psychological damage. Nothing is too good for Cameron."

"Are you being sarcastic?"

"No." He glanced at her. "They value him, they respect him, and they even listen to him on occasion. I got the impression that they would give him anything he asked as long as it was within the rules." He held up his hand. "And I do not know what those rules are. Except that there seems to be a universal one that Cameron not be put at risk. Make any sacrifice but Cameron. I saw it several times, while I was with him. It annoys him at times but he accepts the rule."

"Even when it means Erin's being tortured," she said bitterly.

"Even then."

"Why is he considered so valuable? What makes him king of their world?"

He shrugged. "Probably the same thing that made the committee choose him as Guardian. They looked all over the world and thought him worthy."

"Worthy of what? For God's sake, you talk as if he's some kind of holy man or something. I guarantee you that Cameron is very, very secular."

Hu Chang nodded. "Yes, and yields to temptation on occasion. I was referring more to the worthiness of a knight or warrior. He is the Guardian, after all."

"If he's a knight, he's a black knight."

"You'd have an argument from Erin."

"He has her brainwashed. She'd obviously sacrifice anything for him."

"Not for him. Erin is an intelligent woman and not likely to be fooled even by a man as persuasive as Cameron. It would have to be something above and beyond Cameron."

"But you don't deny that there's a possibility he could have brainwashed her. Even at that think tank in Rome I attended, they didn't have anyone who could do what Cameron can. He's way beyond anyone that our agencies have discovered."

"They might have the potential, but Cameron has had that potential honed and exploited by experts. He was in training for years after he was selected."

"What potential? Just what can Cameron do that he hasn't shown me?"

"I have no clear idea. I was curious and probed where it was safe. He did not mind talking about some things, others he ignored. He was twenty-six when he was chosen to be trained for Guardian. I know he was taught physical disciplines and control by Tibetan monks. I know that he was schooled in weapons, combat, and several deadly martial arts by world-class experts. Evidently, they concentrated on that aspect of his education. He's an amazing sniper, he moves as fast as a cheetah on attack, and he's incredibly strong. When he's not actually on committee business, he does a full exercise regimen every day. He's well educated in a variety of fields. He can be excellent company and has a sense of humor that's sometimes a bit twisted." He paused. "We seemed to mesh. I . . . enjoyed our time together."

"Why not? Your humor is often twisted, too."

"True. But I assure you that Cameron did not brainwash me during my stay with him. We came to an agreement about any mental interference on his part, and he abided by it. I got the impression that he was a little relieved that I had bound his hands. So many temptations . . . When you have a talent like Cameron's, it must be difficult to have to make all the rules yourself regarding restraints."

As Cameron had done with Catherine before he left. "And what if he breaks the rules?"

He shrugged. "Then one must find a way to punish him. In my case, it was not an issue." He was silent a moment. "But it made me think about the trust that committee must have had in Cameron to turn him loose without controls. It was evident he was a free agent and had only a few basic rules. I'd seen a few examples of the almost limitless power and wealth that Cameron could tap when he needed something. He was never questioned."

"Dangerous." She frowned. "What examples? What the hell does Cameron *do*?"

"In one case, he arranged the hijacking of a train on which a troop of soldiers was taking a young Indian computer scientist to Beijing. The boy was exceptionally gifted, and the Chinese government wished to 'honor' him with a scholarship and the opportunity to work in their program. They had lost track of the fact that the boy did not wish to be so honored. The removal of the boy from those soldiers was handled very adeptly, and Beijing was scrambling to find him and still maintain the humanitarian façade."

"So what happened to the boy?"

"You'd have to ask Cameron. I know he was not returned to his parents in Calcutta. Though his parents disappeared themselves about three months later. In the interim, they appeared worried and despondent." He added, "But definitely not overly so. If I were to guess, I'd wager they were settled in another country and situation more to their liking."

"That could be called kidnapping."

"By Cameron or Beijing?"

"Both. I hate youngsters' being used as pawns."

He smiled. "But perhaps this was a rescue by our black knight."

"For what purpose?"

"There is intense competition among international companies and countries over technical brainpower. It's what is moving our world these days. Pity."

"You think that's what's happening here in Tibet? It's a desolate wilderness. Not a viable battleground for that kind of international espionage. You just said that conglomerate made Cameron into some kind of super Guardian. Why would they waste him on this harsh environment in the Himalayas?"

"He spends time here, but he often travels to other countries. He has teams under his orders in a number of cities around the world. He was in Paris twice when I was with him. I believe he goes where he's sent."

"Did he conduct any other raids or similar violent acts while you were there?"

"Not to my precise knowledge." He was silent a moment. "But there were rumors of the killing of a small-time bandit who was harassing a few of his men in a village in the next province."

"He ordered it done?"

"I understand he did it himself."

"But that's against his rules," she said sarcastically. "He might have been hurt or killed."

"Not likely. Cameron kept to the rules. The bandit was shot from a distance of over a thousand yards. I told you that he's a fantastic marksman."

"He appears to be fantastic at several of the skills in which Kadmus prides himself." She thought about it. "If he's that good, is there any reason he couldn't have gone after Erin himself?"

"None but the reason he gave to you."

"Which was bullshit." She was silent again. "If he'd staged a raid on Daksha, what would have been his chances? Could he have done it?"

"In my humble opinion, I believe that he would have run right over Kadmus's men."

"But he didn't do it." She jumped to another subject. "And why would Kadmus be so desperate to get his hands on Cameron?"

"You are full of questions. Unfortunately, I am not equally brimming with answers. I can but surmise. Kadmus has been delving into all kinds of enterprises here in Tibet. Not only thievery but blackmail and kidnapping, and he even has a few legitimate investments. It could be that he is feeling threatened in some way."

She shook her head. "Or more likely that he wants to take over the action. Maybe he thinks if he captures Cameron, it will be a way of doing that." She thought about it. "But Kadmus doesn't even know who he's looking for. He was torturing Erin to give him a name as well as Cameron's location. That's damn weird."

"Yes, but nothing is simple in this matter. I believe Kadmus is searching for a key, and he may think Cameron is that key. In some way, Erin led him to believe that was true. But I was witness to the fact that Cameron makes sure he's invisible when he wishes. Kadmus may have heard rumors about the Westerner as I did, but no one in these mountains would willingly talk about Cameron."

"And neither would Erin. Why would she become involved with that kind of industrial or technical espionage? It doesn't make sense. It would be completely out of character."

And so was the self-sacrifice and torture Erin had been willing to undergo during those months. It wouldn't have been worth it to her for any monetary reward. The more Catherine learned, the more bewildered she became. "So Cameron is some kind of big-time security chief who's not above turning loose his forces whenever he chooses."

"That may be a fairly accurate description, but he's definitely much more complicated. I can only tell you what I know and what I guess." He paused. "Cameron is one of those men who might come along only once or twice in a century. Add in his unusual gifts, and you have a truly extraordinary individual. You will have to make sense of anything else about him yourself. Erin would tell you nothing?"

She shook her head. "She's protecting Cameron." She drew a deep breath. "And I'm angry and resentful, and it may be clouding my judgment. Is he worth protecting, Hu Chang?"

He was silent. "I would like to say no. I do not want you involved with him any more than you have to be. And Cameron can protect himself very well." He slowly nodded his head. "But if the occasion occurs, I believe he may be worthy of Erin or you or even me stepping in to keep him alive."

"Worthy." She repeated the word. "Are we back to the black knight again?"

He just looked at her.

"You're not telling me everything." Her eyes were narrowed. "Have you run out of things you think are safe for me to know?"

"I've told you facts. I've told you logical suppositions. If there are other possible explanations that have come to me in the dark of night, then I will keep them to myself."

"Because you promised Cameron."

"Because ideas that come to one in the dark of night are best left there until dawn."

"Stop being cryptic." She sighed resignedly. "Okay, I'll work it out for myself." She wearily rubbed her temple. "But you're telling me I'll have to protect Cameron just to protect Erin."

"It would seem that's what we will have to do."

Her gaze went to Luke across the room. "He's the only one I should be protecting. You shouldn't have brought him, Hu Chang. I don't know if I can forgive you."

"I accepted that possibility when I told him he could come."

She closed her eyes. "I don't know what's going to happen to us. Even if we get out of this alive, I don't know if Luke and I will—" She opened her eyes and straightened. "Luke and I will be fine. We'll get through it. And I may forgive you when it's all over. But if you ever do anything like this again, I'll murder you."

He smiled but didn't answer.

Because he knew that there was no way she could do without him. He was as much a part of her life and being as Luke. One was born of her body and the other of her loneliness and need.

"Smirking is rude."

"That's why I never smirk."

She looked at the door. "I think Cameron should be back by now. It seems as if he's been gone a long time."

"Not long at all really."

"Maybe I should go—" She met his gaze and nodded. "I'll wait a little longer."

"That would be wise." He got to his feet. "And I will go to my patient and make sure she's doing well. Though it seems impossible that she would not after my expert care."

Catherine lay down before the stove, her gaze on Luke. He was sleeping deeply, his cheeks flushed, his dark hair mussed. Erin had said he was beautiful, but he was so much more. She had not begun to plumb the depths of her son. Tonight had shown her how far she still had to go.

"I love you, Luke. Don't give up on me. I won't give up on you."

She was still lying there, fifteen minutes later, gazing at Luke, when the front door opened with an icy blast.

She stiffened. Cameron. Of course it was Cameron. But it hadn't stopped that first surge of panic.

Cameron smiled as he brushed back his parka as he came into the hut. "No problem," he said softly as he moved toward her. He fell to his knees and held out his hands to the fire. "I was tempted to give you warning while I was coming up the road, but I did make you a promise."

"Yes, you did. What about Kadmus?"

"He and Brasden are scurrying around on the other road leading from the hot springs. That should give us the time we need."

"Should?"

"Kadmus is pushing hard. He'll have his men searching all night. And he may be exploring all his maps and local contacts to see if he can find anyplace you could be hiding. He knows these mountains, and lately he's been making an effort to know them a hell of a lot better."

"Why?"

He shrugged but didn't answer.

"Is it because he knows you're in these mountains?"

"Perhaps."

"Why is he so fanatical about you?"

"He's a madman. Haven't you noticed?" His lips twisted. "He has a passion to be king of the universe. Evidently, he has an idea that if he could get his hands on me, I could help him."

"Could you?"

"Possibly. But it wouldn't come to that."

"Why not?"

"I'd be allowed to kill him."

"Allowed?" Her eyes widened. The word opened an entirely new avenue of thought that she didn't like. "Oh, for God's sake, you're playing games with Kadmus." The anger was searing through her.

"That conglomerate you work for is using him in some way. Just like Venable. He could have sent Special Forces to take Kadmus out, but he was 'useful' on occasion so it never happened. He didn't want to lose a valuable contact. That's what's happening with you, isn't it?"

"In a broad sense."

"Hu Chang says that you could have gone in and gotten Erin out. He said he'd seen you do it before when he was with you. Why didn't you do it? Oh, yes, you couldn't risk your valuable hide. But it was more than that, wasn't it? Your precious committee didn't want you to offend Kadmus."

"'Offend' is not the word."

"So you let him torture Erin."

"Yes, and there's nothing I can say that would absolve me of that in your eyes."

"You bet there's not. Balance a woman like Erin's suffering against corporate greed? How could you live with yourself?"

"The way I live with all the decisions I make every day," he said quietly. "And it wasn't a question of any deals or bribes to keep Kadmus in our pockets. We've never had any dealings with Kadmus. It was just a committee decision that I wasn't able to argue. Under the circumstances, I couldn't go after Erin."

"Why not? What stopped you?"

"Unless I went in alone as you did, I'd have no choice but to confront Kadmus."

"And that wouldn't be according to committee rules, would it? You might damage yourself."

"I'm trying to be patient, Catherine." His words were slow and precise, but his blue eyes were glittering in his taut face. "I'm not accustomed to having to explain myself."

"Because you think you're master of all you survey? You and Kadmus have a lot in common."

"You do manage to make me—" He was silent a moment. "You're right, I have to think twice about risking myself. It's a rule.

And if I organized a raid, I knew what the result would be." He paused. "To save Erin, I would have had to kill Kadmus."

"Good. Then it would all have been over."

"Not for me. Not for the committee," he said. "It would have caused a chain reaction that would not have been beneficial." He shrugged. "Or so the committee decided. I didn't agree with them. I think we can work around it."

"I don't know what you're talking about."

"And you're too angry to care. Actually, there's only one thing that you should accept and understand. Until I persuade the committee to my way of thinking, I cannot kill Kadmus."

"But you hoped that I would do it."

"As you said, it would have all been over."

"If you believed you were right, you should have done it."

"I also believe in discipline."

"Those monks who trained you weren't necessarily correct."

His brows lifted. "You and Hu Chang evidently had a talk while I was gone."

"You knew I'd ask him about you."

"And that he'd answer as long as it was safe for you. He must have decided that I wouldn't harm you if I could help it."

"Was he right?"

His gaze moved slowly from the top of her head, down her face, throat, and breasts. It was unbearably intimate, searingly sexual. "Not unless you ask me to do it."

Heat.

She shouldn't be feeling this sudden surge of sexuality. She was angry with him. She didn't understand half of what he had told her, but she knew she would probably disagree with every word.

None of it mattered.

The heat was there and would not go away.

Tingling.

Swelling breasts.

Breathlessness.

She could feel that same heat flush her cheeks. Why the hell did he have this effect on her? It was pure mindless lust and moments that seemed to strike out of nowhere.

"I won't ask anything of you. Particularly not S and M." She steadied her voice. "But what I will ask you is how soon we can get off this mountain. Kadmus isn't standing still. We shouldn't either."

"We're not standing still. We're conserving our resources and bandaging our wounds."

"When?"

"Tashdon, my helicopter pilot, will be arriving here at about eight in the morning. We'll start down to the plateau at five." He checked his watch. "Six hours to sleep. You'd better get some rest. The descent isn't as bad as going up, but it's still rough." He glanced at Luke. "He did very well. You'd have been proud of him."

"I *am* proud of him."

He nodded. "I could see you in him. The fire. The stubbornness. I was harder than I needed to be on him. I wanted to see what he was made of."

"And you found out?"

"Just you. And the backbone and ferocity of a tiger." His expression was suddenly shadowed. "He reminded me of another young boy I knew once." He got to his feet. "And now I think I'd better go tell Hu Chang when we're leaving and see if he has any warnings or threats to impart regarding you. He's been discreetly restraining himself from glancing at us, but I can feel the disturbance."

She could feel it, too. Hu Chang was sitting quietly beside Erin, but Catherine could read the body language.

She watched Cameron cross the hut and begin to talk to Hu Chang. Hu Chang did not relax, but there was no antagonism in his demeanor. There was obviously a strong bond that had been forged during that time at the monastery. Two strong men with superb intelligence and skills. It was natural that they would become close.

He reminded me of another young boy I knew once.

What boy? Or had he been talking about himself as a young-ster? What had Cameron been like when he was Luke's age? He must have had a huge number of mental and emotional problems due to that freakish gift. Had there been someone by his side to help him through it?

And why in hell was she worrying about Cameron's childhood traumas? She had not had a great childhood either. You just had to survive and learn from it. He had clearly fought through the pain as she had done.

She lay back down and cradled her head on her arm as she gazed at Luke again.

Six hours to sleep. Six hours before the running and the danger began again. You shouldn't be here, baby. No matter what you say, the young should never face that kind of danger. They should only know joy.

But Cameron promised he would keep you safe, Luke. I'll hold him to it. I'd like to say that I could do it alone, and I'll try. But there's no way I'll turn down help from Cameron or Hu Chang or anyone else who will lend a hand.

You're going to live through this no matter what I have to do.

CHAPTER
9

"Those passes up there are like a rabbit warren, Kadmus," Brasden said as he looked down at the map on the hood of the jeep. "There are twice what this map indicates. We could spend a week exploring all of them."

"We don't have a week," Kadmus said curtly. "Have you found any more tracks?"

He shook his head. "No, they disappeared about two miles up the mountain. The roads are almost pure stone from then on." He added, "But we'll get them. It may take a little more time."

"You'd better get them. You let them escape from Daksha. I won't tolerate any more mistakes."

He moistened his lips. "We have to consider that this may have been an alternate plan that Ling put together in case she didn't make the helicopter. Somehow, the CIA must have found out about those hot springs and the connection to this mountain."

"With no records on any scientific chart or historical document?"

"But the tire tracks indicate that they were met when they reached here. Ling had help."

"But not necessarily CIA help."

Brasden frowned. "Who else?"

"Perhaps one of Erin's close and intimate friends," Kadmus murmured. He had been considering that possibility since he had reached this hot spring and seen the tire tracks. It had been hell taking that path from the mountaintop down to the hot spring in the bowels of the Earth. Ling and Erin must have known what lay beyond it, or they would never have made the attempt. How had they known? The old lama that he shot had only a sketchy knowledge. To move as fast as Erin and Ling had, they must have had a firm idea of their direction and destination. "And he could be leading us down the garden path. Ling is going to be frantic to move Erin away from here as soon as possible. Where could a helicopter land on this mountain?"

"The best place would be right here beside the hot spring."

"What's a possible, not the best, place?"

Brasden looked down at the map. "The road widens four miles up from here, and that would support a landing?" His index finger jabbed at another spot. "Or this plateau on the other side of the mountain. But that wouldn't be anywhere close to the direction the jeep was going."

"How do you know? As you said, it's a rabbit warren up there. It could lead anywhere. How long will it take us to get to that plateau on the other side of the mountain?"

He shook his head. "It's rough country. Four, five hours, maybe. We'd only be able to take the vehicle part of the way. The rest of the trip would be on foot."

"Then let's get started."

"There's no proof that they're going to use that plateau."

"There was no proof that they'd use that passage down Daksha Mountain, but they did. Sometimes you have to rely on your gut instinct. I think whoever met them here at the spring decided to try to keep us busy and out of his way."

"The answer could be so much more simple."

"Only for someone who has no feeling on how to grasp the big picture. I know what I'm doing." He stared out at the high ridges of the mountain. "And so does he."

I can feel you out there. Have I at last lured you out of hiding? All those months of toying with Erin, and you wouldn't make a move. But Ling stirred you up. I should thank the bitch. I may do it after I give her to my men, then tear her breasts off. First things, first.

He turned away and strode around to get into the driver's seat of the jeep. "Come on. Leave a token force to guard this road but hold off on searching this area for now. We'll come back here if—"

"You find out you've made a mistake," Brasden finished slyly.

"I've not made a mistake," he said coldly. "The only mistake I may have made is hiring you. It's up to you to prove I didn't." He put the jeep in gear, and the vehicle lurched forward as his foot hit the accelerator. "Get on the phone and start giving orders."

But Brasden would not even do that with the authority that Kadmus would. Some men were born to rule, and Brasden wasn't one of them.

Kadmus looked up at the plateau in the far distance. He felt as if he could almost see a shadowy face in that pale, icy mist. Soon, there would be no almost about it. He would be able to confront that son of a bitch who had eluded him for so long. He would bring him to his knees and make him beg to give Kadmus what he wanted.

Perhaps it was meant to be that Erin had been taken from him. Now everything would fall into place, and he would be able to move forward.

Do you hear me? he asked that ephemeral figure in the mist. *You're nothing to me. That priest I killed called you the Guardian. But you're just an errand boy trying to keep me from my destiny. You think you can whisk those women away from me, then fly away yourself as you've done before.*

Not this time.

The only difference is that I'll have two bitches instead of one to play with. And you to watch what I do to them.

Did you give Ling a pretty gold lotus necklace, too? So childish . . .

And so helpful to me . . .

•   •   •

"It's time to leave," Catherine whispered to Erin. "Do you need me to help you dress?"

Erin shook her head as she sat up. "My shoulder is okay. Just a little sore. Otherwise, I feel . . . good. Your Hu Chang did a terrific job. What time is it?"

"A little before five. Cameron left a few minutes ago with Hu Chang. I think they're checking the trail."

"I'll be with you in a few minutes." She threw back the cover. "Go take care of your son." The rosy light from the stove glowed on Erin's gold necklace as she put on her bra and T-shirt. "I slept well. I have a good feeling about today."

Catherine leaned forward and touched the lotus. "You were right, you didn't lose it. It must have a very strong chain."

Erin nodded and smiled. "Yes, it's very strong." She added, "And so am I. And getting stronger all the time." She was quickly throwing on the rest of her clothes. "Could I have one of those nutrition bars? I'm hungry."

"Sorry. We left them on the bank when we went into the hot spring."

"I have something, Catherine," Luke said.

She turned to him. "I was just going to wake you."

"I've been awake." He opened his backpack. "Hu Chang gave me these when we started out." He pulled out two nutrition bars. "Give them to her."

"I will." She smiled. "This is Erin Sullivan, Luke."

"I know," Luke said gravely. "How do you do, Ms. Sullivan?"

"Pretty well, thanks to your mother," Erin said. "I'm very glad to meet you, Luke." She took a bite of the bar. "Though I didn't expect to see you here." She glanced at Catherine. "And I'm sure Catherine didn't either. She told me she had to get back to you. But it seems you didn't wait for her."

"I have to be here for her." He met Catherine's eyes. "Don't I?"

"That's what you tell me. But it has to go both ways, Luke."

He shook his head. "You took me away from Rakovac and killed him. You don't owe me anything." He got to his feet and stored his sleeping bag in his backpack. "I saw Hu Chang go out with Cameron. May I go find them?"

"As long as you stay within sight." She held up her hand. "Okay, I'd worry. I'm trying to accept that you—" She shook her head. "Give me a break."

A faint smile touched his lips. "I won't go far." The next moment, he'd left the hut.

Catherine immediately followed him and opened the door.

She couldn't help it if she was insulting his independence. She wasn't going to let him go out in the dark with Kadmus somewhere near without knowing he would be able to make contact with Hu Chang.

It was still dark, but it had stopped snowing, and she could see Cameron and Hu Chang standing, talking, fifty yards or so down the road. Luke would reach them within a few minutes.

She shut the door and turned to see Erin watching her.

"He seems to be a nice boy." Erin turned and was quickly dressing. "But, God, I'm sorry that he's here. I wasn't functioning too well when Cameron brought us here last night, but it still came as a shock. I can see that you're devastated. Who's responsible for his being here?"

"Hu Chang. Cameron. Luke, himself." Catherine went across the room and turned off the stove. "And maybe me, too. I can't sort it all out right now. I just have to concentrate on getting him out of here and on his way to the U.S."

"If Cameron had any responsibility for bringing him, he'll make it right."

"He didn't exactly bring him, he just didn't stop him from coming." She paused. "And he promised that nothing would happen to him."

"You see? Everything will be all right." She grabbed her jacket. "Cameron always keeps his promises."

"I can't say I have the same degree of confidence in him."

"And you think I'm a little nuts because I do."

"I don't understand it."

"I did something I wasn't supposed to do." Her hand went to the lotus on her necklace. "He did what he could to fix it." She released the necklace and carefully thrust her arms into the jacket. "And he sent you, didn't he?"

"So he tells me," she said. "I suppose you wouldn't care to say what terrible thing you did that you'd deserve that kind of punishment?"

"It wasn't terrible, it was careless." She pulled her parka over her hair. "But the result was the same." She moved toward the door. "But it's over now, and I have to get over it, too. It will take a long time, but I'll do it. I won't let Kadmus win."

It wasn't over, Catherine thought, and Erin was intelligent enough to know it. But she wasn't going to discourage her any more than she had to by arguing with her. She was glad Erin was managing to keep her spirits up after that hell of a day they'd gone through yesterday. She followed Erin to the door. "No, he won't win. Let's get down to that plateau and get out of here."

* * *

"I assume you're going to tell me what is wrong." Hu Chang's gaze was focused on the twisting path leading down to the plateau. "I do not read minds, but you're not a man to need company on an early-morning stroll."

"But you're always entertaining, Hu Chang." Cameron smiled. "I enjoyed you enormously during your stay with me."

"What is wrong?" he repeated.

"I got word late last night that Kadmus had virtually abandoned the hot-springs road and was taking his men on the road leading across the mountain." He paused. "They're only a few hours away from the plateau now."

"How close is the helicopter?"

"Too close to Kadmus's ETA."

"Can you divert it?"

"Yes, but that would only extend the danger. Our best bet is to get Erin on that helicopter and away from Kadmus."

"You told me that he would still never give up the search."

"And he won't, but it will be a new playing field, and it will give me time to try to persuade the committee that I'm right, and they're wrong."

"What are the chances?" Hu Chang asked. "Can you do a little mental manipulation with them?"

"No," he said curtly. "That wouldn't be honorable. I made promises when I became Guardian. Besides, they think they're doing what they should for the good of the organization. They're all supersmart and claim they have a long-range view. I'm the rebel. I'll just have to contact a few members who are leaning my way and see what I can do."

"Catherine will want to know that there's a threat."

"I'm sure she will. You tell her. I'm heading out now. I'll tell the pilot to touch down and pick you all up. I want you on board and away from the mountain in two minutes flat. I don't think I can manage any more time than that."

"Time? What—" He stopped as he saw Luke coming toward them from the hut. "Catherine's going to hate this for him. She would have preferred a smooth, safe exit."

"I know. I promised her, I'd keep him safe." He smiled and

waved at Luke. "And he will be safe as long as you don't take longer than those two minutes." He turned and started down the road. "I'll be in touch."

"Where is he going?" Luke had reached Hu Chang and was staring after Cameron. He called, "Cameron?"

Cameron looked over his shoulder and smiled. "I'll see you later. Take care of Catherine, Luke."

The next moment, he had disappeared around the curve.

"Hu Chang?" Luke was frowning. "Where is he going?"

"He did not communicate his exact destination, but I believe it had something to do with our departure. So I think that we should follow his example and start down the mountain." He looked at the hut and saw Catherine and Erin coming toward them. "And with all due speed."

· · · ·

"So much for Cameron's keeping Luke safe, Hu Chang," Catherine said as she strode quickly down the mountain. "Kadmus appears on the horizon, and he takes off."

"Kadmus is not on the horizon yet. Cameron said it would be very close."

"But he didn't want to take a chance of an encounter."

"He did not discuss his plans with me. He just said to get everyone on that helicopter in two minutes." He gazed at Erin, who had moved ahead of them with Luke. "She appears better. And she asked no questions about Cameron."

"She trusts him. No matter what he does, she sure it's the right thing. I can't—" She stopped, her head lifting. "What's that?"

He listened. "Vehicles. It appears that Kadmus may be closer than we thought."

"We can't be sure. These mountains echo like crazy. I made that mistake when Erin and I were in the hot springs." She gnawed at her lower lip. "But if we go forward, we could run into Kadmus's men if they get to the plateau before the helicopter."

"Cameron said that it would be close, but we would have the edge and get there first."

"And we should just trust his judgment?"

"Do you have the facts to make your own? Cameron knows these mountains."

And, according to Hu Chang, he was accustomed to fighting in them.

Hu Chang gazed at her. "No time for hesitation. Go back, or trust Cameron and go forward?"

The sound of Kadmus's vehicles sounded aggressively loud in the clear mountain air.

She muttered a curse, and her pace quickened. "Trust Cameron."

•   •   •

"There's the plateau." Brasden gestured up ahead. The first gray of dawn breaking was lighting the sky. "But we've still heard no electronic communication. No radio transmissions at all. If a helicopter is coming in, the pilot is too far out for us to detect."

"Or he's on complete radio silence," Kadmus said. "We'll camp out for a while and see which is true." He gazed thoughtfully up at the footpath leading up and north from the plateau. Then he looked back at the cavalcade of jeeps behind him. The second vehicle was the one carrying the soldiers with the missile launchers. "And then we'll do a little more exploring. How long until we reach the plateau?"

"Fifteen minutes."

"See if we can get it down to ten."

•   •   •

"Four minutes, Cameron," Tashdon said. "I told you I'd be right on time, sir."

"Kadmus will be able to hear your approach in another two minutes. You're going to be busy. You brought a copilot?"

"Ralph Martin. I've used him before."

"No mistakes. They're going to be throwing big stuff at you, but you just obey instructions." He paused. "All instructions."

Silence. "I don't like it, sir."

"You don't have to like it. Just do it."

"Yes, sir."

Cameron broke away.

He didn't have to glance up the trail to know that Hu Chang would be bringing Erin, Catherine, and Luke down to the plateau within a few minutes. They should be rounding the curve at the same time as the helicopter landed.

He reached into his backpack and brought out his case containing the dissembled parts of his Springfield. A minute later, he had assembled it. The he grabbed his AK-47 and started climbing up the rocks and boulders bordering the trail.

Two minutes.

•   •   •

"There's the helicopter," Erin said over her shoulder as she moved around the curve. "He should be landing any—Oh, shit."

Catherine could see what she meant. Kadmus's caravan of jeeps and trucks was barreling up the hill toward the plateau. They should reach it in minutes. She caught a glimpse of a missile being loaded. "Stop. Luke, come back and—"

"Move, Catherine!"

Cameron. Where the hell—

A bullet exploded from the boulders above the plateau!

She saw the driver of the third jeep in the caravan career off the road and over the edge of the cliff.

"Run." She streaked down the hill toward the plateau.

Another three shots.

The tires on Kadmus's jeep blew an instant later. Brasden and Kadmus jumped from the vehicle to the road.

The helicopter touched down.

"Hu Chang?" she gasped.

"Here." He had already passed her and grabbed Erin. "Cameron said two minutes. Get on board."

The door of the helicopter opened, and a man in uniform was lifting Erin on board.

Another shot from the rocks, and the driver of the fourth jeep in the caravan slumped over the steering wheel. But the other soldiers were pouring out of the vehicles and tearing up the road toward the plateau on foot.

"Get that son of a bitching sniper." Brasden's harsh voice. "And I want that missile loaded and off *now*."

"Catherine." Luke was suddenly beside her, taking her arm and jerking her toward the helicopter. "Get on board. Hurry."

But Cameron was alone up there with all those soldiers crawling over the rocks like scorpions. And the missile had to be disabled. She had only her Luger, but she could go down and get the rifle from that disabled jeep and—

"You get on board," she told Luke. "I'll be right—"

But Luke was not leaving her, and she had to get him on board and out of here. She turned and dashed toward the helicopter at a dead run. The next instant, they both dove into the copter.

"Lift off, Tashdon," Hu Chang ordered the uniformed pilot who had opened the door. "Now."

"Not yet." Catherine got to her feet. "That missile. Cameron needs help." She headed for the door. "Get everyone out of here, Hu Chang. I'll go take care of that missile and make sure they don't get—"

"No. Take off, Martin." The pilot, Tashdon, was behind her, tone regretful. "I'm sorry, ma'am. Cameron gave very definite orders."

Pain.

Darkness.

•   •   •

The copter moved jerkily off the plateau.

Good, he'd managed to distract Kadmus's troops and given them the time they needed, Cameron thought. Now to get rid of those missiles.

He aimed carefully.

The first shot took out the soldier loading the missile.

The second shot took out the other soldier.

The third shot hit the gas tank.

The jeep and missiles exploded!

No more missiles.

He glanced at the helicopter. It was still within range of a good shot. More distraction needed. He took his AK-47 and sprayed the oncoming soldiers who had reached the lower boulders below him.

Then he started moving higher on the rocks, deliberately showing himself.

Shouts.

Bullets.

But they were both in his direction, not the helicopter.

Another glance showed the helicopter out of range.

He ducked back behind the boulders and kept on climbing.

•   •   •

"*Kill* that son of a bitch!" Kadmus shouted.

He could feel the heat of the flames from the exploded missile singeing his back as he ran toward the plateau.

Gone.

Erin Sullivan whisked away from him by Catherine Ling. Rage was tearing through him. He had been so close, and she had still managed to make a fool of him.

No, it hadn't been Ling by herself. The man who'd done this damage was still on the mountain. He'd caught a glimpse of him only minutes ago. He'd squeeze his throat until—

Control the anger.

This could be the man he'd been searching for. It's what he'd been suspecting, and the way he'd decimated his men added credence to the suspicions. Now he had to capture him to confirm it.

"Find him," he called to Brasden. "But keep him alive. Do you hear me? I *need* him."

"I hear you." Brasden was starting up the boulders. "And if I can't get my hands on him right away, I may still get him. I took a photo with my phone when we got a glimpse of him a minute ago."

Clever. He wouldn't have thought Brasden would be that clever. "Don't rely on a damn photo. Get him now."

"I'm not relying on anything. You've always told me to have a backup plan. The photo is my backup plan." He stared grimly down at Kadmus. "And I got a photo of the helicopter as it took off. Complete with registration numbers. It could help. Could you have done better?" He turned away and started climbing.

Arrogance, Kadmus thought, trying to stifle his rage.

And he would punish that arrogance as Brasden deserved.

As soon as he could do without the asshole during these next crucial days.

Use him, then kill him.

• • •

"Don't touch him, Luke."

Hu Chang's voice, Catherine realized hazily.

"I said, get away from him," Hu Chang ordered.

Get away from whom? she wondered. It didn't matter. Hu Chang sounded . . . stern. She had to open her eyes and make sure Luke was all right. "Luke . . ."

Luke was not all right.

His eyes were blazing with pure, searing anger. His entire being appeared to be sending off sparks. His lips were pulled back from his teeth. "Let me *go.*"

Then she saw that Hu Chang was standing in front of him, blocking his way.

And the pilot Hu Chang had called Tashdon was lying on the floor of the copter.

"Luke!" She scrambled to sit up. "What's happening, Hu Chang?"

"Ask your son," he said dryly. "Luke, get away from Tashdon and go see if your mother needs water or an aspirin. That's the only help she needs from you right now."

Luke hesitated, and the stormy expression gradually abated. He crossed the copter and fell to his knees beside her. "Is Hu Chang right?" he asked jerkily. "Do you need something? Water?"

"I need to know what happened." She lifted her hand to her temple. The helicopter. They were on the helicopter. They must have gotten away from the mountain. The last thing she remembered was trying to jump out to get to those missiles. They'd been all over Cameron, and he'd—

"Cameron." Her eyes widened. "What happened to Cameron?"

"Cameron will be okay." Erin was suddenly beside her with a bottle of water and two aspirins. "We saw explosions while we were taking off. You don't have to worry about Cameron."

"I wasn't exactly worried. I just didn't want to leave a man behind."

"And you were right," Luke said fiercely. "If you wanted to go get Cameron, then Tashdon should have let you. I would have gone with you." He was glaring over his shoulder at Hu Chang, who was helping the pilot to his feet. "He shouldn't have touched you."

"The pilot." She had to struggle to remember the name Luke had called him. "Tashdon hit me?"

"He had no right to hit you," Luke said. "No one has a right to hurt you."

"You made your opinion clear on that subject, Luke," Erin said dryly. "However, it might be wise to talk before acting." She turned to Catherine. "But I don't believe he's going to listen to anyone but you, and he's been edging toward Tashdon again."

"Why? What happened to Tashdon?"

Luke didn't answer.

Erin shrugged. "Tashdon hit you with the shaft of his gun when you were trying to jump out. Then he took a step back, closed the helicopter door, and tried to say something to Hu Chang." She made a face. "He didn't get the chance. Luke tackled him, then was on him like a cat. He bloodied his nose and gave him a karate chop that put him out. I don't know how much more damage he did before Hu Chang pulled him off."

"Considerable," Tashdon said. "I wasn't expecting it. Keep him away from me."

"He's only a boy," Catherine said. "He's eleven years old."

"Who is almost as tall as me," Hu Chang said. "He doesn't have a man's strength yet, but he has skills that made up for it. He was all ferocity and very intimidating. He knew what he was doing once he got his hands on Tashdon." He looked at Luke. "Didn't you?"

"Karate?" Luke shrugged. "Of course I knew. Rakovac wanted me to know anything that had to do with killing. He wanted me to kill. But I wouldn't do it. I wouldn't do anything he wanted me to do." He looked at Tashdon. "But I wanted to hurt him, and it was easy for me."

"You don't kill someone just because you can," Catherine said.

"He hurt you." He paused. "And I didn't kill him . . . quite."

"I have to go back to the cockpit," Tashdon said. He turned to Catherine. "I'm sorry I hurt you." He added ruefully. "In more ways than one. I was trying to explain to you when I struck you."

"Not the time for explanations," Catherine said. "And I may disapprove of Luke's taking you down, but that doesn't mean that I won't do it myself."

Luke took an eager step toward him.

"No, Luke, not you." She said coldly to Tashdon, "Make your explanations and get out of here. It was Cameron?"

He nodded. "He was sure at some point you would . . . opt to stay and join the fray. He said to be prepared and not let you do it when that time came."

"He told you to knock me on the head?"

"He told me to stop you. I couldn't think of any other way to do it. I didn't mean to knock you out. I just wanted to give you a glancing blow that would get you away from the door." He gazed sourly at Luke. "I'm a pilot. I don't know any of that other stuff. Cameron wanted it done. So I did it."

"It's not always wise to obey blindly," Hu Chang said. "I heard what you said before you struck Catherine and deduced the reason." He added coolly, "Otherwise, you would have had to contend with me as well as the boy. You would have found me even more lethal. Luke knows the method but is obviously controlled by passion. That's sometimes counterproductive. He will have to be mentally and emotionally schooled before he's fully effective. But you might be a good subject on whom he can practi—"

"Stop, Hu Chang," Catherine said. "Let him go fly the damn helicopter. And you will not school Luke in anything lethal. It's bad enough that I'm always worried about you and those poisons."

Tashdon quickly nodded and fled for the cockpit.

"Cameron did it?" Luke was frowning. "He must be lying. Cameron wouldn't do anything to hurt you."

And Luke was willing to blame anyone but Cameron, Catherine thought. Even in the short time that they had been together, Cameron had made a potent impression on her son.

"Not intentionally, Luke," Erin said. "He would only do it to keep Catherine safe."

"But she has a right to do what she wants to do. He shouldn't have told that pilot to hit her."

"Drop it, Luke," Catherine said. The last thing she wanted was for Luke to be aggressive toward Cameron when they saw him again. Cameron had far too many weapons at his disposal. She didn't think he would use them against the boy, but Cameron was unpredictable to say the least. "I agree with you in principle, but I'm willing to withhold judgment until I get an explanation from Cameron."

"That doesn't sound like you."

"No, it does not," Hu Chang said. "It's much too reasonable and logical. At last she must be listening to my sage advice."

Luke shook his head. "I still don't like—"

"Cameron saved us, Luke," Erin said. "Forget everything else. Just remember what odds he took on to help us."

Luke nodded. "I wasn't sure what was happening at the time, but then everything started blowing up." He smiled. "Pretty cool."

"Yeah." Erin smiled back at him. "Cameron is always pretty cool."

Thank heavens Erin had managed to distract Luke. Catherine couldn't be sure of sounding too convincing when her head was throbbing, and she was a hell of a lot angrier at Cameron than Luke. She turned to Hu Chang. "I take it I wasn't out long?"

"No, but you missed the best part."

"That's a matter of opinion. So we should be in Hong Kong in about three hours?"

"That's a good estimation. However, we may not be going to Hong Kong. We'll have to transfer to another flight to go to the U.S., and Cameron may have made other arrangements. Hong Kong may not be safe." He turned away. "But things were in such tumult after we took off that I didn't get a chance to inquire of Tashdon. I'll go up and see if he's regained his composure enough to discuss it with me."

Erin got to her feet. "Since this is all about me, I believe I'll go with you."

Catherine watched them leave before turning to Luke. "I didn't ask you. Are you all right? Did Tashdon hurt you at all?"

Luke looked at her in surprise. "No, Hu Chang told you that I was the one who—"

"But I didn't see it happening. I had to be sure. You were wrong, you know. You should have waited and found out—" Luke was shaking his head. "Okay, I'm not sure I would have waited. I have a habit of acting on instinct."

Luke smiled faintly. "So do I."

She reached out and touched his cheek. "Probably because you're my son. I hope you haven't inherited any more of my faults."

"Who knows if that's a fault? Hu Chang would say it is, but I'm not him. People aren't the same." His smile faded. "You were angry that I hurt that pilot."

"No, not angry. It was a mistake. I just wanted you to realize it and correct it."

He was silent. "I'm not sorry I did it," he said jerkily. "I'd do it again. He hurt you."

"Luke . . ."

"And there's another reason I'm not sorry. You got to see me like I am. I couldn't tell you. You had to see it." He moistened his lips. "I'm not good-natured and full of jokes and all that other stuff. Sometimes when I'm with other kids my age, I just don't get them. I try, but it's like I'm from another planet." He paused. "I felt more comfortable going after that pilot's jugular than I have since you took me away from Rakovac."

She hid the ripple of shock she felt. Poor Luke. She should have seen beyond her own need and fear and tried to make him talk to her before this. "In an emergency, it's natural to go back to the habits of your early training." She smiled with an effort. "And though I didn't actually see it, I feel that I couldn't have had a sharper awakening regarding your present mind-set. Am I going to be faced with anything more mind-boggling?"

"Maybe. I don't know. I don't think so."

"I just wanted to be prepared." She hesitated, then said, "Because

I did something pretty revealing myself when I got on this helicopter. You're not the only one who reacted purely on instinct. Once I got you on board, I was going to leave you in Hu Chang's hands and go back and do my job. You weren't my first priority. I was going to go get those missiles." She wrinkled her nose. "Good CIA. Bad mother."

"Cameron needed you, I didn't. Besides, I was going to go with you."

"Which would have scared me to death." She drew a shaky breath. "So it seems that we've both made mistakes, Luke." She leaned forward and gave him a quick, awkward kiss on the cheek. "But maybe we've learned something. What do you think?"

"You're not mad at me any longer?"

"I told you, l wasn't—" She added, "But I think you should apologize to Tashdon."

"No, he hurt you."

"Not intentionally."

He stubbornly shook his head.

"Okay, I'll let it go." She suddenly chuckled. "And how do you apologize to someone for going for their jugular anyway?"

"I don't know." He grinned back at her. "Rakovac never taught me that." He suddenly frowned. "But I do think that pilot was lying about Cameron. Do you think Cameron's okay? Kadmus's men were pouring up that slope. Tashdon should have let you go help him."

"I thought so, too." She paused. "And I can't promise Cameron is okay. If you'll recall, thanks to Tashdon, I wasn't around to make any judgments. But Erin and Hu Chang think he has a good chance. And Cameron is very clever about getting himself out of trouble. I believe he'll make it."

Luke nodded. "Me, too." He got to his feet. "I've got to go see Hu Chang and apologize. I wasn't polite to him when he was holding me off Tashdon. Hu Chang doesn't like discourtesy."

Catherine remembered that moment when she'd first opened her eyes and seen Luke, looking like a tiger on attack, being held at bay by Hu Chang. "Yes, by all means, I think your behavior definitely warrants an apology."

Luke moved quickly toward the cockpit.

Catherine let her breath out in a weary sigh as she leaned back against the wall of the helicopter. She was glad to have a few moments of solitary silence. She'd been bombarded by panic, shock, and emotion since she'd regained consciousness.

Besides the start of a nagging headache.

Thanks, Cameron. I needed that.

She found herself waiting for a reply.

Nothing.

She hadn't expected an answer, she told herself. She'd told the bastard to leave her mind alone.

Besides, he'd had Kadmus's mercenaries on his trail and was probably having to hide and attack guerrilla style.

So many damn mercenaries.

Erin was Catherine's job. She should have been there to help Cameron get out.

Cameron, it's okay if you just let me know, dammit.

Nothing.

CHAPTER

10

O ut." Tashdon moved through the helicopter toward the rear door. "Everyone out. There's a private jet waiting at the third hangar." He opened the door and jumped out. "The pilot's name is Jack Sen. He's a good pilot and loyal to Cameron. You'll be okay." He helped Erin and Catherine to the ground. "Cameron said he wanted the transfer to not take longer than five minutes. Since I didn't obey his last instructions very efficiently, I'm hoping that you'll cooperate and let me prove I'm not usually a bumbler."

"Heaven forbid you get in his bad books," Catherine murmured. "Hu Chang said that you wouldn't tell him what our final destination was going to be. May we know now?"

He shook his head. "I don't know myself. Cameron only told Jack Sen. He said it was safer."

"He could be right. Luke, Hu Chang. Let's go."

Hu Chang jumped from the helicopter, with Luke following. "Luke, I think since you owe Tashdon a debt, that we should strive to accommodate him." He set off for the Gulfstream jet on the tarmac.

Catherine started after him, then stopped and turned back to Tashdon. "Do you know if Cameron is all right? Have you heard from him since we left the mountain?"

He shook his head. "No, he was probably busy."

"That's what I thought. I just thought he'd tell someone he was safe."

He frowned, puzzled. "But Cameron is always safe."

"Always? Why?"

"Because he's—"

"The Guardian?" she finished mockingly for him as he stopped.

"I don't know what you mean." He added, "I was going to say competent. Cameron is . . . competent."

"No one can argue with that." She said, "And I'm sorry that my son . . . well, I'm not sorry you got what you deserved, but I'm sorry that Luke was the one who did it." She didn't wait for him to answer but hurried and caught up with Erin. "He hasn't heard from Cameron. I thought I'd check." She smiled ironically. "Though he informs me that Cameron is competent. Isn't that a shocker? I'm losing faith in Cameron's personnel choices. He almost slipped and called him the Guardian." She glanced at Erin. "You don't seem surprised that I know that term. I found out a little from Cameron and Hu Chang but damn little. It would help if you'd open up and tell me more."

"I'm not surprised," she said quietly. "I knew you'd dig until you found out all you could. You'll never stop. But I told you that it will have to come from Cameron."

"I have to know. It's the only way I can protect you," she said. "We both know that we're not free yet. We won't be free until Kadmus is dead, and I'll bet he's already started searching again." She added in frustration, "And he knows more about all this than I do, dammit."

"Look, I'll hide out. I'll let you and your CIA people guard me. I'll cooperate fully. I appreciate what you're doing, and I don't want to be a burden."

"Then tell me why Kadmus—" She broke off. She'd gone down that path before and gotten nowhere. New path. "That lotus pendant you wear that Kadmus seemed to be so fascinated with. Where did you get it? Did Cameron give it to you?"

Erin's hand flew to her necklace. "Sort of." She quickly shook her head. "Leave it alone, Catherine. That's out of bounds, too."

"I'll stop questioning you, but I won't leave it alone." They had reached the jet, and she stopped at the steps. "I'm not going to endanger anything or anyone you've suffered to protect, but I *will* know what this is all about. So far I've only been concentrating on getting you free and keeping us alive. But I've got breathing room now, and it's a long flight from here to the U.S. I can think, and I can research. However, it would be easier if I learned it from you."

Erin shook her head.

"Fine." She turned to the small, dapper Eurasian, wearing a brown leather flight jacket who was coming down the steps. "Jack Sen? Catherine Ling. Tashdon tells me that you're the only one who's been advised of Erin's destination. Where are we going?"

"San Francisco." He shook her hand. "Well, actually, an airport east of the city, but we'll have transport for you. Everything will go smooth as clockwork." He had a faint British accent and pleasant manner. "Cameron will have nothing to worry about."

"Thank you. It seems we're all primarily concerned that Cameron suffer as little distress as possible." She started up the steps. "Come on, Erin. Mr. Sen, since we're on a five-minute deadline set by Cameron, perhaps we'd better take off."

• • •

"He got away?" Kadmus asked incredulously. "How could that be? He was alone. He's only one man."

"He just slipped away," Brasden said. "He must have been helped by the villagers."

"You said that the villagers had all abandoned their towns and gone upland."

"What do you want me to tell you?" Brasden asked. "We're still looking. I'm not giving up, but I think we'd better start using those photos." He pulled out his phone and dialed up the photos. "This last one is fairly decent. Anyone who saw it would recognize him. He has a memorable face."

Kadmus glanced at the photo. "Yes, he does." He thought about it. "Start asking questions. I want a name to go with that face." The bastard looked like he was enjoying himself, he thought sourly. That would end when he got his hands on him. "And a location to go with that name."

"It may take a while to find any villagers who will talk about him. We haven't been able to find any—"

"Then leave here and go somewhere that you can find someone who will answer questions."

"Where?"

"Fly over to Yorshoi region. That's where Erin Sullivan was working after the earthquake. I'd bet that's where she made contact with him. There's a chance he's well-known there."

"Right away. What about the registration on the helicopter?"

"I've checked it. The registration number is bogus. But send someone to Hong Kong with a description of the helicopter and see if they can get a lead. I want to get my hands on that pilot."

Brasden nodded. "Though it may be too late for a strike at him. Erin Sullivan is probably well on her way home to the States."

"And will feel all the safer for it." She wouldn't be safe. Things weren't as bad as he'd thought. He might have temporarily lost Erin, but he had a lead on the man who had taken her from him.

He looked down at the photo and the face that was glowing with excitement and recklessness and scorn.

You made a mistake. And you made it for Erin Sullivan.

Or did you make that mistake to protect Catherine Ling? It was a novel idea that had occurred to him and one that was probably without any basis. But it would be interesting if Ling could be used as a weapon against him.

Yes, things weren't nearly as bad as he'd thought . . .

•   •   •   •

"This food is exceptional," Hu Chang said as he took Catherine's tray and gave it to Luke to take back to the well-equipped galley in the rear of the jet. "I spoke to Jack Sen, and he said that Cameron had it catered from the Princess Hotel in Hong Kong." He smiled at Catherine. "You remember the Princess? You had your first meeting with Venable there."

"And you were the one who arranged it for me."

"I wanted you safer than you were selling information on the streets. Though that was no doubt a case of six of one, half a dozen of another." He added, "And Cameron also arranged for a complete wardrobe for all of us to be brought to the plane this morning. Besides that case with the laptop and satellite phone you grabbed as soon as you set eyes on it. He appears to be wanting to meet our every need and wish." He tilted his head. "Or perhaps he wants you comfortable so that you won't strike out at him."

"I haven't struck out at him."

"No, and you were ready to jump out of the copter to save him. But he didn't know then that you'd do that when he provided all of these comforts." He added, "Oh, that's right, evidently he did. He reads you very well. And you hate to be predictable. Is that why you were so angry with Tashdon?"

"I was angry that he'd been stupid enough to do what Cameron told him. And that Cameron had chosen someone who didn't know what he was doing and gave me a headache." She glanced at Luke, who had come out of the galley with some kind of electronic game and dropped down in a seat to play it. "And that it triggered something in Luke that I didn't want to see."

"He's your son, and I saw nothing that I would not approve and embrace." He corrected, "Except a lack of control, and we've already discussed that."

"But you're no more judge than I. We're both flawed."

"I do not like that word. I prefer to call it multiexperienced."

"Call it what you like. We're not normal, and I want a normal life for Luke." She held up her hand. "I know, he made it clear that he couldn't be what I wanted him to be. I just want him not to enjoy killing someone because he thought I was hurt."

"You *were* hurt," Hu Chang said. "And I have no quarrel with his receiving pleasure from punishing the person who did it. I would do the same. And so would you if that act were aimed at Luke or me."

"You see? The case rests. Flawed."

He smiled and shook his head. "Multiexperienced."

She chuckled reluctantly. "Whatever. But it will be better if I get Luke away from this situation as soon as possible. Agreed?"

"Better for your peace of mind. Not necessarily better for your relationship with Luke. You would see that for yourself if you were not so torn by what other people think is correct." He waved his hand. "But I will agree that your heart will be soothed if you're not confronted by other situations like the one with Tashdon. So what is your solution?"

"Find out what is going on with Cameron, Erin, and that ugliness with Kadmus."

"I suspected that would be your answer."

"Of course you did," she said curtly. "But it didn't lead you to point me in the right direction."

"I told you facts and reasonable surmises. I only held back a few wild guesses."

"Which can sometimes be the most valuable of all. Go ahead, hold them back. I'll work around them."

He gave her a pleased smile. "Indeed? I will enjoy watching you."

"Bastard." She settled down in her seat. "Go away. I'm going to take a two-hour nap and clear my mind before I get to work on the computer."

•   •   •

Cameron?

She woke two hours later with the thought of him in her mind like a persistent pop song.

No answer.

Of course not. And there was nothing to worry about. It was just Cameron doing his own thing and ignoring everyone else.

And it was time for her to do her own thing.

She straightened in her seat and reached for her bottle of water. She took a drink and then set it aside and took the computer out of the case and flipped it open.

First, verify what Hu Chang had told her about Cameron's identity being erased. She accessed Langley's database.

Thirty minutes later, she exited the Interpol database. She had also scanned NSA, FBI, and Scotland Yard. It was probably a waste of time to go any further when she was getting the same answer. She sat back and let the information sink home. The sheer power that it would take to make a man invisible on so many fronts was astonishing. They must have believed that Cameron was totally unique to even make the effort.

And who were "they"?

The committee, whoever they were.

Skip that one. She didn't have enough information to even make guesses.

What she did know was that Erin had made contact with Cameron sometime after she had come to Tibet. He had "sort of" given her that lotus necklace, and it had attracted the attention of Kadmus. When had Cameron given her the necklace? She apparently always wore it. . . .

She started to access stories about Erin in the computer. There were a couple photos of her before the earthquake. No sign of the necklace. The day she had received the Pulitzer she'd worn a simple, round-necked dress. No necklace. The next story was a feature about Erin working with the orphans of Yorshoi.

Around her neck was the lotus necklace.

What date?

Six months after she had been given the Pulitzer.

So it was only a fairly recent gift from Cameron.

And during that time Erin had just been doing her job, nothing that was unusual. No contact with Kadmus or his men. She had just been writing stories about the Tibetan people and their problems.

But Beijing didn't like stories written about those problems. It was very bad public relations.

But Venable hadn't thought there was any direct link with Beijing to Erin's kidnapping.

Forget Beijing. Back to the necklace.

She closed her eyes and mentally went over the details of the necklace.

Time to Google it and see if anything it brought up struck a spark.

She typed: Eight-sided lotus.

Good Lord.

The search results appeared to stretch into infinity. Everything from water plants to mythology and ancient history.

This was not going to be easy.

She sighed and clicked on the first link.

How to grow the eight-sided lotus.

•   •   •

"The transfer was made?" Cameron asked. "You saw the plane take off, Tashdon?"

"Yes, as you instructed. Everything went well." He paused. "Well, almost. I only meant to stun Catherine Ling and get her away from the door. But she was unconscious for a few minutes." He added hurriedly, "But she was fine when she woke."

"Not good. That's not what I wanted."

"I know. She was angry, but there was a distraction, and I think that may have made her less upset with me . . . and you."

"What distraction? Never mind." He was too impatient to wait for an answer that would be defensive. He quickly scanned Tashdon's memory. "The boy?" He started to laugh. "I'd be angry with you, but you appear to have had a hard enough time."

"He was a kid. I wasn't expecting—"

"That's when you have to be most on guard. When you don't think you have to be. You did well enough, considering the circumstances. I wouldn't say the same if you'd really hurt her." He changed the subject. "Leave the helicopter at the heliport and get out of Hong Kong. Lose yourself until I tell you it's safe."

"Yes, sir. I'm on my way."

Cameron was still smiling as he closed the connection.

The boy . . .

It was no more than he had anticipated after he had read Luke. He was unusual and on his way to being extraordinary. In the years to come Catherine would have to deal with a boy in her own image. It would be interesting to watch.

She was interesting to watch. Not only that body, which was a constant temptation, but the way she moved, the quickness of her mind.

Even now, she was probably trying to solve the puzzle, go forward instead of sitting still on that long flight to San Francisco.

And she would eventually solve the puzzle. What would he do then? He knew what the committee would say. She wasn't one of the accepted. She hadn't been sanctioned. She was therefore unsafe. There was only one thing to do with anyone in that category.

Kill Catherine Ling?

No!

He violently rejected the thought immediately. There were other alternatives and he would find them. He did not have to—

His phone rang and he smiled as he looked at the ID. Hal Beecham was the only committee member who had never been comfortable enough with mental telepathy to give up his beloved electronic communication. It didn't really bother Cameron. He liked Beecham, and that fault made him all the more human. "Erin Sullivan is on her way to San Francisco," he said when he picked up the call. "The problem is partially solved."

"Kadmus has your photo," Beecham said.

"I know. Brasden got it. I'll take care of it."

"Brasden has started showing it in the villages in Yorshoi region. Will he get your name there?"

"Probably. The villagers are simple people. I said I'll take care of it, Beecham."

"Will we have to do an erasure?"

"A minor one, perhaps. I'll let you know."

"Kadmus is getting too close to you. The committee is becoming troubled."

"There are two solutions to that problem. Let me get rid of Kadmus." He paused. "Or get rid of me."

"Cameron."

"It's very logical."

"I told you that long term, Kadmus is of value to us." He added, "And there's no way the committee would ever let you go. You're one of us. Sometimes, I think you're the best of us."

"Then listen to me. I can't pussyfoot around to keep from killing Kadmus. Now the CIA is involved, and they could take him out in a way that would not be as private as I'd like. Go back and tell them that they have to rethink advance strategy."

"I'll do what I can." He was silent. "It's the first time you've ever allowed a photo be taken of you, Cameron."

"Yes."

"What happened?"

"Kadmus would call it a mistake."

"Was it?"

"No, it was a choice. I needed to get that helicopter safely away. It was important to me."

"Are you too involved?"

"Yes, but I'll make it right. Anything else, Beecham?"

"No, I just wanted you to know that a photo was taken." He added, "And to ask if we could help in any way."

"I'll let you know. Thanks." He hung up.

It was only a matter of days, perhaps hours, before Brasden would have his name. Not that it would do him much good. The erasure of his identity had been too complete and a name would be of little value. But it would give Kadmus a sense of power and confidence, and that would furnish the impetus for him to go forward more quickly.

Adjust.

Go first to Yorshoi and make sure that Brasden wasn't doing damage to those villagers. After that, he should go into hiding for a time. Let Ling and the CIA handle Erin for a while. That would be the safe, approved thing to do.

Would he do it?

Hell, no.

•   •   •

This damn Google search was not only painstaking, it was frustrating.

Catherine rubbed her blurry eyes and closed them for a moment. The frustrating part was the fact that Erin was sitting three rows ahead of her and could answer all the questions for which she was searching if she only would. Catherine had spent over two hours on the lotus search, and she hadn't seen anything that was in the least helpful.

Lightning had not struck.

She opened her eyes. Get back to it. Find a clue. Find a path. Find something that she could bring to Erin and throw at her and see her reaction.

She flipped to the new page.

It was halfway down on the third page.

She had almost skipped over it.

She couldn't breathe as she clicked on the link.

Her gaze raked the page while she frantically made notes.

"Oh, my God," she whispered.

•   •   •

Two hours later Catherine pushed away the computer and reached for the phone. She noticed her hand was shaking. Calm down, the excitement was too extreme. She couldn't be sure that she was coming anywhere close to the truth.

The idea could be completely bizarre. No, it *was* completely bizarre. But that didn't mean that it couldn't have some basis in truth. If the necklace was the key, then this was one answer.

Lightning had struck, and she had to follow it to ground zero.

But first, she had to try to connect the dots. She quickly dialed Venable. "Erin's safe. We're on our way to San Francisco," she said when he picked up. "But Kadmus isn't out of the picture. We're still going to have trouble with him."

"As long as Erin Sullivan is safe and back in the U.S., our job is officially over. Good job, Catherine."

"I told you, it's not over. I'm not going to have Kadmus pick her up and haul her back to Tibet for more fun and games. We have to take him out."

"Give me her location, and I'll have someone keep an eye on her."

"That's not good enough. Kadmus is motivated, and he'll never stop. He has a damn bloody army at his disposal. The only way I can stop him is to find out what's driving him and stage a trap or ambush."

He was silent. "I don't want this to drag on and on, Catherine. When Sullivan gets off that plane, she's no longer our problem."

"She's *my* problem." She drew a deep breath. "But I'll try to wrap it up as soon as I can. But I need some information from you, and I need it quick. You said that Kadmus was pretty wealthy and had several legitimate business enterprises in Tibet as well as all the loot he made from criminal activities."

"That's right."

"Will you e-mail me the list of those legit investments right away?"

"I could do that." He added curiously, "Why?"

"I'm not sure. It may be nothing, or it may be an answer. How quick can you get it to me?"

"Thirty minutes."

"Good. Do it." That sounded too curt and she didn't want him to drag his feet because he was annoyed with her. Besides, he was doing this against his will. "Thanks, Venable."

"You're welcome," he said dryly. He hung up.

She leaned back in her seat.

Thirty minutes.

It was going to be a long thirty minutes.

"Your eyes are brilliant, your cheeks are flushed." Hu Chang was coming down the aisle toward her. "I believe I'm perceiving signs of success." He stopped and looked down at her. "I thought it might be so. It was interesting watching you work these last hours. Would you like to share it with me?"

"No. You weren't overly cooperative about sharing everything with me. You made me dive in and work all the details out for my-self. I may feel generous after I finish putting everything together." She made a face at him. "Or I may not."

"I hope you will," he said. "And you might consider why I was not eager for you to learn too much. I knew I probably could not keep you from tearing away all the veils, but there was the slightest chance . . ."

"You were protecting Cameron."

"No, I was protecting you," he said soberly. The next instant, he had turned and was walking back up the aisle to his seat.

She stared after him. The excitement of the previous moment was gone, quenched by Hu Chang's uncharacteristic gravity. There was no question of his sincerity and she felt a sudden chill.

She moved her shoulders to shake it off. Was he protecting her from Cameron? The path she was following might very well lead to a confrontation with him.

She couldn't worry about it now. She wasn't going to stop until she'd solved all the puzzles and answered all the questions. Then she'd deal with Cameron and Kadmus and anyone else who would prove a threat to Erin.

She just wished Venable would hurry with that information so that she could begin.

Her e-mail alert tinged softly forty minutes later. She hurriedly accessed Venable's message. Not really a message. Just a fairly long list of companies in which Kadmus had an interest. She went over the list of names quickly. She didn't recognize most of them. They were Chinese and Indian, no English or American. She wasn't even sure that she'd find the connection for which she was looking. Kadmus was boldly arrogant but he still might have decided to go undercover with this particular investment. She started checking addresses for each company.

She stopped at the fourth company from the bottom.

Yunnan Province. She had run across that location in the last Google lotus research she'd gone through.

She quickly typed in the name of the Chinese company in Yunnan Province.

She inhaled sharply. Her heart leaped to her throat.

Bingo.

•   •   •

"His name is Cameron," Brasden said as he got off the helicopter and strode over to Kadmus. "I couldn't get a first name. Hell, maybe that is his first name. But I don't think so. Those villagers said that name Cameron as if it stood alone, as if *he* stood alone. They were friendly at first and then closed up the more I questioned them. No one seemed to know anything much about him. Some people thought he was a journalist, others thought he might be a spy from Beijing. Most of them only knew he was just a Westerner who moved in and out of the villages throughout Tibet."

"Did he hire guides?"

Brasden shook his head. "No guides. He visited several monasteries, but I thought you wouldn't want the monks disturbed until you were ready to move on them. It tends to cause a lot of outrage among the people when the monks are targeted. I left a few men to watch the monasteries and see if anyone of his description showed up at any of them."

"No, I'm not ready yet to go after them." He'd had his own experience with those damn religious fanatics when he'd kicked them out of Daksha. They'd clung to the villagers and caused him nothing but trouble. He'd rather go after Cameron at a place easier for him to control. "Keep on searching. You have a name. That should help."

"I also have the name of the pilot who delivered them to Hong Kong. George Tashdon. They transferred to another flight at a private airport outside the city."

"Going where?"

"I'm still working on it." He held up his hand. "I know the name of that pilot, too. Jack Sen. Be patient. I'll have it all for you within a few days." He paused. "Don't you think I deserve a reward?"

Kadmus's gaze narrowed on Brasden. "What do you have in mind?"

"Just a small cut of the pie that you're trying to devour all by yourself. Who is Cameron to you? Tell me, and I'll serve him up to you with all the fixings."

Who was Cameron to him? He was the answer. The guide to everything he'd always wanted to be. If he had Cameron, he could force him to make all the dreams of power come true.

"I'll consider it." Kadmus moved toward his jeep. "Find out where Jack Sen is taking them. Cameron won't risk leaving them on their own. Follow Erin and Ling, and we have a chance of finding Cameron."

I have your name, Cameron. I know what you look like. I know you have a weakness for Erin Sullivan.

I've got you in my sights, Cameron.

CHAPTER

11

How are you doing?" Catherine sat down in the seat next to Erin. "Whenever I looked up from working, you were always snoozing." She set her computer on the table between the seats. "Best thing for you, of course."

"I'm doing fine," Erin said quietly. "These long flights can be exhausting, but I've always been able to sleep on them. From the time I became a journalist, I've always considered that a blessing." She paused. "But evidently you didn't choose to sleep on this one." She glanced down at Catherine's computer. "The one or two times I looked back at you, I saw you pounding those computer keys." Her gaze rose to Catherine's face. "And now you're here and smiling at me and about to pounce. Just what were you doing back there?"

"I was doing searches on the little information that I've been given and trying to make educated guesses." She added, "And 'pounce' is a word you use about an enemy. I'm not your enemy. I'll never be your enemy. You must have a good reason for keeping me in the dark, but I can't stay there. It's not my nature. I had to find a way to let light into the darkness."

Erin stiffened. "And how did you do that?"

Catherine took a deep breath, then threw it at her. "Shambhala."

Erin's eyes flickered. Her lips tightened. "I don't know what you're talking about."

But there had been a definite response, Catherine thought. Erin knew the word, and it had been a shock to her coming from Catherine.

"I'm talking about a place that's said to be a hidden paradise that was supposed to be the center of wisdom in the highlands of central Asia. Its inhabitants' prime goal in life was to store power and knowledge and prepare the way to start life over after the outer world had destroyed itself. Its existence has been rumored for thousands of years in the myths of India, China, and even Europe."

"Really?"

"You haven't heard about it? That's strange when you've been living intimately with the people of Tibet. Shambhala is an essential part of their culture."

"I'm a journalist, not a historian."

"I think you do know about it. But I'm not going to try to make you betray yourself or your word or whatever." She smiled. "That would be pouncing. Instead, I'll tell you how I came around to finding Shambhala." She gestured to Erin's necklace. "I thought that could be the key, so I googled eight-sided lotus and spent hours trying to find a clue."

Erin's hand tightened around her pendant. "A clue to this Shambhala?"

"I didn't know anything about Shambhala. Oh, I might have heard a reference to it sometime or other, but it wasn't on my radar. Until I finally found a reference to an eight-sided lotus that connected it to Shambhala." She slowly shook her head. "It blew me away."

"Why? You said yourself this place is only a myth."

"I said that it was said to be a myth. What if it actually existed?"

"Then it would have been discovered and debunked decades ago."

"Would it?"

"People are always hunting for hidden treasures or lost cities like Atlantis. Do they find them? No, because they don't exist. And because of modern technology and satellites, there's no place to hide any longer."

"Perhaps."

"No perhaps," she said firmly. "Anything else is the stuff of Indiana Jones or *Tomb Raider* movies."

"It's strange you should mention movies." She smiled. "Though the one that could pertain to Shambhala wasn't that recent. It was a vintage classic. *Lost Horizon*. It was based on a novel by James Hilton and was all about a perfect place called Shangri-La. Where people only wished to live in peace. I'm sure you've heard of that particular myth."

"Of course, I even saw the movie on late-night TV."

"Hilton modeled his hidden city of Shangri-La on Shambhala. He borrowed some of his material from the memoirs of Abbe Huc and other Catholic missionaries who explored Tibet and the culture of the lamas in the nineteenth century."

"So he built on one myth to perpetuate another." She moistened her lips. "Shangri-La doesn't exist either though it's become part of world culture. I understand that the Chinese even built a tourist-trap city in Yunnan Province and claimed it to be the location of the Shangri-La in the movie."

"Yes, the Chinese are nothing if not opportunistic. You can even fly into Shangri-La airport. Though the Chinese located their Shangri-La in the Kunlun Mountains and not the Himalayas. But they assured the world that their scientists had studied the topographical features of the entire area, and they were sure they were correct. They did a good, though extremely commercial job, of building their city, and millions flock to the place every year."

"You researched it?"

"I had reason," she said. "Shangri-La was modeled after Shambhala, and I had to know everything about it. Because Shambhala had to be the center of what was happening around me."

"Just because of my lotus necklace?" Erin's brows rose. "You're reaching, Catherine."

"And I don't know all the answers. But I have a feeling I'm on the right track. I think Shambhala exists and that you know something about it. Oh, I don't mean as an actual place. But the idea of creating a perfect world like that, with those values, would attract you. When I thought Cameron was some high-priced security mogul working for an organization that was trying to control the world through technology and political manipulation, I couldn't understand why you'd be drawn to it. From what I knew about you, that didn't compute. But then I ran across this connection with Shambhala. It clicked. What if you thought that this committee was trying to be guided by all those highfalutin goals that are attributed to Shambhala. You're an idealist. I know how persuasive Cameron can be. He could paint you a wonderful picture of this conglomerate trying to save the world, of working to create a new Shambhala. Yes, I think you know a good deal about all of it." She looked her in the eye. "And I think Kadmus wants to know what you know. I believe that's why he wants to find Cameron. Because he's sure Cameron knows even more than you do about the place. I'm not sure he's even aware of Cameron's conglomerate or that committee. He may be looking for Shambhala itself."

"Kadmus is searching for a lost city? That's hardly likely, is it?"

"That's what I thought until I started thinking and putting together the pieces. Kadmus has a king complex, he worships power. That's why he set up headquarters at that royal palace at Daksha. He wants to rule all of Tibet, and if he could manage, he'd branch out into China. But his opportunities appear limited considering his background, and he doesn't like limits. So he began to look around, searching for a way to obtain power without running a risk to his military kingdom at Daksha. I don't know how or why he focused on Shambhala. Perhaps he saw something, heard something that intrigued him." She paused. "And perhaps he ran across someone else who had one of those necklaces and was able to force information out of them. What do you think?"

"I think that you're trying to turn fantasy into reality, and it's not working. Why would he even think that some lost city would be profitable for him? Is it supposed to be some kind of treasure trove?"

"It's possible. Or he might think it possible. The legends surrounding Shambhala aren't the usual stories of hidden treasure. It's a place where physical and psychic powers are blended in a perfect whole. That psychic aspect has been mentioned in the legends for thousands of years. Yes, the ground is supposed to be strewn with gold and silver, and jewels are everywhere. But it's also supposed to be a wonderful place whose people live for a long, long time in beautiful, perfect bodies. They hate war and violence and won't tolerate it. Their main purpose is to store power and knowledge for the time when the outer world destroys itself and comes seeking that knowledge. They also have so-called supernatural or psychic powers and high, high intelligence that enable them to survive and keep the outer world at bay."

"Gold and silver and jewels would appeal to Kadmus. Not the rest."

"But what if that intelligence and psychic ability could translate into producing wonderful products and influence the minds of people in power? That would be a tremendously valuable asset for Kadmus to control."

"If he could do it."

"Kadmus thinks he can do anything. He wouldn't be intimidated. He'd assume that he's the exception to any rule. Did you know that one of his more legitimate investments is a share in one of the most powerful Chinese companies that run several of the hotels and tourist concessions in Shangri-La?"

"No, that could mean nothing or that the idea is an obsession for him."

"I'm voting for the obsession."

"And why would you think that legend is true and Shambhala actually exists?"

"I told you, I don't know if it exists as a real place. Not in this day and age. It would be terribly hard to hide from satellites. In this modern day, I'm leaning toward the idea that it's not a city or country but could be a group of people who might possess some of those qualities and set themselves up to dedicate and maintain that kind of control and skill. Perhaps a conglomerate." She paused. "Or a committee."

Erin was silent.

"And they would need an awesome security force to keep anyone from knowing exactly what they were doing to manipulate the global process." She added softly, "A Guardian at the gates. Cameron was perfect. He has certain mental abilities, and he's tough as hell. But I'm wondering if he had another job. It must be difficult to recruit new blood to keep that kind of organization going. I don't even know what the criteria would be. Perhaps you could help me out there? Let's see, you're intelligent, brave, self-sacrificing. What else?"

"A very ordinary journalist."

"There's nothing ordinary about you. You said Cameron 'sort of' gave you that necklace. Was that to seal the deal?"

"No," she said. "And I have no psychic talents, and I'm fairly smart but no superbrain. So that blows your theory to hell. Cameron did not recruit me."

"Did he try?"

Erin gazed at her with exasperation. "I'm not going to let you lead me down that road. You've convinced yourself that this outrageous fairy tale you've uncovered is true. Well, believe it if you wish, but don't expect me to confirm it."

"It's kind of a nice fairy tale," Catherine said. "Particularly the part about them creating a better world for all of us. I like the idea of a safety net waiting if all we do to keep the world from blowing up doesn't work." She added with a hint of grimness, "Providing that the idealistic purpose is real and that it's just not another giant commercial scam. In that case, the fairy tale would have to be torn apart and burned to cinders. Right now I'm giving it less than 50 percent."

"Because you're cynical?"

"Yes, I guess that's the reason. And I don't like the idea of anyone's hiring someone like Cameron to manipulate everything and everyone to suit himself. I don't want someone in an ivory tower making decisions that I want to make myself."

"Neither do I," Erin said quietly.

"I can see how you'd let that stand in the way. Is that why Cameron couldn't recruit you? You said that you hadn't done what he told you to do. That had something to do with the necklace. He did try to recruit you, right? Did he give you that necklace as an invitation? You weren't supposed to wear it? Did he warn you that you mustn't be seen in it?"

Erin held up her hand. "I only agreed with your philosophy. That was not an admission." She shook her head. "Nor will there be one, Catherine."

"I didn't really expect anything else," Catherine said. "But I don't think I need one. You tried very hard, but you don't exactly have a poker face. I may not have hit a bull's-eye but I came very close." She got to her feet and picked up her computer. "I'll let you relax now. I have a word to say to Hu Chang." She started to leave, then stopped. "And though you have great faith in Cameron, there must be a little doubt in your mind about the people behind him. Because you really do want to believe the fairy tale." She smiled. "Maybe that's one of the qualities that are important in their recruits. The ability to believe in fairy tales. I'd never make the first cut."

She moved down the aisle toward Hu Chang's seat. He was watching her, and when she stopped beside him, he said, "You disturbed Erin. Was it necessary?"

"Yes, I needed confirmation. It was a bizarre idea, and I wasn't totally at ease with it."

"Bizarre? Now I wonder what that could be."

"Shambhala."

"Are you watching to see my reaction?"

"No, you're harder than Erin. You would show nothing. But now that I've broken through the barrier, I think you'll talk to me. Is this conglomerate bad business?"

"I have no idea. Like you, I worked my way through to the same conclusion. Cameron could be doing idealistic work in a wicked world. Or he could be a paid operator with no conscience who carries out corrupt missions."

"He seems to be close to the monks in the monasteries."

"Is he deeply religious? Is he recruiting the lamas and monks? Neither to my knowledge. He's more interested in the plants and brews that they concoct. If he's after anything but intelligent conversation from learned individuals, I'd say it was their expertise and discoveries in the field."

"I've never felt anything like those blankets Cameron wrapped around Erin and me. They were incredible. They completely blocked the cold. He said a friend invented them."

"There may be quite a few friends providing inventions and discoveries if the people in the organization are both intelligent and gifted."

"And that young Indian boy Cameron hijacked off that train going to China might have been tapped to become one of the new breed of gifted in the organization."

"It's possible," Hu Chang said. "It occurred to me at the time." He paused. "And now you're excited, and your mind is working triple time. I was afraid of that. Before you were only concerned

with Kadmus. Now you've got your eye on Cameron and his em-
ployers. Much more dangerous, Catherine. They won't permit you
to reveal anything about them to the CIA. The only way they've
survived and flourished is because they were virtually invisible."

"I don't know enough about Cameron to reveal anything. All I
have is vague suspicions, nothing concrete." She added, "And I won't
betray Erin. She went through hell to protect Cameron. But that
doesn't mean that I'm not going to dig until I find out whether I
should go after him."

"You may not have to dig. You may be able to ask him yourself.
Cameron won't leave Erin unprotected." He shrugged. "And he
seems to be able to read you very well. If he thinks you're on the
attack, he won't wait for you to make the first move."

"He reads everyone very well." She paused. "But he promised
me that he would stay out and not intrude unless there was some
threat to me or Erin. Can I trust that promise?"

"As I told you, he's kept his word to me. But I don't know if he
would if he sensed a danger to himself."

"Is he able to do that?"

"It wouldn't surprise me. How else would he sense the danger to
you? I don't know. Cameron doesn't want me to know what other
talents he possesses. I imagine he feels more at ease if the people
around him aren't aware of anything more than he has to show them.
I've always been comfortable with that."

"I'm not."

"No, you want everything spelled out. Cameron would find
that difficult. And I didn't mean that Cameron was using any mental
tricks to read you. He could probably stay out and just use what he'd
already found out about you. He was interested enough to make a
thorough exploration. He even wanted to see how you and Luke
interacted."

She stiffened. "Luke? That's not good."

"Because you think that he could manipulate your relationship if he chose? But there's always that threat when dealing with Cameron. I find it a trifle bittersweet that he can never get away from having that hang over the heads of anyone with whom he has a relationship."

"And I only find it terrifying."

"Yet you're far more empathetic than I am. And you're always challenged to find a way to work around a problem that appears unsolvable. Why aren't you reacting like that toward Cameron?" He added softly, "I am very curious to know why you're afraid of him when I can't remember anyone else who intimidates you."

"I have my moments." She changed the subject. "When will we arrive in San Francisco?"

"About two hours."

"Then I think I'll go back and talk to Luke for a while." She wrinkled her nose. "If I can tear him away from that electronic game. He seems fascinated."

"He likes puzzles," Hu Chang said. "Like his mother. By all means, go talk to him. He may be feeling a little insecure after giving you that jolt with Tashdon."

"I'm the one feeling insecure." She turned and moved back down the aisle toward Luke.

And she was definitely feeling insecure about Cameron's unusual interest in Luke. She had felt an instant of pure panic that had turned into the beginning of fierce anger.

Yet you're far more empathetic than I am.

Hu Chang was right, her response wasn't characteristic. None of her responses to Cameron were characteristic. She had been on the defensive since the moment she had seen him and felt that first explosive bolt of sexual attraction. The knowledge of what he was and what he could do had only compounded that initial burst of wariness. His effect on her mind and body was incredibly sensual.

She had only to look at him, talk to him, and she felt weak, breath-less. Every time she had to make an effort to block it, to stop feeling and fight it.

Empathetic? Yes, she had empathy for Cameron. She could feel what he was feeling because what he was feeling was lust. The electricity between them was like a powerful wall that she wanted to reach out and touch, wrap herself, sink into the flames.

Oh, God, if he was eavesdropping now, then she was lost.

Get control. You've been able to keep steady and not do any-thing stupid or unprofessional. She didn't even know whether he was one of the good guys or a master criminal. She didn't care, she realized with shock. All she wanted to do was go to bed with him. She'd worry about the rest later.

Wrong. Worry now. Walk away.

He was too dangerous to her, maybe too dangerous to Luke.

She had reached Luke's seat, and she smiled with an effort. "Hi, I thought I'd come and let you teach me that game that you're find-ing so cool. Hu Chang just pointed out to me that we both have a passion for puzzles."

HONG KONG

Blood.

The blood was staining the floor and the rush mat where Jack Sen's mother had been doing her prayer ritual.

Her throat had been cut.

Cameron gazed down at her and felt the anger begin to surge through him. She was white-haired, small and fragile. She had not had to die. She would have told what Kadmus wanted to know with very little torture.

Or perhaps she would have not told where her son had taken Erin and Catherine. Maternal protectiveness was an amazingly strong feeling. He had just encountered that particular emotion in Catherine.

At any rate, the sight of the old lady's blood-soaked body filled him with rage. A waste of an innocent life. And he'd had a part of the ugliness that had been brought down on her. The innocent were often savaged by Kadmus, but Cameron's not being permitted to kill the bastard had caused this particular atrocity. The domino effect had started and wouldn't stop until Cameron halted it.

Banish the anger. Think. The old lady had not been dead long and consequently any information she'd told Kadmus or Brasden might not have been acted upon. The flight to San Francisco would not have landed yet. Damage control.

Don't contact Catherine as his instincts told him to do. She would be angry, too, and it might lead her to act when he preferred her to hide until he could get to her.

Hu Chang.

Two minutes later, Cameron had made contact with him. *"How long before you land?"*

"Another hour. You are well, I trust? You left us in rather tumultuous circumstances."

"I'm safe. But you may not be. I'm at the home of Jack Sen's mother, and her throat's been cut. The place has been ransacked. It's reasonable to assume that she told Kadmus everything she knew. I don't believe they would have killed her unless they were satisfied with the information she gave them. They would have toyed with her longer."

"Sen lived with his mother?"

"Yes, and he wouldn't have given her details, but he might have thought it safe to mention San Francisco."

"Then we may expect a welcoming committee?"

"Possibly. Or they may not have had time to rally their troops. The flight is going to land at a private airport. The minute it hits the ground, get Catherine, Erin, and Luke off the plane before it taxis to a hangar. Run and keep on running until you leave the airport behind. Tell Sen to taxi to the

hangar and stall for at least fifteen minutes before he opens the door. If he thinks any of Kadmus's men are at the hangar, tell him to stay put and call the police. Sen was supposed to take you to a safe house, but scratch that. Do you know anyone in San Francisco who might be safe shelter for Erin?"

"I have a few acquaintances who might qualify." He paused. "This is going to cause Catherine to be upset."

"Tell me about it."

"I believe it best that I not involve her until the last minute. Then she will only be concerned about saving Luke and Erin and not planning long-range."

"Wise man."

"That goes without saying. But that doesn't take wisdom, only the knowledge of my Catherine." His tone hardened. "I do not like the fact that Sen was vulnerable and that you're having to scramble to keep Catherine safe. I thought better of you."

"I don't like it either. Sen has always been trustworthy before. He might have gotten careless." He added wearily, "I suppose no one is trustworthy who has people he cares about."

"And whom do you care about, Cameron?" Hu Chang asked quietly.

"Why, no one," he said with bitter mockery. "That's why I'm considered so trustworthy." He was silent for a moment. "But the committee may lose faith in me shortly. They made a wrong decision, and they won't back down. I may have to force the point."

"What do you mean?"

"Just what I said. I'm on my way to San Francisco. Keep everyone safe until I get there." He broke the connection.

He shook his head regretfully as he glanced once more down at the elderly woman on the floor. Then he strode to the back of the house and slipped out the same alleyway he'd entered.

Dammit, he didn't like having to rely on Hu Chang to pull his irons out of the fire. Everything had been planned, and he'd been in total control. That's the way he liked it, the way he had to have it. He had told Catherine that, he remembered. It had made her angry and indignant. But, then, she was always indignant and angry with him. It was the nature of their relationship.

And after they had sex, it would be the same. He could not imagine anything different. He could imagine many erotic and bizarre acts with her, but her character would not change. And that would make every coming together all the more exciting.

And they would come together, he thought recklessly. The chance he was taking might very well be the end of him. He deserved a reward after all the punishment he'd taken over the years.

He deserved Catherine Ling.

.   .   .

"My mother?" Jack Sen's face was pale with pain as he glanced at Hu Chang in the copilot's seat next to him. "You're sure?"

"Cameron was sure," Hu Chang said gravely. "I regret to be the bearer of such grievous tidings."

Sen's lips twisted. "The sons of bitches." His eyes glittered with moisture. "She was gentle, kind, always smiling . . ."

"Are you willing to do as Cameron asked? There may be an element of danger for you."

Sen jerked his attention back to Hu Chang. "I'll do it," he said hoarsely. "I almost hope they are waiting at the hangar. I have my gun, and I'll use it if anyone gets in my way."

Hu Chang nodded. "Do what you must. But Cameron said to tell you to disappear. You can't help him any longer."

"I understand." Sen drew a deep, shaky, breath. "But I may be able to help my mother's soul. Someone should pay." He glanced at Hu Chang. "I'm on the approach. We should be landing in five minutes. Go back and get ready."

Hu Chang got up from the seat. "We will be ready." He hesitated as he opened the door. "But you should know that I received the impression that Cameron is planning on making them pay. Why not leave it to him?"

Sen didn't answer.

Hu Chang shrugged as he left the cockpit. He had done his best. Sen would do what his heart and mind dictated. His own job was to make their escape from the airport as speedy and seamless as possible.

He must get Catherine moving and not have second thoughts about going to the hangar with Jack Sen.

His demeanor must be perfect and reflect urgency, gravity. Maybe even desperation. Yes, desperation would be good.

He moved swiftly down the aisle. "Gather your possessions, Catherine, Erin. Quickly. Luke, help them!" His voice was hard, whiplike, and the desperation was there. "Sen tells me all hell has broken out, and our plans have to change."

•   •   •

Hu Chan threw the door open. "Out." He jumped to the ground and helped Erin to the tarmac. "Run." He jerked his head toward the woods to the west of the airport. "Head toward the woods, not the airport. Luke, go with Erin and help her." He saw him hesitate, and said impatiently, "I'll take care of Catherine."

"Right." The boy dashed past him and caught up with Erin.

Catherine glanced back over her shoulder at the plane, which was already starting to taxi. "I don't like this, Hu Chang. All you said was—What the hell went wrong?"

"Later," Hu Chang said. "There's no time. I see lights beyond those trees. We need to get through the woods to the nearest street and get a taxi." His pace increased. "Run! Don't lose sight of Luke and Erin."

She instinctively obeyed. She ran across the runway and headed for the woods. Luke had stopped, waiting for her. She motioned for him to go on. Then she put on speed to make sure that he would. She caught up with him, and, five minutes later, they were tearing through the trees. It took them all another five minutes to traverse the rough ground and ditches to make it to the street that bordered the stretch of trees.

Lights. Noise. Neon signs.

"Taxi," Hu Chang said. "Now."

"I'll get it." Luke stepped into the street in front of the wave of traffic.

"Luke!" Catherine started to go after him.

"Hey, I'm a kid. Sometimes it come in handy." Luke grinned at her as he waved down a taxi. "No one wants to mow down a kid. Rakovac used me that way all the time."

"Well, I'm not going to use you that way."

"Get in the cab, Catherine." Erin opened the passenger door. "The deed's done. Argue later."

Catherine was already heading for the cab. "I wasn't going to stage a protest. I just had a—" She broke off as she heard the high keening of a siren. "What's that?"

"The sound of foolish disobedience." Hu Chang jumped into the seat beside the driver. "Get in the cab." He turned to the taxi driver. "Chinatown. I'll give you the exact address later."

An ambulance and two police cars roared past the taxi as Catherine got in the back with Luke and Erin. "They're turning in up ahead at the airport terminal," Luke said. "I wonder . . ."

So did Catherine. Another ambulance roared by as the taxi started negotiating the traffic. She gazed at Hu Chang. "What did you mean about disobeying?"

"Jack Sen quite probably disobeyed Cameron's orders. I was wondering if he would. I hope he survived."

"What orders?"

"To lie low and call the police if there was a threat."

"What threat?" Her gaze shifted to the airport entrance they were passing. "You're saying that Sen—"

"I'm only saying Jack Sen had a weapon." He gazed meaningfully at the taxi driver. "And that I will discuss it with you later."

Catherine leaned back in her seat. She had a sinking feeling that Sen might be hurt or dead. But there was no way of knowing or even guessing until she could get Hu Chang to talk. And that wouldn't occur until they had reached their destination and could have a moment of privacy. "Chinatown? Who's in Chinatown?"

"Several million Chinese and other interesting cultural and racial blends."

"Who are we going to see?" she asked impatiently.

"A woman of beauty and intelligence who is an old and valued friend." He told the driver, "Just let us out at a restaurant on Clement Street. We'll make our own way from there." He turned back to Catherine. "To my friend, who might be persuaded to welcome us into her home."

"Don't you have any old and valued friends that aren't women?"

"A few. But women appear to be drawn to me, and I find them fascinating. My relations with men always seem to have an element of antagonism. No doubt they recognize a superior male in me."

"No doubt," she said dryly. She looked back over her shoulder, at the flashing lights of the ambulance at the airport entrance. Had Jack Sen been hurt or killed? Perhaps there was something that she could have done. Hu Chang should have told her what was going on instead of rushing her away.

"He made a choice," Hu Chang said as he saw her expression.

"But you didn't let me make one."

"I told Cameron I would keep you safe." He looked at Erin. "And you were not the only one at risk. Erin and Luke—"

"I know." She raised her hand to interrupt him. "And maybe you're right. But I can't be sure of that."

"We will have a discussion when we arrive at Chinatown, and you can make a determination."

"You promised Cameron?" Erin had focused only on that part of the conversation. "He reached you? He's all right?"

Hu Chang nodded.

Naturally, Erin would zero in on the well-being of her superhero, Catherine thought. She had not had the same response. Somehow, she had felt she would have known if anything had happened to Cameron. Crazy, unreasonable, but perfectly in sync with everything else that had gone on since she had encountered him.

"That's good," Luke said. "I thought that he would be. Cameron is a cool guy."

And maybe Luke had that same sense that he would have known that Catherine did. She hoped it wasn't true. She didn't want him to be that close to Cameron in any way.

Dangerous.

Dangerous for Luke. Dangerous for her.

CHAPTER
12

CHINATOWN

Bright lights.
Crowded streets.

The spicy sweet-sour smell of food.

A restaurant painted red with a gold dragon on the door.

"Let us out here. We will walk the rest of the way." Hu Chang paid the driver and got out of the cab. "Come along. It's not far. It will give my friend time to prepare for us."

Catherine watched the driver negotiate his way through the busy traffic. "And the name of your friend?"

"Celia Mekong." He was making a telephone call. "Ah, Celia. I have guests and perhaps a few problems. May I bring them to you? You have no commitments?" He smiled at her answer. "We will be there within twenty minutes." He hung up. "She is bored and delighted to have our company." He started down the street. "However, she must get rid of one of her commitments and prepare for us. So we will stroll slowly and enjoy people watching. The Chinatowns of America are like no others."

Luke and Erin were already walking ahead and looking into shop windows.

"Commitment?" Catherine asked.

"Celia is a courtesan."

Catherine's eyes widened. "She's a prostitute?"

"No, a courtesan. There is a vast difference. You will understand once you meet her."

"I don't have to understand. All I have to know is that Erin is
safe with her."

"As safe as the circumstances permit. Until Cameron takes care
of the root of the matter."

"Kadmus." She said, "I'm not sure Cameron is going to take care
of him. He told me that was on the forbidden list."

"He may have changed his mind. I received that indication."

"Well, I can't rely on him. I have to be ready for Kadmus when
he comes." She gazed directly into his eyes. "Or his men come, as
they did tonight. Why did we have to go on the run? Tell me what
happened at the airport, Hu Chang."

"What you've probably deduced, but I'll fill in the details."

She listened quietly, and when he'd finished, she didn't
speak for a moment. "And we don't know if Jack Sen is alive or
dead."

"He didn't have to confront Kadmus's men. I told him that I
believed Cameron was going to address the problem."

"Would that have been good enough for you? It was his mother
who was murdered, for God's sake. It wouldn't have been good
enough for me." She paused. "I need to know if there's anything I
can do for Sen."

"I will contact the airport and local hospitals and try to find out
where he was taken. Or I will have Celia call a few people she knows,
and they will be able to tell her." He smiled. "People are always eager
to do favors for Celia."

"Good." She was silent. "Cameron said he was on his way?"

"Yes."

"I don't know if I want him to come. I thought we might be done with him. He . . . disturbs me."

"I know. Then you must decide if you're willing to tolerate the disturbance for his help in keeping Erin safe."

"I don't need his help. All I need is a little time to work things out for her."

"Kadmus isn't going to give us time. And you have both Erin and Luke to protect. Help would not come amiss."

"You want Cameron to come?"

"I want you to come to terms with him. Take what you need, give what you wish. But do not hide from him."

"I'm not hiding." Or perhaps she was. And perhaps Hu Chang was right. Confront Cameron and take what she needed.

What she needed . . .

Tingling heat.

She pulled her gaze away. "I'll think about it."

"I know you will." He nodded up ahead. "There is Celia's house on the corner."

"That store?" She could see a plate-glass window displaying exquisite Chinese statues on ivory pedestals and beside it a finely carved mahogany door. "It's not what I was expecting."

"Once you get beyond that door, you will see a house that would rival any mansion in the city. The interior is absolutely stunning. But Celia's clientele quite often would prefer to be seen going into a store that can be explained rather than a luxury apartment. One of her main attractions is that she always protects the customer." He corrected himself. "Well, not main attraction, that is the product itself."

"How did you come to know her?"

"Several years ago, she was being held in a bordello in Calcutta by Li Pradka, a criminal who was scum of the Earth. She was his pride and joy. A prize he only let be sampled by special friends and clients. Celia was superbly talented, and it was considered a rare treat if she came to your bed." He smiled. "But Li Pradka annoyed me, and I decided he had to be punished. So I arranged to take Celia from him and give her a life of her own."

"Did she want to go?"

"Oh, yes, she told me later that she was only waiting for the opportunity to kill him and flee the city. It was not a life that she would have chosen for herself. She'd grown up in Greece and been kidnapped by one of the sex-slave traffickers. Li Pradka had bought her from them."

"Poor woman."

"She never pitied herself."

"Yet evidently she felt she had to go back to prostitution."

"She was not forced to do anything. I set her up here in the city with enough money for schooling and living expenses."

"Then why—"

"Ask her yourself." He motioned to Erin and Luke, who were looking at the Chinese artifacts in the window. He moved to the door and frowned as he looked at the digital-numbered lock. "I know the code for this lock, but Celia gives very few people the code. I believe we'll not use it. We must respect her privacy." He knocked on the door. "And she will not be shy about answering."

"Hu Chang!" The door was thrown open, and the woman who stood there took Hu Chang's hand and drew him into the house. "Why can't you give me notice? Do you think I wait around for you to come visit me? I'm a busy woman." She kissed him lightly on the cheek. "Actually, I do wait for you. I have no other friends that I value as much." She turned to Catherine. "And who are you?"

"Catherine Ling."

The woman was stunning. Shining red hair, green eyes, and golden skin that seemed to shimmer in the light. Her features were beautifully symmetrical and her body graceful and sexual at the same time. She was dressed in a black jumpsuit and looked sleek and sensual as a cat. Celia Mekong might be somewhere in her thirties, but it was difficult to determine. You were only aware of the dazzling total and just wanted to keep on looking.

"Thank you for allowing us to come here." Catherine gestured to Erin. "Erin Sullivan. And this is my son, Luke."

"I'm happy to have you." Her white teeth flashed as she smiled. "Hu Chang always brings me wonderful surprises." Her brow knitted as she stared at Erin. "I've seen you before. Or perhaps a photo?"

"Perhaps," Erin said. "I'm a journalist, but in this day and age, the journalist is sometimes part of the story. It shouldn't be that way, but that's the way it is."

Celia turned to Luke. "And you're such a handsome young man. But you're also probably much more complex and interesting since Hu Chang brought you. Welcome."

"Thank you." Luke was smiling awkwardly, and he was looking at Celia with a bedazzled expression.

Catherine stared at him in bemusement. Good God, even boys as young and cool as Luke fell under Celia's spell.

"We've had a long trip, Celia," Hu Chang said. "I'd be grateful if you could furnish us with rooms and hot showers."

"Of course." She gestured toward the exquisite wrought-iron staircase. "There are several bedrooms on the upper floor. I assume you'll wish to be close together if there are difficulties. You take the room I usually give you, Hu Chang. Perhaps Ms. Sullivan and Catherine Ling could share the second suite. There are two queen beds in that apartment. And let young Luke take the next room down the hall." She waved a hand. "You know where everything is, Hu Chang. Why don't you take Ms. Sullivan and Luke up and get them settled?" She smiled at Catherine. "Will you come to the kitchen and help me make a pot of tea? We can take it up to them."

Catherine nodded. "If you like."

"I do like." Celia whirled and headed down the hall. "Come along."

Catherine glanced at Hu Chang and shrugged. "I'll see you later. I guess I'm on kitchen duty."

"I expected that Celia wouldn't let you disappear right away." He gestured for Luke and Erin to go before him up the stairs. "Did I mention that she's very curious?"

He didn't wait for an answer before he started up the stairs.

Catherine gazed after him for a moment before turning and heading after Celia.

The kitchen was all stainless steel and exotic granites, beautiful woods and soft lights glowing in crystal chandeliers.

Celia was already pouring water into a huge brass carafe. "You don't mind helping me, do you? If you're tired, I can do it myself."

"You seem to be doing it yourself anyway. Why am I here?"

"You're very blunt." Celia looked up and smiled. "Because I can't resist getting to know you. I've heard of you for many years."

"From Hu Chang?"

"Yes, he doesn't come to see me often, but when he does, there is usually a mention of Catherine. He regards you as his dear friend. Hu Chang does not make many friends." She set the tea to brewing. "And I decided I must make sure you're worthy of his friendship."

Catherine smiled. She was finding the woman's frankness appealing. "And how am I to prove it to you?"

"Tell me what you feel for him." Celia looked her directly in the eye. "I will know if you lie. I have great experience with liars."

"What do I feel for him?" Catherine was silent, thinking. "I think he's part of me, but it's a part that I may never know completely. He's my friend who will never leave me, who will never let me know loneliness, who can finish my sentences almost before I begin them. He came to me when I was just struggling to stay alive and taught me why staying alive was important. How to reach out and grasp the joy of every moment. I've put my life on the line to save him, and I would do it again tomorrow." She ended simply, "Because I would not want to live in a world that held no Hu Chang."

"Very eloquent," Celia said slowly. Then a warm smile lit her face. "But truthful, I think. I believe Hu Chang is safe with you."

"I'm glad you're satisfied."

"Not entirely. Do you sleep with him?"

Catherine blinked. "No, I told you, he's my friend."

She shrugged. "Friends sometimes make the very best lovers. They care about your pleasure. That's very important. You have a son. Was your relationship with your husband very close? Was he your friend as well as your lover?"

"You have no right to ask me that."

"But the fact that you don't want to answer indicates that he might have been one but not the other," Celia said shrewdly. "I will make my own guess which it is."

"Terry was a wonderful man, older, but a good lover. He was my mentor when I first became an agent with the CIA. We wanted the same things, a home, a child, a normal life."

"He was a friend," Celia said triumphantly. "I knew it."

"How nice that you can make a judgment on my marriage from only a few words," Catherine said dryly.

"I'm very clever about reading people. I've had to be. My life has been filled with men who lie and cheat to get what they want. I've learned to know how to keep them from getting it," Celia said. "Ask Hu Chang."

"I'd rather ask you," Catherine said boldly. "You've had no compunction about asking me personal things. Now it's my turn."

Celia's brows rose. "You think I'll object? Not now that I know that Hu Chang has reason to trust you. I'm not ashamed of anything I've done in my life. Go ahead, ask me."

"Did *you* sleep with Hu Chang?"

She threw back her head and laughed. "I knew that was coming. You're as curious about me and I am about you. No, I did not.

Though I did offer and was refused. I think that, in spite of the fact that he's very worldly and the wisest man I've ever known, he's burdened by a conscience. I couldn't convince him that I wasn't offering out of gratitude."

"Why did you offer?"

"He's exciting, like a mystery that has no end. He'd be a very good lover. I wanted to try him . . ." She shrugged. "But it's probably better that I didn't. I have a tendency to try to control men. That wouldn't work with Hu Chang. And if it did, he would no longer be my friend."

"I don't think you'd need to worry. Hu Chang can't be controlled."

"I don't think so either. But sex is everything, sex rules the world. I've only met two men since I discovered that truth who I wasn't able to control with sex." She grinned. "It was a devastating blow to my ego, but I recovered."

"Who were they?"

Celia shook her head. "I don't reveal names. All my clients are confidential. They can trust me."

Catherine was silent a moment.

"Ask it," Celia said softly. "It always comes down to this question. Ask it."

"Why are you doing this? You're obviously very bright. Hu Chang gave you money. You could have gone to school and become anything you wished."

"This is what I wish," Celia said quietly. "When Hu Chang took me away from that bordello in Calcutta, I was very grateful, but not for the reason you would think. I didn't consider myself a victim whose body was raped and ravaged, a helpless sex slave. Yes, I felt that way when I was sold to Li Pradka. The first month was hell. But then I discovered something that I hadn't known about myself. I didn't hate what was being done to me anymore. I was liking it . . . I was *loving* it."

"What?"

"You're shocked. I can't help that I don't think like you. I'm intensely sexual. I *need* sex. I learned to divorce myself from the individual and just enjoy the act. The only thing I hated was that I had to take, not give."

"I don't understand."

"I had to submit and respond. I don't like submission. I wanted to be the one in control. I wanted to be so good at what I was doing that my partner would do anything to keep me from stopping. So I took another step and began to learn how to be that good. I talked to prostitutes at the bordello, I experimented, I read books. From the Kama Sutra to Marquis De Sade. I studied sexual pleasure in all forms. Some I liked, some I didn't. But I learned them all, and in the end, I made them my own." She got a tray down from the cabinet. "I wasn't a victim by the time Hu Chang decided to rescue me. Any man who went to bed with me played by my rules because he knew the rewards. He was eager to let me guide the play. Occasionally, I was sent someone who was so twisted that I had a few problems, but I found a way to keep him subdued." Her tone was without emotion. "But it pointed out that I had to get away from Li Pradka. I was very grateful when Hu Chang took me away from Calcutta." She took out an exquisite teapot of Chinese origin. "Isn't this lovely? It was a gift from a sheik from Kuwait. I usually don't accept gifts. A sum is just paid into my bank account for a designated period. Additional gifts sometime makes the client feel that he's the giver. But this pot is very old, priceless, and it pleased me."

"It's amazing." And so was Celia. Her frankness was only matched by her cheerful matter-of-factness. "And did the sheik please you?"

She chuckled. "When I schooled him a little. One of the reasons I enjoy the first time is that it stimulates my mind as well as gives me release. By the second time, I know to what lengths of excess I can drive him that will make him mine."

"You speak as if your clients are stallions."

"They all think they are. And if I can make them go away believing that they're the greatest stallion in the barn, then I've done my job."

"And you actually don't mind being—"

"A whore?"

"Hu Chang calls you a courtesan. But I'm having trouble distinguishing the differences."

"Most people do. Economically, it means that I'm paid enormous amounts of money. I can demand a price for a night or two that would buy an apartment building. For a week, the price is enough to enrich my investment portfolio to the tune of over a million. I've slept with some of the richest and most influential men in the world." She poured water over the tea leaves. "The difference for me is that I have a vocation and a skill and that I enjoy my life. I enjoy sex." She paused. "And I can't do without it. I need it frequently and varied. I tried to slack off for a while after I came to San Francisco. I even went to a therapy group. But they were all too gloomy and troubled. I wasn't either. So I figured I could make a better life without them. And I did. I'm doing very well. I hired a private investigator, who is also my agent. At first it went slowly, but then word spread." She made a face. "Don't let anyone tell you that men don't talk if they've found a fantastic lay. I made sure it was discreet, and my investigator checked out every client to make sure that I wouldn't run into something I couldn't handle."

"Which doesn't appear to be likely."

"It wasn't. After these last years, I have a fat stock-market portfolio that assures me security and I'm very, very wealthy."

"But still not tempted to retire."

"Why should I? I told you, it's my vocation . . . and my pleasure. I love every minute of the sex act. It's hard to explain to you—" She searched for words. "I'm . . . superb. You can't imagine the power. There's no one better at what I do. Sex means everything to men. It's like being a queen."

"Just so you don't abuse that power."

"I've never been tempted. I don't need to play those games." She set lemon, cream, and sugar on the tray. "I'll take the tray. You get the door." She glanced at Catherine as she picked up the tray. "How do you feel about me now after our little chat?"

"What do you mean?"

"Pity? Disgust? Threatened? Some women feel antagonistic toward my profession."

"I don't feel any of those emotions. I still don't understand, but I'm trying. My mother was a whore, and I grew up on the docks where she and her friends plied their trade. All I knew was despair and drugs and men who hurt my mother. The life killed her when I was a little girl. She was a true victim. I've never run across anyone on the other end of the scale."

"I'm sorry," Celia said gently. "I know that was hard for you. I've been there. It tends to scar . . ." She moved toward the staircase. "Do you have trouble with sex now? I'll help if you like."

Catherine blinked. "What?"

"You saw only the women around you as sex slaves. I'll teach you a few tricks and moves that will ensure that will never happen to you."

Catherine chuckled. "A queen, not a slave?"

"Exactly. It won't take long. You won't be anywhere near as expert as I am, but you'll be extraordinary."

"Thank you for the offer," she said solemnly. "But I believe I'll pass."

"If you change your mind . . ." She started up the stairs. "I was troubled that your husband was a friend, not lover. I thought that there might be a problem. I know Hu Chang wishes only the best for you. I thought I might help give it to you."

"If I decide I need to be queen of the bedroom, I'll let you know." She was silent, then said, "I'm truly not unappreciative. You have a good heart, Celia."

"That's true," Celia said. "And I think you may, too. We will become good friends and give each other many gifts."

"But you don't accept gifts."

"Only from friends. Knock on that first door. We will let Hu Chang set up this tray and call Erin Sullivan and your Luke. We have labored enough."

"But I'm certain you took your reward," Hu Chang said as he opened the door. "Is your curiosity satisfied?"

"Yes, but it didn't go only one way." She handed him the tray. "Catherine was also curious. But now all is well, we're on our way to friendship, and we both know that you're safe."

"I knew that before." Hu Chang looked at Catherine. "I called the local hospital and could get no information. So I called Venable and let him probe. Sen is at St. James Hospital. Two men are dead. Jack Sen is wounded but not badly."

"Thank God. Though who knows what will happen to him once the police start questioning him."

"Police?" Celia asked. "Serious trouble then, Hu Chang?"

"Very serious."

"Don't just leave it at that," Catherine said impatiently. "She should know the danger." She turned to Celia. "Jack Sen was our pilot. His mother was murdered when they questioned her about where he was bringing us. He could have avoided the people who did it, he chose revenge." She added bluntly, "I can't promise you they won't come after you, too."

"I'm glad you told me," Celia said. "But it won't change my decision. Running away from anything is always a form of submission. What can I do for you? Do you need a car, a jet, a boat? I have many clients who would be happy to make me happy."

"I will let you know," Hu Chang said. "There are decisions to be made. I'm content that you're providing us with a place to rest and make those decisions. Now I will go and get Erin and Luke so that they can partake of your wonderful tea." He paused at the door.

"Venable said to tell you his own decision still stands, Catherine." He gazed at her inquiringly. "And that decision was?"

"He wants to cut Erin loose." She poured tea into a cup. "I won't let him do it. I just have to figure out a way to force the issue."

"Another decision to be made." He moved silently down the hall. But the next moment, they heard him open a door, and call, "It is time for tea, Luke. You will enjoy it. Your hostess is expert at many, many wonderful skills, and that is one of them."

"What else does she do?" Luke asked as he moved down the hall. "Besides tea, I mean."

"She knows many exciting, intricate secrets. Perhaps, if you're very polite and kind, she will show them to you someday."

"Oh, Lord," Catherine murmured.

"Not before eighteen." Celia's eyes were sparkling with mischief. She tilted her head consideringly. "Or maybe sixteen if he is ready . . ."

·   · .   ·

Catherine and Erin's suite had been dark for nearly thirty min-utes, but Catherine knew Erin wasn't sleeping. She could hear the sound of her restless movements and light, shallow breathing in the next bed.

"Catherine?"

"I'm awake. But I hoped you'd give it up and go to sleep."

"I can't sleep. What are we going to do about Jack Sen?"

"We'll think of something. His life could be ruined if the police arrest him, and he has to go through that nightmare. Venable can make people disappear if he needs it to happen. Maybe I can convince him that he needs Sen to be whisked off the scene."

"Maybe." Erin was silent. "I was really happy that I was away from that damned palace. I was almost giddy. But I'm coming down now. Death. Everywhere I turn, there's death. And it's all connected to me."

"I won't deny you're the center, but I'd stake my life that you're not responsible for one particle of it."

"I am, you know." Her voice was faint in the darkness. "I wore the necklace. Cameron told me not to wear it."

Catherine stiffened. "He did?"

"He said to keep it safe and send it to him if I needed him or if I changed my mind."

It was the first time that Erin had indicated that Catherine's guesswork might have a basis in fact. Don't push it. Keep everything low-key. "Changed your mind?"

"I wanted to change my mind. I really did. Such a beautiful dream. You'd think it was beautiful, too."

"Would I?"

"But you can't believe in dreams, can you? You're afraid that they'll interfere with your reality. I was like that once. Hell, I'm a journalist. I deal in facts. But since I've been working in Tibet, I've been changing. The life is so simple, it has a kind of purity. It lures you into thinking that all life should be clean and simple, with rules that everyone obeys. A world without men like Kadmus and countries that want to blow everyone to kingdom come."

"That's the way it should be," Catherine said. "But you're right, it's only a beautiful dream." She had to move slowly, carefully. "Why would Cameron tell you not to wear that necklace?"

"He was trying to protect me. He said that he couldn't be sure that it would be safe for me." She was silent a moment. "I know you want me to tell you everything, but I can't do it. I don't have that right. But you've risked your life for me. Your son's at risk now, too. I can't treat you as if you were a stranger. I trust you. I consider you my friend."

"I am your friend."

"And because you're my friend, I can't let you go on thinking that Cameron is totally ruthless. It's not true."

"I saw those wounds on your body. He could have stepped in and stopped it."

"He told me when he gave me the necklace that he couldn't help me if I didn't do what he told me." She went on in a rush, "He's not what you think. Oh, yes, he's tough, and maybe he wants his own way. But if you could have seen him the way I did at the earthquake site at Qinghai, you'd know how wonderful he is."

"He was at Qinghai?"

"Yes," she said. "I was there with the monks trying to rescue the people buried under the ruins of the villages. We had little help from the Chinese soldiers because they had developed altitude sickness. The second day, we had to make our way down a trail that was almost nonexistent to reach a buried school. When we finally made it, I saw that a man was already there working with a pick to clear the rubble. I was stunned. I couldn't imagine how he had gotten down there. But the monks weren't surprised. It was Cameron, and they knew him. And during the next twelve hours, I got to know him, too. Though he never told me his name. It didn't bother me, it wasn't a time for names. It was a time to get those kids out. And I didn't get over being stunned for that entire twelve hours. He started giving orders, telling us exactly where to dig. I knew later that he was mentally communicating with the children buried beneath that rubble. At the time, I thought he was either a domineering bastard or maybe that he was some kind of earthquake-retrieval specialist. But every time we dug where he told us to dig, we found a child. We kept digging. There were two dead in that school, but we were able to save eleven. Eleven who would have probably died if left much longer to the elements. We had to bring three up to the top on stretchers. Cameron worked as hard as we did to get those kids up that trail. No, harder. His energy was amazing. But when we got near the top, he stopped and said for us to go ahead and that he'd go back down and check out the school for any more survivors. That was the last I saw of him. We worked at that earthquake site for another three days, and I never ran into him." She fell silent. "But I already knew the kind of man he was. During that time, he was tireless and smart and gentle with the children. He was larger-than-life, and that's what we needed at Qinghai."

"You must have impressed him, too." She paused. "Because he looked you up and came after you, didn't he?"

She didn't speak for a moment. "Yes."

The answer was so brief that Catherine knew there would be no elaboration. She had told her story about Cameron because she wanted Catherine to stop condemning him. But what had transpired later was too private for her to divulge. "I worked very hard trying to put the puzzle together. Will you tell me if I came close?"

Another silence. "You're very clever, Catherine." She turned over on her side. "Good night."

"Good night."

It was answer enough. Erin wasn't about to go any further. So at least the bare bones of the answers she'd drawn had come close to the truth.

Maybe.

But she thought Erin was done with deception. She'd done all she could to protect Cameron and the people he represented, but she wouldn't lie to Catherine. Complete disclosure was something else. She was still stubbornly silent.

Because Erin had been caught up in a dream, a beautiful dream . . .

•   •   •

"I need to know where Jack Sen is, Catherine."

Cameron, she realized drowsily.

Then she came wide-awake. "I thought you were only to come visiting by invitation only, Cameron. You woke me."

"I'll make sure you go back to sleep. And I'm suspending that promise for the duration. Things are going to get very edgy during the next few days. Where is Jack Sen?"

"At St. James Hospital. Why didn't you link with Hu Chang as you did before? He could have told you."

"Because I wanted to be with you. And I've decided that it's time I did what I wanted to do. I tried to get through to Sen, but they must have drugged him. I just knew he was hurt."

"And he's in trouble. I don't know when the police will transfer him to county facilities."

"I'll take care of him. I just had to know his location."

"What are you going to do?"

"At the moment, nothing except make a few plans and preparations. I'm in a jet over the Pacific and won't arrive in San Francisco for another six hours."

"You took a jet? I'm surprised you just don't don your Superman cape and zoom faster than a speeding bullet. And what will you do when you finally arrive here?"

"I won't let Jack Sen be punished anymore for doing a service for me. He's already suffered enough."

"I was going to ask Venable to do—"

"That's not the way I operate. Keep Venable out of it. I'll handle it."

She stiffened. "I'll do what I think best."

He was silent. "I know you will. But don't start a chain of actions I'll have to dodge around."

"You mean don't get in your way."

"That's another way of putting it." He smiled. "Any other time, I'd be delighted to have you in my way. It would be pure pleasure having to deal with you."

"Deal? In what way?"

"Mentally or physically or both." His voice was soft, infinitely sensual. "I've had quite a few hours on this plane to think about all the things I want to do to you. Would you like to see a few?"

Heat.

Her stomach clenched, and she found it hard to breathe.

"No."

"I believe I'll show you just a glimpse. I owe you for that Superman crack."

"You should be used to it. I'm sure other people resent the—"

He was over her, his hand parting her thighs, his lips on her nipple. Then, with one plunge, he was inside, huge in her tightness, hot, moving, lifting her with each thrust.

Madness. Frantic need. Every nerve and muscle in her body convulsing as he moved.

The scene changed.

He was still inside her, but her wrists were cuffed above her head. She couldn't move, but the erotic need was now even more intense. He was moving slowly, his fingers plucking, teasing, doing things to her that were indescribable. The muscles of her stomach were tensing, convulsing. Her very helplessness made the acts even more arousing. She wanted to move, take him, all of him. Draw him into her make him—

He was gone from her body.

And she was left panting and frustrated and wanting to kill him.

"You son of a bitch."

"Which one did you like better?" He was smiling. "I was wondering about that exotic variation, but your response was pretty close to equal. Which makes me think that you're going to be a magnificently diverse lover."

"Not your lover."

"You're angry and indignant at the moment, but did I do anything you didn't want, except stop? You're still wanting it, and that isn't me, it's you." He added, "And that was very close to how it's going to feel, only better. I took as much of your physical sensory potential as I could gather to make it absolutely real and good for you."

"Real? You said you were doing it to punish me."

"I lied. I did it because I had to have you. I've wanted you from the beginning, and I had to show you what we're like together." He added

softly, "I can't wait to taste your breasts, to get inside you. You want that, too. We're both hungry and a little wild with it. It has to happen soon, Catherine." His eyes were glittering with that wildness, and she could feel the hot, sweeping lust melt deep within her. He saw it, felt it, and his voice hoarsened. "No force. No games. Your rules."

She swallowed hard. Her heart was beating so hard, she couldn't breathe. She couldn't even argue that what he'd said wasn't true. She was hot, shaking, her breasts still taut and aching.

She wanted him.

"Then that's all I needed for now," he said. "I want you to remember that I've never wanted a woman the way I want you. I think about you all the time. I don't think it's going to go away even after we have sex. It's like a crazy, aching fever and not like me at all." He leaned back in the chair, and his beautifully shaped, sensual lips were curved in a rueful half smile. "That's a big admission for me. I regard it as a weakness. Enjoy it. I'll see you soon."

He was no longer with her.

And she wanted him back.

She wanted him in her body, she wanted his hands touching her, bringing her to the point of climax and past it. She wanted to stare at that beautiful, sensual face and watch his mouth, listen to the deep masculinity of his voice. Feel him, see him, taste him.

She drew a deep, uneven breath and forced her clenched hands to relax.

Block it. Block *him*. Though she didn't believe that he had anything directly to do with what she was feeling at this moment. He had left her, dammit. It was a lingering aftereffect from that searing explosion of carnal need.

She tried to relax her muscles, but it wasn't easy. Her entire body was ready for sex. She wanted to blame it on Cameron, but she knew it wasn't entirely his fault. This had been coming from the moment she had seen him in that cozy library he had mentally created for her, looking so damn sexy that she had been immediately turned on. Which was completely uncharacteristic of her. He had said what he felt for her wasn't at all like him. Well, this wasn't like her either. She didn't like it. She wouldn't have it.

Only what could she do about it when she was unable to fight it? She didn't even want the desire to go away, she just wanted it satisfied. Celia had said something like that, and she hadn't understood.

Now she understood. Only Celia was enamored with the act itself, and Catherine was lost in a barbaric sexual fascination for one damnably difficult man.

Work on it. Take apart the physical response and try to make sense of it and then downplay it. Or go back to sleep and push it away. That would probably be the best solution. Then when she woke, she would be busy and not thinking of Cameron.

But he was on his way. He would be here soon. She would see him.

She felt an aching burning start between her thighs at the thought.

But she'd be surrounded by people, there would be a job to do. Neither of them would be concerned with anything but Kadmus and keeping Erin safe. It would be okay.

If she could just get to sleep. If she could keep her heart from beating so hard. If she could make her tense muscles relax. If she could forget the feel of him in her body.

It was going to be a long night.

CHAPTER

13

You don't look as if you've slept well." Hu Chang's eyes were narrowed on Catherine's face as she came into the dining room for breakfast the next morning. "Sit down and have a cup of tea." He poured her tea and handed it to her. "Was something bothering you?"

"You mean besides Kadmus breathing down our necks and Venable dragging his heels about giving Erin protection?" She picked up her cup. "Do you blame me for lying awake and trying to find a way out?"

"I never blame you for anything. I was just inquiring."

Catherine turned to Erin. "It's going to be all right. I'll handle Venable. I didn't really lie awake fretting about it."

"I wasn't worried. I don't have as much confidence in Venable as you do. If he bowed out, it wouldn't mean that much to me." She smiled. "Besides, Cameron is coming."

"Yes, he is." She looked down into the tea in her cup. "He should be here anytime now."

"You're very certain," Hu Chang said. "Is there reason for that certainty?"

She looked up and met his gaze. She knew that Hu Chang had

been aware that Cameron could reach out to her when he wished. Why try to hide this last invasion? Perhaps because it had been so intensely personal. "He was six hours away last night. He wanted to know where Jack Sen was. He couldn't reach him."

"And Cameron wanted *you* to tell him where he could find Sen," Hu Chang said. "Interesting."

She didn't answer. "Where's Luke?" she asked instead. "He usually doesn't sleep this late."

"He didn't this morning either," Erin said. "He was going out in the garden with Celia when I came down. He was telling her all about some new fertilizer he and Hu Chang had concocted." She smiled. "She acted totally fascinated."

"No act," Hu Chang said. "She has a great zest for living, and she likes Luke. Her garden is a postage stamp compared to Chen Lu's, but she's a very enthusiastic gardener." He lifted his own cup to his lips. "She's very enthusiastic about everything that interests her."

"I've noticed that tendency to—"

The doorbell rang, and Hu Chang quickly rose to his feet. "If you're not mistaken, that may be Cameron. I'll let him in."

"You know the code?" Catherine answered her own question. "That's right, you said you did. What was I thinking? No one is closer to Celia than—"

"You all look very comfortable." Cameron was standing in the arched doorway of the dining room. "It's a shame to disturb you, but we've got to get moving." He reminded Catherine of a storm wind as he came into the room. "There were only two men at the airport last night, but Kadmus will have half a dozen more searching for you by now."

"I gave the taxi driver an address on Clement Street, several blocks from here. With all its alleys and byways, Chinatown can be a very confusing place," Hu Chang said. "It will take him time."

"And how do you know how many men Kadmus can muster here in San Francisco, Cameron?" Catherine asked.

"Kadmus has an entire West Coast operation here that handles art artifacts and drugs he channels through here. Mark Nagle usually works out of L.A., but he's on tap for any job Kadmus orders him to do. He has a sizable team and enough corrupt influence in city government to be troublesome. It was Nagle who ordered those scumbags to grab you at the airport." He turned to Catherine. "Where's the boy?"

"In the garden."

"I don't want him to go anywhere alone, even in this house. I don't want Kadmus to have any chance of getting his hands on him. He's your Achilles' heel." He met her gaze and added curtly, "Which makes him my Achilles' heel."

She stiffened. He had been so sharp and businesslike since he'd appeared that she'd thought it was going to be okay. But the electricity between them was suddenly tangible. "I'll take care of my son."

"We'll all keep an eye on him, Cameron," Erin said quietly. "Though he takes pretty good care of himself."

"Don't rely on it." For the first time since he'd entered the room, he smiled. "How are you, Erin?"

"Better in some ways. Not so good in others. I want the killing to stop."

"It will. Give me a little while."

She nodded. "I know you're doing your best."

He turned back to Hu Chang. "I figure that you'll be safe here for perhaps another twenty-four hours. That should give us enough time. I have to take care of Jack Sen, but then I'll be able to concentrate on Kadmus."

Catherine said dryly, "Meanwhile, as you said, he'll be concentrating extremely hard on us. He'll be very glad that you're planning a diversion."

"Twenty-four hours," he repeated.

"And how are you going to 'take care' of Jack Sen?" She didn't wait for an answer. "Oh, that's right, Hu Chang said that you have teams all over the world just waiting to obey your every word." Her voice was faintly mocking. "Are they better than this Nagle Kadmus turned loose on us?"

"John Blake is a good man," Cameron said quietly. "And the people he uses to help me are also very good." He met her eyes. "Would you rather I go up against Kadmus's pet snake, Nagle, by myself?"

She shook her head. "No."

"Good, because it wouldn't happen. Blake's men will go into the hospital and get him at lunchtime when the staff is busiest. He'll be taken down to the morgue and put in an ambulance to be driven off the property. I'll have him on a private jet back to Hong Kong an hour later. He'll be taken to a private hospital in Tibet to recover."

"You make it sound easy," Catherine said. "There will be police guards and security and nursing staff at that hospital. It's not going to be so simple."

"Money makes everything simple. The guard at the door will be suddenly taken deathly ill and rush to the bathroom to throw up. He's already been furnished with a pill to make sure that happens and protect him from sellout accusations after the fact. The head nurse will keep everyone away from the area by slowing paperwork at the desk and keeping the nurses on duty busy down the hall, helping with the meal distribution. It will take three minutes to disconnect Sen's tubes and get him out of the room, down the hall and into the elevator. One minute to get him to the garage level. Another minute to transfer him to the ambulance. By that time, there will be a ruckus when they discover Sen's gone. But the ambulance will be out of the garage and driving down the street while they're still scrambling."

"Bribes," Catherine said. "No violence?"

"That wouldn't be efficient. I always prefer money whenever possible."

"How much money?"

"Substantial. Some would say astonishing. Enough to sway any-one to take a chance if they thought they could get away with it. It was particularly important in this case because the time factor was so short. I didn't know exactly what method I'd be using to extract Sen before I found out he was in the hospital. I had to notify Blake, the head of the team here, that a fix had to be made immediately. But he made it happen."

"I only talked to you seven hours ago."

He smiled. "I told you, Blake is very, very good. He had every-thing else in place about the actual exit plan from when I contacted him before I left Hong Kong."

"Then you clearly knew before you got on that plane that Sen wouldn't obey your orders," Hu Chang said.

"There was a possibility that he would." He shrugged. "But I had to prepare damage control in case he didn't."

"I still might be able to persuade Venable that we should get Sen out," Catherine said.

"I'm sure you could persuade a leopard to change its spots, but we don't have time. If we don't get him out, then he'll be taken to jail. Or Kadmus might order him killed in the hospital to set an example for killing two of his men. It wouldn't take nearly as much money as I spent to bribe someone to put a lethal dose in his bot-tle." He met her eyes. "I can't risk Venable's saying no to you."

"And you're sure this Blake will be able to get him out of San Francisco?"

"The chances are 85 percent positive. I've had him do similar jobs for me before here in San Francisco. He's very good at extrac-tion."

"Extraction," she repeated. "Like the young Indian boy you ar-ranged to be extracted from that train on the way to China?"

He grimaced. "Hu Chang has been talking."

"A little," Hu Chang said. "The circumstance warranted it. In the end, my loyalty is not to you but to Catherine."

"Understandable." Cameron said to Catherine, "Yes, that was considered an extraction. I sanction and personally do a good many." He made a chopping motion with his hand. "And I do it well. So you should feel comfortable that Jack Sen will just be another one in a long list."

"I'm not comfortable," she said bluntly. "I want Sen to be out of danger, but I don't want any innocent people hurt. Can you guarantee that won't happen?"

"No, but I've done everything I can to assure that it won't." He paused. "Look, I'm going to be in constant contact with Blake throughout the extraction. I'll be in a car a few blocks from the hospital when that ambulance pulls out of the garage. If anything goes wrong, I'll be there to take charge. I'll follow the ambulance to the airport and be there until Sen is on the plane and off the ground."

"That will be a risk for you." Erin frowned. "Kadmus won't care a damn about Jack Sen if he finds out you're anywhere near him."

"Then hopefully he won't. Though there's a strong possibility that the hospital is being watched. What will be, will be. I'll adapt."

"How fatalistic," Catherine said. "And stupid."

"I'm sending Blake in to do the job. It may not be as clean as I'd like. I have to back him." He added softly, "I'm touched you care."

Heat.

Push it away.

"You didn't worry that much when Erin was in trouble. You didn't go near her. You were only concerned about your precious rules."

"Catherine," Erin said sharply. "I told you that—"

"Hush," Cameron said gently. "I don't need you to defend me." He said to Catherine, "You're right, but I've decided I have to change the rules. Kadmus has to be stopped no matter what anyone else thinks. But I have to make sure there are no hostages when I make a move. Jack Sen could be a hostage."

Catherine was silent, studying him. He was telling the truth. At least, she thought he was being sincere. How did she know with all those mental tricks?

"You know," he said. *"And all the tricks are over. We're so close now, I can't stop being with you. But I won't lie, and I won't manipulate."*

She pulled her eyes away from him. "No, I don't like hostage situations either, but I don't like the idea of your running the risk." She forced a smile. "You have a few unique talents. I might have use for you later."

"I have every intention of letting you use me later. I'm leaving now. I should be back here by three, and we'll start moving toward Kadmus."

She stood up. "I'm going with you." The words had come out of nowhere and caught her by surprise. "You may need backup yourself."

"No." He turned and moved toward the arched door. "Stay close to the house and don't let—"

"Cameron?" Celia stood in the doorway with Luke beside her. Her eyes were wide with shock as she stared at him. "What are you doing here?"

"Just leaving." He smiled at her. "It's good to see you again, Celia. I take it that Hu Chang didn't mention that I was involved in this problem he threw at you?"

"No. I prefer not to know details where Hu Chang is concerned. You're . . . a surprise."

More than a surprise, Catherine realized. She had never thought Celia would ever lose her composure, but she was coming very close.

"And so are you," Cameron said. "More beautiful than the last time I saw you. And generous, as usual. Hu Chang couldn't have chosen anyone better." He turned to Luke. "I hear you've been busy. I got a very irritated report from Tashdon about you."

Luke stiffened. "He said that you told him to hurt Catherine. You didn't, did you?"

"No, but I told him to stop her. I didn't want her hurt. It evidently didn't translate well."

Luke frowned. "She had the right to do what she wanted. I would have helped her." His expression cleared. "But I'm glad you didn't mean anyone to hurt her. I didn't think you'd do that."

"I've just been getting advice from Luke about my garden," Celia said. "But it's time to eat. We came in to get breakfast orders. I'm a magnificent cook. Won't you change your mind and stay?"

He shook his head. "Thank you, I have things to do. Another time."

Celia smiled brilliantly. "Anytime."

Catherine inhaled sharply. That intimate smile could not be misinterpreted.

My God, they were lovers.

"No. You're reading too much into—Dammit, I can't get through to you. Your mind is all over the place."

"Lovers."

"Catherine, it's not—"

"It doesn't matter to me. I don't care."

"Cameron has to go, Celia," Catherine said. "Could I help you make breakfast? I'm sure I'm not as good as you, but I'll play kitchen help."

Cameron was silent a moment. "She'll have to find someone else to help." He smiled recklessly. "Have you forgotten, Catherine? You've just offered to be my backup. I've decided to take you up on it." He went back, grasped her wrist, and pulled her to her feet. "Let's go."

She could see Luke staring at her with a puzzled expression. If she struggled or caused a scene, she didn't know what his reaction would be. The last thing she wanted was for Luke to confront

Cameron. "If that's what you want." She smiled at Luke. "We'll be back in a couple hours. Why don't you help Celia?"

He nodded. "I will."

She glanced at Hu Chang. He was very still, his eyes narrowed on her. "You handle everything here, okay?"

"With my usual splendid efficiency and understanding." His glance went to Cameron. "And you will do the same, I trust."

"You can count on me trying my utmost to do that," Cameron said.

The next moment, they were out of the room and in the hallway. She immediately pulled her wrist away. "That was unnecessary. Why did you do it?"

"Because if I'd left you for the next four hours to come to your own conclusions, you'd have developed a mind-set that I'd have had to use a diamond-tipped drill to get through." He opened the front door. "It was easier to confront the problem now."

"There is no problem."

He led her to a dark blue Mercedes at the curb and opened the passenger door. "Not now that I have you where I can control it. We have a couple hours waiting at the hospital for Blake to do his job. I should be able to get through to you by then."

"All you should be concentrating on is getting Jack Sen away from here."

"And I would, if it weren't for you, dammit." He started the car. "But it's not happening. So I'll have to—"

"Adapt? Isn't that what you said?"

"Multitask. Now be quiet and let me get to somewhere that I can talk to you."

"Why do you have to go anywhere special? After all, you're a double threat as far as communication is concerned."

"Evidently I'm not communicating too well at the moment," he said grimly. "We should be at the hospital in fifteen minutes. Just don't start building your mental scenarios until we get there."

"This is completely unreasonable. I have no interest in—"

"Fifteen minutes."

It was closer to ten minutes when he pulled into a curbside parking space across the street from the hospital with a clear view of the garage exit. Not really clear, she thought. It had started to rain, and the large drops driving against the windshield would have made it hard to see the exit anyway. They were completely cocooned in the rain driving against the car.

He put the Mercedes in park and turned to face her. "Yes, Celia and I had sex several years ago," he said curtly. "We were not lovers, the way you would define it. There's no reason for you to go off the rails like this."

"I agree. What you did with her or any other woman should mean absolutely nothing to me." She unsnapped her seat belt. "I was just surprised. I suppose I shouldn't have been since you obviously had her house code. It didn't sink home when you walked into the dining room."

"I've never used the code before. She gave it to me when I put her on her flight home from Bangkok."

"Hu Chang said she's almost fanatically cautious about giving that code out. You must have been special to her."

"Special? No, more in the line of unfinished business."

"I didn't mean to pry." She wasn't looking at him. "You don't owe me any—"

"Hush." His hands were suddenly tightly grasping her shoulders. "I know I don't owe you anything. I'm straightening this out purely for my own benefit. Something's going on between us, and I won't have it destroyed almost before it begins."

"There's nothing to straighten out." She still wouldn't look at him. "There's a sexual attraction, of course, but that wouldn't give me any right to resent anything you do now or have done in the past. We're both mature adults who live their own lives. This brief encounter will lead nowhere and shouldn't be perceived as—"

He muttered a curse, then she was in his arms, his mouth on hers, his tongue playing wildly, deeply, with her own.

Heat. Tingling between her thighs. Breasts taut, swelling.

Her mouth was opening wider as she made a sound of need deep in her throat.

Fight him. This is crazy. Crazy . . .

Her blouse was open and her bra unfastened . . .

"Catherine." His hands were cupping her breasts, then rubbing, pulling at the nipples.

She lunged upward as she felt his teeth gnaw at her nipple.

Need.

His hands were squeezing, his mouth moving. "Beautiful . . . Give me more."

She couldn't help but give him more. Her breasts were swelling with response to that erotic stimulation, pushing against his lips, his tongue. She moved closer, lifting, offering. "That's right," he murmured. "Let me have them. Let me play . . ."

Not play, she thought hazily. Her whole body was on fire, and he was drawing a response with his mouth that was driving her crazy. But maybe it was play to him. Maybe he knew what he was doing to her and—

"No." She jerked away from him, her eyes blazing. "What the hell are you doing?"

"What you want me to do." He was breathing hard, his cheeks flushed, his eyes glittering. "What I want to do. Don't give me that bullshit about being civilized, mature adults. What we're feeling is purely barbaric, with nothing civilized about it." He watched her tuck her breasts back into her bra and start to button her blouse. "I want to be inside you. If you'd let me, I'd pull you in the backseat right now. It's raining so hard no one could see us. But I wouldn't give a damn if they could see me over you, in you. I *need* you."

And she needed him. She had never needed anyone like this

before; the intensity was taking her breath, melting her. She shook her head. "I . . . give a damn."

"I know. I can see it." He moistened his lips as he gazed at the curve of her breast as she buttoned her blouse. "And that's why I'm holding on." He drew a deep breath. "Believe it or not, this isn't my usual—" He stopped and started again. "I don't know why you have this effect on me. It must be a punishment for past sins. It's not happened before." His lips twisted. "And I assure you I'm usually civilized and mature in my sexual encounters. I can't allow myself to be anything else."

"Because you're the Guardian?" Her voice was shaking, and she steadied it. "And the Guardian has to behave with discretion and obey all the rules."

"Not with you. I can't do it with you."

"This is going nowhere." She looked away from him. "And it's partly my fault. I behaved irrationally about Celia, and it sparked something that—"

"Oh, yes, it did. And I would have behaved just as irrationally under similar circumstances. Rationality doesn't exist in the same ballpark as barbaric. That's why I had to scoop you away until we could clarify." He held up his hand as she opened her lips to speak. "And I know that you're going to say again that it doesn't matter. Be quiet, and listen to me. I have to tell you exactly how much it doesn't matter. First, I'm very highly sexed." He grimaced. "You might have guessed that fact. Because of my duties, sexual activity has to meet all the discipline requirements that guide the rest of my life. I can't allow myself to have normal relations. So I arrange time with women who ask no questions and want no strings."

"Prostitutes."

"Of the highest caliber and discretion." He added, "When Hu Chang asked me to help him with the monks at the monastery, it was necessary that I read him. Celia came up several times in his memory. She was intriguing."

"I can imagine."

"A few months later, when I needed a woman, I arranged for her to spend a week with me in Bangkok."

"A week? From what I hear, that would have been an expensive week."

He shrugged. "I have money. Do you think that I would have been hired as Guardian if there was any chance of my being bribed? The first thing the committee did was make sure that I had a billion or two."

"Billion?"

"It was nothing to them, Catherine. It was nothing to me, either, except when I needed something."

"Like a courtesan. Was she worth it?"

"She was probably the most skilled woman I'd ever had. I enjoyed her."

"Then I'd say she was worth it."

"Except that she had one fault I couldn't accept. She wanted control of me. I couldn't allow anyone sexual dominance. It would have been dangerous. She tried all the time she was with me, in a variety of delightful, intricate ways to overcome resistance. She even offered to stay another week with me."

There were only two men I found I couldn't control, Celia had said.

Cameron was evidently one of them.

"Couldn't you use a little of that mental manipulation to persuade her to stop?"

"No, she never knew I was capable of anything that wasn't totally normal. I preferred it that way."

"Why?"

"Normal isn't bad. On occasion, it can be a relief."

"And stop the prostitutes from talking about certain odd behavior?"

"That, too."

She was silent. "You didn't have to tell me this. It's not my business."

"It *is* your business. I told you, I haven't felt like this before. I felt more for you when I had my mouth on you just now than I did for Celia when she was screwing me. That makes it dangerous as hell for me, and I have to come to terms with it. I don't know what path we're on, but I'm not going to let you go until we both find out."

"It's my choice, too." She steadied her voice. "You're this big mystery man, and I don't even know if I like what you do or what you stand for. It's all clouded. I don't know you."

He gazed at her. "Do you want to ask me questions? It's dangerous. You're an outsider and have not been sanctioned. I don't believe I could ever hurt you." He smiled crookedly. "But there are others who could step in and save me from myself if given the command."

"Outsider? Bullshit. Do you think I'm afraid of all that hogwash?"

"No, I don't think you're afraid of anything, and I embrace that courage." He paused. "But you have to tell me. You have to say the words."

She stared at him. He would not have warned her if he hadn't thought there was danger. Was she willing to say those words and run the risk?

Yes, for Erin's sake.

And, yes, for her own sake, too.

"I do want to ask you questions. Will you tell me the truth?"

"Yes, but I may not answer everything if it's something that would harm the committee or what they stand for." He leaned back, and said softly, "Ask me, Catherine."

"I want to know about you. Why did you want to become this mega security chief?"

"I didn't. It wasn't a question of choice. But when it came down to whether I'd let anyone else do it, I couldn't turn it down. I was the right person. The committee knew it, and I knew it."

"Because of the mental abilities?"

"That was a big part of it. There were only two other men in the world who even approached my abilities. One was CIA, and he wasn't stable." He nodded at Catherine. "Venable didn't display his best stuff with that Italian girl when he brought you all to that mental-telepathy seminar. He had someone much better he'd hoped to bring along, but he couldn't trust him not to freak with all of those agents bombarding him." He added, "The other man was my brother, who would have been a decent choice."

"Your brother?"

"Yes, Brad and I were discovered by a member of the committee in an orphanage in the Miami slums. We were being isolated and kept away from the other kids because the people who ran the place thought we had mental problems. You couldn't blame them. Brad and I both had certain talents, but we didn't know how to control them. We were confused and frustrated and had temper tantrums." He grimaced. "Evidently, our parents didn't know what to do with us either. They left us beside a road outside Boca Raton in the middle of the night."

"If you were isolated, how did this committee member locate you?"

"The committee is always on the hunt for anyone with unusual talents. They regard psych talents the way they would a mathematical genius. They want the best of the best in their corner. They believe it's the way to move people and society in the right direction. He'd heard stories and was looking for us. He took us out of the orphanage and put us with a young teacher, Nell Coledge, who had been trained to deal with kids like us. We lived with her for the next several years."

"Was it better for you there?"

"Night and day. She taught us to handle being freaks and even accept it with humor. We both grew to love her."

"Did she belong to this great committee?"

"No, she was just someone who believed in them. She was the one who tried to explain to us why being Guardian was so important. I couldn't see it."

"Could your brother?"

"Brad was much more idealistic than I'll ever be. He actually wanted to be Guardian."

"Then why isn't he?"

"He didn't get the chance. He was tortured and murdered when he was eighteen years old."

Cameron's tone was without expression. Yet Catherine could sense the pain.

"How?"

"He was kidnapped and taken to Iran. They're building their own psych think tanks there. Brad and I were both on their radar, but he was easier to grab. I was older, and my training made me fairly formidable."

"Why would they kill him?"

"The Iranians didn't know how to handle what they had in Brad. They tried to force compliance. He wouldn't do what they wanted, and they went too far. He bled to death before they could save him."

"Dear God."

"I wasn't sure there was a God at that point. He was the person I loved most in the world. I couldn't see why God would take him away." He voice was suddenly bitter. "And then I realized that if that could happen to Brad, then there was something terribly wrong with the world as I knew it. I told the committee if they wanted me as Guardian, I'd do it."

"I don't understand all this Guardian business."

"From what I've read in your mind since I got here, it seems you've already figured most of it out for yourself. I'm sent to take care of security problems, to keep anyone from knowing about the committee and what it's trying to do. I also try to recruit those with talent of all kinds and descriptions who have the right moral character and mind-set and send them to the committee to train and incorporate into the organization."

"And what is the committee trying to do?"

His lips turned up at the corners. "Are you afraid I'm going to say that they want to take over the world like something from a James Bond movie?"

"It occurred to me."

"No, go back to what you read about the myth of Shambhala. What was the purpose of those who lived there?"

She thought about it. "Supposedly to live in peace and gather riches and knowledge. Because they knew that the world around them would grow worse as time went on and destroy itself. Then Shambhala would be there for those who still remained and came seeking the way to rebuild and live an enlightened life." She gazed at him skeptically. "Are you telling me that this huge conglomerate capable of doing all the things that you say it can do would spend its time and resources on trying to save the world?"

"No, they don't believe civilization as we know it can be saved. They just want a shot at building the next one."

"Crazy."

"If you say so."

"What's the name of this conglomerate?"

He shook his head.

"Then do you believe they're really trying to do what they say, or are they working under the table for their own ends?"

"I wouldn't be Guardian if I didn't believe they're doing what they think is right."

"But you could be brainwashed. They had you and your brother from the time you were young and impressionable. And your brother's death could have tipped the scales."

"It's a difficult task to brainwash anyone with a convoluted brain like mine." He smiled. "If you think it's crazy, you have to think I'm crazy, too."

"It's a cold world out there, and big business is even colder."

"And what if the business was started decades and decades ago and created with that one underlying purpose?"

She shook her head. "I still can't believe it."

"I didn't think you would. Questions over?"

"No, you say you also recruit. You were trying to recruit Erin, weren't you?"

He nodded. "She was a perfect candidate. Intelligent, talented, strong, idealistic. The committee could have helped and used her in a hundred situations."

"She wouldn't like to be used."

"Only with her consent and cooperation. Force is what the committee is battling against."

"Except where you're concerned."

"But then I'm the Guardian," he said simply.

"Which means that the gloves are off, and all the rules are your rules."

"I told you that from the beginning."

"I didn't realize that you were out to remake the world as we know it."

"After Brad died, I decided I didn't like the world the way it was being run. Why not change it?" He was studying her expression. "You're getting more upset. No one is targeting innocents, Catherine. There has to be a balance to keep the operation from crashing down. Sometimes that balance is very delicate, and I have to make decisions how to maintain it."

"So you go out and kill someone."

"Is it different from your having to take down one of the bad guys? Don't you have to make judgments?"

"Yes. It's just that you seem more . . . autocratic."

"I am what I am. Are we finished?"

"No." She added honestly, "But my mind is so messed up right now I need time to absorb."

"Then by all means absorb." He leaned back and gazed at her. "It's a wonderful mind and not that messed up even now. It was the first thing that attracted me to you when I was searching for someone to go after Erin. Such a clean, beautiful mind with none of the static most people broadcast." He smiled. "Of course, that particular attraction faded into the background in short order. Lust is a very domineering master. Perhaps someday I'll be able to combine the two, but it may be a while."

Lust.

Yes, it was with her now, again. She could feel a flush heat her cheeks. "Listen, Cameron. I'm not going to lie to you. It would be stupid to tell you that I don't want you to—" She moistened her lips. "You can see I do, damn you. But I'm not going to do it."

"I know. Not now. It's not the time. Now that we've crossed the first barrier, I can wait. I just had to clear up the Celia hurdle."

Good God, she was disappointed, she realized, shocked.

"Me, too," he said thickly. "And don't think I'm not going to have you as soon as I can justify doing it. I'll be thinking of all the ways that we can try. Not that I haven't been doing that already. Every time I have a moment to myself, you're there."

"I don't have any moments to myself without your butting in," she said tartly. "You said that you wouldn't do that. It's totally unfair, Cameron."

"I'll try to stay out as much as possible. It's difficult when I feel so close to you." He paused. "And I'm not sure if there's a threat. I have very strong protective instincts. That was one of the reasons I was chosen as Guardian."

"That's not a good excuse for snooping," she said dryly. "I don't care if your instincts say go for it. I'm the one who should be able to block you from doing it."

"I'll try, Catherine. That's all I can promise."

She gazed at him with exasperation.

"I've learned to be disciplined, and usually it works," he said quietly. "But I'm not disciplined with you. It all goes out the window."

"Why?"

"It's not only the sex. Though God knows that's a gigantic part of it. I feel as if I'm turning a new page with you. I don't know what I'll find, but I know it's going to be important to me. And sometimes what you make me feel blows that discipline to hell." He reached out and touched her lower lip with his forefinger. "I know you don't feel the same, but there are moments when you come close. I think that's why I slip inside. I need to know that I'm not alone."

Alone. She knew about loneliness. Her life had been nothing but loneliness before she met Hu Chang. How much worse must have been Cameron's loneliness. He had been shut in isolation and rejection most of his childhood. Even after he had been put with the woman who had raised him, he must have come to realize how different he was from everyone else. That was loneliness in itself.

"Stop feeling sorry for me. I do just fine." Then he smiled. "Or maybe I should tell you to go ahead. I don't mind sympathy if it makes you melt like this. It could lead in all kinds of interesting directions."

"No, it can't. And you're snooping again." She slapped his hand away from her mouth. "And I'm not melting. You're the last person I'd feel sorry for." But she couldn't resist asking, "Hu Chang once said that he thought that you were relieved when you were forced to not use all that mental firepower. Is that true?"

"He's a wise man. It's both relaxing and a little annoying. I get impatient." He tilted his head. "You have the most beautifully shaped lips. I keep wanting to touch them. And your breasts are magnificent. My tongue still tingles from—"

"Cameron."

He nodded. "I know, later." He turned on the windshield wipers, and the interior of the car was flooded with daylight, destroying the cocoonlike intimacy. "We still have forty-five minutes before Blake should start the action." He was gazing at the entrance of the hospital garage. His hands closed tightly on the steering wheel. "He's probably in the hospital now seeing to the stretcher and getting it up to Jack Sen's floor."

Her gaze was narrowed on his face. "You're on edge. You said you trust Blake."

"I do. I just want to be there, doing it myself." He grimaced. "That's what I always want, but it's against the rules. Only occasionally are the circumstances just right for me to be able to step in. I have to remain the invisible man."

"Frustrating. It would drive me crazy."

"You bet, intensely frustrating. But I've become accustomed to—" He stopped, and a reckless smile suddenly lit his face. "But why should I have to put up with it on this job? I've already broken the rules. Why not break a few more?" He opened the driver's door and got out of the car. "Get in the driver's seat. Come and pick me up when I run out of the garage."

"What? You can't interfere with a plan in motion. It would screw everything up."

"I won't interfere." The rain was pouring down his face, and his dark hair was already wet. His expression was alive with vitality and that excitement. "I'll just be there on the spot and get them out of the garage faster."

"And not be the invisible man," she said softly.

"Right. Will you wait here and pick me up? Will you be there for me?"

She didn't want to sit here and wait. She wanted to go with him.

He shook his head. "Not this time. I need you to be on call outside the hospital. Will you do it?"

She made a face as she nodded resignedly. "I'll be there for you."

"That's what I wanted to hear." He smiled brilliantly as he turned and walked toward the garage. "I don't know anyone who I'd rather have beside me, but this will have to do."

"But you did it again," she called after him. "Stop that snooping . . ."

He waved and disappeared into the garage.

The rain was falling harder again, closing out the sight of the garage entrance. She turned on the windshield wipers once more. She had to *see*, dammit.

She checked her watch. Forty minutes until the action started. Then it would probably escalate at warp speed. Cameron had said five minutes, if everything went well.

But she would be on the alert from this time forward. She had never trusted that every detail in an operation would necessarily go well. Cameron was brilliant, and his plan was probably just as brilliant, but there were usually slipups. She would watch and make sure that Cameron was not caught in one.

She had promised to be there for him.

CHAPTER

14

Catherine checked her wristwatch.

Forty-five minutes.

They should be in the garage by now.

Forty-six minutes.

She felt tension grip her.

Soon.

Unless something had gone wrong.

An ambulance tore out of the garage, tires screeching, as it turned and barreled down the street toward the light on the corner.

Yes.

She put the Mercedes in gear and stomped on the accelerator. The car jumped forward, and she drove toward the garage entrance.

Come on, Cameron, I'm here for you. Where the hell are you?

"Right here." He ran out of the garage and jumped into the passenger seat. "Let's go!"

She was already moving. She glanced sideways at him as she went through the light on yellow. His eyes were glittering, his mouth taut, and she could almost feel the tension and excitement. He was loving this. "Everything went okay?"

"Right on schedule. Blake did very well. And with me helping with the transfer, we had Sen out of the garage two minutes early."

"It must have been like the pit team at a car race." She glanced in the rearview mirror. "We're not being followed."

"They're still scrambling. There will be someone tearing out of that garage any minute. Turn left at the next street."

She turned left. "Where do I go from here?"

"Set your GPS for Celia's place. We should get off the street. Someone could have seen you scoop me up in that grand getaway." He smiled. "You had a certain dash about you. Have you done this before?"

"Once or twice." She set the GPS. "In Colombia. There always seemed to be a reason for a getaway down there." She started following the GPS guidelines. "Were you really useful, or were you just enjoying yourself?"

"Both. They could have done it without me. But Kadmus's local team had a man stationed down there waiting to see if someone would show. He came out from behind a car when he saw me disabling the security cameras in the garage and the elevator. He had a knife and an attitude. I took care of him and gave Blake a little extra time that bought them insurance."

"And had a good time."

"Life is always more exciting on the edge." He glanced challengingly at her. "Isn't it?"

She couldn't deny it. She had lived on the edge all of her life. At one time, she had thought she wanted peace and normalcy, but that had faded into the background as life exploded around her. "As long as something is accomplished."

"How very solemn and dutiful. But today you didn't know exactly what could be accomplished, and you wanted to go with me anyway."

"I don't like to sit on the sidelines."

"And I would have loved having you beside me," he said. "Any-time. Any way. I usually have to fight alone, and I like it that way. But it would be different with you."

It would be different with him, she thought. He wouldn't try to keep her from doing what she'd been trained to do.

Or would he? He'd said he had highly protective instincts.

"You'll have to see, won't you?" he asked.

"Out," she said succinctly.

He smiled. "I'm working on it."

"And one other thing that's puzzling me. Why didn't you have one of Blake's men come down earlier to disable those cameras?"

"I wanted to do it myself."

"Why?"

"I wanted to make sure that those cameras showed what I wanted them to show. I disabled the ones that were trained on the elevator and the ambulance. I kept the one that showed me taking out Kad-mus's man and heading for the elevator."

"That's crazy," she said, stunned. "You spend all your time try-ing to avoid being recognized or connected to anything that might have a police investigation."

"There are exceptions to every rule." He paused. "I had to show myself to distract Kadmus's men when I was trying to get you off the mountain. A photo was taken, and by this time, he knows my face and name."

"No," she whispered.

"That's what the committee says. They're not pleased. But they can rectify the problem with a little high-priced erasure. But I might as well use the fact that Kadmus now knows who he's looking for as bait."

"You mean using yourself as bait."

He nodded. "Before he had only Erin to go after here in San Francisco. But after he sees the security disks, he'll know I'm here protecting her." He glanced at her. "Don't you think that might draw Kadmus out of his palace on the mountains to come here and go after me personally?"

"Yes. And he might not bring an army with him, but you can bet he'll have enough firepower to be damn intimidating. Nagle will have to step up to the plate. But how's he going to get hold of that security disk?"

"The police will pull the disks, and Kadmus will pay to get a copy of what's on them. That's what I'd do."

"But you have unlimited funds for bribery."

"Kadmus will pay whatever he has to pay to find Shambhala." He tapped his chest. "And right now, he sees me as the key to Shambhala."

"Does he really think of Shambhala as the proverbial pot of gold?"

"He sees the power, he's been watching and knows that I've been plucking the brightest, the most talented brains in the world. That's an incredibly valuable asset in itself. As for the myth that there are untold riches stored in a hidden city, perhaps he believes that, too. He certainly believes that he deserves to be emperor of his world, and the Shangri-La myth riveted his attention enough to invest a sizable amount of his ill-gotten gains in it." He thought about it. "Yes, he probably does think there is an actual Shambhala."

"And is there?"

He didn't answer for a moment. "That's been the argument for centuries. Is Shambhala an actual place? Or is it a mythical concept that philosophers developed of a perfect world that might save us all?"

"You're not answering me."

"No, I'm not, am I?" He leaned back in the seat. "Now chauffeur me back to Celia's, and we'll wait for Blake to call and tell me Sen is on a jet back to Hong Kong." He added grimly, "And then we'll start getting a plan together to bring Kadmus down."

•   •   •

"Jack Sen had been taken from the hospital. Someone snatched him from beneath the police guard's nose," Brasden said as he hung up the phone. "And one of Nagle's men was killed in the hospital garage."

"Son of a bitch," Kadmus said. "I don't give a damn about that bungler. I told Nagle to stake out that hospital. He was supposed to either get his hands on anyone who tried to get Sen away from the police or follow them and try to get Erin Sullivan. Did they do either?"

"No." He held up his hand as Kadmus started to curse. "It was evidently a crack team who did the job. The lookout in the garage was supposed to call upstairs to the lobby if he spotted anyone." He shrugged. "But it seems someone spotted him first. The ambulance carrying Sen got away clean as a whistle. Nagle is outside the garage questioning everyone about what they saw at the time. He said two nurses saw a dark-haired man jump into a blue Mercedes that skidded to a stop near the garage entrance."

"License plate?"

"Not so far. Listen, give me a minute. The police are pulling the video cameras out of the garage. That may tell us something. Shall I give Nagle the okay to spend the money to get a copy? It will be steep."

"Get them," Kadmus said curtly. "And get Erin Sullivan. I've got to have a bargaining chip when we locate Cameron. Have you heard anything about him yet? Do you even know if he's still in Tibet?"

"No word. But we have the photo that we've been showing around. I'll find a lead." He paused. "Providing I have the motivation."

Kadmus stiffened. "I'm tired of this, Brasden. I've put up with your damned arrogance for too long. One more word, and I'll have you shot."

"Not do it yourself? Ten years ago, you wouldn't have been

afraid to go after me. But you've changed. You've gotten softer."
He said silkily, "And I've gotten stronger. You've let me take over
running your little army, and now they listen to me, not you."

"The hell they do."

"Would you like to call my bluff?" Brasden's hand rested on the
butt of the pistol in his holster. "Go ahead."

The bastard was too sure of himself, Kadmus thought. He had
been so absorbed in getting that crucial information from Erin Sullivan that he had ignored the possibility that Brasden could be insin-
uating himself into a leadership position. Had he really undermined
Kadmus's power with his men? Loyalty could be bought with promises and extra pay as well as intimidation. It was possible.

Be cautious until he could determine the consequences.

"Motivation?" he repeated slowly. "What motivation?"

"I'm tired of doing all the work and having you take the biggest
percentage of the profits."

"Percentage? You work for me. I hired you to do a job."

"That's not good enough any longer. I want 50 percent of every
fee I earn for you."

"Screw you."

"And I want to start with the money you're trying to squeeze
out of Erin Sullivan . . . and this Cameron. You want me to find
them? Then don't make me go at it blind." He reached in his pocket
and pulled out something shiny and gold and very familiar. "I went
through your desk last night and found this pretty piece." He dan-
gled the chain of the lotus necklace. "I remember you took it from
that priest you killed three years ago. You were angry because you
said he died too soon."

"Give me that!"

"And then you had us take Erin Sullivan. You tried very hard
not to let her die too soon. I want to know what we're supposed to
be looking for."

"You son of a bitch."

"Tell me, Kadmus. I'll still let you have half of whatever I find."

And he was supposed to believe him? Kadmus hadn't survived all these years by being taken in by a prick like Brasden. Play him, then take him down. He was silent a moment. "You have me over a barrel. We . . . may be able to work together."

"Tell me," Brasden said again.

"You won't believe it. It takes a man with vision."

"Tell me."

"I've heard rumors for forty years about a city in these mountains that has a treasure trove of jewels and gold. At first, I didn't believe it; and then I began to wonder why shouldn't it be true when so many people I ran across thought it existed? After all, I'd always known that I was meant to rule. It's my destiny. It could also be my destiny that I came to these mountains so that I'd find a place worthy of me. So I started searching for clues to find Shambhala."

"The priest," Brasden prompted.

"That priest I took the necklace from told his children about a wonderful place he would take them to one day. Yes, where there were jewels and gold and wonderful, wise people. He said that he was one of the chosen, and he'd been given the pendant by one of the wise ones who would lead him to the place of wonder." His mouth twisted. "Old fool. He only talked about it. He stayed in his sod hut in that village when he could have gone to Shambhala."

"Shambhala . . . I've never heard of it."

"Because you're an ignorant fool. Like that priest. He didn't die quite right away. Not before he told me that those who were given the necklace were the sanctioned who would be permitted to join the wise ones in Shambhala. It was given to him by a man, a Westerner, but I wasn't able to get a name. He kept calling him the Guardian. And I couldn't get any other information out of him. I would have done it if I'd only had the time. But he cut his throat with a knife one of the villagers slipped him."

"You actually believed him?"

"It's true," he said fiercely. "There's a Shambhala, and it was meant to be found by me."

"Or me," Brasden said. "If it exists."

"It exists. Find Cameron, and he'll take us to it."

"Us," Brasden repeated. "That sounds like a partnership."

"I'm not a fool." It would be a partnership until Kadmus rooted out any Brasden supporters among his men and destroyed them as well as Brasden. "There's kingdom enough to share in Shambhala. Just find Cameron."

Brasden stared thoughtfully at Kadmus, then contemptuously tossed the lotus necklace to him before he turned on his heel. "I'll find him."

•   •   •   •

Erin and Hu Chang were the only ones in the library when Catherine and Cameron got back to Celia's house.

Catherine felt a jolt of anxiety. "Where's Luke?"

"In the kitchen with Celia," Erin said. "He's helping her with the dishes. I offered, but she chose Luke. They seem to have bonded."

"Did you really think that I'd let anything happen to him?" Hu Chang asked. "He wasn't at all happy that you left without him. I thought it best to keep him busy." He glanced at Cameron. "He wants to believe in you, but Tashdon made that hard. I'd go and reinforce to him that you'll never hurt Catherine." He paused. "If that's possible?"

"Not only possible but certain." He turned and headed for the door. "Tell them about Sen, Catherine. I'll go make sure that we don't have any trouble with Luke."

"I should be the one who—" But he was gone, and Catherine shrugged and turned back to Erin and Hu Chang. "Jack Sen is on his way to an airport outside the city, where he'll be put on a flight to Hong Kong," she said curtly. "Everything went well. Except Cameron killed one of Kadmus's men staked out in the garage." She told them briefly about the security cameras and Cameron's decision to let himself be recognized. "Now we're waiting for word that Jack Sen is on that flight." She added, "And then we wait to see if those security-camera videos are compromised and will target Cameron. Cameron said Blake has contacts in the police department who might be able to let us know."

"It appears that Cameron is changing his modus operandi," Hu Chang said dryly. "Exposing himself on camera is most unlike him. And so is guaranteeing your safety. Life and death are always ebb and flow depending on his duties as Guardian."

"That doesn't mean he won't change his mind," Catherine said. "But perhaps it does mean that he's thinking that his precious committee isn't always right." She looked at Erin. "He must have gone through a lot with you. He'd have to be completely callous not to have it affect him."

"It did affect him," Erin said. "I could feel his pain as he did mine. But he won't betray what he believes in. I wouldn't want him to do that."

"Erin, I don't know what to say to you," Catherine said helplessly. "What the hell is so worthwhile to you that you'd go through what you did to keep from sacrificing it? I can't comprehend it."

"I think you know more than you did when you left here this morning," Erin said shrewdly. "Cameron has a way of blowing away the mist and making things clear."

"That's Cameron. He's in a class by himself. I'm talking about you. What makes it that important to you?"

"The dream," she said softly. "And the people who are willing to work and sacrifice to keep it alive. I wasn't brave enough to do it. What Cameron goes through must be terrible at times. I think that's why I wore the lotus necklace when I knew I shouldn't. I wanted to show support even though I didn't have the courage to become one of them." She met Catherine's gaze. "You'd have the courage. I can see you and Cameron together fighting for a cause."

"Only if I believed in it." She added gently, "And you have an enormous amount of courage."

"I have endurance. It's different from having the guts to take a step into the unknown." She paused. "But I've been thinking about it, and I may have grown during the last months. I hope that's true."

"You didn't need to grow. You're a person who—"

"I just talked to Blake," Cameron said as he strode into the library. "Sen's flight took off ten minutes ago. He'll arrive in Hong Kong in eighteen hours and be taken to a secure hospital just across the Tibet border. We won't know about the security disks for several hours." His eyes were glittering, his face taut. "But by that time, we should have most of the preparations made." He looked over his shoulder. "Isn't that so, Luke?"

Good God, Catherine thought as she watched Luke come into the room. Her son had the same expression of barely restrained excitement as Cameron.

Luke smiled at Catherine as he stopped beside Cameron. "He's trying to make you think that he and I are planning this together. It's not true. But he promised to make sure I'd be part of it." His smile lingered as he looked up at Cameron. "And that's enough for me."

Cameron returned his smile. "Smart boy. You see right through me."

"No." His brow furrowed. "But it's funny you should say that. I've been thinking that sometimes I get a crazy feeling that *you* see right through me."

Cameron's smile faded, and he gave a low whistle. "You might have to give him to me for a few tests, Catherine."

"No way," she said flatly.

He shrugged. "We'll talk later." He turned to Hu Chang. "The first thing to do is get the Mercedes away from the front of Celia's house and placed in a spot that will throw out a red herring for Kadmus to pick up as soon as the Mercedes is identified from either the security cameras or any witness accounts. I'll take care of it. By now that cabdriver who brought you to Chinatown will have given a description of all of you to Kadmus's men. We don't want you to be seen again until the right time. Stay here with Celia." He glanced down at Luke again. "Take care of Catherine. I'll be back soon."

"You told him that before. We'll take care of each other. Just as we always have," Catherine said coolly. "Where are you going to drop the Mercedes?"

"I'm not sure. I have an idea, but I'll have to call and have a little research done." He smiled as he turned and headed for the door. "But I'll be sure and ask your approval."

Bastard, she thought as she watched the door close behind him. What research? She hated that he had left her behind. He was right that it wasn't smart that they be identified, but that hadn't stopped him from practically yanking her out of this house this morning.

But that hadn't had anything to do with cool calculation. That had been fire and smoke and lust that had driven both of them to the brink.

She could feel her body start to ready as she remembered just how intense that lust had been.

No. Don't think of it. Particularly with Hu Chang's gaze fastened on her. Cameron wasn't the only man who could read her emotions. She turned to Luke. "I haven't had breakfast yet. Cameron and I were a little busy. How about going with me to the kitchen while I fix something?"

He nodded. "Cameron told me how good you were at being a getaway driver." He followed her out of the library. "He said he thought you enjoyed it."

"Did he? It was serious stuff."

"Did you enjoy it?"

"Maybe. A little." He was looking at her. "Okay, maybe a lot. But it's not something that most people with any intelligence would want to do."

"But you're very intelligent."

"You're grinning. Are you making fun of me?"

"Yes." He paused. "And I like it that you told me the truth. Truth is important."

"And do you think that Cameron told you the truth?"

"Yes, there are things he's hiding, but he's mostly telling the truth."

"You might have to give him to me for a few tests, Catherine."

Oh, shit. It's not going to happen, Cameron.

"And do you trust him?"

"I believe that he won't let you be hurt."

"I'm not the only one involved in this, Luke."

"I think everyone else will be all right, too. I just know that you'll be okay, and Hu Chang is always fine. And that's the only thing that's important to me."

"Then widen your horizons." She stopped at the kitchen door. "Erin is very—"

"I thought you might be coming for a snack." Celia smiled from where she was standing by the AGA stove. "Cameron said that you hadn't eaten. I tried to convince him to let me fix him something, but he was in a hurry. But now I have you."

And Catherine had forgotten that Celia might still be in the kitchen. She could feel herself instinctively tensing. "Thank you, but I can fix myself something to eat. We've troubled you enough."

"I wouldn't think of it." Celia's smile was both brilliant and genuine. "I love to cook. I took a Cordon Bleu course in Paris, and I scored off the charts. You can't cheat me out of the satisfaction. Luke will tell you how good I am."

Luke nodded. "Breakfast was great."

"You see, and he's a very tough critic." She turned to the refrigerator. "I'll make you an omelet par excellence. Luke, please go out to my herb garden and pick fresh rosemary and bring me a garlic bulb."

He nodded and moved toward the kitchen door.

"He's a sweet boy," Celia said as she took out eggs and milk and set them on the granite bar. "And very smart. If I was able to have children, I'd wish for a son just like your Luke."

"You can't have children?"

"No." She shrugged. "When I was sold into that whorehouse in Calcutta, they performed an operation that made it impossible. Pregnant whores are not commercially profitable, you know."

"No, I didn't know." She was appalled. "I'm sorry."

"So was I." She broke a egg into the bowl. "Not at first. The last thing I wanted was to become pregnant by any of those men who used me. But later, when I was in control of my life, I felt cheated. No one had a right to take that from me."

"I would have been furious. I would have killed someone."

She nodded. "I was angry and sad. But I couldn't let it dominate my life. It's not who I am." Her glance shifted to the door through which Luke had vanished. "But every now and then, the sadness comes back." She stirred the second egg into the mixture. "You're lucky, Catherine."

"I know that."

Celia raised her gaze. "But you may not be lucky with Richard Cameron. Be careful."

Catherine stiffened. "It's obvious you were lovers."

"I'm sure that Cameron told you that it was a sexual liaison only."

"Why do you assume that?"

"Because I saw him with you. I can read his expressions, his movements. I studied him for a long time when I was with him. He became something of an obsession with me because I couldn't get him to commit."

"You mean that you couldn't control him."

She nodded. "He's fantastic sexually." She made a face. "I hate to admit it, but maybe better than me. I might have given him a second week free if he'd agreed to—Nah, that wouldn't have been professional. I keep personal and business strictly compartmentalized." She glanced at Catherine. "But I could handle Cameron. I don't know if you can. You're strictly an amateur, and I've never seen Cameron as aroused as he was with you this morning. It was . . . unusual."

"Most people are amateurs compared to you."

"But most people don't have to deal with Cameron." She frowned. "Look, don't fight him or push him away. It will only make him more intense and determined to get his own way. Just take him and enjoy it." She added ruefully, "And I promise you *will* enjoy it, Catherine."

"Thank you for the advice," she said reservedly.

"Which you're not going to take."

"I have other things to do than worry about Cameron's sexual needs and attitudes. That's not why we're here, Celia. The entire world isn't about sex."

"No, but it rules." She added softly, "Everything else comes and goes, but sex and passion are always there. For a moment, an hour, a decade." She repeated, "It rules, Catherine."

"I don't agree."

"You will." She stirred the mixture. "You have your son here in the house. There's a summerhouse on the other side of my little garden that will allow you and Cameron privacy. You're welcome to use it. I'll tell Cameron."

"Don't you dare."

"I always dare. It makes life more interesting." She turned to Luke as he came into the kitchen. "Ah, you've brought some fine specimens." She took the garlic. "Could I talk you into eating another small omelet, Luke? Your mother won't want to eat alone. That's one of the things that I learned in cooking school. Everything tastes better in good company."

He nodded and sat down at the table. "I'm hungry again."

"Young boys are always hungry," Celia said. "Or so I've been told. It will just be a few minutes . . ."

DAKSHA PALACE

"I've just heard from San Francisco." Brasden threw down a photo. "No word on the interior security cameras yet. But this was taken by the outside camera by the garage entrance. Nagle was able to negotiate a copy on this one while the police are examining the others. It's a shot of the car that pulled up shortly after the ambulance took off. It's a little hazy and dark from the rain. Familiar?"

"Cameron." Excitement was soaring through him. "The bastard looks like he's having a hell of a good time." He looked closer. "And the driver is Catherine Ling."

"Right."

"Did you get the license?"

"It didn't show up in the videos, but it's a rental car. We're checking."

"Find it. Find him. You were looking in the wrong place. He's not here in Tibet." His hand crushed the paper on which the photo was printed. "He followed Erin Sullivan. She must mean more to him than I thought. She was free of me. Why go after her?"

"But he's with Catherine Ling," Brasden pointed out. "Maybe he has business with her and not Sullivan." He smiled. "Or not. She's a beautiful woman. Not everyone is obsessed by your mystical city."

"But Cameron is obsessed by Shambhala. No woman could take its place." He glanced at Ling. "Still, it would do no harm to probe a little deeper into Ling and see if we can use her as a weapon. See to it."

"Please," Brasden said. "Say please, Kadmus."

Restraint. He had been looking into Brasden's claim that he

could take over his forces at any time. There was some evidence that Brasden did have some influence with the men and he had to be careful. He did not want an uprising at this crucial moment. But he had already started to reinforce his power, and he wouldn't have to put up with Brasden for much longer. "Please, see to it."

"I'll do it right away."

"And arrange for me to get to San Francisco right away. I'm not going to trust anyone else to zero in on Cameron." He smiled gently, imagining all the torture he was going to inflict on this asshole. "If you please, Brasden."

CHAPTER
15

"A ren't you two going to bed soon?" Catherine shook her head at Luke and Hu Chang sitting over the chess board before the fire in the library. "It's almost midnight. You've been playing for hours."

"I almost beat him the last game." Luke didn't look up from the board. "I'm close this time."

"Not close enough." Hu Chang smiled. "But you're making it interesting." He glanced at Catherine. "Run along to bed. I'll tell you how I triumphed in the morning."

Luke snorted. "Someday I'll beat you. Maybe tonight."

"A competitive spirit is good. A humble spirit is even better."

"I don't think so."

Hu Chang chuckled. "Actually, neither do I." He moved his knight. "No word from Cameron, Catherine?"

"No," she said curtly. "Not unless he contacted you."

Hu Chang shook his head. "I believe any communication will be with you from now on. I sensed a change today." He waved his hand. "Now go away and do not distract me. I'm having to concentrate on this game. I did not think he'd reach this degree of expertise for another year."

She shook her head ruefully as she left the library and closed the door. Luke had been changing, making all kinds of advancements, since the day she had arrived in Hong Kong. It was even surprising Hu Chang. He was busily adjusting and accepting. She must do the same.

God, it was hard. It was like dealing with an adult and she wasn't ready for that yet. She needed a little time to—

"Good. I was hoping I wouldn't have to search the house for you." Cameron had blown into the hall like a strong wind. His eyes were glittering, and Catherine could almost feel the tornado of excitement and exhilaration that surrounded him. "Come on." He grabbed her wrist and was pulling her toward the front door. "I have something to show you."

"What?" They were outside, and she was having to half run to keep up. "Where are we going?"

"The trap. I've found the trap." They had stopped beside an orange-and-blue motorcycle, and he handed her a helmet and large-lensed protective glasses. "Tuck your hair under the helmet." He was putting on his own orange-striped helmet and dark glasses. For the first time, she noticed he was still in the jeans he'd worn earlier in the day but had somewhere acquired biker boots and a black leather jacket. He got on the bike and revved up the engine. "Jump on."

She got on the broad seat of the bike behind him, her arms around his waist. "Where's the Mercedes?" she asked as he tore down the street. "And where did you get this motorcycle?"

"The Mercedes is discreetly dumped in a place that will lead Kadmus to step into the trap. The bike I bought from a man in a bar along with his gear." He smiled. "It's as close as I could come to a bona fide disguise that would allow us to move around Chinatown. The young people love their bikes. Not surprising, considering the terrible traffic."

He was right—the helmet and glasses were a decent disguise.

"It took you long enough. If you'd taken me along, I could have split up the search by—"

"And I would have been distracted," he interrupted. "I didn't need you. I got everything done. Now be quiet and enjoy the ride."

And she was enjoying the ride, she realized suddenly. Why? A roaring motorcycle wasn't the place to enjoy a conversation and yet she was having no difficulty hearing or communicating. Cameron? It didn't feel like intrusion but that didn't mean it wasn't a more subtle form of manipulation. Hu Chang had said he didn't know the extent of Cameron's skills.

Oh, what the hell, if it was an intrusion, it was minor.

"I'm glad you've decided to give me the benefit of the doubt," Cameron said. "Now relax and enjoy. I haven't ridden a motorcycle for years. Have you?"

She tried to remember. "Once when I was in Moscow trying to track down Luke." Her arms grasped him tighter. "It was no joyride."

"No, nothing about that time contained any joy for you. But it's over, and you have Luke."

If Cameron didn't lure him into his camp, she thought dryly. He seemed to have an incredible amount of magnetism where her son was concerned.

"I wouldn't try to take him away from you," he said quietly. "And I won't use him as a pawn. You have my word on it."

"Is your word any good?"

"Yes." He added simply, "Because it's all I have that doesn't belong to the committee. I have to keep something for myself."

"And yet you're going to go against them when you kill Kadmus."

"It's an exception. In most cases, I'm in agreement with them."

"Why do they want to keep the bastard alive?"

"He's a big investor and financial force in keeping that tourist town of Shangri-La going. There are a few reasons why the committee wants all the public attention fixed on that town the Chinese swear is the location of Shangri-La."

"Because it's not the true location?"

He was silent. "How can a mythological place have a true location except in the imagination?"

"How indeed?" she whispered. She laid her cheek on his back. She could feel the silky smoothness and smell the leather of his jacket against her flesh. "Or perhaps they want the entire myth to have a tawdry image and be totally discounted."

"I said there are a few reasons."

"And some you're not going to divulge," she said. "That's okay with me. When I really want to know, I'll go searching for myself. In the meantime, it's enough to know that you realize that your committee isn't right all the time." She added, "And that you're willing to help me take Kadmus down."

"Oh, I'm definitely willing to help you do that." He swerved around the corner, and they were suddenly bombarded by light and tourists and music. "It will be my pleasure." He paused. "By the way, I like the feel of you lying against me."

She started to straighten, then stopped. She liked the feel of him, too. Why cheat herself? "How far away are we?"

"About six blocks. In three blocks, I'm going to cut left and start going down the alleys. We'll be able to ditch the bike in the alley and climb the fire escape to get into the building."

"What building?"

"The home of Moon, Stars, and Heavenly Wonder," Cameron said gravely. "And, hopefully, the place where we'll be able to bury Kadmus and Brasden." He cut left and roared down the neon-lit street and then turned the bike into darkness.

Glowing feline eyes. Garbage cans. Foul smells. Alley. They were in the alley.

After ten minutes of weaving in and out of the maze of alleys, Cameron brought the bike to a stop. "We're here." He got off the

bike and lifted her off the seat. "Come on. Let's get moving." He set
her on the ground and jumped up to bring the fire-escape ladder
down. "There's an open window on the third floor. I'll go first. I
climbed the ladder before, and it's none too steady. If you feel it going, yell, and I'll grab for you."

"Don't worry, I'll bellow loud and strong." She watched as he
climbed the steps until he reached the first-floor landing. She loved
watching him move. He was all animal grace and clean definition.

He glanced down at her. "Coming?"

"Right behind you." She was climbing the first steps as she
spoke. She said maliciously, "I wanted to give you a chance to fall
before I risked my valuable neck."

"Very wise." He had turned and was rapidly climbing. "I feel
just as cautious about risking your neck and other delectable body
parts. It would be punishing myself." He had reached the third
level and turned to look down at her. His eyes were gleaming with
mischief as he reached out a hand to her. "Give me your hands. I'll
pull you the rest of the way up. It will be quicker."

"Are we in that much of a hurry?" She let him grasp her hands.
He pulled, then dropped her hands and grasped her waist and swung
her the rest of the way up to his level. Strong, he was so strong. She
remembered what Hu Chang had said about his daily workouts to
keep fit for the task of being Guardian.

"No real hurry." His hands lingered a moment on her waist
before he dropped them and turned to the window. "I just wanted
to touch you again."

"This is serious business, Cameron."

"It's not serious until there are bullets flying. This is prelimi-
nary stuff that allows a bit of pleasure." He opened the window and
slipped over the sill. "There are three boxes piled under the window.
Be careful not to send them crashing when you crawl in."

He was gone.

She heard nothing in the darkness beyond the window.

She followed him across the sill and felt for the boxes with her feet.

Found.

She stood on the top box and dropped catlike to the floor.

"Good. No sound." Cameron was beside her. "I just disconnected the security system. We can move through the place without worrying about motion alarms."

"Where the hell are we?" She was peering around her, trying to pierce the darkness. "Boxes. Lots of boxes." She stopped. "And I smell something . . . chemicals."

He handed her a penlight. "Gunpowder and coated papers. Keep the beam down. But look around. I want you to memorize the area. You can never tell when you'll need to know where you are at any given minute."

She shined the beam of the flashlight around the room, and up to the ceiling, where she saw a gleam of light. Stars? Yes, there was a large rectangular skylight that occupied a good half of the ceiling. Night sky and stars. She lowered the beam to the room itself. There seemed to be a wall of cabinets or closets against the far wall. Other than that storage wall, the place was stacked high with various-sized boxes. Some were open, some were sealed.

She took a step nearer one of the boxes. The Chinese print on the lid jumped out at her. *Moon, Stars, and Heavenly Wonder.* And beside it a red-and-gold fireworks display.

Her gaze flew to Cameron's face. "This is a fireworks factory?"

"The top two floors. The street floor is a collection of souvenir shops." He moved toward the freight elevator. "This floor is mostly storage. Let's go down to the second floor. I saw some offices down there."

She followed him. "What did you have in mind for this place?"

"The trap. We're going to let Kadmus discover that we're using this place as a safe house. We can probably expect him to attack with a full crew. In order to lure him into a trap where we have the advantage, we'll have to find a way to eliminate a large number of his men. You get the picture?"

"Boom. Fireworks. Explosions. Yes, I get it." She frowned. "But I'm not sure I like it. This building is in the middle of the city. How are you going to stop the big boom from blowing up a block of prime real estate and the people inhabiting it?"

"I'll work it out. There's a vacant lot next door that may have potential."

"No, don't give me that. I have to *know.* I remember a fireworks factory that blew in Vietnam years ago. The death-and-injury count were terrible. I won't accept being part of a catastrophe like that."

"I don't have all the details in mind yet." He met her eyes. "But I promise you there won't be innocents killed. It won't be another Vietnam. Is that enough for you?"

"And what about the people who own this property?"

"The owner's name is Kim Po. I have a man at his home right now making him a deal that will set him up for life."

"Money, again."

"You object?"

"I prefer bribery to violence." She wrinkled her nose. "It's just that the quantity of money you appear to control is a little mind-boggling. Of course, there are crime syndicates like the Mafia who are able to dig deep to get what they want, but you're one man." She tilted her head. "Or maybe this conglomerate is really a crime syndicate."

"You don't believe that."

No, she didn't. Incredibly, she was beginning to believe the concept or reality of Shambhala as the mystical, idealistic place about which Cameron and Erin had told her. "I can't see you in the Mafia. You wouldn't pay any attention to the 'family.' You like control too much. How are you going to bait this trap?"

"You and Hu Chang bring Erin here through the front door of

the shop entrances. By that time, Nagle's men will know they're in Chinatown and be on the alert. They'll probably have photos of Erin . . . and you."

"You won't be with us?"

"I'll come in through the back fire escape. I don't want Kadmus to think that he can gather me in with one scoop. The bait has to be a little less tempting, and you have to have something to offer."

"I won't let Erin be exposed to that bastard again. No risk to her, dammit."

"There won't be a risk. All she has to do is show up and be seen entering the factory. There's a basement exit that leads to the restaurant next door. I'll negotiate with the owner to have one of Blake's men there to take Erin to safety."

Catherine frowned. "I still don't like it."

"Erin will like it," he said quietly. "She'll want her part in getting rid of Kadmus. Don't cheat her of that because you want to protect her."

"Just make sure that she'll be out of any action. When is all this supposed to happen?"

"Today is Tuesday—everything should be in place by Thursday. Sooner if Kadmus moves faster than I'm expecting."

"Thursday. It will all be over day after tomorrow . . ." She got off the freight elevator on the second floor. "You've obviously scoped out the building already. You don't have to tag along with me. I'll look around on my own."

He stepped back and gestured. "Be my guest. I'll wait upstairs. I want to put the alarm back on, and that's the only window I've taken off the motion detectors."

"Twenty minutes." She moved quickly into the darkness. Several cubicles that would serve as offices, an assembly line with several stools. Boxes. Lockers. A Coke machine . . .

She arrived back at the third floor seventeen minutes later. She got off the freight elevator and moved toward where Cameron was

standing by the window. He was only a blur in the darkness lit from the faint light streaming through the skylight. "They'll have to come in from the shops on the street. It's not likely they'll use the fire escape to break into the other floors. They're too easy to guard."

"Unless Kadmus is more clever than we think."

His voice sounded . . . strange.

She stopped, her gaze searching the darkness to see his face. "Is something wrong?"

"No."

He wasn't telling the truth. The air was thick, crackling with whatever was disturbing him.

"Let's get out of here." He lifted her up on the top box under the window. "Go on. I'll see you down there. I'll take care of the alarm."

She was already jumping the last few feet to the alley when he reached the fire escape at the second floor.

She hadn't had a chance to look around when they first arrived and took the opportunity to do it now. Garbage cans, boxes with the Moon, Stars, and Heavenly Wonder fireworks signs and, several yards toward the street, the blue Mercedes.

"So this is where you dumped it," she said, as Cameron jumped down beside her. "It definitely looks out of place in this alley. It should be easily spotted if anyone is searching."

"They'll be searching." He got on the motorcycle. "I guarantee it." His voice held a tension that hadn't been there before. "Come on, let's go."

She frowned as she swung her leg over the bike and slid onto the seat behind him. Her arms slipped around his waist. "There *is* something wrong. What did you see up there after I left?"

"Nothing." He started the bike and roared down the alley toward the street. "It was just a long twenty minutes waiting for you."

"Seventeen."

"Whatever."

"It's not as if I wasn't efficient. I just needed to make sure there wasn't anything that might trip me up when—"

"I know that." He was silent. "I suppose I was counting on going with you. It would have kept me busy, and I wouldn't have had time to think."

"You mean worry? I thought you had it all planned. It's not—"

"I mean think. Anticipate. Imagine. I leaned against that wall waiting for you with the darkness surrounding me." He said jerkily, "Guess what I was anticipating, Catherine?"

She didn't have to guess. Her heart was beating hard, and she felt the taut muscles of his back against her breasts. His words had come out of nowhere, but they were not really a surprise. Somewhere deep within her, she had been waiting for them.

"You're not answering," he said softly. "Do you want me to tell you?"

"Don't play games." Her voice was uneven, and she stopped to steady it. "You've already given me a glimpse before of how your mind works. It's all about sex."

"Not all, but when I'm anywhere near you, it comes close. I was very controlled on the ride here. That's amazing. As I told you, I have no discipline where you're concerned." He paused. "And you were touching me."

As she was touching him now. Her breasts pressed against the smoothness of the leather jacket, her arms holding tight around his taut, corded waist. Her upper legs curved under his and the center of her sex jammed against his buttocks. Only their thin layers of clothing separated warm skin.

Not warm. Hot. Her entire body was flushed, readying.

"I'll tell you anyway." His voice was hoarse. "I could smell you in the darkness, just a lingering hint of soap and shampoo. You were nowhere near me, but your scent was still there in the darkness. The same scent that drifted to me when you were behind me on the bike. The same scent I'm smelling now." He gunned the bike.

Speed. Jarring contact against his body. Wind whipping her face.

"And I thought how I wanted that scent closer to me, how I wanted to drink it in and get drunk on it." His words were soft as velvet, and yet she was aware of a subtle, erotic abrasion. "And I began to think how I could make that happen. I thought about this bike and that it was all wrong for you to be behind me. I wanted you to be in front, with your legs wrapped around my waist, so that I could bury my face in your hair."

"Rather distracting," she said unevenly. "And definitely unsafe."

"It gets worse . . . or better. You're naked, and I open my jacket so that I can feel your breasts rub against me. Your nipples are hard and taut, and I want my mouth on them. But I know it's not going to be enough. So I make an adjustment, and I'm inside you. I can feel you. I start to move."

"My God, Cameron." Her voice was shaking. "Stop."

"Because you're feeling me inside you, too? That's no reason. You like it, don't you? You feel the jarring of the bike, the occasional sharp bump, but it's all part of me and you and the rhythm. It's driving you as crazy as it's driving me."

Crazy? Yes, and breathlessly erotic, with white-hot sexuality. She found herself clenching, fighting the emptiness. "Are you doing something to my head, Cameron?"

"Not this time. It's only words."

And visions brought to life by those words.

"Close your eyes," he said. "Let it come to you. Let me come to you. You know it's going to happen. Why are you fighting it?"

"Dammit, because I don't fall into bed with every man I find sexually attractive. There has to be a reason, there has to be order to my life."

"Then I'll give you a reason," he said roughly. "You want your son protected? I'll see that he's safe from Kadmus and everyone else.

Not just now but for the foreseeable future. I'm probably the best-qualified and expensive Guardian he could ever have. Is that reason enough?"

"I didn't say price. I said reason."

"Then you'll have to decide if what I bring to you is reason enough." She could see his hands clench on the handlebars. "But decide soon, or I'll start fighting dirty. I don't want to do that with you." He said curtly, "We're halfway back to Celia's place. You haven't got much time."

"I have as much time as I wish. I won't be pressured, Cameron."

"Pressured? I'm not pressuring you. It's the last thing I want. I know that's a one-way street." He drew a deep breath. "I've just got to have you. You tell me how to do it."

She didn't answer. Her mind was in chaos. She put her cheek on his back again. Leather, jarring contact, his words, which were sending deep tremors throughout her body. Feelings and visions were splintering into glittering shards all around her.

Her thighs resting against Cameron's. She wanted to move them, rub against him.

Her breasts were taut, swollen, full.

I wanted my mouth on them, Cameron had said.

Cameron's imaginary scenario was suddenly her own.

Her body naked against him, her thighs parted to accept him into her body.

She could *feel* him.

She bit her lower lip to keep back a groan. She clenched hard, and he must have felt the movement ripple through her body. "Stop fighting," he said thickly. "You won't regret it. I'll give you anything you want from me. Stack up a dozen reasons, and I'll knock them out one by one. Are you afraid of me?"

"No." She was more afraid of herself and this fever that seemed to be possessing her. She could feel the waves of pure lust jolting through her. She could feel the flush heating her cheeks. She was shaking, wanting to draw him closer, wanting to tear off her clothes and make that naked vision reality. "Of course not."

"I can't take this," he said harshly. "Celia's is just ahead. I'm parking a few houses down." He drew the motorcycle to the curb and turned off the engine. "I've got to have my hands on you." He pulled her off the bike. "Don't argue. You want it, too." He pulled her toward the walkway leading to Celia's backyard. He'd gone only a scant four yards when he released her wrist and jammed her up against the brick wall of the house. "God, I hope you want it. I can't cheat and find out." His mouth was on hers, opening it, tonguing wildly. "Not this time. Not with you." His body was arching, hips rubbing catlike, pushing her back against the rough bricks. "Tell me you want me, Catherine."

Want him? She was dizzy with wanting him. She couldn't breathe. She was on fire.

"Tell me," he said roughly. "I have to know. I can't find out any other way."

"That must . . . be very frustrating for you." She reached up and started quickly unbuttoning her blouse with hands that were shaking. "Hell, yes, I want you. And if you don't do something about it, I'm going to drag you down right here. This is too much to—" His lips were covering hers again. Tongue to tongue. Teeth nibbling, biting, tasting, possessing.

"Not here." He lifted his head. "Come on." He grabbed her hand and pulled her toward the back garden. "I got a text from Celia. There's supposed to be a summerhouse . . ." He glanced at her. "Oh, shit. Bad timing?"

"No, she told me the same thing." She was half running to keep up with him. "I don't care if she thinks she can set up arrangements for you. This isn't about her."

It was about need and the most intense desire she'd ever experienced, she thought hazily. She had to have him, and nothing else mattered.

"That's what I was trying to tell you." He threw open the door of the summerhouse and pulled her inside. Darkness. Moonlight streaming through long, arched windows, couches, and chairs with some kind of print upholstery. "This is the only thing that's important." His fingers were flying over the buttons of her blouse. "I have to—"

He wasn't being quick enough. "I'll do it." She kicked off her shoes and brushed his hands aside. "I don't need you for this."

"Whatever." His jacket dropped to the floor. "Just so you need me for—" He inhaled sharply as she came naked into his arms and began to rub against him. "Dear God." He closed his eyes. "I'm so damn close. Give me one minute."

"I don't want to—" She moved away from him. She was panting. Her skin felt burning, aching yet satin smooth, inviting touch. Inviting *him*. "Where's your control, Cameron?"

"I don't know," he said jerkily. "I don't have it with you. Everything's different with you." He was naked, pulling her to the couch and tipping her down onto softness. "The first time is going to be fast. I'll make it good, but I can't—" He parted her thighs and sank into her.

Deep.

Hot.

Hard.

She groaned through clenched teeth, and her nails sank into his shoulders.

But he was groaning hoarsely, too, and moving, lifting her to meet every thrust, turning her, taking every bit of her.

Madness.

Striving.

Her stomach was clenching to give more, take more.

But she couldn't take more no matter how she tried. And it was driving her insane.

She held him frantically tighter. "Cameron."

"I know." His tongue was in her mouth, taking deep. He raised his head. "Now . . . I'm sorry . . . it has to be now."

"Sorry?" Her teeth sank into his shoulder. "*Do* it."

He went deep, deeper than before. She hadn't thought it was possible, but he was pinning her and stroking with an intensity that was causing her mouth to open in a silent scream.

Deeper.

Round.

Deeper.

Frantic.

She climaxed!

And the scream was no longer silent but had become a broken sobbing of sheer pleasure and relief.

She was only vaguely aware of Cameron's low cry and his body stiffening above her. She was lost in a haze of pure physical sensation.

He was leaving her.

She instinctively tried to keep him inside her.

"Shh, not right now." He pushed her away and kissed her breast. "Rest, then I'll make this up to you."

What was he talking about? Oh, yes, something about control or lack of it. But none of that was important now. What was important was that she felt empty without him and wanted him back, wanted the rhythm and the madness back.

She watched him move off the couch, the moonlight playing on that beautiful, strong body like a shadow lover. But she wanted to see more of him. She was feeling a crazy sense of possession. "Turn on the lamp."

"No, I don't want anyone looking down from the house and noticing that we're here." He took out his penlight, turned it on, and put it on the end table by the couch. "But I want to see you, too."

The beam was only a little brighter than the moonlight, but she could see him. Oh, yes, superbly masculine and totally sexual. Purely sensual, muscular, tight belly and buttocks. And now that she had what she wanted, she was feeling a little awkward about it. Or perhaps it was because the first frantic, feverish need was subsiding, and her head was clearing. "It's okay. You're right, the light's not necessary."

"The hell it's not." His gaze was slowly going over her. "You're magnificent, you know. All gold and sable and grace. I want to take my time and memorize every gorgeous inch of you." He knelt before her, and his hands cupped her breasts and lifted them to his mouth. "Because I can't see time or opportunity allowing us another occasion like this anytime soon." He sucked gently, then teethed the nipple. "And you may decide I'm not what you want. I'll try to rectify that clumsiness I showed last time, but it's your decision."

His teeth were causing her nipple to harden and the need to return. And he had to know it. She said, "You're being very meek, but I think you're full of shit."

He lifted his head and smiled. "Partly. I have no intention of giving you or this up. I just have to find a way to keep it going that won't interfere with your independence." He parted her thighs, widened them, and began stroking the soft hair. "I admire and respect your independence. Did I ever tell you that?"

She was losing her breath again. "I can't remember its coming up."

"I do. But it's going to get in the way. I found out something tonight. I kept thinking . . . mine."

"How barbaric and completely chauvinistic. What about *your* independence?"

He grinned. "That doesn't bother me."

"I'm sure," she said dryly. "Because you consider it totally inviolate. Not fair, Cameron."

"No, but I'm trying to give as much as I can." His fingers started gently plucking. "I know I can't have it all my own way."

Heat was spreading from his fingers to her entire lower body, and she had to steady her voice. "Why even discuss it? It's only sex and really has nothing to do with who we are. Who I am. This isn't me. Do you think I do this all the time? You managed to sweep me away, and I'm still dizzy from it. But I'll come to my senses. So will you."

"Will I?" He leaned forward, and his lips touched her belly. "I don't think so. I'm caught. I don't even want to be free." He licked delicately. "So I'll just have to find a way to have you. Get used to the idea."

She closed her eyes as her entire body started to ready. "It's only sex," she repeated. "And you'll become bored. I'm just another woman in your life."

"Neither of us is going to become bored." His fingers were moving down. "We started out with something pretty incredible, and I'll keep fanning the flame until it gets so high, it will burn us both to touch it."

She was burning now. His fingers were doing something strange, wickedly erotic . . . "Cameron."

"You like that?" He rubbed his cheek against her belly, and she felt the faint bearded roughness. "I told you I'd take my time from now on. Providing I can keep control. I believe I can hold on. I told you I was forced to limit sexual encounters to prostitutes, and that may have advantages for you. I was taught many, many ways. There are so many things I can do with my hands and mouth . . ." Pressure. Two fingers. His thumb. "And I can do them for hours and hours." Three fingers. He pressed hard with his thumb.

She cried out and lunged upward as an explosion of pure lust shot through her.

"Shh, it's just starting." He was rubbing, pressing, pinching. "I love to see you like this. Will you believe that it's the only control I want to have over you?"

Her head was moving back and forth on the couch in an agony of need. "No, I don't—believe you."

"Well, right now." He whispered, "And perhaps, if I bring you enough pleasure, you'll let me share that beautiful mind while I'm inside your body. That would be spectacular. There's a thousand sensations and emotions I could give you if you permit me to do that."

"No." She could barely speak as she clenched helplessly around his fingers. "Dangerous."

"Not if you trust me."

She shook her head.

"You're trusting me to do this to you. That's only another step." He looked up at her and coaxed, "It would please me. Sometimes I think I love that mind of yours better than I do your body." He leaned forward and licked her nipple. "And then I realize that I can have both if I work hard at it."

"You can't have either." Dear heaven, his fingers, intricate, knowing . . . She hadn't known anyone could do that . . .

"Yes, I can. Just look at us. Right now, this is strictly on loan. But I'm working toward making it a permanent arrangement." His lips returned to her belly. "But you're distracting me, I'm not working hard enough. I have to see if I can make you want to please me as much I'm pleasing you." His breath was warm and heavy as he moved down. "What do you think, Catherine?"

Don't scream. Don't scream. Don't scream.

She screamed.

CHAPTER
16

Something was wrong.

Something was missing.

Cameron wasn't with her.

Catherine's eyes flew open.

No, he hadn't left her. He was standing in front of the window staring out into the darkness.

Still naked, buttocks tight, shoulders back, and legs slightly parted.

"What are you looking at?" She raised herself on one arm. "Is it getting light?"

"No." He looked over his shoulder. "Not for another hour or so." He smiled. "I was just putting space between us, so that I could give you a little rest. But you didn't doze long."

Because she had grown so accustomed to his body next to her, in her, that it had disturbed her not to have him there. During those last hours, the sexual intensity had been unremitting, and they had not been able to get enough of each other. She had never known that animal wildness and mindless need. The various forms of exotic play he'd used to bring her to the edge of sexual madness had been fantastic and exhausting. She had never responded to anyone as she had

Cameron. Even now, looking at him, she felt a heaviness and swelling in her breasts and a deep throbbing where his hands had brought her to climax so many times before he'd allowed himself to thrust inside her.

Madness, indeed. She drew a shaky breath and sat up on the couch. "I've got to get back to the house."

"We have time." He looked away from her again. "You didn't let me share your mind. I wanted very badly to do that, Catherine. Were you that much afraid of me?"

"No, you were taking enough. You didn't need to take that, too."

"I would have given, not taken, Catherine. I could have taken anyway, but I didn't want you to throw it back at me later. I'm trying hard. You don't know how hard." He turned and strolled toward her. "Let me show you that I can give. I want you again."

She could see that. She looked away from him and got to her feet and turned to gather her clothes. "No, it's over. I'm a woman with responsibilities. I don't go creeping into a house at daybreak. Particularly not when my son is in that house."

"I'll be quick." He was behind her and reached around to cup her breasts. "You want me, too."

"Yes." And if she stood here and let him touch and rub against her, she would give in to that need. She had been helpless before Cameron's skill and her own sexual attraction toward him all night. It had to end. She stepped away from him. "But I don't always do what I want." She felt his gaze on her as she headed quickly toward the tiny bathroom at the back of the summerhouse. She closed the door and leaned against it. She'd give herself a few minutes before she washed and started to dress. God, she wanted to open the door and go out there and begin that sexual rhapsody all over again.

She wouldn't do it.

Cameron was dangerous to her in too many ways.

She stepped to the vanity and began to run the water. It was over. Leave him and become Catherine Ling again.

Ten minutes later, she braced herself, opened the door, and came out of the bathroom. Cameron was sitting on the couch, still naked, gazing at her without expression.

"You're still barefoot," he said. "Your shoes are under the couch. I saw them a minute ago. You'd better put them on before you leave. Bare feet aren't suitable for creeping into houses either. Much worse than the idea of coming in at the crack of dawn."

"I was just coming out to get them."

"I'll do it." He got up and picked up her shoes and brought them to her. "What sensible shoes." He knelt down and picked up her foot and slipped them into the flat. "You have wonderful, shapely feet. I didn't pay enough attention to them tonight. The feet have a number of pleasure zones." His fingers moved teasingly on her instep as he put her other foot into the mate. "Next time."

She didn't answer as she turned toward the door. "You'll let me know when you hear anything about Kadmus?"

"Of course; nothing has changed in that direction. I'll do my job. You'll do your job. Erin will be saved. Kadmus will die." He was suddenly beside her and whirling her back against the door. His eyes were glittering, and he was no longer without expression. Anger. Frustration. Desire. Yes, definitely desire. "But everything has changed with us, hasn't it, Catherine?" His voice was hoarse and clipped. "You can walk away, but you're not going to forget me. You're going to remember everything I did to you and with you. You're going to know that every time I look at you, I'm going to remember the taste of your breasts and want to take them out and hold them. You'll know that if I get a chance, no matter where we are, in a car or a room or even in a ditch, I'll do what I did tonight. I knew I wasn't going to have another chance for hours alone with you. But I'll make do." His lips covered her own, savage, open, taking, giving. "And you'll want it and take *me*. Because neither one of us can help what we're feeling." He turned away. "Now go and be a good mother to Luke, a good friend to Hu Chang, Venable's best agent. In the end, we'll be together, and you'll be just mine. I'll try to stay away from you for a while so that I can look at you without showing how I'm feeling." He added tightly, "Which probably won't happen."

"Cameron. I don't—" There wasn't anything to say, and the atmosphere was too charged. She had to get away from him. She turned, opened the door, and flew down the walk toward the house. She tried desperately to remember the code she'd been given for the back door.

Yes, that was it. She keyed in the numbers, and the door swung open.

She was inside in the darkness of the foyer.

She tried to catch her breath as she started for the staircase down the hall. She was passing the library, where she'd watched Luke and Hu Chang play chess all those hours ago. It seemed a century. She felt changed. Her body felt . . . riper. She had the odd sensation that Cameron was still with her, a part of her.

It would go away. It had to go away. She would wake in a few hours, and she would have a hell of a lot of erotic memories but not this feeling of being possessed.

But what if it didn't go away?

•   •   •

Brasden received a phone call just as they were getting off the private jet at the airport in San Francisco. "Keep questioning him. He might have been paid to keep silent about Ling's destination." He hung up and turned to Kadmus. "Nagle found the taxi driver who picked up Sullivan, Ling, Hu Chang, and some kid at an airport north of the city. He took them to a destination in Chinatown. But he was told to let them out in front of a restaurant, and he saw them walking down the street as he was driving away."

"No address?"

Brasden shook his head. "But a general location. Nagle is questioning everyone on the street and trying to pin it down. It's reasonable that Ling would choose a safe house in an Asian neighborhood. She grew up in Hong Kong and must have local contacts."

"Or maybe she's trying to throw a red herring into the mix," Kadmus said. "Who is to say she didn't leave Chinatown after that taxi let them out?" He frowned. "A kid?"

"There was a kid that got on that helicopter on the mountain. There were several reports."

"I thought maybe it was one of Erin's village charity cases who she wanted to hide away from me. But she could have dropped him in Hong Kong. Why take him with her to the U.S.?"

Brasden was looking at the dossiers on his phone. "Catherine Ling has an eleven-year-old son, Luke."

Kadmus chuckled. "And she would definitely take him out of my reach if she could. I'd gut the little son of a bitch. I'm just wondering why the hell he was with them on that mountain." He shrugged. "But that doesn't matter right now. He's with her here in San Francisco, and that opens all kinds of possibilities. Erin Sullivan has a soft heart toward children. Maternal love would be a powerful weapon where Ling is concerned. I can use the kid." He strode toward the car waiting by the hangar. "Find him."

"I will." Brasden strolled after him. "But there's an order to these things. The kid will be with his mother, and we know she's with Richard Cameron. After all, he's your prime target. We'll continue looking for the blue Mercedes Cameron used. When we find it, everything may come together. I would have thought you'd have learned that after all these years, Kadmus."

"I've forgotten more than you've ever learned," Kadmus said. "You're going at it backwards. Find the kid. He was with Hu Chang and Sullivan in the taxi. Ling is going to have to leave him with someone if she's not with him. If we grab the kid, Ling will hand us Cameron."

Brasden was silent. "You may have a point. We'll see how it goes."

"It better go damn quick. Scour those streets in Chinatown and find someone who knows something." Kadmus got in the passenger seat of the Cadillac. "And get me Ling's cell-phone number. I want a way to contact her when I'm ready."

"No problem." Brasden got in the driver's seat and started the car. "It will take a few hours, but I can get it."

"You're being very accommodating," Kadmus said sarcastically. "What's happening?"

"I don't mind cooperating. I just had to make sure that you realized I had the upper hand. I told you, I want a percentage, not the entire pot. I'm willing to listen to you on occasion. I'd prefer to be the silent partner who skips away if the situation becomes too hot to handle." He smiled maliciously. "And watches from a distance as they tear you limb from limb."

Kadmus didn't reply.

Smother the rage. It would only be for a little while. He would be able to deal with Brasden soon. He was getting closer all the time to the prize. They were in the same city as Cameron and Cameron could lead him to Shambhala.

And the key to Cameron was no longer Erin Sullivan, who had proved to be such a disappointment.

It was Catherine Ling and a boy named Luke.

•   •   •

"You slept later than I thought you would," Hu Chang said when Catherine came into the dining room. "It's nearly ten."

"I was up late." She sat down and poured herself a cup of tea. "Where's Luke?"

"With Erin and Celia in the garden. He's playing badminton with Celia."

"What? Badminton? I can't see him playing that. I always imagine women in old-fashioned long white gowns and big hats playing the game."

"Badminton is an Olympic sport these days, and the play can become fairly intense. Not the way Celia plays it. She prefers it slow and easy. But she has a tiny garden, and badminton fits the area requirements. Besides, she likes the game." He added dryly, "Of course, after playing with Luke, she may change her mind. He doesn't know how to be slow and easy. And he can sometimes be overenthusiastic. He's like that with every competition."

"Did he beat you at chess last night?"

"No, but he came exceptionally close. He wanted to start playing after breakfast, but I told him to go outside and clear his mind."

"I'll take my tea and go out and join him." She started to get up. "It may be the only time I get the chance before you take him back to that library."

"Have your tea," Hu Chang said. "You look like you need it."

"Do I?" She smiled with an effort. "I'm fine." It wasn't the truth. She had woken an hour ago with a strange languor and a feeling of emptiness. It had filled her with panic. She did not want to have any lingering sensations from her time with Cameron. She wanted to be totally sharp and completely her own person. She had jumped out of bed, showered, dressed, and come down to face her world. "As I said, I had a late night. Cameron came to the house after I left you and Luke. He found the place he wants to set his trap for Kadmus." She sat down again and lifted her cup to her lips. "It's a fireworks factory on Clement Street. Moon, Stars, and Heavenly Wonders. Weird name, isn't it? Three floors and shops on the street level. Cameron was already in the process of buying it from the owner, but wanted me to see it and make sure I was familiar with every floor."

"Yes, very weird name. And did you examine it thoroughly?"

"Yes, of course. I won't have any problems when the trap's sprung."

"No, I have the utmost confidence in you when it comes to overcoming problems of that sort." He took a sip of his tea and leaned back in his chair. "But sometimes other problems of a more personal nature tend to challenge you. Did you face a few of those last night, Catherine?"

She met his eyes. Wise eyes, eyes that could see into her soul. She would not lie to him. "Yes." She moistened her lips. "He makes me—I've never met anyone who—He's different. I have to fight for control with him all the time. Sometimes I lose. I don't like that, Hu Chang."

"No, you wouldn't." He paused. "But evidently he sometimes loses, too. Can you imagine how difficult that must be for him? He's the Guardian. He has to win. He was chosen and trained to win."

"Then let him go and win with someone else." She steadied her hand as she raised her cup to her lips. "I'm my own person. I can't let him dominate me. I won't let him take and take, no matter how I—" She stopped. "I don't want to talk about him any longer. All I know is that we have to get Kadmus and make sure Erin is safe." She got to her feet. "And we have to do it right away. I want to go home with Luke and be what I am and not what Cameron wants me to be." She drank the last of her tea. She was already feeling better and more herself now that she had talked to Hu Chang and voiced her thoughts. "Now I'm going out to the garden and see my son. Do you want to come with me?"

"Delighted." He rose to his feet and followed her toward the French doors. "I believe the sun is shining. We haven't had much of that since we arrived. Celia always says this city is wonderful, but I could use less fog and more sun."

The sun *was* shining. The brilliant rays were glinting on Luke's dark hair as he leaped to hit the shuttlecock over the net at Celia. Catherine stood in the doorway, watching them for a minute.

Then Luke saw her and stopped. "Hi, Catherine. Want to play?"

She shook her head. "I've never played badminton." She made a face. "I've never really learned to play any games. I didn't have time when I was growing up."

He grinned. "Neither did I. But I've been learning since you brought me home. Come and play. I'll teach you."

She stared at him in surprise.

"Yes, go on and play, Catherine," Hu Chang murmured.

Come and play. I'll teach you.

Was a door opening? She had been the one teaching Luke since they'd rescued him from Rakovac. She'd tried to supply all he needed and give him everything he'd missed. But he'd told her that she had to accept him for what he was.

Now he wanted to teach her.

Did he mean come and play, be my friend, not my mother, not my teacher? She didn't care if she was overanalyzing it. She'd take it.

She smiled and started toward him. "You probably just want to have an easy mark. Celia looked like she was pretty good."

"I've been savaged. Your son is a whirlwind." Celia grimaced. "Please, take over for me."

Catherine took the racquet Celia handed her. "Okay, Luke, show me how to play this game."

·   ·   ·

"She's not very good at this, is she?" Cameron asked Hu Chang from where he stood at the French doors. His gaze was on Catherine across the garden. She was laughing, her cheeks flushed, and she leaped forward, then sent the ball into the net. "I'm surprised. She's always seemed so competent at everything."

"She's only been at this for a couple hours," Hu Chang said quietly. "And she doesn't care if she doesn't win. She's playing with her son. She figures she's already won."

"I can see that." Cameron had never seen her like this. She looked almost as young as Luke. No wariness, no edge, just pleasure. He felt a surge of warmth that was rare for him. "I . . . like it."

"She doesn't care if you like it or not," Hu Chang said. "And I like her like this, too. I don't want her disturbed."

Cameron's glance shifted from Catherine to his face. "Do I detect antagonism?"

"I haven't decided. I usually don't interfere with Catherine's choices. But you seem to have pulled out all the stops, and you're very formidable." He added thoughtfully, "Now, if you'd just walk away, it would solve a lot of confusion."

"I'm not going to walk away."

"Then I'll just have to observe the situation and see if she regains her equilibrium. I believe that will be the way to handle it. Everything may resolve itself."

"And if it doesn't?"

"The usual conflict that occurs between men such as us."

"I would regret that." He meant it. Those months with Hu Chang had brought him both relief and camaraderie. "I've not met anyone in all my years as Guardian whom I respect as much as I do you."

"And I also. I do not know whether you're right or wrong, but there are few men in this weary world who would battle so hard for a cause. I found it refreshing. I would hate to remove you." He smiled. "But we will not discuss this yet. Catherine is in no danger of hurt while she concentrates on saving Erin. I assume you came to talk to her about plans to do that?"

"Yes." His gaze went back to Catherine, and he felt again that strange warmth. He wanted to keep her smiling with that childlike enthusiasm. "But I can tell you as well. She's busy."

Hu Chang's brows rose. "Interesting. And unusual for you. I believe that's a step back."

"Perhaps you don't read me as well as you think." He turned to face him. "I've had a report from Blake. Kadmus and Brasden arrived here a few hours ago."

"Kadmus. Then you did manage to draw him here. How did you know he'd arrived?"

"Blake bribed one of Nagle's team to come over to his camp. He'll be very useful."

"Without question," Hu Chang said. "What comes next?"

"We bait the trap. I'm moving Catherine, Erin, and you to the fireworks factory tomorrow night. She told you about it?"

"Yes. What about Luke?"

"He stays here with Celia, where I can surround him with protection. I'll have Blake assign several of his best men to him."

"You may have trouble with that plan. Luke will want to protect Catherine."

"He'll have to forget it. I'll try to find something for him to do that will be safe. I gave her my word I'd take care of him."

"Indeed? Then I'll gladly leave that task to you. After all, you are the Guardian." Hu Chang's tone verged on mockery. "And I assume that the man you have in Nagle's camp will be able to give us warning when Kadmus intends to attack."

"Yes." He paused. "And also give Kadmus any information I might want him to have."

"What information?"

"I'll have to see. No plan is foolproof, there's always ebb and flow. Just when you think every detail is set, something comes along to blow it apart." He gave one last look at Catherine and turned away. "Tell her I'll get back to her with any new info."

"Or you can let me know. I'm always here for you, Cameron."

"Or for Catherine." Cameron smiled recklessly over his shoulder. "Always for Catherine." He strode through the hall toward the front door. "But I don't like to take steps back. I believe next time, I'll deal with the lady herself."

•   •   •

"Thursday. Tomorrow night," Erin repeated the words after Catherine. She shivered. "Tomorrow night, Kadmus will be dead. Tomorrow, I can go back to living a normal life. It doesn't seem possible."

"It's possible." She added firmly, "It's going to happen, Erin. Cameron set it up, and he may be many things that irritate the hell out of me, but, according to Hu Chang, he doesn't make mistakes. He's a master manipulator."

Erin smiled faintly. "I know. But he never tried to manipulate me, Catherine. You've always accused him of being responsible. How can I convince you that he only gave me a choice, a wonderful choice?"

"That caused you months of imprisonment and torture." She held up her hand as Erin opened her lips to speak. "I believe you . . . sometimes. When I'm far away from Cameron and not exposed to all that power and charisma."

"You keep struggling against him." Erin shook her head. "Relax and trust him, Catherine. You're a good deal alike. You could understand him if you gave him a chance."

She only understood the power and the hypnotizing force of both his body and personality. There was no way she could relax or trust Cameron. Yes, they were alike, but there was a secret place within both of them that neither would surrender. "I trust that he'll get the job done in setting the trap for Kadmus. That's the only thing that's important." She turned and headed for the staircase. "Now I need to shower and change. That son of mine showed no mercy, and I feel like a wrung-out dishrag."

"But you enjoyed it," Erin said quietly. "And so did he. It was nice to watch the two of you."

"Yes, I enjoyed it." She had felt younger than Luke as she had played. "And maybe next time, I'll be able to take that rascal."

"I was so busy laughing at the two of you that I didn't even notice Cameron talking to Hu Chang."

"Neither did I." She started up the stairs. She couldn't decide if she was relieved or disappointed that Cameron had not waited and spoken to her.

Relieved, of course.

"Catherine."

She looked down at Erin still standing in the hall.

"Trust him," she urged softly. "I'm not blind. I've been trained to watch and listen and draw conclusions. Your relationship will never be the same as mine with Cameron. There's nothing cerebral or spiritual in what you are together. But that doesn't mean that you can't give him what he needs." She paused. "He's very much alone, Catherine."

"His choice. He's the Guardian." She turned and started climbing the steps again. "And I can't imagine anything worse than giving up my life and career to trail behind him when I don't even believe in what he's doing." She glanced down as she reached the top step. "And you evidently didn't either. You refused him when he tried to recruit you for Shambhala."

"I'm not sure I would now." Erin smiled. "I've been thinking about it. I'm stronger than that day he gave me the choice."

"Then you go and keep the arrogant bastard from being lonely."

"That wouldn't be my job. As he explained it, I would have my own duties and rewards." She turned away. "It sounded . . . wonderful."

Catherine shook her head as she opened the door to the bedroom. She could see how Erin would embrace a life of giving herself to the cause of peace. She was as much a peacemaker as Catherine was a warrior.

"Catherine."

She turned to see Luke standing at his bedroom door. His hair was wet from the shower, and he was smiling. "You did good that last game."

"Liar. But I'll get better. When we get home to Louisville, I'll start practicing."

"It's not really worth it. What about tennis?"

"What? I'm just learning badminton."

"Sam has been teaching me tennis for the past couple months. I'll show you what he's taught me."

"Whatever." She smiled at him. "It will be fun. You're opening new doors for me, Luke."

"I . . . liked it. I'm glad we came here." He moved past her and started down the steps. "I've got to go down to the library and meet

Hu Chang. You've been pretty busy. Are you going to be here for dinner?"

"Yes, but you'll be so absorbed, you won't even know I'm here."

He didn't look back. "I'll know, Catherine."

She felt a warmth surge through her as she watched him go down the steps. He had said he was glad they had come here. He was so resilient that he was able to ignore the bad and embrace the good. It was a great gift. She couldn't say that she was glad. Last night with Cameron had shaken her world, and the looming danger was terrifying.

But for these few hours with Luke, she had been so happy that all the tension and worry seemed worth it. It had brought them together and even cast a glow on the future.

So maybe it had been worthwhile coming to Celia's house. But now she had to concentrate on getting out of this house and doing what she had come to this city to do. It would be—

Her cell phone rang, and she glanced at the ID. Venable. She punched the access. "No, I haven't dropped Erin Sullivan, and I'm not going to do it. Have you changed your mind?"

"No, I'm right, and you're wrong," he said. "I called to tell you that your private access information has been breached. It was done by someone who was good and had contacts in the Agency."

"Kadmus?"

"Possibly. Whoever it was wanted your telephone number very badly."

"Evidently, I may be about to be contacted," Catherine said. "I'm flattered. I've been pretty much ignored since I snatched Erin. I must have made more of an impression on the bastard than I thought."

"Enough to be targeted. Be careful, Catherine."

"My phone is blocked. He can't track me unless I actually pick up. That means I won't be able to pick up while I'm in this house with the others." She was thinking quickly, sorting out options. "But he wants contact. I need to give him what he wants. Can you put a tracking device on my phone for the next twenty-four hours so that I can grab his signal?"

"I've already done it."

"Thanks, Venable." She hung up.

What did Kadmus want from her beside the obvious? Revenge? Information? She was clearly going to find out.

And what then?

Go after Kadmus herself? Or stick with Cameron's plan for tomorrow night? Tomorrow night might be too late. She had an idea that Kadmus was impatient and hungry. Impatient men were prone to mistakes. Cameron has set up his scenario and just assumed she would go along with it. Maybe she would. But she would have to think about it and maybe do a little reconnoitering of her own.

Her phone rang. Private number.

Is that you, Kadmus? Probably. But you can't have me. Not yet.

He was as impatient as she'd thought. But if he'd called once, he'd call again.

Soon.

And she'd be ready for him.

CHINATOWN

CLEMENT STREET

WEDNESDAY

9:35 P.M.

Call me, Kadmus.

She gazed at her reflection in a shop window that sold Chinese toys. Pretty, genteel toys. Nothing Luke would appreciate. She didn't look very genteel herself. She had aimed at appearing to be a casual tourist. She wore a loose white blouse, had bound her hair up beneath a colorful scarf, and was wearing large tortoiseshell glasses.

Call me, Kadmus.

She'd been moving around Chinatown for the last hour, waiting for a call that had not come. Though she had stayed principally in the alleyways and away from anywhere that she might be recognized. It was irritating that Kadmus had not seen fit to call when she was perfectly placed now.

Four blocks from the fireworks factory.

A good sixteen blocks from Celia's house.

If Kadmus tapped her phone, he would definitely trace her to this area, and it would be a smooth way to make a connection to the factory if they decided to use Cameron's plan. It might be assumed she'd come from the factory safe house.

And the distance to Celia's house should be safe for everyone there.

Just call and get this over with, Kadmus.

Five minutes later, the phone rang.

Private number.

Be cool. No eagerness.

She let it ring three times before she picked up. "Is that you, Kadmus? I hear you've been exceptionally inquisitive. I'm flattered you think that I'm worth all the money you must have spent."

"I'm only going to talk for a few minutes," Kadmus said. "I know you probably have a trace, bitch."

"And you don't? Talk, Kadmus."

"I want Cameron. You're going to give him to me."

"He's not mine to give. Find him yourself."

"You were with him when you took that scumbag, Jack Sen, from the hospital. What did Cameron promise you to help him? Money? Treasure? Death to your enemies? He's very good at promises. But don't bank on his keeping them. I've already killed one man he promised to take under his wing."

"Did you torture him as you did Erin?"

"Yes, the fool killed himself rather than betray Cameron." He paused. "I should have gone another route and tortured his children. But I learn from my mistakes."

She tensed. "What are you saying?"

"You have a son, and you have him with you. You apparently can't bear to be parted from him. Give me Cameron or I'll not only kill your boy, I'll cut him into pieces . . . very slowly."

She drew a deep breath, trying to suppress the anger . . . and fear. "You bastard. Luke has nothing to do with this."

"I really don't care," Kadmus said. "I'll take him, or Erin Sullivan, or your friend, Hu Chang. Anyone who stands in my way. *You* stand in my way, Ling."

"You can't touch him. You have no idea where he is now."

"I'll find out. I have photos of all of you. I have men searching the city. I'll find your Luke, then you'll come begging to trade Cameron. But it might be too late. If I find Cameron first, I won't have a use for the boy. He'll be in my way, and I'll kill him." He added persuasively, "What do you care about Cameron? Let me have him and keep your son. I'm hanging up now. I'll call you tomorrow evening. By that time, I should have my sights on you. It might be your last chance to deal." He hung up.

Move!

Three minutes would have been enough for him to get a fix on her location. There would be someone here within a few minutes or less.

She accessed the tracking device as she started trotting down the street, then ducked into the alley. It gave her a general location somewhere near the park but had not had time to pinpoint the exact location, dammit. She hadn't really expected to get lucky. She ducked into an alley and ran toward the brightly lit street at the other end. Stay away from Celia's and keep running until Kadmus's men gave up the search.

Run.

Don't get near Luke until it was safe.

Oh, God, when would it be safe for him?

That bastard, Kadmus. He had meant it when he'd said he'd chop him into pieces. Look what he'd done to Erin.

Watch.

Run.

She darted in and out of alleys and streets for the next ten minutes.

She finally stopped and drew a deep breath. She'd not seen any signs of pursuit, but that didn't mean that she was free to go back to the house. Give it another ten minutes.

"Or fifteen."

She whirled to see Cameron walking down the alley toward her.

She could only see him dimly, but his grim expression was not to be mistaken. She braced herself. "Ten should be enough. I haven't seen any signs of Kadmus's men." She moistened her lips. "And I do have on a disguise."

"Not much of one." He stopped before her. "That scarf only makes you look more exotic."

"I considered wearing a wig, but I decided the scarf looked more casual. I think it works." Why was she standing here talking to him about wigs? she thought impatiently. "Why are you here?"

"Because you're here," he said roughly. "And because you didn't see fit to tell me that you were playing Kadmus alone."

"It was a recent development. I thought it had potential." She paused. "I don't have to ask how you knew about it."

"It was too dangerous trusting you to be cool and reasonable after last night. I had to know what you were thinking." He added, "And what you were doing."

"And you found out. I'm sure you eavesdropped on my conversation with that bastard." Her lips twisted. "Am I a threat to you, Cameron? Kadmus wants to use me as one, and he's determined to find my Achilles' heel. What do you generally do to threats?"

"That wouldn't apply. It's not the same."

"You'd destroy them."

"It's not the same," he repeated.

"No? Then what should I do if Kadmus does get his hands on Luke and wants me to hand you over to him?"

"Do as he said—betray me and save your son."

"No!" Her eyes widened in stunned horror. She had not expected that answer. "That's not acceptable either. You're the Guardian and supposed to be able to solve all this kind of ugliness. What good are you?"

"Good enough to take on Kadmus. So betray me and let me do it. But that won't happen. I promised you that I'd take care of your son."

"Kadmus said that your promises aren't worth a damn."

"He lied."

"I know," she whispered. "I think I know, Cameron."

"He shook you. He made you afraid," Cameron said harshly. "I could feel him doing it. I wanted to kill him."

"So did I." She smiled with an effort. "I hate being afraid. I can usually control it. But there's no rhyme or reason about any threat to Luke. I react instinctively." She straightened her shoulders. "And I can take care of my own son, Cameron. You go take care of yourself. I was hoping against hope that I might be able to zero in on Kadmus's location, but that didn't happen. Which means we'll have to go along with the plan for tomorrow night." She started to turn away. "Now I'll go back to Celia's. I found a roundabout way to get there when I was wandering around waiting for Kadmus's call that should be safer." She looked back at him. "I suppose you were tuned in to that, too?"

He didn't answer.

She shrugged. "It doesn't matter."

"Everything matters." His hand was on her wrist, whirling her to face him. He tore the scarf from her hair and the glasses from her face and tossed them on the ground. Then she was in his arms, pressed against his body, his hand cupping the back of her head against his chest. "When it's between us."

Her heart leaped, and she went still. No, don't touch me. Don't let it be like last night. She was feeling vulnerable enough right now.

"Shh." He was rocking her, his face buried against her temple. "I only want to hold you, help you. Don't fight me."

She couldn't fight him. He had never been like this with her. He was showing her the same exquisite tenderness she had seen him show Erin that night at the hot springs. It was like being stroked with velvet, and that tenderness was flowing into her and taking out all the pain.

"If you'd just accept me, I'd never let you be hurt again," he said thickly.

Just one more minute, then she'd step away from him. "Oh, yes, that would be just fine," she said unevenly. "No responsibility for what I do or the safety of my son. All I have to do is act like a robot and permit you to run my life."

"It's not like that."

"I think it is. It's like your damn committee, who are trying to bring peace as they perceive it to the world. They do it by stealing brains and talent and cocooning the chosen to wait for the rest of us to destroy ourselves." She moved away from him. "Only I wouldn't be chosen, Cameron. I'd rather be in the trenches trying to keep the bombs from falling and the madmen from inheriting the Earth."

"So did I at one time." He didn't try to touch her again, but she felt as if she could still feel his hands on her, hear his heart beneath her ear. His eyes were glittering, and the tenderness was no longer there. Intensity. Passion. Lust. This was the Cameron of last night, and she could feel her body begin to respond in the same way. He said recklessly, "And screw the committee, I choose you. No one would question me."

"I'm sure they wouldn't. You seem to be all-powerful in their eyes." She turned away and grabbed her scarf and glasses from the ground where he'd thrown them. "Well, I don't choose you."

He wasn't following her as she'd thought he might. He stood watching her as she hurried away from him.

"You will, Catherine," he called softly. "You will."

CHAPTER
17

No sign of her," Brasden said when Kadmus came in from the balcony of his hotel room. He went over to the coffee table where a map of the city had been placed. "But with the phone trace, we've narrowed down these blocks in Chinatown." He drew a wide circle. "So the chances are that Sullivan and Ling are still in a safe house somewhere in that area."

"And Cameron may be with them," Kadmus gazed down at the circle on the map. It looked like such a small area that he felt a sudden surge of savage pleasure.

I'm closing in on you, bitch. Just a few steps more, and I'll have you.

"I've doubled the men we have patrolling Chinatown and made sure all of them have photos. They'll call if they see them on the streets or get any reports about anyone of their description."

"Good." He smiled. "I'll be happy if they can move the timeline forward. But I've *got* her. It should take only one more phone call to narrow her location down even more."

"If she'll take the call."

"She'll take it. She's not as tough as you led me to believe. I could tell that I frightened her with talk of the boy. When she picks up the phone, we'll start closing in. She's so scared, she'll keep the boy with her. Once we have him, she'll cave."

"You're very sure."

"Because I have a destiny, and I know that she's not going to be able to stop me." He could feel the power coursing through him. "None of you will be able to stop me."

"Unless you decide to betray me," Brasden said. "But I'm sure you're not thinking of that any longer." He turned and moved toward the door. "We're cooperating so nicely these days."

Kadmus didn't answer as the door closed behind him. Brasden was a dead man. He'd sealed his fate a long time ago and wasn't worth thinking about.

He had told Brasden that he had a destiny, and that grand destiny was looming closer with every passing moment. He had never been more certain than after that call with Ling.

Ling was the path to Cameron.

And Cameron was the path to Kadmus's destiny.

He pulled the lotus necklace that Brasden had tossed so contemptuously at him out of his pocket. He caressed the pendant with a gentle finger.

Destiny.

Shambhala.

THURSDAY

3:37 P.M.

"What's happening, Catherine?" Erin was standing in the doorway of the library looking at Hu Chang and Catherine. "When do we leave? You've not said a word to me today."

Catherine had been afraid of this confrontation.

"I was busy with Luke. I wanted—" She shook her head. Erin

deserved the truth. "I was trying to think of a way to tell you that you're out of it."

"What?" She stared Catherine in the eye. "The hell I am. I'm in this up to my neck. Why does Cameron want me out?"

"He doesn't, I do," Catherine said. "Look, there's no use your going to the fireworks factory tonight. I told you Kadmus seems to have changed focus. Leave it up to Cameron and me."

"And my humble self," Hu Chang said. "Whose help is magnificently useful and erases the need for anyone else."

"No way," Erin said flatly. "You're not closing me out. If you leave me here, I'll be knocking on the door of that damn Stars, Moon, and Heavenly—whatever. This is more my fight than anyone else's."

"You're not needed," Catherine said. "I don't want you to go, Erin. And it may not be necessary now. I told you, Kadmus is narrowing his sights on me at the moment. I can be the bait."

"I'm going. I'll let you whisk me out of there as you planned because I don't want you to risk yourself trying to protect me. But I *will* be part of this, Catherine."

Catherine sighed. "You're a very stubborn woman, Erin."

"Yes." Erin's warm smile suddenly lit her face. "Hey, if Kadmus couldn't break me, you don't stand a chance. What time?"

"After dinner, as soon as we can slip away." She paused. "Luke is not to know."

"Trouble."

"Dammit, he's going to be safe here. Cameron promised me that the place would be surrounded by Blake's guards and that he'd check on him frequently." She didn't like it, but she had no choice. Other than tying Luke up and stuffing him in a closet, Cameron's solution was the only logical and safe one. "I'll only be gone a few hours. I'm hoping Celia can distract him."

"Distraction is certainly her area of expertise," Hu Chang said. "But she's limited in Luke's case."

"I didn't need to hear that," Catherine said. "Or maybe I did. I just hope she'll rise to the occasion." She got to her feet. "I can't change your mind, Erin?"

She shook her head. "We've traveled this path together. I won't leave you now."

Catherine gazed at her with frustration, deep affection, and a trace of panic. They were so close to assuring Erin's permanent safety, but tonight, anything could happen.

She smiled with an effort. "Just stay close as you did in that hot spring, and we'll be okay."

She nodded. "And I promise I won't duck my head under the water."

"See that you don't."

But what they might encounter tonight could be far deadlier than anything they'd yet faced together.

God, keep her safe. She's gone through so much. Give her a break tonight.

7:40 P.M.

Celia gazed at Luke uncertainly. He'd been much too quiet for the past thirty minutes.

Luke turned away from the French doors to look at her.

"Where's Catherine?" he asked uncertainly. "And Hu Chang? Something's happening, isn't it?"

"Something is always happening," Celia said. "But nothing for you to worry about."

"I saw men on the street at the front of the house and one near the corner. Who are they?"

"No one to concern you. Cameron has the house surrounded by several lethal-looking men who he assures me will take good care of all of us."

"Why should he do that? Where's Catherine?" Luke repeated. "I haven't seen her since dinner. And Hu Chang, he always—"

"You'll have to ask Cameron. He said he'd come around and check on you later." She smiled. "He's gone to a lot of trouble. He evidently cares a great deal for you, Luke."

"I like him, too." He added, "Most of the time."

"I feel the same way." Celia laughed. "But you may have more reason. He's turned your life upside down."

"No, he hasn't. I'm the one who decided to go after Catherine when she left Hong Kong." His gaze went to the garden. "There are two men out there near the summerhouse. Are they more of the men Cameron assigned to us?"

"Yes. Stop worrying. Come into the kitchen with me, and I'll make you a cup of jasmine tea."

"I'm not worrying. I just have to know what's happening." He didn't turn around. "Catherine's gone to that fireworks factory she was talking about with Erin and Hu Chang, hasn't she?"

She went still. "I don't know about any fireworks factory. I don't ask, and I prefer not to be involved." She paused. "How did you happen to hear about it? I can't see Catherine's discussing it around you."

"She didn't. I heard them talking, but I didn't hear it all. I didn't know it was tonight. She should have told me." His hand tightened on the French doorjamb. "She should have *taken* me. But I knew she wasn't going to do it."

"So you decided to do a little eavesdropping?" Celia asked shrewdly. "What did you hear, Luke?"

"Enough. She should have taken me. We should be together. I should be able to take care of her."

"I'm not sure how mothers usually think, but I don't believe that's the way it goes, Luke." She shrugged. "Anyway, it's too late. You'll have to make the best of staying with me until Cameron gives me a call. He made it very clear that all of these guards were here to keep you safe and sound."

"And what about Catherine?"

"Cameron will make sure that nothing happens to her."

"But that's not his job, it's *mine*," he said fiercely. "Catherine belongs to me."

"Discuss it with him." Celia moved toward the kitchen. "I believe he may have a different view. Now I'll go in the kitchen and start the water boiling. We'll have tea, and I'll try to keep you amused for the next few hours. I'm not good at chess, but I'm one great poker player." She hesitated at the door. "She'll be fine, Luke," she said softly. "You'll have lots of time to take care of your mother when you get a little older. I'll call you when the tea is ready."

What was she doing babysitting a boy like Luke? Celia thought with frustration as she moved toward the kitchen. She liked the kid, but she knew nothing about what made boys his age tick. He was older in some ways than the men who were her customers, and there were depths that she had not been able to reach. But she couldn't treat him as she did—

Her phone rang. Cameron.

"I don't like this, Cameron," she said crossly. "You told me to keep him busy. You didn't tell me that he has some kind of obsession about protecting his mother. How the hell am I supposed to soothe him and make everything alright?"

"Soothe him?" Cameron repeated. "Why?"

"He knows what's happening, dammit. He eavesdropped and came up with answers that didn't compute when he didn't see Catherine after dinner. I don't know if I can—"

"He knows about the fireworks factory?"

"He mentioned something about it."

"Shit," Cameron snapped. "Where is he now?"

"In the dining room. I just left him glaring at two of the guards in the garden that you sent over. I'm in the kitchen making jasmine tea and trying to lure him with a poker game."

"You left him alone?"

"He's in the next room."

"Celia, go and find him," he said slowly and precisely. "Now. Keep him with you until I get there. Don't let him out of your sight."

"I'm on my way." She moved back down the hall. "But it's not as if—"

The dining room was empty.

"He's not here," she said blankly. "I'll go upstairs and see if he went to his room."

Cameron muttered a curse. "Do that. And then go out and see if any of those guards saw him. I doubt if they did. Luke has had experience evading surveillance. He's probably on his way here to the fireworks factory."

"He said he had to protect Catherine. It was his job." She paused. "And not yours, Cameron."

"Just call back if you find him." He hung up.

Running up the stairs, she hoped she would be able to call back with good news. She didn't like the idea that she had failed to keep Luke safe. She'd be a lousy mother. There was supposed to be some kind of instinct that told you when a kid was wandering off.

But Luke was not the usual kid, and if he had left, it was deliberate.

Be in your bedroom, Luke. Don't let me be responsible for losing you. Or worse. Cameron had been very curt. She didn't even want to think about what else could happen to Luke.

FIREWORKS FACTORY

7:45 P.M.

"I'm going to go and check out a few things, Catherine," Cameron said as he got off the third-floor freight elevator. "I won't be long. And I'll be monitoring you."

"What? Now?" She stared at him in bewilderment. "Kadmus should be calling any minute. Where are you going?"

"Something has come up that I can't put off." He moved toward the window leading to the fire escape. "I have to see to it."

"Orders from your damn committee?" she asked. "Did they find out that Kadmus is going down?"

"No." He was swinging out onto the fire escape. "It's nothing like that." His face was without expression. "Look, I've put Blake's men in the shops across the street, and they'll come if they see anything suspicious. I should be back before Kadmus puts in an appearance."

He was gone.

"Most unusual," Hu Chang said from across the room where he was sitting with Erin. "But I'm sure that we can handle everything without Cameron if it comes down to it. After all, we are extraordinary people."

"And Cameron is a secretive bastard who thinks no one is extraordinary but himself." She drew a deep breath and moved toward the freight elevator. "I'm going to go check all the floors and make sure we're locked up tight. I want to hear any entry."

"Would you like me to go with you?" Erin asked.

She smiled. "No, you're bait. Stay with Hu Chang. That's all you should have to do tonight."

"It doesn't seem like much." She looked around the dark warehouse. "I don't like sitting here doing nothing."

"Then Cameron should have taken you with him. Maybe he would have told you what the—" Catherine stopped. It wasn't Erin's fault her superhero was behaving as if he was the only one who was capable. She was just nervous and on edge and wanted this meeting with Kadmus over. She pressed the elevator button. "I'll be right back."

•   •   •

He had to move swiftly, Cameron thought.

Head toward Celia's neighborhood.

Stay off the main streets. If Luke was heading toward the fireworks factory, he would not be doing it stupidly. The way he'd been brought up was close to the training of a guerrilla fighter according to what Cameron had learned about the boy. Luke would find out his destination, discover how to get there, then proceed in a way that would not endanger Catherine.

That meant alleys and side streets.

But Cameron had no time to go on the usual hunt. He had to get back to Catherine.

And he had to find Luke quickly.

He tried to reach out and locate him.

Nothing.

He had touched the boy's mind once on that mountainside when he had first met him. Once was usually enough to locate him and go in again.

Usually. There was nothing usual about Catherine's son. He had sensed signs in the boy that were definitely above and beyond the ordinary.

Concentrate . . .

There he was. He *had* him. Luke's mind was not as clean and singing as Catherine's, but he was better than nine-tenths of the people Cameron encountered, and he had the same crystal sharpness. And that sharpness was leveled at Catherine.

"She should have taken me with her." Rage. Indignation. Fear. Not for himself but for Catherine. "I explained it to her. Why didn't she listen?" Then the emphasis shifted. Find the fireworks factory. It should still be several blocks away. He had checked the address in Celia's phone book before slipping out of the house.

Keep off the main streets. He didn't see why anyone would be interested in him but he'd been taught by that bastard, Rakovac, to never take anything for granted.

And to never be sure that you weren't someone's next target.

Target.

He was feeling a tenseness between his shoulder blades.

He glanced over his shoulder.

A dark-haired man in a yellow Windbreaker jacket and scarlet baseball cap was a block behind him. He was moving fast and with purpose.

Luke didn't like it. See if he had reason to worry. He cut down the next street and started trotting.

He took another glance behind him.

The man in the yellow jacket had just rounded the corner.

Luke could feel his heart jump.

Lose him. He couldn't lead the man to Catherine.

He turned into an alley near an all-night movie theater and began to run.

Cameron kept in close contact though there was little to monitor. During these first frantic minutes, he wouldn't be able to control Luke, and he had to wait until he could insert guidance without letting him know that it was being done. The kid was doing well. The last thing he wanted was for Luke to go into shock and throw him off with Kadmus's man on his heels.

But the man was gaining, and he had to get Luke away from him.

Luke didn't know the streets, alleys, and general terrain, but Cameron did. There should be another alley in the next block, and if Luke took it, he'd pass a six-foot cedar fence bordering the backyard of a butcher shop. Time to take control.

•   •   •

Luke's breath was coming in harsh pants as he ran down the street. Why *couldn't he get away? He had no doubt that man in the yellow jacket was after him. And he had seen him talking into a cell phone. That meant he could expect one or more of the man's scumbag buddies to be after him, too.*

Maybe he should double back to that movie theater and slip inside and go out the back exit. No. Maybe not.

No, definitely not.

Where, then? Right or left at the next corner.

Right.

He turned right and quickened his pace. He saw a small alley in the middle of the block. He might have to take it.

Yellow jacket was gaining on him again.

Take the alley.

That seemed right, he could only rely on instinct.

He turned down the alley.

•   •   •

"Ellis says he just got a visual on Luke Ling," Brasden said as he turned to Kadmus. "He said the kid was on Clement Street and heading east."

"Is he sure it's Ling's kid?" Kadmus could feel his excitement rise. "Is he following him?"

"Yes. He said there was no missing the closeness to the photograph. He said to alert the rest of the team that the kid's wearing a blue sweatshirt, jeans, and tennis shoes." He grimaced. "But the boy saw him and took off. Ellis is right behind him."

"He can't lose him. I'll castrate the bastard if he screws this up." He pushed back his chair from the table in the bar where he'd been waiting for word. And what a good word it was, he thought with fierce pleasure. Everything was coming together. He was right on Ling's heels, and with any luck, he'd be gathering in her brat to use to negotiate. What a fool she was to let him run around and right into Kadmus's hands. But she wouldn't have let him go far, so the circle must be narrowing even more.

He moved toward the door. "Let's go, Brasden. We'll head for the place where Ellis spotted the boy and I'll make my call to Catherine Ling. We'll be able to zero in on her when she picks up." He chuckled. "And I may have ammunition by that time that will make her cave even before I get my hands on her."

"She'll know that we'll be able to find her within five or ten minutes," Brasden said. "She might not pick up."

"But she will. She wants to take me down as much as I do her. It's only a question of who will get there first. And if the boy's not with her, she'll be worried. That gives me an edge." He glanced at Brasden. "I always have the edge. You knew that when you first came to work for me. You seem to have lost that realization somewhere along the way."

"And you seem to have forgotten that you're now in a vulnerable position with me."

"Oh, I haven't forgotten." He smiled blandly. "I'll have to attend to that problem right after I deal with Ling and her son."

*   *   *

The alley was pitch-dark.

Luke's heart was pounding, his lungs struggling for air as he ran. He could see the brightly lit cross street up ahead.

No yellow jacket yet.

He was passing a cedar fence.

Go over it.

He slowed, uncertain.

Better to go on to the street?

No, go over it, then double back to the street where he'd entered the alley. It might catch the hunter off guard and let him lose him.

He veered to the side and began to climb the cedar fence.

The soles of his tennis shoes dug into the wood as he shinnied over the fence and jumped to the ground on the other side.

He knelt there, listening.

Running footsteps, muttered curses.

Then the steps passed on down the alley.

Get up, move. Take advantage of the moment of confusion. Yellow jacket might come back and check on the fence.

He jumped to his feet and ran back toward the butcher shop. He was out the gate and turning left at the street.

Go straight for another couple blocks then turn east again, he thought. Try to find other alleys and byways that would lead toward the fireworks factory.

It had been the right thing to do. He was on the right track.

He didn't know why he was so certain, but there was no doubt in his mind.

He just had to follow his instincts, and he'd be okay.

.   .   .

Catherine glanced at her watch. "It's been forty-five minutes. Where the hell is Cameron?"

Hu Chang shrugged. "Why are you concerned? He said he'd left men across the street if there was a problem."

But they weren't Cameron, she wanted to tell him. He was trained in mayhem and was a bloody expert at this kind of trouble. She had wanted him here, dammit.

"It's time you took Erin down to the basement, Hu Chang. Get her out that passage to the next building. We've got to keep her safe."

"And leave you here alone? I don't believe I could tolerate that scenario. Think of another one."

"Cameron said he'd be back. You weren't having any trouble with the idea of that before."

"That was before I knew I had to leave you alone."

She drew a deep breath. "Okay, take Erin out of the building and get her safely settled with Blake's man. Then come back to me. Does that work for you?"

"Not entirely." He was silent. "But it will have to do. Erin is no warrior and should not be here. If it's to be done, it must be done immediately." He turned and moved quickly across the room. "Call me if there is danger."

She heard the freight elevator going down two minutes later. They should be out of the building within another few minutes, she thought. Hu Chang could move at warp speed when he wished.

It was good that he was taking care of Erin. Good that he was no longer in the building. It had been a good decision to send them away now.

The darkness was oppressive and lonely.

For God's sake, this was her job. She had been in similar situations dozens of times since she had become an agent. What difference did it make if Cameron was with her or not? None at all. She
could handle it. She would just sit here and wait for Kadmus to call
or the action to start.

Eight minutes later, the telephone rang. She let it ring only two
times before she answered. "You've only got one minute before I
hang up, Kadmus. I'm not going to give you Cameron or Erin, so
this call is useless."

"Useless? No such thing." Kadmus sounded almost amused.
"And one minute will be sufficient. I'm in the proverbial catbird seat,
and I'm ready to go after you, Catherine." He added softly, "And,
when I get you, you're going to tell me everything I need to know.
Do you know why?"

"Evidently you're going to tell me."

"Because I'll have the boy. I'm tracking him now. What a fool
you were to let him go wandering around Chinatown. Or did he
just slip away from you?"

She lost her breath. "You're bluffing."

"Why, I believe you didn't know."

"You're lying."

"He's wearing a dark blue sweatshirt, jeans, and tennis shoes.
Familiar?"

Oh God, yes. It was what Luke had been wearing at the dinner
table this evening. She closed her eyes as waves of sickness rolled
over her.

"I should have him at any minute. If you don't tell me where to
find Cameron, the pain I caused Erin will be nothing to what your
son suffers."

"You don't have Luke. You won't have him." She had to hang
up. "And if you or any of your men try to hurt him, you'll be a
dead man." She hung up.

She only had five or ten minutes before Kadmus and Brasden would have their men surrounding the factory.

But Luke was somewhere out there in the streets. Kadmus didn't have him yet.

Yet.

From what Kadmus had said, Luke was being followed. She had to guess Luke had somehow found out about the factory, and he must be on his way here.

He'd be coming straight toward Kadmus.

No!

She was across the room and jumping on the three boxes at the window. She climbed out on the fire escape. She took a glance around. No sign of Luke. No sign of Kadmus or his men.

Not yet.

She had to make sure. She called Celia. "Listen, Celia, is Luke with you?"

"No, of course not. I'm sorry, Catherine, but I told Cameron that I had no idea the boy would—"

"You told Cameron?"

"Yes, when he called to check on—"

Catherine hung up the phone.

Cameron had known Luke was not at Celia's and not told her. He had set off on his own to find him without a word to her.

She was going to kill him.

She flew down the fire escape.

"Cameron! Do you hear me? If there's one time you should be in my head, it's now, you bastard. Where the hell are you?"

"At the end of the next alley over. I'm handling it, Catherine. I'm taking care of Luke. Go back to the factory. I'll bring him to you."

"I'm not going to do anything but safeguard my son. I'm on my way to you. You have Luke?"

"Not yet. I've been leading him toward me."

"Not yet? Kadmus knows about him."

"I know, Luke's had one of Kadmus's men on his tail since Spring Street."

"How close?"

"Luke's lost Kadmus's man twice, but the guy's pretty savvy. I've had to do some gentle guiding to keep Luke avoiding him and on the right path." He paused. "But Luke's too close to the factory now. I'm going to have to step in and permanently rid him of his tail."

"This is my job. Why the hell didn't you tell me what was happening?"

"Because I knew you'd go after him, and there wasn't any way that you wouldn't be recognized if you were spotted. That wouldn't be good for you or for Luke. I had a chance of leading him here without Kadmus's knowing about him."

"Well, it didn't work."

"I've kept him alive so far, haven't I?" He paused. "I won't let him be hurt, Catherine. I made you a promise."

"You keep that promise," she said fiercely. "But I'm not relying on you. How close is that scumbag following Luke?"

"Very close. And Luke is thinking about doing something rash. I'm trying to keep him—"

Cameron was no longer there.

Panic.

Catherine tore across the street and down the alley.

Luke.

Oh, God, she could see Luke at the far end of the alley. But he wasn't running, he was standing still, slightly crouched.

On the attack? He was just a boy. But he had attacked Tashdon on the helicopter. No, Luke, please don't do—

Too late.

A man in a yellow jacket had rounded the corner.

Luke sprang forward and gave him a karate chop to the neck.

But the man recovered and whirled away from him.

He was cursing as he pulled out his gun and aimed it at Luke.

"No!" This was a nightmare. She jerked her own gun from the shoulder holster. Let her be in time.

Cameron.

Suddenly there, out of the darkness, incredibly fast.

He dove between Luke and his attacker.

A shot.

Cameron jerked.

Had he been shot?

No, Cameron leaped on the man in the yellow jacket and with two moves stunned him with a blow to the neck before slicing his throat.

Cameron pushed him off and turned away as the man fell to the ground. He turned to Luke. "Are you okay?"

Luke nodded, his eyes on the dead man. "You did that very well."

"And you need a few lessons," he said grimly. "I'll have to see to it."

"Luke." Catherine was beside them. She wanted to yell and hug him and slap him and—"You're sure that you're—" She lifted a shaking hand to her temple. "You shouldn't be here. This was the wrong thing to—"

"Move." Cameron told Luke as he started back down the alley. "You, too, Catherine. Kadmus is going down, and we don't have time for anything but making sure of that. She's right, Luke, you shouldn't be here. But you are, and we can't leave you here and have Kadmus or one of his crew get his hands on you. You're coming to the factory with us." His tone was cold and sharp. "And you're going to obey orders, and you're going to help blow Kadmus and his team to kingdom come. Is that clear?"

"Yes, sir," Luke said. His eyes glittered with excitement. "That's all I wanted. I'll do what you say. Come on, Catherine. Let's go. Where is this place? I got all turned around in these alleys."

"But you got here," Cameron said. "You go on ahead with Catherine. I'll watch your back."

"You're giving a hell of a lot of orders," Catherine said, looking over her shoulder as she reached the end of the alley. "And what if I don't want to go on—" She stopped as she saw a spreading stain on the side of his shirt. "Blood. Is that your blood or his?"

"Probably a little of both."

"He *did* shoot you."

"Flesh wound. It's not bleeding much. I've had worse. Nothing to worry about." He added, "And we don't have time for you to give me first aid. I'm figuring we have eight minutes tops before we have to deal with Kadmus." He smiled. "And now that you have Luke here, you'll want to put him down as soon as possible. Catch up with him. Get going."

She took one last look at the trickle of blood seeping from Cameron's wound. The wound that he had taken to save Luke. There was no way she'd let that blood be spilled for nothing. She whirled and started running after Luke. "I'm going. Don't you *dare* bleed to death, Cameron."

·   ·   ·

"We've got the trace." Brasden handed the map that he'd circled to Kadmus. "It's a fireworks factory on Clement Street." That's where Ling took the call."

"*Yes.*" Kadmus's hand clenched on the map. "Get Nagle and his men over there. Seal off all the entrances. But I don't want anyone touched until I get there. What do you hear from Ellis about the boy?"

"He was still tracking him when he checked in ten minutes ago. He said that the kid was sharper than he'd thought he'd be but he thinks he'll have him soon."

And Kadmus would probably have taken the boy's mother even before Ellis grabbed the kid.

"How long will it take me to get to that factory?" he asked.

CHAPTER

18

U p," Catherine said curtly to Luke when they reached the fire escape. "The third-floor window is open. Hurry."

Luke was already climbing, not looking back as he moved swiftly up to the third floor.

Catherine gave a glance at Cameron, who was several yards behind them. She couldn't tell if he was really watching their backs or if that wound had weakened him. She couldn't worry about it now. She was right behind Luke and reached him just after he'd ducked through the window.

"I was beginning to worry, Catherine." Hu Chang stepped out of the shadows as she jumped to the floor. "You didn't mention that you'd planned any extracurricular activities before I left with Erin." He glanced at Luke. "But plans have a habit of changing when Luke appears on the scene. How did that occur?"

"He eavesdropped on our conversation when we were discussing the factory this afternoon," she said curtly.

"Yes, I've spoken to him about that grievous character flaw before," Hu Chang said. "I was hoping that our discussion had solved the problem."

"Five, six minutes, maybe. It's quicker to walk than to go get the car."

Kadmus started down the street in the direction of Clement Street.

Did you hear that, Ling? You have six minutes. Then you're mine.

"You shouldn't have tried to keep me from going with Catherine," Luke said fiercely. "I'd do it again."

"No, you won't. But that's not important now," Catherine said. "Is Erin safe?"

"Yes, I slipped her out of the building to the restaurant Cameron had set up to take her in. She's safe."

"Good, then you can take Luke out the same route."

Luke adamantly shook his head. "No, Catherine."

"Don't argue. There's no time to—"

The sound of splintering glass from the first floor.

"It appears time has run out," Hu Chang said quietly.

Her cell phone rang. It had to be Kadmus. She punched the access.

"I've found you, Ling," Kadmus said. "Did you hear that glass breaking? My men are pouring into the building. I've told them to search every nook and cranny until they find you and Erin. Then we'll have a discussion about what I'm going to do to your son if you don't give me Cameron."

Kadmus obviously didn't know yet that his man was dead and he had no chance to get his hands on Luke. No chance? Luke was right here in front of her, and Kadmus was breaking down the doors.

She had to play him, keep him thinking that was true, lead him into the trap. "You'll lose men if you have them come after me. I won't go down easily. I won't let you take Erin." She paused. "But I can't let you hurt my boy. Perhaps we can come to an agreement."

"Agreement?"

"I won't give you Erin Sullivan, but if you promise that my Luke won't be hurt and will be returned to me, I might be able to tell you where you can find Cameron." She could hear shouts and loud footsteps coming from the second floor, and she said quickly, "But you have to call off your men and come to talk to me yourself."

"I don't have to do anything that I don't want to do."

"The hell you don't. I'm very good at what I do, Kadmus. I'll not only kill off enough of your men to discourage them, but there's even a chance I'll be able to get out of here. At the least, I'll cause enough of an uproar to have the police crashing in here to see what's happening. Make a deal, Kadmus."

Silence. "I'll talk to you. Where are you?"

"Third floor."

"Brasden and I will be on our way up in a few minutes." He added mockingly, "You remember Brasden, don't you, Ling? He has very vivid memories of you. He can hardly wait to see you again." He hung up.

She whirled on Luke and Hu Chang. "Get Luke into that storage closet across the far wall. Right now."

Luke was frowning. "Catherine, I don't—"

She turned on him, and said fiercely, "Luke, don't *argue* with me. I've been trying to do what you want, be what you want. I've been almost afraid to do anything for fear of losing you. Well, that's over. You say I don't know you. Maybe that works both ways. But it's time you got to know me and what I do. In situations like this, I'm the one who runs things. Now do what I tell you."

Luke stared at her, then turned on his heel. "Come on, Hu Chang." He said over his shoulder, "But if I see you having trouble, I'm not going to stay there, Catherine."

She could hear the elevator begin to move. "Go!" She glanced at the window. Cameron should have been here by now, but who knew what Cameron would be doing at any given time? She would have to run her own show.

The elevator stopped just before it reached the third floor. "I have an AK-47," Kadmus called. "Throw down your weapons on the floor, or I'll blow you to hell, Ling."

"No way. I'd be helpless."

"Put them down."

There wasn't much she could do with her .38 against an AK-47 anyway. She would still have the knife in the holster on her calf. "You win." She put her gun on the floor. "My gun is on the floor in front of me."

"Good." The freight elevator started to move again, and Kadmus and Brasden came in view. The darkness was suddenly pierced by the brilliant LED lantern Kadmus was holding in one hand. True to his word, his other arm cradled an AK-47.

Brasden was carrying a Smith & Wesson automatic, and he smiled maliciously as his gaze zeroed in on Catherine. "I've been waiting for this, Ling."

Kadmus lifted the lantern so that's its beam would light every corner of the darkness. "Where's Sullivan?"

"I wouldn't risk her life. When you called me tonight, I got her out of here." She stepped forward. "She's suffered enough, you bastard. It's not her fault my son is on your kill list."

"He might not have to die," Brasden said. "Kadmus is a reasonable man, and I might be able to persuade him to let the boy live. Providing you give us Cameron."

"Us?" She turned to Kadmus. "I thought Brasden was only a glorified errand boy in that ragtag army of yours. Do I have to deal with him, too?"

"Yes," Brasden said before Kadmus could answer. "Kadmus and I have come to terms regarding the future of our relationship. Tell us about Cameron."

Catherine ignored him, still staring at Kadmus. "Is that true?"

"Brasden has been very helpful in tracking you down."

That was no real confirmation, and she could sense antagonism. She might be able to work with it. "I won't be telling you anything about Cameron until you prove that it's worth my while. I don't even know that you've managed to get your hands on Luke. He can be very clever."

"He's just a kid," Brasden said. "Our man Ellis is smart and experienced. Your Luke won't have a chance."

"Won't?" she repeated. "That means you don't have him yet. You lied, Kadmus."

"I exaggerated, and you fell for it. Women are always vulnerable where their emotions are concerned." He smiled triumphantly. "But I have you now. So it doesn't matter. Ellis will bring the boy here and—"

Brasden's cell phone rang, and he picked up. "Brasden." He listened and muttered a curse. "*Find* him."

Kadmus stiffened. "Brasden, that didn't sound good. You told me—"

"Ellis is dead," Brasden said curtly. "About two blocks from here. Throat cut. No sign of the boy."

"What? You told me that Ellis was so good. He couldn't deal with an eleven-year-old kid?"

"It's not my fault. Ellis was good."

"It seems you have nothing to offer me, Kadmus," Catherine said. "I suppose I should thank Brasden for being an incompetent bumbler."

"I can offer you your life." Kadmus's hand tightened on the AK-47. "And it's damn funny that Ellis was killed only two blocks from here. It wouldn't have taken you long to run out of here to rescue the boy."

"You're reaching. I wouldn't have had the time."

"But you tell me you're so good." He gave Brasden a cold glance. "And you succeeded in making a fool of Brasden at Daksha. You might have managed to pluck your son away from Ellis. But where would you have found to stash the little bastard?" He raised the lantern high again and slowly let the beam play around the walls. "I wonder . . ."

She felt a jolt of panic. Any minute he might decide to go and investigate those storage cabinets. She couldn't wait any longer. "It's stupid to think that I'd be able to—"

She kicked the lantern out of his hand, and it crashed to the floor. The glass smashed, but the bulb remained lit as it rolled toward the elevator.

Catherine dove behind the stacked boxes as Brasden let loose with a spray of bullets from his automatic.

"Be careful, you fool," Kadmus yelled. "Do you want to set those fireworks off and have us all go up in flames?"

It was what Catherine had hoped he'd think. She'd made preparations earlier in the evening and ensured that these wooden boxes were filled with relatively harmless fireworks. But if Kadmus let go with that AK-47, it would shred those boxes and anyone sheltering behind them in seconds.

"She's not armed, Brasden," Kadmus said. "Go after her, dammit."

Catherine slid her knife out of her leg holster.

Then she reached for one of the cherry bombs from the pile she'd earlier readied and started lighting them.

"Come on, bitch." Brasden was moving toward her. "Kadmus may want you alive, but I don't give a damn about his screwy ideas about Shambhala. You're a dead woman if you give me any trouble."

She waited.

Just a little closer . . .

First, distract him.

She raised up and started tossing the cherry bombs.

Blam! Blam!

Two exploded in front of Brasden.

"What the—"

The next one hit him in the chest and exploded, burning him.

He screamed.

Now he was off guard. She scrambled to her knees and threw the knife.

It sank deep into his chest.

He tottered and dropped to his knees. He was moaning as he tried to lift his gun.

He didn't get the chance.

His body was suddenly riddled with bullets, tearing him to pieces.

"Fool." Kadmus stood over his body with his AK-47. "He couldn't even perform a simple kill." He kicked Brasden's body. "But I didn't want you to kill him. I've been reserving that pleasure for myself." He stared into the darkness. "You've used your knife and those pitiful fireworks. I doubt if you have anything more lethal. I won't be as easy to put down as Brasden." He started forward. "I won't kill you. I'll just wound you. Then I can take my time and—"

The skylight above them exploded and shattered in thousands of shards of glittering glass.

Someone had jumped, hurled himself through the glass.

Cameron!

He rolled in a ball toward Kadmus, then grabbed him around the knees and brought him down. But Kadmus's AK-47 was swinging viciously at Cameron's head as he hit the floor. Cameron ducked and straddled him.

Catherine was on her feet and diving for the gun she'd been forced to drop on the floor.

Dammit, but she couldn't use it without running the risk of hitting Cameron. Kadmus was fighting viciously, and he still hadn't released that AK-47.

"Get away from him, Cameron," she called desperately. "Let me take my shot."

Kadmus stiffened and went still for an instant. "Cameron?" He stared up into Cameron's face. "I've got you?" His voice was hoarse with excitement. "I was wondering if you'd come to try to help Ling." His fist slammed into Cameron's stomach with brutal force. "I've got to be careful not to damage you too much. I need you."

"Too bad," Cameron said. "I don't need you. Yes, I did come for Catherine, but you're my primary target."

"My hand's wet." Kadmus looked down at his fist. "You're bleeding." He smiled fiercely. "That's good. It means you're weak. I'll take you, then I'll get Ling with the AK-47."

"Not that weak." Cameron lifted his hand and backhanded him. "You like weak, don't you? I remember how much you enjoyed using those ropes to play with Erin. Do you know how often I was tempted to come and use them on you?"

"But you didn't." His hands gripped Cameron's neck. "Because you knew that I was too strong for you. You knew that I was destined for Shambhala. I was meant to be there, and you were keeping me from it. No more, Cameron."

"No more," Cameron whispered as he struggled to break Kadmus's grip. "You do have a destiny, and I won't keep you from it any longer." He broke Kadmus's hold, and his hands grasped Kadmus's neck. Cameron stared him in the eye. "Not Shambhala, never Shambhala." His hands tightened, cutting off air. "Hell, Kadmus." He twisted sharply. "That's your destiny."

Kadmus's neck snapped and broke.

Dead, Catherine realized, as Kadmus's body went limp. Relief surged through her as she moved toward Cameron. He was getting off Kadmus's body as she reached him. She said, "He said you were bleeding. You told me that you were okay."

"That was before I jumped through that skylight," Cameron said dryly. "Actions like that tend to aggravate a wound."

"Let me see it."

"Later." He grabbed Kadmus's legs and started to pull him toward the freight elevator. "But you can help me get Kadmus and Brasden on that elevator. I don't want to bleed any more than necessary."

She was dragging Kadmus's upper body. "Why do you want them on the elevator?"

"We're going to send them both down to the second floor to rendezvous with those ten or fifteen men Kadmus told to wait for word to attack. It should cause a satisfactory amount of confusion and give us a chance to get away from the factory before they recover." He opened the elevator gate, and they pushed Kadmus inside. "Now for Brasden." He smiled at Catherine. "I was impressed. I was watching from the skylight, getting ready to jump. You handled him very well." His brows rose. "But cherry bombs, Catherine?"

She shrugged. "You use what you have on hand." She strode back toward Brasden's body. "And I wasn't expecting help from above."

"You didn't need it," Hu Chang said as he came out of the darkness. "I thought I might have to intercede, but I'm glad I didn't have to do it. I was quite busy trying to keep young Luke from breaking out of that storage closet. He didn't have the same faith in you that I do."

"I have faith in her," Luke said as he came to stand beside Hu Chang. He added simply, "I was just scared."

"So was I," Cameron said. "But can we stop talking and get Brasden's body on that elevator? We need to get out of here."

"I'll help," Luke said quickly.

Catherine opened her mouth to protest but then closed it. It might not be what she wanted for Luke, but this was minor compared to the violence to which he could have been subjected tonight. "Hurry."

Hu Chang smiled. "Very wise." He helped Luke drag Brasden's body toward the elevator and glanced at Cameron. "I heard that you were bleeding. I'll take a look at it once we're out of here."

Cameron shook his head. "I don't wish to insult you, but I have to deal with physicians the committee authorizes." He smiled. "Unless I'm bleeding to death. Which I am not." He slammed the gate of the freight elevator shut and pressed the button. He whirled and headed for the window exit. "I'll go first and clear the way. I saw some activity down there when I was on the roof." He had reached the window and swung his legs over the sill. "Hurry. Don't waste any time."

Catherine pushed Luke ahead of her and watched him climb to the window.

"After you, Catherine." Hu Chang bowed.

An uproar from the second floor. Shouts.

Nagle had opened the elevator door.

She was at the window and looked back to make sure Hu Chang was behind her.

"Catherine." Luke was looking down at the alley below him. "Cameron."

"What's wrong with Camer—"

Nothing was wrong with Cameron, she saw. He had evidently been confronted by three of Kadmus's men in the alley and he was fighting them off with the speed and skill of a Jackie Chan. She had never seen anyone with that degree of lethal karate technique. He had the three men down in less than a minute.

"Neat," Luke murmured.

"Keep going," she said.

"I hear the elevator," Hu Chang said from behind her. "Evidently, the lack of leadership didn't confuse them enough to stop them."

"They're drones," Cameron said as he reached up to give a hand to help Luke to the ground. "Nagle had orders, and he'll try to obey them. He doesn't know who will take over for Kadmus but he'll want them to use him and his team." He added grimly, "But his men won't have the brainpower to make good decisions, and we've thrown them into a turmoil. That's why I wanted to be out of that building. Blake's men were breaking into the first floor and I called and told them to get out, too." They were all on the ground now. "Let's get away from it." He started down the alley at a dead run. Hu Chang, Luke, and Catherine followed.

Shouts. Curses.

Catherine looked back over her shoulder. She could see shadowy figures at the third-floor window. Someone was trying to climb out on the fire escape.

Shots.

A bullet struck the brick wall next to her.

More shots.

"Run," Cameron said tensely.

Those shots . . .

Didn't they realize the danger of those shots? Just one random shot could ignite those fireworks.

Another shot.

The factory blew!

Not all at once, a series of explosions as it moved from box to box on the third floor.

Then, as it reached the main fireworks supply, the explosion shook the ground.

Luke was knocked to his knees by the blast.

She pulled him to his feet and kept on running.

Explosion after explosion.

Then just the crackling suction of flames.

She stopped and looked back.

The factory was totally engulfed in fire. From the street shops to the third floor, the entire structure looked like a garden house in hell.

She was only vaguely aware that Hu Chang and Luke were standing beside her, staring at the inferno. "No one could survive that fire . . ." She looked at Cameron. "You told me that it wouldn't be like that horrible fireworks blast in Vietnam."

"And it isn't," Cameron said. "I had the majority of the gunpowder and chemical papers moved out of the building. And I placed the other explosives in such a way that it caused them to principally implode. It won't hurt anyone outside the factory. The only deaths will be Kadmus's men who caused the blast." He smiled crookedly. "And the fire is so intense that even the firemen won't try to enter the building to save them."

She was staring at him. "But you knew they'd react like that. Nagle's drones you called them. You wanted it to happen."

He shrugged. "I'm the Guardian. If Nagle's men hadn't died, they'd have been in my way again next year or the year after. It was the efficient way to handle it."

She shivered at the sheer, cool calculation that had brought Cameron exactly what he needed to happen. Yes, those men in that building had been murderers and a threat to them, but they really hadn't had a chance against him. "You're very formidable, Cameron."

"It's what I was hired to be." He met her gaze. "Don't expect anything else of me." He cast one more look at the burning factory and turned to Hu Chang. "Get them out of here. The place is going to be surrounded by fire trucks and police any minute. Take them back to Celia's. I'll call Blake and tell him that it's safe to take Erin back there, too." He glanced at Luke. "I have to leave for a little while to get this wound sewn up and bandaged. You take care of Catherine for me."

"I won't do it for you. I'll do it for myself." Luke paused. "And I'm sorry that you got shot because of me. I wouldn't let it happen again."

"Not if I had the schooling of you."

"Which you won't," Catherine said as she started toward the street down the alley. She stopped and looked back at him. "You won't let us help you?"

He smiled and shook his head. "Rules."

"Heaven forbid that we interfere with your committee's idiotic rules."

"The rules are actually meant to protect me. No one is more vulnerable than when under the care of a doctor. I'll let Hu Chang know where I am and what's happening." He moved quickly past them and turned left at the street. The next moment, he had disappeared around the corner.

Luke was gazing after him. "Should we have let him go? I'm kind of worried."

"Feeling responsible?" Catherine asked. "Now you know how I feel about you. Responsibility does lead to interference. We may not like it, but it's the human response to caring for someone."

"You didn't answer me," Luke said. "I think you're worried, too."

She nodded jerkily. "But we can't do anything to help Cameron against his will. He doesn't belong to us. He doesn't belong to anyone." Except to that damned committee that appeared to be the center of his existence. She drew a deep breath. "As soon as Hu Chang finds out where he's staying tomorrow, I'll go check on him. Okay?"

Luke nodded soberly. "He could have died for me, couldn't he, Catherine?"

"Yes." If Cameron hadn't interceded, she might not be talking to Luke right now. She was passionately grateful, but it was mixed with anger and frustration and even . . . fear.

He's probably the most dangerous man either of us will ever meet, Hu Chang had said.

There were so many intricate facets to Cameron's personality that left her dizzy and wanting to come closer. And then he'd suddenly reveal another, more lethal, side that put her on her guard and made her step back.

"Formidable," she had called him.

Tonight he had shown that he was all of that and more.

•   •   •

Catherine was dressed and downstairs at ten the next morning.

She met Celia in the hall. She was carrying a Louis Vuitton suitcase and looked stunningly smart.

"Going somewhere?"

Celia nodded. "I have an engagement in Monaco. I would have canceled it if things had not worked out for you all last night." She smiled brilliantly. "But now I won't have to put him off, will I? That's good, you're all charming people, but I do like to be the center of attention."

"And deservedly so." She reached out to shake Celia's hand. "Thank you for everything, Celia."

"You're being generous." She made a face. "I didn't mean to lose your son. Maybe it's just as well I can't have children."

"No one could have stopped Luke if he was determined on leaving."

"I like him. Send him to me when you need him schooled."

"That's what Cameron said," Catherine said dryly. "I'm sure you didn't mean the same thing but everyone seems to believe that I can't teach Luke what he needs to know."

Celia laughed. "Well, we all have our talents. Take advantage of us." She opened the door. "And the offer still stands if you need a little schooling yourself."

"Thanks, but no thanks. Good-bye, Celia. I hope you have a pleasant trip."

"Always." Celia waved as she went down the steps toward the waiting car service. "Most of the time we get what we're looking for in this life. Me? I look for joy and a hell of a good time."

Catherine was smiling as she turned away from the door. Celia had led a life that could have embittered and poisoned her. Instead, she had learned who she was and looked for that joy. Perhaps not one person in a million could have made that adjustment, but Catherine was glad that Celia had been able to do it.

Her smile faded. No, joy was difficult to pluck from ashes. It had been a restless night, and the memories of Kadmus, Brasden, and those other deaths had stayed with her.

But she had to remember that Erin was now safe and able to go back to her old life.

Cameron? She doubted if he'd ever be safe. But she hoped that wound he'd suffered for Luke was as minor as he'd told her. She needed to keep her promise to Luke and go and check that out for herself.

She moved toward the dining room to see if Hu Chang had heard from Cameron.

CHAPTER
19

Catherine came into the library and slammed the door.
"Well, that was a complete fiasco, Hu Chang," she said with exasperation. "All I wanted to do was to see Cameron. No big deal, right? Why the hell couldn't I see him? I tried to visit him in that fancy suite at the Ritz-Carlton and ran into three guards who politely told me to go to hell. Is he under some kind of house arrest or something? That damn committee told him he couldn't kill Kadmus." Her hands clenched into fists. "I think it had something to do with Kadmus's being a driving economic force in keeping that tawdry tourist town of Shangri-La alive and an active distraction."

Hu Chang nodded. "It would make sense. Since Shangri-La was based on the idea of Shambhala, the existence of that tourist trap kept anyone from looking past it to the new world the committee was trying to create. A bit of sleight of hand. Yes, I can see that would suit the committee just fine."

"And keep a monster alive to do it. Cameron was right to take him out. But now he's cooped up with those goons, and that committee is calling the shots. Are they going to take him somewhere and—"

"Easy," Hu Chang said. "You may be bristling with protective indignation, but I assure you it's uncalled for. It's not house arrest, it's protective custody. The committee isn't going to let anyone near him until their doctor clears him and declares he's able to defend himself."

"He didn't seem to be hurt too bad. Was he pretending?"

"Probably not. But I imagine this entire episode has upset everyone surrounding Cameron. They consider him very valuable. They're not taking any chances with him."

"Chances? They're treating him as if he's heir apparent to a throne."

"Hmm. They do, don't they? Interesting thought. It would explain many things. I wonder . . ." He shrugged. "At any rate, you need not worry about him."

"I wasn't worried about him. He saved Luke. I just wanted to thank him before I left for Kentucky tomorrow. Luke wanted to see him, too."

"Yes, he told me. He seems to think highly of Cameron." He tilted his head. "And I don't believe Cameron manipulated that opinion in any way. They appear to have developed a certain camaraderie."

"Who could blame him?" she said curtly. "He comes swooping down like some comic-book hero and saves the day. Even Luke would be dazzled."

"You weren't exactly standing on the sidelines," Hu Chang commented mildly.

"It's difficult as hell for a mother to dazzle her own son." She paused. "And Cameron pretty well dazzled me, too. In a fight, he's everything you told me he was."

"As he would tell you, it is what he does," Hu Chang said. "So you will try to see him again?"

"No, I'm not running through that gauntlet to get to him. It's probably better that I contact him later."

"And will you do that?"

She was silent. "Maybe."

His eyes narrowed on her face. "You're relieved you didn't get to see him."

"He's . . . difficult to deal with. I don't need difficult now. I just want to go home with Luke and see if we managed to come a few steps closer among all this craziness."

"Cameron will be more difficult to avoid."

She shrugged. "He's a busy man." Her mouth twisted. "Heir apparent, remember?" She turned and started for the stairs. "Now, I've got to go up and tell Luke that we were turned away at the gates. He'll be disappointed. Are you going to come to Louisville with us?"

"No. I have had a request from Erin. She's leaving for Hong Kong early this evening and asked if I would accompany her. She's going to Daksha Mountain and thought I might be of assistance with language and customs."

"What?"

"Kadmus practically destroyed that village and the people who lived there when he took over the palace. Erin wants to see if she can help them get back on their feet." He shrugged. "And I have nothing to do for the next few months."

"Erin didn't tell me."

"You've been a trifle preoccupied," Hu Chang said. "And I imagine Erin has quietly been thinking and planning about what to do with her own life." He turned away. "I will bid you and Luke farewell before we leave."

"You'd better." She grinned at him over her shoulder. "Since you've chosen that barren Daksha and not Louisville to spend those months."

"It is a question of need. Erin is stretching and flexing new muscles. Growth has always fascinated me." He added slyly, "You must make an effort to give me something to pique my interest. I would hate to become bored with you."

"Bored? Why you—" But Hu Chang had disappeared into the library.

She shook her head ruefully as she continued up the stairs. She had not known how much she had wanted Hu Chang to go with them to Louisville until this moment. He was comfort and security and a bastion against loneliness. She needed that right now. But she would never tell him of that need. He would draw too many conclusions, and they would all have to do with Cameron.

But then, everything seemed to be connected with Cameron. Which was why she was grateful she hadn't had to see him.

But one of those connections had to do with Erin Sullivan, and she had to see Erin.

The bedroom door was open, and Erin was packing her suitcase. "Erin?"

"Hi." Erin looked up and smiled. "How is Cameron?"

"I wouldn't know. He's being protected by a trio of hulks who look like a Mafia squad. I guess I looked too dangerous to risk within the presence."

"Really?" Erin threw back her head and laughed. "That's funny. I guess that means I shouldn't even try. Too bad. I wanted to say good-bye." She shook her head. "But it doesn't matter. It's never really good-bye with Cameron."

"Hu Chang says you're heading back to Daksha." She shivered. "I wouldn't think you'd be able to bear the memories of what you went through there."

"I don't think I'm strong enough to go back to the palace yet, but the village is different. I think that it may . . . cleanse me."

"I hope so." Her gaze went to Erin's throat. "You're still wearing your lotus necklace."

"I always will."

"Does that mean that—" She stopped as Erin shook her head. "No?"

"Not yet. I'm closer. I may find my answer at Daksha."

"Whatever you decide, I hope that answer includes me, Erin." She crossed the room and gave her a kiss on the cheek. "Because I believe that you'll always be my friend and part of my life now. If you need me, call."

Erin's eyes were moist as she nodded jerkily. "I will. Thank you for everything, Catherine. You'll always be with me." She cleared her throat. "And I'm sorry I'm stealing Hu Chang from you. I need him."

"And you can obviously be as ruthless as Cameron when you have a plan." She smiled. "It's okay. You trumped me this time. Hu Chang's admiring your energy and growth." She paused. "So do I." She turned and headed quickly for the door. "Good-bye, Erin. Take care."

She didn't wait for a reply. She was having trouble holding back the tears. She and Erin had gone through so much together. She admired her gentleness and toughness and the idealistic dreams that Catherine would never have.

She would miss her, dammit.

•   •   •

Cameron was there in the darkness, she thought drowsily.

She could *feel* him.

She opened her eyes.

"I wish you would," he said from the bedroom doorway. "In many interesting and carnal ways. It's a state much to be desired."

All drowsiness left her. She scrambled to sit up in bed. "Cameron." She reached over and turned on the lamp on the bedside table. "What the hell are you doing here?"

"I understand you paid me a call this afternoon. I felt it was only polite to return the visit." His lips tightened. "You didn't see fit to leave a message."

"Why should I? I wasn't welcomed with open arms by those gorillas."

"They were under orders from the committee. The doctor was with me at the time, and they didn't want anyone to interfere with him."

"As if I would." Her gaze went over him. He was dressed in jeans and a white shirt with sleeves rolled up to the elbows. He looked strong and tough and was emitting the same electric force as always. "I only came to see you to make sure that you were all right. After all, you did save Luke." She met his gaze. "But I don't have to ask that, do I? You look as if that bullet hadn't even touched you."

"It touched me." His hand went to his side. "I told you, flesh wound. The doctor wanted to keep me penned up for a day or two, but that wasn't going to happen. The committee is always over-careful."

"Hu Chang says you're a shining star in their firmament," she said sarcastically. "They wouldn't want you either dimmed or sent into outer space. Did they object to your taking down Kadmus?"

"They didn't like it, but they got over it. I just had to present them with a fait accompli."

"I imagine you do that quite a bit. It makes me wonder who's running the show."

"For God's sake, I've no desire to do anything but my job as Guardian."

"But those duties could encompass many—"

"I didn't come here to talk about the committee or their plans for me," he interrupted impatiently. "I won't waste time when I know damn well we don't have it." He strode toward the bed. "Come on."

She tensed. "I'm not going anywhere."

"Yes, you are. I don't like all the things that are zooming around your mind. I could stay here, but it might not be either quiet or calm. In fact, you can count on high-octane disturbance. You wouldn't like that with Luke only a few rooms down." He grasped her arm and pulled her from the bed. "So it's the summerhouse."

"No!" Memories of those erotic hours in the summerhouse

were flooding back to her, the heady sexual games that had kept her captive.

"Yes." He looked her in the eye. "Look, I'm not going to touch you if you don't want me. But I'm going to talk to you. I stopped at Luke's room on the way here to you and told him good-bye. You wouldn't want him to hear anything that would make him defensive. He might feel bound to come in and confront me."

He knew she wouldn't permit Luke to be put in that position. She tore her wrist from his grasp. "I'll go with you. But it's not going to be your way, Cameron. This is only going to make me angry."

"I know." He bowed slightly and gestured for her to precede him. "But there's no time for me to negotiate. I have to do what I have to do. I found out from Hu Chang that you're on your way to Louisville."

"Found out in your usual fashion, I suppose."

"Yes, Hu Chang has no objection to an occasional intrusion as long as I make it a rare occurrence. Not like you, Catherine."

"With me, your intrusions have not been all that rare," Catherine said as she reached the bottom of the stairs. "And this particular one strikes me as being particularly obnoxious."

"Because you're on guard, and you don't want to be put in a position where you might be tempted to lower it." He opened the garden French door for her. "And that's all I'm offering here. Not force." He smiled. "Temptation."

"After you got your way and positioned me correctly to receive temptation."

"As I said, I don't have much time."

"It's not going to work, Cameron."

"Then I'll go away and try again another day." He opened the door to the summerhouse. "There's always tomorrow."

"Not according to your doctrines of Shambhala. Your committee thinks we're all on our way to destruction."

"But tomorrow will still exist, and it will be a brighter day."

Cameron closed the door of the summerhouse behind them. "And I'll never stop trying, Catherine."

The darkness was overwhelmingly intimate, with only the faint moonlight pouring through the windows. She could see his shadow only a few feet away, the white of his shirt, the muscular tightness of his body.

It was happening again. The anger didn't matter. Her body was responding. She had to get out of here.

"Say what you have to say," she said jerkily. "I'll listen, then I'm gone."

"I've already said what was important. But I said it in the middle of our hunt for Kadmus, and I have to make sure that you know that nothing has changed." He reached out and turned on a lamp near the armchair he was standing beside. The soft glow illuminated him, his eyes, his mouth, the broad shoulders taut beneath that white shirt.

She drew a shaky breath. Don't let him see how the sight of him affected her. Shit, he probably knew.

"I know how you affect me." His gaze ran over her. "I like that sleep shirt. It clings in all the right places. I'd like it more if it were lying on the floor at your feet."

She moistened her lips. "Yes, I want to screw you. That doesn't mean I will. I have a life. I can't let you do this to me."

"Do what? Pleasure?"

"It's more than that. I have a tendency to . . . lose myself. That mustn't happen."

He didn't speak for a moment. "I told you, that's not why I brought you down here. Sex with you is magnificent, but I can do without it . . ." He grimaced. "If I have to. But I have to talk to you. I can't let you go without doing that." He dropped down in the easy chair. "So stop standing there like an animal at bay and sit down and let me do it."

She gazed at him warily, then went to the couch and sat down. "I'm listening."

"I don't want you to go to Louisville. I want you to go with me."

She gazed at him incredulously. "Back to Tibet?"

"Perhaps. I may not go back there for a while. Kadmus is gone, and that eliminates a lot of problems in the area. I think I'll be sent to Copenhagen to take care of a few troubles that have popped up there." He met her eyes, and the intensity enveloped her, held her. "I don't want to do without you. I want you with me."

"You want me to trail behind you like a camp follower does a soldier? No thank you, Cameron."

"It wouldn't be like that." His hands clenched on the arms of the chair. "I just have to have you. I'll give you anything you want. There's nothing in the world you can't have that money will buy. I know you'd be giving up a lot. I'd try to allow you freedom and independence. I'd make arrangements for you to have Luke with you."

"How very kind of you."

"I'm trying, dammit," he said harshly. "Just state your terms."

"I don't have terms. You've been spending too much time with prostitutes." She could feel the flush heat her cheeks as shock turned to anger. "And how long would you want me with you, Cameron? A week, a month, a year?"

"I don't know," he said. "Do you want me to promise you forever? I can't do that. This is too new for me. All I can say is that I can't imagine not wanting you."

"But if it didn't last long, that would be okay, wouldn't it? Because you're securing my future with all those billions of shekels your committee rains down on you." She added fiercely, "You're offering me a lousy deal. And you're insulting me. I'm more than just a good lay. Go to hell, Cameron."

He was silent. "I thought that would be your response. I had to make the attempt before I tried anything else. It's not an insult, Catherine. It's the best I can do under the circumstances. I can't follow you to Louisville right now. I don't have that choice."

"Who asked you to do that?"

"No one," he said wearily. "It was just a thought. You'd probably call the local police on me for harassing you."

He sounded tired, rueful, sad, and unlike the Cameron she knew. She found her anger fading away. "I might. But I can't see you in Louisville. I can't see you anywhere that I belong. You have your own damn life, running around on mountains in Tibet, or kidnapping geniuses off trains in India, or fixing troubles in Copenhagen. That's not my life. I don't believe in it. I wouldn't want to share it."

"Have you finished?" Cameron asked quietly.

She nodded. "May I go now?"

His smile was twisted. "Yes, I promised you, didn't I?"

Again that faintest hint of sadness . . . and loneliness.

Hu Chang had said he was lonely.

Well, she wasn't about to follow him and become his mistress to keep him from being lonely. He was an expert at taking care of himself.

But anyone would say that so was she and she had been lonely most of her life.

"What are you waiting for?" he asked. "I won't try to stop you."

"I know, you gave your word."

And he valued his promises. It's the only thing that's really mine to give, he had told her. Yet he had untold wealth at his disposal and the power the committee gave him was mind-boggling. She didn't really know how he thought or how he felt about anything but his dedication to the Shambhala cause and his passion for her. Both of those emotions were clear. His history had formed such a complex mixture of qualities and experiences that it might take years to say she truly knew him.

She did not have years to pierce that wall. She had a son, she had a life. She was working on surviving her own past and making a decent future.

And she still had that son because Cameron had stepped in and taken a bullet for him.

She had been passionately grateful to him for saving Luke. Somehow that gratitude had become lost in her other emotions toward Cameron. How could that have happened?

Because it had made her feel vulnerable, and she couldn't afford to feel any more vulnerable toward him. Yet it was all part of the total of what she felt for Cameron. What she had to come to terms with before she left him.

"Get out of here," Cameron said roughly. "I'm trying to hold on, but it's not going to last long."

She could see that. And she knew that when that dam broke, it would overwhelm both of them as it had before. She would feel helpless and lost and want only—

What was she thinking? She sounded like a victim, *his* victim, and that would never be true. She had choice and power, and she would learn control.

"I'm going." She got to her feet. "But not just yet." She came toward him and stopped before his chair. "Because I have to come to terms with you, Cameron. All through our time together, you've been intimidating me."

"The hell I have. You're tough, Catherine."

"Oh, I fought it. Maybe it was those damn mind tricks that threw me off." She looked him in the eye. "Or maybe it was that I'd never wanted anyone sexually the way I did you. It made me feel helpless, and I hated it. Anyway it all added up to intimidation."

His eyes narrowed. "Is this leading somewhere?"

"Yes, out of confusion and into the bright light." She took his face into her hands and stared into his eyes. "First, I just realized I don't have to be intimidated by you. I'm no victim."

"You're damn right you're not."

"Second, I want to tell you I'm grateful to you for saving Luke. I'll never forget it."

"I don't want your gratitude. I made you a promise."

"Whether you want it or not, I'm grateful. Accept it. Third, I will not go with you and be your mistress. Accept it." She bent forward and kissed him, hard, open, passionate. "Also accept that anything I do isn't because I'm grateful; it's because I want to do it. Not forever, not permanent, just for tonight. There's no reason why I shouldn't have you. I'm taking what I want if you want to give it." She stepped back, pulled her sleep shirt over head, and dropped it on the floor. "Understood?"

"Oh, my God." He reached for her and she was suddenly on his lap and his mouth was on her breast.

She could hardly breathe. She could feel his teeth and his tongue and that suction that nearly drove her crazy. "No." She was sitting astride him, unbuttoning his shirt, then her fingers were on his pants, freeing him.

She cried out as he sank deep, her arms holding him with all her strength, and her body moved.

Taking. Taking. Taking.

His mouth was on hers as he tumbled her to the floor.

He lifted her hips to take the thrust.

Deep. Deeper.

Full of him . . .

His mouth on her breast, drawing, biting.

Fire.

Breathlessness.

Deeper.

It was a fever. It was need.

A need that was met and satisfied and ignited again, and again.

And it went on forever.

Or maybe it was only hours that seemed forever.

Silk on her bare skin . . .

She opened her eyes as he carried her over to the couch and settled her there. He gently tucked the silk comforter he'd taken from the chair over her. "You like the feel of silk against you? Sharp and soft, it's very sensual." He drew the end of the comforter slowly, teasingly, over her breasts and smiled as he saw the response. "I learned a few interesting things do with silk cords and raw silk. Remind me to show you." He dropped a light kiss on her lips. "I don't want to leave now, but I'm not going to do anything to push my luck. I told you that you could be in control." He was dressing quickly. "I did understand you, Catherine. Perhaps more than you understood yourself."

"Intimidation, again . . . You're wrong, I understood what I wanted, and I took it." And she wanted him again. He was putting on his shirt and the ripples of muscle were sleek and—"You're bleeding again!" Her gaze was on the bandage on the left side that was wet with fresh blood. "I forgot about your wound. Why didn't you tell me?"

He grinned. "Surely you jest? Even if I'd noticed it, I wouldn't have run the risk of you stopping to soothe and rebandage me." He came back to her and pulled the silk comforter down and kissed her breast. "And it gave me a chance to prove I'd give my blood for you." He rubbed his slightly rough cheek against her. "I would, you know. To the last drop."

"Bullshit." She pushed him away. "Your committee wouldn't permit you to donate even a pint of your precious blood to the Red Cross." She sat up. "You're too essential to their splendid cause."

"It is splendid, Catherine." He got to his feet. "You'll come to believe that, too, someday."

"No, I won't. And that's another prime reason for me to leave and let you go back to being Guardian. We'd never agree."

"We've just spent a number of hours in complete agreement." He turned and headed for the door. "And we will again."

"You said you understood. It's over now. I told you, it was just for tonight, Cameron."

He smiled as he opened the door. "I can be patient. I can let you go for a while. I was planning on it anyway. I'll either come after you, or you'll come to me."

Her brows rose. "*I'll* come to you?"

"Oh, not running to jump into bed with me. That would be too much to hope for. But you're CIA and as Guardian I have frequent encounters both bad and good with the CIA. I leave them alone as long as they don't interfere, but they're becoming increasingly troublesome."

"Or is it you who are becoming troublesome?"

"The dangers are increasing, and I have to make adjustments for them." He shrugged. "Either way, it's more likely to bring us together."

"Or put us on the hunt for each other."

"But that could be exciting, too."

She felt a thrill of that excitement at the thought. How would it feel to be on the hunt for Cameron with his superb talents and training?

"You see?" Cameron said softly. "It can't be over. We'd miss too much."

She believed him as she gazed at him standing there. He had so many different faces. Guardian, warrior, crown prince of never-never land. Memories were flooding back to her of Cameron in a dozen different scenes since he'd come into her life. That first moment when she'd seen him before that fireplace in what she'd thought was a hallucination, the moment when he'd lifted her from the hot spring, the moment in the Mercedes when he'd first touched her. How many other such moments could be on the horizon? "If we don't kill each other."

He chuckled. "Point taken. But it's not likely." His laughter faded. "I don't think I could bear it." He started to leave.

"Wait."

He looked back at her.

"I once asked you a question. You never really answered me. Is Shambhala a real place? Is there a true Shangri-La?"

"What do you think?" His smile was brilliant, telling nothing, promising everything. "Come with me and I'll take you to see for yourself."

The next moment, he was gone.